THE ANIMAL HOUR

Also by Andrew Klavan

As Keith Peterson

The Scarred Man
Rough Justice
The Rain
There Fell a Shadow
The Trapdoor

As Andrew Klavan

Don't Say a Word
Son of Man
Darling Clementine
Face of the Earth
The Animal Hour

Screenplay

A Shock to the System

THE ANIMAL HOUR

ANDREW KLAVAN

POCKET **STAR** BOOKS

New York   London   Toronto   Sydney   Tokyo   Singapore

A Pocket Star Book published by
POCKET BOOKS, a division of Simon & Schuster Inc.
1230 Avenue of the Americas, New York, NY 10020

ISBN 0-671-74011-3

First Pocket Books paperback printing November 1993

10 9 8 7 6 5 4 3 2 1

POCKET STAR BOOKS and colophon are registered trademarks of Simon & Schuster Inc.

Cover art by Keith Birdsong

Printed in the U.S.A.

This book is for Spencer

I would like to thank Erica Newton, M.D., for her medical advice and her tour of Bellevue; Barney Karpfinger, for his sage counsel and unwavering support; and my wife, Ellen, as always, for everything.

PART 1

NOBODY'S SWEETHEART

"Where am I going? I don't quite know.
What does it matter where people go?"
—A. A. Milne

NANCY KINCAID

It was going to be a lousy day. She was sure of that, even before she vanished.

She felt rotten, for one thing. Sodden, as if she were coming down with the flu. The subway rocked and chattered its way downtown and the motion made her head feel like an accordion, going in and out. And it was rush hour. Monday morning, 8:45. Every seat on the train was filled. Commuters stood packed tightly in the aisle, pressed flat against the doors. She stood in the middle of them. She clutched her purse tight under her arm. She gripped the metal pole with her free hand. Gray shoulders, black faces, lipsticked mouths—they pressed in close to her. The smells of them: sharp cologne; flowery perfume; sweat and shampoo and sickly sweet deodorant. They mingled in her nostrils. They clogged her brain. The train swayed. The bodies jostled her.

Oh man, she thought. *This is going to be the worst.*

The train stopped at Prince Street. The doors slid open on the long station's yellowing walls. The crowd on the platform struggled briefly with the crowd in the train. Faintly, over the noise, she heard the sound of a Dixieland band. She caught a glimpse of it through the doors. A white man blowing a trumpet, his cheeks ballooned.

> "painted lips, painted eyes;
> wearin' a bird of paradise . . ."

3

I know that song, she thought. *Dad used to sing that song sometimes.*

The title eluded her for a second. Then the trumpet brought it home: "Nobody's Sweetheart."

> "It all seems wrong somehow.
> Cause you're nobody's sweetheart now."

The doors slid shut. The train jolted on. The music had made her sad, nostalgic: like a glimpse of sunlight to the prisoner in her cell. She closed her eyes as the train rocked, as the people pressed against her. Oh God, she prayed without much hope; oh God, make it the weekend. Okay? I'll just open my eyes and poof, it'll be Saturday. Okay? C'mon, you crazy guy, you God. Let 'er rip. You can do it. You're the big guy. Ready. One, two, three. Poof.

She opened her eyes. That God. He had a lot to answer for, if you asked her.

She stuck out her tongue and made a gagging noise. It was drowned completely by the rattle of the train.

Leaning against her pole, she went on thinking about the weekend. Only five days away. Then Friday night would come around. She and Maura could go down to the Village. Dress bad. Something tight, something black. Sit at a bar, at Lancer's maybe. Drink espresso, pretend to like it. Pretend they weren't just this side of virginity. Pretend they might meet some guys. Or maybe they actually would meet some guys. You never knew. Maybe some half-scary Village type, some poet or something, would take the barstool next to her. A shaggy-haired poet with a haggard face, a bulky sweater . . .

"Canal Street," the motorman called over the speaker. "Watch the closing doors."

She was washed this way and that by the tide of commuters getting off, getting on. She gripped her purse, gripped her pole. The train coughed and chugged away again. The black tunnels whispered at the window. She peered into the middle distance. She began expanding on this poet idea. She liked it. She could picture him. A barrel-chested grizzly bear of a guy. A guy who thumped when he walked. Talked in gut-

4

turals, cursed all the time. But with these warm brown eyes just for her—he was a regular puppy dog when he took hold of her shoulders, when he gazed down at her. You hadda love him, in spite of everything.

She stared into space as the subway sped on. *Woof,* she thought.

Late at night, she would wake up in the little bed in his attic studio. She would lie quietly, naked under the single sheet. Oh, Mom would just have fits if she slept in the nude at home. But Mom—her sedate, little dumpling of a Mom—would be far away. She would be in her faded Gramercy apartment. And silver-haired Dad would have turned off the cable news. Would have stood up by then and stretched and said, "Ah well, no sense waiting up for her." And taken his beer to bed.

But her poet would be awake still. Sitting at his desk in the midnight garret. While she lay on her side, naked under the single sheet. Pretending to be asleep, watching him secretly. He would be hunched over his notebook in the circle of lamp-light, his pen moving feverishly, his eyes feverishly bright.

"This is the animal hour," he would write.

The slow October flies, despairing on the porch chairs,
blink into the shards of the sun they see setting.
Blue and then a deeper blue ease into the air . . .

And she would wait and watch beneath the thin, stained sheet. And he would get tired finally. He would lay his pen down finally and rest his head against his hands. And then she would stir, she would whisper to him: "Come to bed now, darling." She would peel the sheet back . . . Oh, Mom would definitely croak if she saw it. Even he—even her poet—would get a laugh out of it. He would stand up in his lumbering way. "You were such a good little repressed Irish Catholic girl when I met you," he would say. "What have I done to you?" And then he would lumber toward her, ready to do it to her again.

"City Hall," the motorman called.

She came to the surface with a goofy smile. *Oh hell,* she thought, letting her breath out. *Nancy Kincaid's Romantic*

5

Fantasy Number 712. The train stopped. The doors cracked open. The passengers flooded out into the station. She let herself be washed along.

Dull-headed, still vaguely dreaming about her poet, she joined the parade. The March of the Rush Hour New Yorkers. Gray suits, tidy dresses, legs striding along the platform, footsteps pattering in unison. Up the concrete stairs, knees high. Out into the vaulted gallery under the Municipal Building. A squat newsy, waving his papers, leaned into her face.

"Mother Eats Baby!" he shrieked. "Get the *Post!*"

She blinked, her daydream blown away. *Thanks ever so much,* she thought. She dodged around the screaming toad. Wove through the stout columns. Broke out into the open air.

Oh yes, that was good. The open air. She sucked it in as she waited for the light to change. Cool, cool leafy air. October air. Above her, the sky was big and blue. The cars spat past the great building's sweeping colonnade. Here and there, marble courthouses loomed like temples over the roadway. Across from her, City Hall showed white through the red leaves of the oaks and the yellow leaves of the sycamores in the park.

The lights changed. The cars pulled up, snorting to go. She hurried across the street toward the park, toward the Hall.

She cut into the park. Seedy old park. Concrete walks curving through littered patches of grass. Homeless men hunkering on the green benches. Men in suits charging past her toward the small Hall. Policemen paced on the Hall steps, under its tiers of arched windows, its peeling dome, its statue of Justice with her scales. The wind blew and the leaves rained down from the sycamores all around her. They stirred and swirled on the paths. Nipped and chattered at her feet like Disney squirrels. The fresh air had made her head a little clearer now, but that nostalgic sadness was rising inside her again.

When you walk down the avenue,
I just can't believe it's you . . .

6

It was just—what?—five months ago, she thought. Five months ago she had been in college. Just last May. She had hurried just like this across the small campus on the West Side. She could remember the weight of her dance bag over her shoulder, the feel of her leotards snug under her clothes. Had she really thought she was going to be a dancer then? Had she really believed that? The daydreams—the ones about going to auditions, winning parts. "You. The girl with the blue eyes. The part is yours." The feeling of strong hands closing on her waist in the spotlit dark. The footlights washing everything away as she was lifted off her feet. The sound of applause. Loud, loud, long-lasting applause. Had she ever really thought any of that was going to become real?

Nah. Probably not. At least, she wasn't sure anymore whether she had. She couldn't remember.

It all seems wrong somehow,
Cause you're nobody's sweetheart now . . .

She passed the Hall, came out of the park onto Broadway. The office building was right across the street. A tall thin tower, white stone, ornate as an altarpiece. Filigree scrolling up the arched windows. Gibbering gargoyles peering out over the high ledges, grinning viciously.

Anyway, she had taken the job with Fernando Woodlawn the first chance she got. She hadn't been out of school a week. Her father said Woodlawn needed an assistant and, bingo, she had agreed to interview for the spot right away. No dance auditions, not a one. Not even any of the dance classes she had planned to take. And as for "You. The girl with the blue eyes," you could pretty much forget about it. Oh, she still looked at the trade papers now and then. She still told herself she'd start classes again next week, next month; start going to auditions—soon, real soon. But basically, she knew it wasn't so. Basically, she had become the personal assistant to an attorney friend of her father's, and that was pretty much that. *Christ,* she thought as she reached the curb, *I haven't even moved away from home.* Her mother had said, "You can still stay here while you're looking for an apartment."

And though she had looked for an apartment one Sunday afternoon, she soon found there wasn't enough time for that and, of course, she wanted to save her money too and, well . . . there she was.

NANCY KINCAID LEARNS TRUTH ABOUT SELF! COW-ARDICE EATS FUTURE! Get the *Post!*

She stepped off the sidewalk. Dashed into a break in the Broadway traffic. Ran to the opposite curb. There was a deli there, on the ground floor of her building. Its plate-glass window was decorated for Halloween with paper jack-o'-lanterns and snarling skeletons. On one side, a huge black bat with a phosphorescent stare darkened the glass. She could see her reflection in it. She paused to look herself over.

She was a small, slender woman. Still with a girl's figure really. Still with a lot of girl about her face too. It was a round, open face. Too broad and flat, she thought. Too strong in the jaw. But she had curly red-brown hair that tumbled to her shoulders and softened the effect a little. And her eyes —not only were they a delicate china blue, but they appeared very frank, very straightforward. Her friend Maura always said they made her look intelligent and honest.

The subway ride had left her a tousled mess. She brushed at her hair. Smoothed down her imitation camel hair trench-coat. Adjusted the green tam-o'-shanter on the crown of her head. *Intelligent and honest,* she thought. Not as good as, say, smoldering and mysterious. But there must be some guys who like intelligent and honest. Somewhere. Maybe.

She let out a sigh. Went into the building, plucking her compact from her purse as she shouldered through the door. She redid her lipstick, waiting for the elevator. Smoothed away a smudge of mascara.

> Painted lips, painted eyes.
> Wearin' a bird of paradise.
> Oh, it all seems wrong somehow . . .

The decorated steel door of the old elevator slid open. She stepped into the little box. Just before the door clapped shut, she pulled off her tam and stuffed it into her trench coat pocket. More businesslike. Less schoolgirl.

She rode up to the twelfth floor. Stepped out into the reception area of Woodlawn, Jesse and Goldstein. Old aqua sofas. A coffee table covered with copies of the *Law Journal*. A heavyset black woman reading a newspaper behind a pane of glass. Nancy waved to her. The woman hardly glanced up as she buzzed her through the low wooden gate.

Here there was a single broad hall, a row of offices on either side. Gunmetal desks and maroon swivel chairs behind walls of windows and brown wood. Everything buried under papers. Folders and briefs stacked in the corners of everybody's floor. Open file cabinets, skewed bookshelves. Pretty dingy stuff, all in all. Nancy remembered that she'd been shocked the first time she'd seen it. How could these be the offices of the great Fernando Woodlawn?

She had heard about Woodlawn since she was a child. Every time his name was in a newspaper, Dad would go on and on about him. *I always knew he was destined for big things! A real world beater! A true legal mind!*

Poor Dad, she thought. The sweetest, gentlest man in the world really, but as a lawyer he was never much more than a maker of wills. And as a politician, he was downright proud to be a licker of envelopes for his beloved Democrats. His sole claim to fame was that he had gone to Brooklyn Law School with Fernando. "Lifted many a beer with the man between one class and another." Dad just never stopped being proud of that. He took personal satisfaction in Fernando's big real estate deals. His meetings with the mayor. His battles with the governor. He even bragged about the patronage jobs Fernando had sent his way when he needed them. "All I ever had to say was, 'I'm a little short this quarter, Fernando,' and by God, within a week, I'd have more assessment appeals on my desk than I could handle."

Poor Dad.

Well, she thought—she walked along the empty corridor toward her own office down at the end—soon Dad would have cause to be even prouder, God bless him. She wasn't allowed to tell him yet, but it seemed fairly certain that Fernando was on his way to Albany. The governor, it was pretty much agreed, was through. He'd been taking a slow-motion nose dive in the polls for over a year, and the new tax hikes he was going to need to balance the budget were sure to finish him off. If the Democrats were going to stay in power, he'd either have to step down next year or risk a humiliating defeat at his own convention. So the field was open—and guess who was at the starting gate. If the new Ashley Towers project got approved this week, Fernando would be able to farm out enough legal work to the party leaders to virtually assure himself the nomination. And with the state Republicans completely in disarray, Governor Fernando was looking like a very good bet.

Nancy's head throbbed again as she thought about it. It was going to be hell this week. It was going to be just like last week. The inside lines ringing. The conversations in whispers. The sudden bursts of shouting. "I want it! Now! Let's go! Let's go!" She had begun to live in terror of the next harsh hiss over her intercom. "Nancy! Come here! I need to talk to you!"

There was a photograph on Fernando's wall—it was visible through the glass as she passed it now. It was a two-page spread cut from an article in *Downtowner* magazine. The article had run about four months ago. It was the first interview in which Fernando had hinted at his intention to run for the statehouse. "Floating the balloon," he called it: it was the start of all the craziness. The magazine's photographer had come to the office and spent the whole day following Fernando around. And Fernando had charmed the kid as only he could. Shoulder slaps, racy jokes; he even took the kid and his girlfriend out to dinner when the day was through. The result was that photograph. Practically a campaign poster. Fernando, leaning forward over his desk, with a wide-angle view of downtown Manhattan spread out behind him. Fernando's shirtsleeves rolled to his elbows. His thin forearms corded and throbbing as he thrust himself forward. His whole wiry frame seemed coiled, ready to spring over the desktop and into the lens. And his thin face, the blade-sharp features—they were burning like a laser with his craving and

10

his glee. It was Governor Fernando, all right. And the sight of that photo as she went by actually made Nancy's stomach boil with anxiety.

With another sigh—almost a groan—she turned into her office. Her gunmetal desk, of course, was neat as a pin. Papers properly stacked in the corners. Computer keyboard lined with the desk's edge. Even her monitor was tilted expectantly toward her chair.

She tossed her purse down on the desk and headed straight for the window. She was beginning to feel muzzy again and wanted some more of that fresh air. She grabbed the bottom of the heavy wooden frame and sent it rattling upward. She stuck her head out into the smell of dying leaves and car exhaust.

From twelve stories above, she could hear the cars honk softly down on Warren Street. She could even hear the sound of synchronized footsteps on the sidewalk, the Monday morning march to work. She glanced to her left. On the ledge just beside her, there was a gargoyle. He was a clownish gnome of white stone. He wore a peaked cap. His face jutted out over the street. He stared down at it. His features were frozen in unpleasant, wild-eyed laughter. She turned away from him, turned to the right. Craning her neck, she could just get a glimpse of Broadway. The clustered sycamores in the park. The Hall's white dome. Justice holding her scales above the yellow leaves.

She breathed in the air gratefully, her eyes wide. She glanced back in the other direction.

The gargoyle had turned its head. It was grinning directly at her, its twisted face six inches from her own.

"Yikes!"

She pulled inside double quick. She backed away from the window, her hand to her chest. She could feel her heart fluttering against her fingers. Then she stopped. Her mouth open, she shook her head. She laughed.

"Whoa," she said aloud.

What a *weird* thing to see! God! She felt her forehead with the back of her hand. Maybe she had a fever or something.

"Jeepers," she whispered.

Well, then she went right back to that window. She stuck her head out again. For a second, she was half afraid the thing really *would* be staring at her.

Or creeping toward her. Oooh, she thought.

Luckily though, the creature was back in its proper place. Grinning down at the street below. Just as stationary as a piece of stone ought to be. She smiled at it.

"Excuse me, may I help you!"

The voice came suddenly from behind her and, bang, she started and cracked her head on the windowsill.

"Yowch. Darn it," she said. She wheeled back into the office, rubbing her scalp hard. There was a woman there now. She was standing in the office doorway.

She was a black woman. Slim and busty. Fashionable in a bright red dress made vivid by her dark skin and her red lipstick. The woman was holding a folder under one arm. She was regarding Nancy with an expectant smile.

For a moment, though, Nancy could only continue to rub her head. "Hi," she said through her teeth. "Boy, that really smarted."

The black woman just hung there, her smile just hung there. "Is there something I can help you with?" she said.

"Uh . . . no," said Nancy, a little confused. "I don't think so." She dropped her hand to her side finally. "Why do you ask?"

"Well, I . . . I mean, are you waiting for someone?" the black woman said.

"Uh . . . no. No. I'm supposed to be here. You must be new. This is my office."

The black woman gave a puzzled little laugh at that. "Well, no it's not, actually," she said. "I think you've made a mistake."

Nancy gazed at her blankly.

When you walk down the avenue . . .

She blinked. "Uh . . . Excuse me? I'm sorry. What do you mean?"

"I mean, I think you've made a mistake," the black woman said. "This is definitely not your office."

Slowly, Nancy glanced around her, surveyed the place. Had

she wandered into the wrong cubicle? "I'm . . . pretty sure this is the place," she said more slowly. "Isn't this Nancy Kincaid's office?"

I just can't believe it's you . . .

The black woman stared at her for a long moment. The stare seemed dark. Deep. Empty.

Oh, it all seems wrong somehow . . .

"Well . . . yes," the black woman said after a long moment. "Yes, it is Nancy Kincaid's office." And then she shook her head. Once. Slowly.

"But you're not Nancy Kincaid."

AVIS BEST
————————➤

The phone rang. The baby started crying. The Shithead started pounding on the door.

For a moment, Avis did not know which way to turn. She stood in the center of the bare white living room, a small, paralyzed figure under the ceiling's naked bulb. Her hands were in the air, her fingers splayed. Her sweet, pale face seemed frozen.

The phone rang again and again. The baby kept crying for her. The Shithead hammered the door hard and now he was shouting too.

"Avis! Avis, I know you're in there! Open the goddamned door, Avis! You're my fucking wife, now open the goddamned door!"

Avis put her hands to her hair—short curls of dirty-blonde hair. She blinked once behind the huge, square frames of her glasses.

13

"Avis! I'm telling you! I know you're there!"

The baby's crying, she thought. *Get the baby.*

She could hear the rhythmic wails from the bedroom: "Aah! Aah! Aah!"

The kitchenette phone shrilled in between. And *wham! wham! wham!* went the Shithead's fist.

"It's my baby too, Avis! You can't keep me away from my own goddamned baby!"

But Avis stood there, stunned, yet another moment. It had all happened too quickly for her.

Just thirty seconds ago, she had been sitting in the empty room quietly. She had been perched on the canvas chair before the folding card table. She had been resting her hands on the keys of her portable Olivetti, staring at the page peeling off the roller. It was the last page of her report on *Thirty Below,* a thriller novel set here in New York City. She wrote reports like this for a living. She read novels and wrote synopses of them. Then she wrote her opinion on whether or not the novels' plots would make good movies. She sent these reports to the office of Victory Pictures, so that the Victory executives could pretend that *they* had read the novels and had opinions. She was paid sixty dollars for each report.

On this report, on this page, she had just typed: "This exciting urban thriller—reminiscent of *Marathon Man*—could be a good vehicle for Dustin Hoffman." She had been sitting in the canvas chair, staring at that sentence.

Dustin Hoffman, she had been thinking. *A good vehicle for Dustin Hoffman. I don't know how I'm going to pay my rent next month, and I'm writing about vehicles for Dustin Hoffman. How am I going to buy diapers for my baby, Dustin Hoffman? Tell me that, you stupid millionaire sitting by your pool someplace drinking champagne! My little baby doesn't have good clothes to wear, Mr. Dusty, Mr. Dust-man, and if he were on fucking fire YOU WOULDN'T PISS ON HIM TO PUT HIM OUT AND MY LIFE IS SHIT, YOU MOVIE STAR ASSHOLE! What am I going to do?*

That is what she had been thinking. And her glasses had been beginning to fog with tears. And she had been thinking about how, if she hadn't married the Shithead, she would have graduated from Kenyon this past year. And she would've come to New York and been a set designer instead of the wife of a starving actor. And she would not have allowed herself to get pregnant before her husband had even landed a paying role. And she would never have known what it felt like for a nice girl from Cleveland, Ohio, to lie curled on the kitchenette floor, trying to protect her womb with her arms while her husband punched her head again and again and again because it was her fault, all her fault, all of it, all of it . . .

A good vehicle for Dustin Hoffman, she had been thinking. *Well, hot shit.*

And then the phone had started ringing. The baby woke up and started to cry. The Shithead started pounding on the door.

"When I get in there, Avis, you are going to be one sorry girl, you understand me? If you don't open this door right this second . . ."

Now, finally, her paralysis broke. She started for the bedroom, for the baby.

"Get the hell out of here, Randall," she shouted over her shoulder. "You can't come in here. Just go away."

"Avis! Goddamnit!" He hit the door hard—with his shoulder it sounded like. The chain lock bounced and rattled.

The phone kept ringing.

"Aah! Aah! Aah!" the baby cried.

"I'm coming, sweetheart." Avis pushed open the connecting door and ran into the bedroom.

It was just like *The Wizard of Oz.* Stepping from the living room into the bedroom: it was just like the scene in the movie *The Wizard of Oz* where Dorothy steps from her black-and-white Kansas house into the colorful world of Munchkinland. The living room was Kansas. The peeling white walls, the faded parquet floor; the card table, the chair, the bare bulb in the ceiling. The bedroom—the nursery—that was Oz, or Munchkinland or whatever. There was a riot of color and decoration here. The walls were plastered with Mickeys and Goofys and Kermit the Frogs. The floors were lined with toys and cushions, unicorns and rainbows. And so many dangling

mobiles—elephant mobiles, lamb mobiles, airplane mobiles
—that Avis had to push them out of her way as she ran to
the crib by the bright window.

My apartment, she thought frantically. *A good vehicle for
Judy Garland.* She reached the side of the crib.

The baby was waiting for her there, standing, gripping the
crib's top rail. He was a sturdy ten-month-old boy with sandy
hair and blue eyes. He had pushed aside his handsewn quilt
and was jumping up and down amid his embroidered pillows.
The moment he saw her, he stopped crying. His puckered
face smoothed and cleared. He broke into his huge, half-
toothless, baby grin.

"Gee-ee-ee," he said.

"Oh!" Avis breathed. "It's da baby! Did da baby come to
say hello? *Hello* to da baby!"

"Agga agga agga agga," the baby said.

"This is bullshit, Avis!" She could still hear the Shithead
screaming through the other room. "You cannot keep me
out! This is not legal!" And—*wham!* It sounded like he hit
the door with his whole body this time.

The phone shrilled again, insistent.

"Agga agga agga agga!" said the baby.

"Oh, da baby." Avis hoisted him quickly out of the crib,
held him against her shoulder.

"I'm gonna break this fucking door down, Avis, I mean
it!"

He hit it hard again. The phone rang.

"Oh God," Avis whispered.

She held her baby's head gently as she rushed out of Oz,
back into the living room. She blinked hard as her tears made
the bare Kansas walls blur. She ran toward the kitchenette,
toward the phone on the wall.

"Avis!" He was now hammering rapidly against the door
with his fist: bang-bang-bang-bang-bang-bang without stopping. "A-vis!"

"I'm going to call the police, Randall!" she called out,
crying. "I'm serious!"

"Go ahead!" The fist kept hammering. "They'll agree with
me! You know they will! Go ahead!"

The baby made a small, frightened noise against her shoulder. She patted his head as she ran. "It's all right," she whispered breathlessly.

"Avis!" Bang-bang-bang.

The phone on the wall rang again just as she reached it. She snatched it up. Held it to her ear.

There was nothing. Then a dial tone. The caller had finally hung up.

"Oh shit!"

She slammed the phone down. The Shithead flung himself against the door so hard, so loudly, that she spun to face it. He did it again. The door seemed to bulge inward. She backed against the wall and stared at it. Where the fuck was Dustin Hoffman now?

"You hear me, Avis?"

The baby was starting to whimper, afraid.

"Ssh," Avis said. She stroked him. She bit her lip as the tears streamed down her cheeks.

Randall slammed into the door. She gasped. She thought she heard the wood cracking.

"Avis, goddamn it!"

"All right!" she shouted. And now the baby started crying. She stroked him, jogged him up and down. "All right, that's it!" she screamed.

The Shithead pounded wildly. The door cracked and jumped in its frame.

"Avis!"

"That's it!" she screamed. "Stop it right now, I swear to God, or that's it, that's it! I'm calling Perkins."

On the instant, the pounding stopped. The screaming stopped. The room went silent except for the baby's tentative cries. Avis held the boy against her shoulder, bounced him up and down. "Ssh," she whispered. "It's all right now. Ssh." She sniffled. She took a quick swipe at her nose with her knuckles. More loudly, she said, "Do you hear me, Randall?"

The silence went on for another second. Then: "Damn it, Avis," he said. But he did not shout now. He said it quietly. "Damn it."

"I'm serious," Avis said, jogging her baby. "I mean it. I'm going to call him. I'm going to call him right now."

"Goddamn it," came the voice—the suddenly little voice —from behind the door. "Look . . ." And then: "Goddamn it . . . Goddamn it, Avis, what do you have to pull shit like that for?"

"I mean it," Avis called back. "I'm picking up the phone. Just go away, Randall. I'm picking up the phone right this minute."

"A-vis," the Shithead whined. "Come on. Come on, I mean it. Don't do stuff like this. I mean it."

"I'm dialing him. I'm dialing Perkins right now."

The baby had lifted his head from her shoulder. He was looking around with wide-eyed interest. "Pah?" he wondered softly. The baby liked Perkins.

"Listen, Avis, could we just talk?" said Randall through the door.

She gritted her teeth. She hated this, the way he sounded now, the humiliation in his voice. She wanted it to stop. She wanted to leave him some pride. Maybe she *could* let him in, she thought. Even if he was a Shithead. Maybe they could just talk, just through the chain maybe. Just for a minute. She closed her eyes, took a breath. She forced herself to go through with it. "The phone is ringing, Randall," she called.

"Shit," he said softly through the door. But he tried one more time. "You know, I'm going to call my lawyer, Avis. I am. I'm gonna call my lawyer on this right now, today, as soon as I get home."

She pressed her lips together, almost overwhelmed with pity. She knew Randall didn't have any lawyer. She knew it was just something he said whenever he felt helpless and weak. The tears that had pooled in her glasses spilled out now in little streams. And still, she made herself go on. "It's ringing, Randall. It's ringing right . . . Hello! Perkins? Hi, it's me, Avis."

"All right, all right," Randall said quickly. She could hear him moving away from the door now. She could hear his voice growing fainter. "All right, but I'm serious, Avis. You're gonna hear from my lawyer on this. You can't just do this. I got rights. I got rights, you know."

But then there were his footsteps on the stairs. Tumbling down the stairs quickly. Practically running. She could imagine Randall shooting a terrified glance back over his shoulder as he skittered past Perkins's door on the landing below.

"Pah?" said the baby, looking around with his big eyes.

Avis held him away from her so she could look in his face. He stared at her, wondering.

"Pah!" she said, blowing on him.

The baby thought that was hilarious and let out a loud laugh, kicking his legs.

Right beside them, the phone rang loudly. Avis jumped. The baby thought that was hilarious too. The phone rang again. Avis let her breath out, shook her head. The baby laughed some more.

"Ah ha ha!"

"Very funny," Avis told him.

She caught up the phone as it rang a third time. She wedged the handset between her chin and shoulder. She held the baby out in the air. Made a face at him through her tears. He wriggled happily.

"Hello," she said. She sniffled.

"Oh, Avis," came the voice on the other end, an old woman's voice, quavering. "Oh, Avis. Thank heavens. You're finally there. It's Ollie's Nana, dear. I need him. I'm desperate. There's been a catastrophe."

NANCY KINCAID

"What's that supposed to mean?" she said. She laughed. "I'm not Nancy Kincaid—what does that mean? Who am I then? Am I supposed to guess?"

But the black woman in the doorway did not laugh. She was not even smiling anymore. She simply stood there, poised and stylish. Her folder under her arm. Her hip jutting a little in her red dress. Her gaze still empty, still unfathomable. Nancy (because she was sure that she *was*, in fact, Nancy Kincaid) found herself shifting nervously under that gaze. Her weight went from foot to foot. Her hand flicked to her hair.

"Come on," she said. "Seriously. What is the problem here?"

The black woman raised one hand: a mature, professional gesture. "Look," she said. "You can't be in here without permission. All right? That's all I know. If you want to wait outside in the reception area, maybe when Nancy comes in you can discuss it with her, otherwise—"

"But I *am* Nancy. This is my office. Christ. I mean, I think I know who I am."

"Well—I'm sorry. But whoever you are, you can't stay in here." The black woman did not waver. Her gaze did not waver. "You'll have to go out into the waiting room. Please."

"I can't believe this." Open-mouthed, Nancy looked around for support. Through the glass partitions, she could see down the row of offices. She could see an older woman hanging up her coat on a stand. A man in shirtsleeves opening his briefcase on his desk. People were going about their business, getting down to work. Only she, of all God's children, was being persecuted here by the Demon Secretary of Warren Street. She turned back to the black woman. "You know," she said, as the idea dawned on her, "I don't think I know *you*. Do *you* work here?"

"Miss, I don't have time for this right now. If you want to—"

"Do you work here?" Nancy said. "I mean, this is ridiculous. Why are you bothering me?"

"Albert." The woman had turned, had called the name down the corridor. Nancy glanced to her left and saw the man in shirtsleeves look up at the call. He was a young man with coiffed brown hair. He was wearing a blue-striped shirt with a red tie and jolly red suspenders.

"Is that you calling, Martha, my love?" he said.

"Albert, could you come in here for a moment?"

Jesus. This woman won't give up, Nancy thought. But she was annoyed to feel a little clutch of fear in her stomach. As if she were a high school kid standing up to a teacher. "Look, can I just get to work now please?" she said, a little desperately. "I mean, this is ridiculous. I would like to have my office to my—"

"Albert." The young man had joined the black woman in the doorway. The black woman—Martha—was indicating Nancy with one red fingernail.

"Yes, oh entrancing one," Albert said.

"This woman has come in here without permission."

"Horrors!"

"She says she's Nancy."

"What?" To Nancy's dismay, the young man, this Albert, looked up at her and let out a surprised little laugh. "She says she's Nancy?"

"Nancy Kincaid?" Nancy said. She felt the blood rushing to her cheeks. "Fernando Woodlawn's personal assistant? Jesus, you guys! I don't know what's going on here but . . ." Then, as Martha and Albert gazed at her, she stopped. Two other people had come up behind them. A tall woman with tinted hair. A doughy blob of a man in a gray suit. They were standing on their toes, looking in at her over Martha's and Albert's shoulders. Nancy looked from one to the other, from one stare to the other. Her mouth was still open on her last word as the whole thing became clear to her. "Oh," she said finally, drawing out the syllable. "Oh. Oh, very, very funny. Very funny, people." And her cheeks really did turn scarlet now. She felt as if her whole body was blushing and she thought: *Damn him!* "All right," she said. "Where is he? Where's Fernando? What is this, like, some kind of trick he pulls every year at Halloween or something? Break in the new girl? Is he hiding under the desk or recording this or something? Come on. You got me. I'm humiliated, hooray. Enough is enough."

She was trying hard to keep her composure, not to show how irritated and embarrassed she was. But this was something that truly bugged her about her ever-lovin' boss. This sixteen-year-old jockstrap humor of his. The fact that she was an overprotected Catholic girl was just the big joke of the world to him. It was just so, so funny. Practically every day, he went out of his way to mention some bodily function or other in front of her. As if she'd never heard of it before. Then he'd shout out to everyone, "Look. Catholic School is blushing." And, of course, that *would* make her blush. And then she was always supposed to laugh and roll her eyes and demonstrate that she could take a joke.

"You've had your fun," she said now, controlling her voice. She was feeling hotter, more ridiculous, more annoyed by the moment. "You can all go back to Fernando and tell him I blushed and looked stupid, okay? Now I have a lot of work to do this morning, so if you don't mind . . ."

But the people standing in the doorway said nothing. They answered her, all four of them, only with those gazes. Empty and unfathomable stares; stares in a waxwork; unwavering. Nancy felt herself tighten as it went on and on. She felt her whole body tighten with the frustration of it. The frustration—and something else. That clutch of fear again, that cold contraction in her stomach.

It all seems wrong somehow . . .

She swallowed. She put her hands on her hips. She was aware of the silence lengthening. She was aware of the whisper of traffic in the room. The faint Warren Street patter and shush coming in through the open window behind her. She was aware that she was just standing there, jutting her chin at the four of them as they confronted her. She could not think of anything else to say.

"What's going on here?"

The voice broke the moment. It was a loud voice, deep and authoritative. The cluster of people at the door slowly gave way. A new arrival shouldered his way into the room between Martha and Albert.

Nancy cried out at the sight of him: "Oh!" She felt a great warm bath of relief. "Henry! Thank heavens!"

Henry Goldstein, the firm's junior partner, was now standing just within the office. He was a short man, but broad-shouldered; well formed in his gray suit. He had a full head of silver hair and chiseled good looks that went with his voice: a look of authority. He was searching around him for an explanation. He turned to Nancy.

"Listen, Henry," she said at once, "would you please get the Fernando Brigade here to curtail the sidesplitting hilarity and let me get to work? We've got the community meeting later today and Fernando's gonna kill me if I don't have his charts put together before lunchtime."

She checked herself, kept herself from babbling on. She waited. Henry Goldstein lowered his brows at her. He cocked his head. "I'm sorry?" he said. Uncertainly, he glanced over his shoulder at Martha.

"She keeps saying she's Nancy Kincaid," said the black woman with a shrug. "She came in here without permission and now she says she's Nancy and this is her office. She says she won't leave."

Slowly, Goldstein inclined his proud chin, as if to say: Ah, I see; I understand everything. He turned back to Nancy. She caught her breath as she saw the caution, the wariness that had now entered his hazel eyes.

"Henry . . . ?" she started to say.

"Just take it easy, Miss," Goldstein answered her. He held out his hands toward her.

To calm me! she thought. *He's trying to keep me calm!*

"No one wants to hurt you," he went on.

23

Nancy's mouth fell open. She backed away from him. From all of them. All of them just kept staring at her. Martha with her blank brown eyes. Young Albert with his alert features. The tint-haired woman and the roly-poly man—their curious glares on her like spotlights.

What the hell is this?

She took another step back and felt the cool air from the window against her calves.

"No one wants to hurt you," Goldstein repeated. "All we want is for you to step outside into the reception area. We can talk about everything out there. Okay?"

Nancy shook her head. "I don't . . . I don't . . . understand. I mean . . ." That muzziness—the feverish haze that had been with her all morning—it was rising inside her again. She felt as if her head were expanding. She blinked as her thoughts clouded. "I . . . I mean . . . Don't you know me? Don't, uh, don't you know who I am?"

The stocky little Goldstein took a small step toward her. His hand stayed in front of him, to ward her off now too. "We can talk about all that right outside, Miss. Right outside in the waiting room. Okay? We'll all talk about it together and figure it all out. No one wants to hurt you."

Nancy put her hand to her forehead, trying to clear it.

"We're all your friends," Goldstein said.

Well, she thought wildly, *that's certainly reassuring.*

Now Albert was coming forward also. He took a long, vigorous step around the far side of the gunmetal desk. "Watch out behind you now," he said. "Don't get too close to that window."

"Look . . . Look, I'm a little confused, I . . . I don't know what's going on . . . I came in here, I . . . I mean . . ." She shook her head. The fog was filling her mind. She couldn't stop it. *I'm babbling,* she thought. *Stop babbling.* "Look, I just, I'm feeling a little sick today or something . . . if you could just let me . . . If you could just . . ." She didn't finish.

"No one's going to hurt you," said Goldstein, sliding toward her. "We'll just take you outside."

"Look, if you could just . . . I mean, I *am* Nancy Kincaid!" she said weakly.

Somehow, someone had moved right up beside her. She heard his voice, a new voice, a soft, warm voice, right at her elbow. "Hey," he said, "this is ridiculous. Why don't you just shoot him?"

Startled, she swung around to face him. "What do you mean, shoot him? I'm not just going to shoot him, how can I . . . ?"

She stopped. No one was there. No one was standing there at all. There was only the file cabinet in the corner. The open window. The ledge out over Warren Street. The faint plash of traffic. The faint clatter of falling leaves in the park on Broadway. And no one . . .

Nancy stood where she was. For a long, long moment, she just stood: half turned; her mouth open. She stared at the file cabinet, at the window. Her eyes darted from one to the other, and to the wall, and to the floor, trying to find someone, anyone, any*thing,* that might have just spoken to her.

A voice? The thought blinked in her mind like neon as she stared. *A voice telling me to shoot him? Did I hear that? Oh shit. Oh, that is not good. That is not a good thing at all.*

"Martha," Goldstein said. She heard him speaking to the secretary in slow, authoritative tones. "Martha, I want you to call the police. From my office. Right now. Right away."

"Right."

Slowly—still staring, still wide-eyed—Nancy (She *was* Nancy, damn it. Wasn't she?) turned to face them again. Goldstein was closer to her now. Creeping up on the near side of her well-groomed desk. Albert was coming around the far side, edging toward her. There were more people in the doorway too and some out in the corridor, a whole audience of them. And there was Martha in her red dress. She was just turning to push her way into the crowd. Just tearing her fearful gaze away from Nancy and turning to push her way to the phone in Goldstein's office. To call the police.

"That—That won't be necessary," Nancy heard herself whisper. She could barely squeeze the words out past the stricture in her throat. Her head had begun to throb again. All her thoughts seemed to have dissolved into a thick mist that hung over her mind, over everything. She swallowed hard, but her throat was dry. Her lips were dry and stiff. "That's not necessary," she said, a little louder.

Martha paused. She glanced doubtfully at Mr. Goldstein.

"I'll . . . I'll just go," Nancy said quickly. She had to get out. She had to get some air, clear her thoughts. *What the hell . . . What the hell . . . ?* "I'll just . . . I'll go, okay? Just let me go." *Shoot him?*

Goldstein lifted a hand toward her. "Are you sure you don't want us to call someone for you? I think you could use some help, Miss."

Shoot him? "No, no, I'm . . ." She bit her lip, fighting back the tears. "I'm fine," she said. She could not look at him. She looked at the desktop in front of her. She could not look at any of them, could not meet their eyes. "I'm just not feeling very well right now, I'm . . . I'm sorry. I . . . I don't feel well."

They were all looking at her. She knew they were all looking, staring at her. She felt naked in front of them. *God!* she thought. *God, I mean . . . I mean: God!* She reached out quickly, snatched her purse off the desktop. She clutched it to her chest as if for protection. "I'm just not feeling very well," she said. "I'll just go. That's all. Please."

She scuttled forward quickly. The crowd parted in front of her. Hell, they jumped out of her way, jumped to either side. They couldn't leave the path clear fast enough. She hurried through them. She was vaguely aware that Goldstein was following her. That he and Albert had come around just behind her, on either side of her. They flanked her as she hurried out of the office. They escorted her down the corridor. Past the dingy offices behind their glass partitions. Past the photo of Fernando framed by the city. Out again through the low gate, through the reception area. With everyone behind her, everyone staring at her, watching her go.

What . . . ? she kept thinking, as she hurried to the elevator, as she stared at the floor in front of her, as she clutched her purse. *What . . . ? What . . . ?*

Mr. Goldstein pressed the elevator button for her. She stood in front of the door, clutching her purse, her head bowed, like a supplicant with hat in hand. It took an unbearably long time for the elevator to arrive, and she thought, *What . . . ? What is it? What is happening here?*

When the door finally slipped open, Nancy charged inside. She spun around, her back against the steel wall. They were all still there, just through the elevator door. They were all in the reception area and beyond it, behind the low gate. Goldstein and Albert and Martha in her red dress. They were all gazing at her as she cowered in her box. Those empty waxwork gazes fixed her. And she clutched her purse, praying that the door would close.

Then the door closed. Clapped shut. And Nancy's knees buckled. She sagged, sticking her tongue out as her stomach roiled. She slid halfway to the floor. Then she crouched there, grimacing, staring into space and gritting her teeth as her eyes brimmed over with tears.

The elevator started down to the ground.

"What?" she whispered.

Then she coughed once, and started to cry.

OLIVER PERKINS

Perkins staggered to the toilet. He grabbed the light-string next to him and yanked it. The bathroom's bare bulb went on. Naked, Perkins stood above the toilet bowl. He squinted sleepily at his penis, waiting for the piss.

The bottom of the toilet bowl was covered with some sort of brown crud. It darkened the toilet water, so he could see his face reflected in it. The light from the bulb behind his head threw the reflected face into silhouette. Beams of light-bulb light radiated from the silhouette in a golden halo. His reflection looked Christlike, the beams fanning out from his shaggy hair.

Look, Ma, Perkins thought, *I'm a demigod.*

Then the piss broke from him. It splattered in the toilet water. The reflection was obliterated.

Perkins gave a soft snort as the stream of piss ran. He smiled with one corner of his mouth. Even through the haze of his hangover, he could see the poem in this: the reflected Christself pissed into oblivion. Even though his brain had turned to sand, he could tell the poem was good. He could feel it rising in him as he stared down into the bowl. Just a wordless rhythm, at first. Not a poem yet, just the sound, the beat of a poem. He felt it mushrooming up out of his chest as he pissed. He felt how white it was. He felt how it was spreading itself within him, spreading like wings, rising up out of him. He felt the words starting to clamber aboard, the rhythms becoming syllables.

There . . . he thought. *There* . . .

But already, the poem had begun to falter. It was dissolving. The wings were atomizing. The solid white of it was melting away.

And the stream of piss was faltering too. It pattered in the water loudly. Perkins tried to hold on to his poem, but it was no good. It plummeted. Dropped off the edge of him into nothingness. All of a sudden, it was just gone. He was empty inside. He sprayed the toilet water with a few last squirts.

Oh well, he thought casually. *No more good poems for you, sonny boy.*

But the truth was, it made him feel black and lonesome. Standing there naked on the mossy bathroom tile, his poem gone. It made him feel a huge, yearning, vasty lonesomeness. As if he were standing at the bottom of a canyon, searching amid the rocks for another soul on earth.

He took his dick in his hand and waggled a drop off it. From behind, he released some of the hangover gas twisting in his gut.

There had been no good poems for two years now, he thought. Two full years this month. There had been nothing worth publishing since the river house. Since Julia and the October evenings.

He reached down to flush the toilet. The water gushed away, though the weird brown stuff remained. He sighed. There were still some days when he thought it was kind of romantic to be a dissolute Village poet. Then there were days like this one: when he thought he was going to vomit until his ears bled. He twitched the string to turn off the bathroom bulb. Then, tugging one more bit of dribble off his pud, he stalked back into the other room.

Avis Best was there. She was just climbing in through the window, her baby under her arm. Perkins waved to her wearily, his eyes half closed. He made his way to the mattress on the floor. He flopped down on it with a groan.

By that time, Avis was standing by the window. She was staring around the room, her mouth open. Behind her, a line of blue sky showed through the bars of the fire escape. She held her baby on her hip. The baby played with her face as she stood there gaping.

"Jesus Christ, Perkins," she said.

Perkins rolled onto his back on the bare mattress. He flung his arm over his eyes. He felt black and lonely and dry, his whole body stuffed with gritty sand. "Oh, Avis," he said pitifully. His head hurt too and he was beginning to feel nauseous.

"Oh, really," Avis said. "Do you mind telling me what you're trying to do to yourself?"

He shook his head slightly. "I don't remember. But it must be something really awful."

"Sure looks like it."

"I just hope I don't deserve it."

"Pah! Pah! Pah!" the baby cried out. He had noticed the naked figure on the bed. He was twisting in his mother's arms, straining toward the man, reaching out.

"All right." Avis let out a breath. She started picking her way to the mattress through the mess. "Look at this place." Even in the dim western light from the window, she could see it was a disaster.

It was just a studio, just the one large room. A subway map

29

taped to the wall. A framed drawing of Whitman. A poster from the Keats House one of his girlfriends had brought him from Rome. There was a writing desk with a Spartan wooden chair. A dresser. A few canvas chairs, a couple of standing lamps. There was the mattress, bare on the floor.

But mostly, there were books. There were books everywhere, gray and dusty. Piles of them lined the walls, two deep, three deep, four. Stacks of them rose up at random in the center of the room like stalagmites. Books covered the desk and all the chairs. Even the bookshelf—Avis thought she remembered a small bookshelf here somewhere once—was buried now under the books.

And then there was the rest of it. His bedcovers splayed everywhere. His jeans over a chair back, his sweater over a tumbled mound of Dostoevskys. His underpants tied around a lamp.

Gimme a break, Avis thought sourly.

And bottles of Sam Adams beer lying in the gaps all around. Empty bottles made of brown glass: Wherever she looked, her eye fell on one. She bumped one with her toe as she reached the mattress, sent it rolling with a clink into an illustrated *Quixote*.

She lowered herself to the mattress, sat down next to Perkins. Perkins dropped his arm and gazed up at her pitiably. She tried to keep from glancing down at his nakedness, but she couldn't help it. He was a sturdily built man with a hairy barrel chest and muscular arms. He wore his black hair long and had an angular face, pouched and lined at thirty-one. She found his eyes—his brown eyes—seductively miserable.

She placed the baby on his chest. He held the chunky little kid steady. The baby gave a big smile and pawed him. Perkins suddenly blew up his cheeks and the baby looked up at his mother in surprise and laughed.

Avis smiled. She touched Perkins's forehead, brushed his hair with her fingers. "How bad is it?" she said softly.

"Oh . . ." He wrinkled his nose at the baby. " 'My heart aches, and a drowsy numbness pains my sense, as though of hemlock I had drunk.' How's by you?"

"Okay, I guess. So-so."

"Baga baga baga, pah, pah, pah," said the baby. He slapped Perkins's chest. Perkins gave a grunt and lifted him into the air. The baby squealed and wriggled.

Perkins lowered the baby and kissed his neck. He was comforted a little by the softness of the baby's skin and hair, and by the fact that the kid liked him. With a great effort, he propped himself up so he could set the baby on the floor beside the bed. Then he let go and the baby started crawling away.

"Stick to the classics," Perkins said, "and don't put your fingers in a socket."

The baby babbled his farewells and crawled off among the books.

"My advice to the generations," said Perkins. He lay back heavily on the mattress. He took Avis's hand. He looked up at her. The small features of the valentine-shaped face, hovering over him, soothing. She brushed at his forehead again, smiling down at him. He felt his cock stir at her cool touch.

"Your Nana called," she told him gently.

He closed his eyes. "Oh boy."

"She says she couldn't reach you. She says your phone is off the hook."

"Jesus. I don't even know where it is. Was it urgent?"

"Oh, I don't know. You know Nana. It's a catastrophe."

"Oh no."

"I told her you'd be over there in an hour."

Perkins kept his eyes closed. He felt her cool fingertips. "Maybe I should call her," he murmured. "Maybe I can find the phone."

"No, her nurse was just coming. She wants you to come over."

"Okay," he said. It was barely audible. His mind was drifting now. He was thinking now about Avis. He was picturing her: the way she had been on the one night he had had her. He remembered her lying facedown on his mattress, sobbing into the pillow. He had stood over her, breathless and helpless. He had just finished dealing with her husband. His knuckles were pouring blood. After a long time, he had knelt down next to her. He wanted her to stop crying, and he wanted her, and he did not know what else to do. His breath caught when she lifted her hips to let him work her leggings down. She had parted her legs too when he stretched out on top of her. All the while he was rocking in and out of her, she had held his hand in front of her and sucked the blood off his fingers. He had murmured to her, and he thought he heard her whisper something. He didn't catch it though. She would never tell him what it was . . .

The memory was giving him an erection. He opened his eyes. He saw Avis steal another glance down him. She nearly smiled, but then she took her hands away. She stood up quickly. Grabbed his bedsheet off the floor and dropped it over him.

"You could get dressed, you know," she said. "You could pretend that I was here."

"I know you're here," he said. The light was bad, but he thought he saw her cheeks color. Anyway, she hurried across the room to the baby, who was stretched across *The Idiot* now, chewing on Perkins's sweater. She got the sweater from him. Draped it over her arm.

"You do this too much, Perkins," she said.

"I got carried away. Don't clean up."

"You get carried away too much." She lifted his jeans while the baby watched her. "It's like every night, every other night."

"It's not every night. Avis . . . Don't clean up. I'm telling you." He tried to get up, but the movement shifted the sand in his head. He could only sit on the edge of the mattress, his feet on the floor. He covered his face with his hands. "Oh man!"

"I'm telling *you*, Oliver," Avis said. "It's getting to be a real habit."

He forced himself to look up at her. She was placing his clothes on top of the dresser now. Then she was tugging the laundry bag out from underneath the dresser, stuffing in his underwear.

"Avis, would you not do this, please."

"Well, look at this place, Ollie."

His shoulders sagged. He shook his head dismally. He

turned and squinted dismally at the window, at the strip of blue sky. "I don't know," he said finally. "I gave a reading at the café last night."

"Well, that's no excuse." She had moved across the room to pry her son's fingers from the base of a standing lamp. "Everyone always . . . oof! . . . loves your readings."

"Yeah." He grunted at her. "All those old poems. The same ones over and over. I had to wash away the taste of them. I could feel them stuck in my throat."

"Oh, Oliver, come on."

"Two years, Avis. Two years this month since I wrote my last good one."

"And getting tanked every night is going to help a lot."

He sighed. Sat silently.

"Shit," Avis muttered. He glanced at her. She had been restacking a toppled pile of Greek histories and had come up with something. She examined it a moment, turning it in her fingers. "I guess someone lost this," she said. She tossed it across the room to him.

He caught it in his cupped hands. An earring. Turquoise on hand-hammered silver. Something bought on the street in the East Village probably. "Not one of yours, huh?"

"You know it's not." She showed him her back, walking toward the kitchenette.

Perkins gazed down at the earring, trying to remember. He had a vague flash of the café. The black microphone in his face. The cool neck of the beer bottle in his fist. Candlelight in the white wine at the tables. Faces at the tables, young men, young women's faces; the grizzled chins of the old Village denizens; the candlelight in their eyes.

Avis flicked on the light in the kitchenette. "I hope it's a girl's, that's all," she said darkly.

"There was someone." He studied the earring.

"You said you weren't going to do boys anymore. It's dangerous—especially when you're too drunk to think."

"Cindy," he said. "Or Mindy. Maybe it was Mindy . . ." He looked up then and saw her in the kitchenette. He flinched. A dolmen of encrusted pots and dishes rose out of the sink.

Avis was sponging some red slime off the countertop. A roach was scuttling for a crack in the caulking.

"Well, I'm sure she was a nice girl," she was saying. "She probably just had to get back to school in time for recess."

"Avis," said Perkins. "Would you put down the fucking sponge."

"You want eggs?"

"Oh, don't make me breakfast. God, Avis, don't take care of me. I mean it. This is your whole problem."

"I'll get a psychiatrist first thing tomorrow. You want them scrambled?"

Perkins let out his breath, dejected. His chin fell to his chest. There was the baby. Crawling over a Sam Adams to get to his foot. Smiling up at him from his hairy toes, waiting for some attention.

Perkins reached down and picked the baby up. The baby put his arms around the poet's neck. "Yeah," Perkins said quietly. "Scrambled is fine."

He lay down with the baby on top of him. He blew out his cheeks again to make the baby laugh. But now the kid had noticed the buttons on the mattress. He was climbing down off Perkins to see if he could get some to eat.

Abandoned, Perkins lay where he was, staring up at the ceiling. He licked his lips, picking up the faint taste of dried vomit. He listened to the running water in the kitchenette. The clattering of pots as Avis cleared them. He listened to the baby gurgling. The loneliness settled down over him like a blanket.

Two years, he thought. Not since the river house. He had sat on the porch there in the evenings and watched the view. The green Catskills rising against the pale and darkening sky. The beaver pond lying in the meadow just below, a black oval in the high grasses. He could see Julia floating on her back down there. Her long body white beneath the black water, her breasts breaking the surface of it. Her white thighs lifting and falling lazily as she kicked along. Sometimes he heard an explosive whap! as a beaver slapped its tail against the water to warn the others she was coming. More often, the creatures swam right over to her. He could see their Vshaped wakes, the domes of their heads. They would bump their black noses against her side and make her smile.

And Perkins would sit on the porch, balancing a pad on his lap, twirling a pen in his hand. Soon, the evening star would shine dimly in the big sky above them. Other stars would show through the tendrils of mountain mist. Raccoons would waddle to the pond's edge and drink while Julia floated with the beavers. And deer too would sometimes step from the grass and bow their heads gracefully to lap the water. There had seemed to him a luxury of life and death, night coming like that. And just as the light was almost gone, he would begin writing.

This is the animal hour.
The slow October flies, despairing on the porch chairs,
blink into the shards of the sun they see setting.
Blue and then a deeper blue ease into the air,
and bats suddenly dive and butterfly up out of the trees . . .

His last good poem. The last poem in the collection.

"Christ." He groaned, his head going back and forth on the pillow. He rubbed his eyes with both hands. He yawned. "So what did Nana want anyway?" he said.

"What?" Avis was at the sink, the water running. She glanced over her shoulder, holding a pot under the stream.

"I said, What did my grandmother want?" Perkins called. "What was the big catastrophe?"

"Oh," Avis called back. "It's your kid brother again."

"Zachary?" Perkins came up slowly onto his elbow. "What the hell's the matter with Zach?"

Avis shrugged. "You know how Nana is."

"What?" he called. He couldn't hear her over the water.

"I say you know how Nana is," Avis shouted back to him.

"Agga agga agga," said the baby, climbing up Perkins's back.

Avis placed the clean pot in the drainer. She shouted: "Apparently, he's disappeared."

35

NANCY KINCAID

Deep breaths, she thought.

She was sitting on a bench in City Hall Park. One in the line of green benches that bordered the park path. She was sitting under sycamores. Their yellow leaves rattled above her in the breeze. Brown leaves and red leaves clattered by her feet along the pavement.

Through the trees, to her right, was the parking lot and the domed, white-stoned Hall. A garden of grass and hedges was to her left, a fountain spraying up out of it. Before her were the tall office buildings on Broadway. Their windows caught the sun, flashed white through the red leaves of the oaks by the sidewalk. She could hear car engines gunning and the rumbling of buses, and the patter of pedestrians too. She could see the streaks of traffic through the low branches.

She huddled in her tan trench coat. She bent over her knees, her arms crossed high on her thighs. She felt nauseous.

Just take deep breaths, she told herself. Deep breaths.

And don't hear voices.

Right. Deep breaths and no voices. And no gargoyles either.

Yeah, lose those gargoyles too. Woof.

She nodded: right. She took slow, steady, deep breaths. She tried to concentrate on the gray asphalt of the path in front of her. As soon as this pea soup blew out of her head, she thought . . . As soon as her stomach settled . . . she would take stock, she would figure this out.

You're not Nancy Kincaid.

The black woman's voice had been so . . . unwavering. She rocked a little on the green bench. She pulled her crossed arms in tighter to her middle.

The park was quieter now. The determined men in suits had stridden away, and so had the women in their curt dresses. She lifted her eyes along the curving path. Over the row of wire garbage cans in the path's center. Over the leaves stirring around the cans. She could feel how the place had emptied. It heightened her hovering sense of panic. To think that all those people were at work now. Bent to their desks, swiveling in their chairs, sipping their coffee in the bosoms of their normal days. She alone was here. And the occasional workmen bopping past. And the policemen—in the parking lot and on the Hall steps just visible through the trees.

And the beggars. The homeless men. They hunkered on benches across the way. They hunched or stretched on some of the benches beside her. There were over a dozen of them. In black coats, or wrapped in soiled blankets. In stained, baggy pants. With shirts like rags. White faces, black with grime. Black faces, gray with dust. Eyes balefully glaring.

I'll bet some of them *hear voices too,* she thought.

She shuddered. Took in another long pull of the autumn air. Her mind was beginning to clear a little now. That cottony feeling between her ears was starting to thin out. Her stomach was still up in her throat, but she didn't think she was going to vomit anytime soon. She began to release her grip on her middle. She straightened slowly. Sat up against the bench back, her purse by her side.

Yeah, I'll just bet they *hear voices all the time,* she thought.

She let her breath out in a long stream. So what now? She gazed fuzzily toward the red oaks near Broadway. What the heck, she wondered, was she supposed to do now? Go home? Explain things to Mom?

Why, you're home early, dear.

Yeah. Everyone at work said I wasn't me.

Oh that's too bad. Have some soup. It'll make you feel better.

She gave a short laugh. That was no good. She had to go back to the office, that's all. She had to talk to someone who knew her. Or prove to someone that she was who she was. *I mean, I am Nancy Kincaid,* she thought; *that ought to work to my advantage a little.* She imagined herself trying to explain this to her coworkers. She imagined herself being quizzed. The silver-haired, authoritative countenance of Henry Goldstein leaning in toward her. *I'm twenty-two years old,* she told him. *I work for Fernando Woodlawn. I'm his personal assistant. I live on Gramercy Park with my mom and dad. My mom, Nora, who does part-time work at the library. My dad, Tom, who's a lawyer.*

She tilted her head back carefully. Looked up over the crowns of the trees. She saw the tip of her office building against the cloudless sky. The faint design of its stonework, the shape of its gargoyles, jutting, still. There was a lull in the noise of traffic. She could hear the hiss and splash of the fountain in the grass plot to her left. She gazed at the building a long moment.

I have always lived in Manhattan, she told Henry Goldstein in her mind. She imagined herself sitting across a desk from him. He leaning back in his chair, finger laid across his lips. His stern eyes narrowed at her. *I grew up here,* she said. *You can ask anyone. Ask Maura. She'll know me. Maura and I have known each other forever, since we were babies practically. We still see each other almost every weekend. She doesn't have a boyfriend either, that's why. I know: It's arrested development. When you grow up in the city your parents tend to be overprotective. And there's the Catholic school thing too, like Fernando says. I mean, not that we're virgins or anything . . . But that's another story.*

To be really honest, I'm sometimes afraid Maura will meet someone before I do. I mean, a guy. It's not that I'm jealous or anything, it's just . . . Well, you know how girls are: I'd never see her. I mean, I don't know what I'd do if I didn't have her to talk to. Jesus. I mean, we went all through high school together. And believe me, St. Ann's was no picnic. We were even in elementary school together for two years when I was transferred to . . .

She came out of her fantasy suddenly. She thought a moment. Her lips parted.

. . . transferred to . . .

She felt it again. Like something inside her turning sour: a jolt of fear.

I was transferred . . . I went to elementary school . . .

She lowered her head. Lowered her eyes from the Broadway rooftop. Her mouth open, she scanned the park aimlessly, as if looking for the answer. She scanned the benches across the way. The dark bundle shapes of the homeless men, the hot eyes glaring out of them: Her gaze passed over them unseeing. She shook her head, as if to jog the answer loose.

I went to elementary school at . . .

But she couldn't. She couldn't remember. Nothing came. She could not remember where she had gone to elementary school.

God, that's weird. That's so weird.

It made her skin go cold. She tried to think back to it, picture it in her mind. A long brick building. Children filing in through the glass doors. No. No, that wasn't it. There was no connection. She felt the small bumps rising on her arms.

You're not Nancy Kincaid.

And the chill radiated out from the cold core of her. Sweat gathered under her tam, under her hairline. It rolled down her temple, down the back of her neck.

Oh, this is ridiculous, she thought angrily. *This is stupid. I know who I am. I can prove who I . . .*

She stopped. She wiped her lips with her palm. She looked down at the purse on the bench beside her. A big purse of black leather. She swallowed hard. Of course she could. She *could* prove who she was. She could prove who she was to anyone.

Idiot. Why hadn't she thought of that before? Up there, in the Woodlawn offices, with those unwavering gazes melting her knees. Why hadn't she just taken her wallet out? Shown them her identification, the picture on her driver's license? *I'm not Nancy Kincaid, huh? Well, who's that, clown? Meryl Streep?*

With an exasperated shake of her head, she brought the purse onto her lap. She unzipped it. At the same moment, she saw something move. She caught it out of the corner of her eye. She glanced up.

It was one of the homeless men. On one of the benches just across the path. Opening her purse must have attracted him. He was stealing a look at her under his brows. He was a slack-faced white, with long hair hanging in filthy, yellow knots. His scabby lips hung open. His eyes were half closed. Now, she saw, he was pushing off the bench, working to his feet.

Damn, she thought. She ought to get out of here, do this someplace else.

But she snatched her wallet out of her purse. She had to see her own ID. It was ridiculous, but she had to be sure. *I mean, a person ought to remember where she went to elementary school.*

She took a quick check of the beggar again. He was standing now, making a great show of ignoring her. Muttering to himself importantly. Examining the green bench he'd been sitting on. Fingering some of the newspapers he'd been using as blankets, as if he might've left something behind. As if he had anything to leave behind. I'm just standing up, he seemed to be saying. Nothing to do with you, Miss. But even now, she could tell, he was edging across the gray path. He was edging toward her.

It made Nancy nervous. But she couldn't wait. *Something* was wrong, after all. *Something* weird was going on. It wasn't just the people in her office. There was the gargoyle, her elementary school . . .

Why don't you just shoot him?

Yeah, and that: the voice. There was some kind of glitch in her brain this morning. A fever or something probably. Maybe she'd eaten some bad mayonnaise—her mother had always warned her about that. Whatever it was, she wanted to see her ID *now*. She wanted to make sure she wasn't completely nutso.

She opened her wallet. Again, she looked up quickly to check the beggar. He was on his way, all right. Casual as could be. His hands in the back pockets of his dusty black slacks. His black coat flapping in the breeze over his rag of a shirt. The yellow leaves showered down around him. The red oaks behind him set off his dark shape. He kicked the leaves at his feet idly as he shuffled toward her across the path.

Damn it, she thought again. She looked to her right, toward City Hall. There was still a cop in the parking lot, pacing along the line of government cars. And under the branches of the trees, she could see the legs of the cop on the Hall's steps too. They were definitely within screaming distance.

She went back to her wallet, angry at the bum for frightening her like this. Just because she opened her purse didn't mean he had to get some money from her. *I mean, cripes.*

She unsnapped the wallet's card pouch. She felt her heart speed up a little. An accordion of plastic holders spilled out onto her lap. Immediately, she saw her mother's picture. Tubby little mom, laughing, waving the camera away: *"Don't point that silly thing at me."* And there was her father, all silver haired and red faced; his crinkle-eyed grin.

Yes, yes, yes, she thought. A bus surged loudly on Broadway. Then, as the rumble of it died, she heard the beggar's footsteps coming closer on the path. She went through the plastic holders quickly, searching for her driver's license.

There was her MasterCard. Her name was on it, at least —Nancy Kincaid—right there at the bottom. And there was her Visa: same name, same girl. And then: bingo. The license. She closed her eyes for a second with relief after she saw it. Her picture. Her face. With its strong chin and the broad cheeks and the clear, honest eyes. The same old familiar face she had just seen reflected in the deli window. And there was her name—her own name—Nancy Kincaid—right there by its side. Proof positive. She was who she was.

Well, who the hell else would I be? she thought. She gave another exasperated shake of her head. But she smiled too. The knots inside her were starting to loosen.

Then she remembered the beggar. She glanced up. She caught him midway across the path. He stopped beside a garbage can. Studied its contents, muttering darkly. Just checking out the garbage, lady. Don't mind me.

I better get out of here, she thought.

She folded up the plastic accordion. Popped it back into her wallet. Snapped the wallet shut. All she needed to do now was to go back to her office. Talk to someone who knew her. Someone who was willing to listen.

And don't hear any more voices.

And nix those voices, right. But she wasn't worried about that anymore now. She felt sure it was going to be all right. Just a flu or something. A fever. That bad, bad mayo. She put her wallet back in her purse. She pushed it down deep, as if to protect it from the oncoming beggar. Just as soon as she could go back and speak to Henry Goldstein, as soon as she got everything straightened out, it would be . . .

On the instant, she went cold again. Her heart went cold. Her skin prickled with it.

Something . . .

Her fingers had touched something. Something in her purse. Something hard. Something black and chilly.

What the hell . . . ? she thought—but somehow she already knew.

The sounds of Broadway traffic seemed to recede from her. The plash of the fountain, the rattle of the sycamore leaves above. Even the sweetly cool autumn breeze that stirred her hair on her brow seemed to be blowing far away.

What . . . ?

Her fingers were groping over the object in her purse. Feeling out its shape. Tracing it along its cold black surface.

Then, almost without meaning to—without wanting to— she took hold of it. She brought it up. Up from the bottom of the purse on her lap. Past her compact, past her Kleenex, past her lipstick, past her keys. All her relief was gone. The sickly chill of her fear, the tight twist of her fear, had come back redoubled. The sweat dropped off her as she looked down, onto her hands. She stared at what she held.

A pistol?

It was a .38 caliber revolver. A nasty-looking little piece. Snub-nosed, black, ugly. Its compact shape seemed coiled on her palm somehow. As if it were ready to spring out, to strike. Her hand shook as she held it. Her lips moved silently as she stared at it.

What the hell . . . ? A pistol?

Why don't you just shoot him?

She shook her head slowly. She raised her eyes.

The beggar stood there before her, blotting out the sky. His large, dark shape hung over her. His hot white eyes burned down into her. The smell of him, the gutter smell, the sour, living smell, snaked its way into the freshness of the October air and turned it rancid.

Nancy stared up at him, clutching the gun just inside her purse. The beggar smiled. His lips cracked open. His teeth showed, yellow and skewed. He held his hand out to her. Nancy caught her breath. She wanted to call out, but couldn't. The cry stuck in her throat.

"Don't forget now," the beggar said. His voice was a long, slow screak. He leaned down toward her. "Don't forget: eight o'clock." He winked. "That's the Animal Hour."

OLIVER PERKINS

"I find it very discouraging," said the old woman slowly. "When I was a little girl, I was always such a nervous Nell. Always worrying about this and that. About getting sick, about growing old. I used to wish I *was* old. So I could *stop* worrying about it. So I would be calmer. And look at me."

Perkins looked away from the window. Smiled at his grandmother over his shoulder. She sat slack and shapeless in her satin bergère. Her hands—all twigs and blue veins—trembled atop the pink blanket on her knees. Her watery eyes were lifted to him.

"I'm a catastrophe," she complained.

"Hey," Perkins said. "Am I gonna have to throw you down the stairs again?"

"Oh, just hush." Nana's voice was soft and quaky. "You know it's true. A little crisis and I'm crumbling practically in front of our very eyes."

"There's no crisis. And you'll still be here crumbling when I've died of old age." He turned back to the window. Elegant in its walnut frame, wide and ceiling-high. He gazed through it at a broad view of West Twelfth Street. "Who will you complain to then?" he said.

"I don't know," Nana murmured behind him. "It *is* going to be a problem."

Perkins laughed—then grimaced. A bolt of pain had shot up his temple. He touched the spot with his fingertips. Avis's breakfast of scrambled eggs and coffee had settled his stomach somewhat. Woken him up a little. But his hangover was still beating at his forehead, a living pulse inside his skull. *O for a draught of vintage!* he thought, *that hath been cool'd a long age in the deep-delved earth. Or maybe just a really cold beer and a babe with a soapy washcloth* . . . He massaged his head, squinting out the window.

Out there, five stories below, a woman pushed a stroller under the frail elms that lined the sidewalk. A student in a sweatshirt hauled his books past the brick apartments. And there was another mother, Perkins noticed, tugging her son along by the hand. The dawdling boy was dressed in a black cape. His face was whitened with makeup. Red droplets were painted around his lips. And Perkins thought: *That's right. Today is Halloween* . . .

"Why are you rubbing your temple, dear? Do you have a hangover?" Nana asked him.

"That depends," he said. "Are you gonna nag me about it?"

"Well, yes."

"Then I feel great."

"Well, I ought to nag you. Drinking all the time. And Zachary with . . . all his things. And now this . . . this disappearing. I just don't know."

Shaking his head, he turned from the window and faced her. He stuck his hands in the pockets of his jeans. Propped his butt on the windowsill. He smiled down at the old woman with her old room around her. *Fading into her faded delicacies,* he thought. Becoming one with her chairs and their scrolls and cabrioles and palmettes. The lampstand statuary. The Persian rug. The silver candles on the carved mantelpiece of the fireplace. Bathed all of it in the sad autumn gold of the light through the elegant windows.

"You make me feel like a terrible old failure," she said.

"I'm warning you," he told her. "I go through grandmothers like gravy."

"Oh." She waved him off feebly. "I'm sorry I ever took you two in."

"Yeah, well . . . you've got that right."

"Hmph." She turned her head to one side and shot him a flirty moue. He snorted. The fleshy pouches around her eye sagged heavily. The skin of her cheek hung slack on the high bones. There was wild hair sprouting from her upper lip. The hair on her head was thin and yellow.

She was old even then, he thought. Even sixteen/seventeen years ago. When his mother died, when he and Zach had gone to live with her. She must've been over seventy already. A quivery dowager, a doctor's widow. He could remember her hands fluttering in the air before her face. These two grandsons she had suddenly acquired crashing and tumbling through the MacDougal Alley mews, and her voice trilling: "Oh boys! Oh! Boys! Boys!"

"You *are* sure he's all right, Ollie, aren't you?" she said suddenly.

"Positive, kiddo." He pushed off the window and went to her. "I saw him Friday. He was happy as a clam."

"And that's happy."

"What, clams? It's one laugh with them after another."

She reached a hand up to him for comfort. He pressed it between his two palms. Rubbed it to warm the cold, loose flesh. Bent to blow his hot breath over the brittle sticks of fingers.

"Stop worrying so much," he whispered. "You know it's not good for you."

"Well, I can't help it," said Nana sadly. "I'm a nervous person. I've always been a nervous person. What am I supposed to do? *Not* be a nervous person? *That's* not very good advice."

"There's no talking to you, you wicked old witch." He lay her hand gently back on the blanket. Hanging his own hands on his pockets again, he strolled farther into the room. "I'm telling you. He's probably on assignment somewhere. Or maybe he's off somewhere getting ready for the parade or something. He's gonna be in that big parade tonight."

"What parade?"

"Tonight. The Halloween parade."

"Oh. That." She raised her eyebrows at the windows. "I thought that was only for . . . Well . . . You know."

"Butt fuckers."

"Yes. And those men who dress up as women."

"Well, it is mostly." Perkins was behind her now, wandering toward the edge of the Persian rug. In his bulky sweater, with his long hair flopping around his eyes, with his hangover throbbing, he felt oversized and unkempt. All those appointments and furnishings, all petite and just-so around him. "But Zach's magazine has a float this year or something. He's gonna play King Death. He's got a skull mask and everything."

"King Death?"

"He was all excited about it when I saw him." He circled past the low teakwood table. The framed portrait photos on it of himself and Zach. He glanced absently down the entrance to a long hallway. Nana's bedroom was down there and, across from it, a back door that led to the freight elevator and the fire stairs. Staring down the hall, he was thinking about seeing Zach on Friday. Zach in his skull mask. And Tiffany. *Goddamned Tiffany,* he was thinking. *Goddamned Tiffany.*

"And he's seeing his doctor, his psychiatrist," Nana said over her shoulder.

"Well, I didn't ask him but I guess so. He looked happy, Nana. He looked fine."

"Well, as long as he's not taking those . . . horrible, horrible drugs . . ."

He had wandered back along the sofa now to where he could see her from the side. He saw her shudder, her hands clasping each other. He saw her shake her head at those nasty old drugs, her lips pressed together tight. He smiled sadly with one corner of his mouth. Sometimes, some moments like that, she was just his mother to the life. The same birdlike tremolos. The same ardent, wide-eyed worries; her sacred fears. That wringing movement of the hands—he could remember his mom doing that. *Oh, don't let Zachary get too cold, Ollie.* He wanted to throw his body around the old woman, to fend off the hovering archangel.

She had the same heart as his mother too. The same problem: That's where Mom got it from. Normally, it can be kept fairly stable, the doctor had told him. But it's unpredictable. The valve can close suddenly and . . . Perkins had to shut his eyes a moment to fight off that last image of his mother. The way he'd found her: stretched out on her side between the sofa and the coffee table. Her short hair spilled over her cheek. Her thin arm flung out over her head. The saucer upside down on the rug and the cup on its side and the small spurt-stain of tea on the white shag. A weak valve. The same damn thing.

"Really, Nana," he heard himself say. "Do me a favor: don't get all upset over nothing."

"Well, but, Ollie, that's what I always do."

"Well, but, Nana, it isn't good for you. Jesus."

She tried to draw herself up, but sagged again almost at once under her anxieties. "Well, why did Tiffany say the mews? She said you had to go to the mews."

"Oh . . . Tiffany."

"Well, she's worried about him, poor thing."

"Well, she should've waited. She shouldn't've called you. I'd've plugged my phone in eventually." He muttered this. He knew Nana liked Tiffany. The closest thing she had to a granddaughter-in-law. Still. "She should've kept trying," he muttered again.

"But she was very specific," Nana insisted. "She said you had to go to the mews. She said she was sure he must be there."

"I know, I know."

47

"And that's where he always went to take the drugs. So why would she say that, Ollie?"

"Forget it, Nana, really." *God* damn *Tiffany,* he thought. "He's not on the drugs. I just saw him."

"I wish someone would buy that place," she said, meaning the mews. She pressed her hands down on the blanket. The yellow strands of her hair trembled at her ears.

He walked over to her. He crouched down by her chair. She turned her head to him. Her thin, shriveled face. The loose flesh on it quivering. The water in her eyes threatening to overflow.

"I'm serious now," he said to her. "You keep this up, I'm gonna have to start breaking some old lady bones. You've gotta calm down."

"He *thinks* too much," Nana said. "That's his problem. Your mother was just like that. He thinks and he worries about nothing at all. All those strange books he reads. And all that talk about . . . about God and salvation and I don't know what else." She reached out weakly, patted his hand where it held to the arm of her chair. "That's why you were always such a comfort to me, Ollie. You never believed in anything."

He laughed again, ignoring the pain. "Yeah." He pushed off her chair. Stood. "Maybe that's why I don't have anything to say."

"Oh now."

He reached out to her, smiling. Laid the back of his hand softly against her cheek. She leaned against the hand, closing her eyes. Perkins looked down at her. His smile fell away. She was so still like that. Her eyes closed. Her breathing barely visible. He could feel the fading furniture around her. The fading pictures. The fading gold in the light. It was pretty well close to unbearable.

He took a deep breath, let it out unsteadily. "Don't . . ." He had to clear his throat. "Don't worry, Nana. Please. Okay? I promise. I'll go right over there."

NANCY KINCAID

Nancy stared up from the bench. The beggar hovered over her. The blue sky, the yellow sycamores, the path, the other benches, the Hall, they were all erased. He filled her vision. His slack jowls, his glaring white eyes, pressed down on her.

Eight o'clock. Don't forget now. That's the Animal Hour.

Her pulse beat loudly in her head. It drowned the honk of horns, the Broadway buses. The rattle of leaves and the footsteps on the street were gone. There was just the tom-tom of her pulse in her head, all through her.

Eight o'clock . . .

"What?" She had to force the word out. "What did you say?"

That's the Animal Hour . . .

The beggar held his hand out, grinning, glaring at her.

"What?" she said again, more loudly; shrilly.

He spoke in his thin cackle. "Can you spare a quarter, Miss? Just a quarter—fifty cents—for a cup of coffee."

Nancy tried to breathe. She tried to catch her breath. *Jesus, am I going nuts? What did I hear, what did he say?*

"Please, Miss. A quarter. Just something for some coffee."

She became aware that her wrist was aching. The gun. She remembered all at once that she was still gripping the gun. Holding it just within the mouth of her leather purse.

Christ!

She made a small noise. Looked down, stared down. Saw the ugly black weapon in her hand.

Christ! Christ!

49

She dropped the thing as if it had burned her. She clutched the purse shut with both hands, all ten fingernails digging into the leather.

Then she raised her eyes, fast. The beggar had shuffled in even closer. The sour, rancid smell of him, of his piss and his sweat, clogged her nostrils.

Why don't you shoot him? Why don't you just shoot him? Oh shit, she thought. *This is definitely getting out of hand.*

"Just a quarter, Miss. Come on," the man said.

"I'm sorry." She managed a breathy whisper. Her breath was fluttering in her chest. "I'm sorry, I'm not feeling well. I'm . . . I'm sorry . . ."

She tried to stand up. He bore in on her. He held her so close to the bench she couldn't straighten her knees. The smell of him gagged her. His grin—his chancred lips—seemed an inch from her eyes.

"Please," she said.

She twisted her body sharply. Twisted away from him, away from the bench out into the path. Her head felt as if it were spiraling down. The yellow leaves blowing and whirling in the air made her stomach turn. For a moment, the trees around her seemed to keel over. City Hall seemed to tilt up on its side and fall back again.

"You can spare a quarter, Miss," said the beggar. "I know you can." He came at her again. He held his hand out. His ragged shoes chafed the path.

"No," she said. She pressed one hand to her head. Clutched the leather of her purse so tight with the other that her fingernails bent painfully. "No, no, no, I'm going . . . I'm going . . ."

Nuts, she thought. *I'm going nuts. This is how you go nuts.*

"I have to . . . I have to . . . go. I'm sorry."

She spun away from him unsteadily. Clutching that purse closed as hard as she could. As if the mouth of it might tear itself open. As if the gun might jump out of it. As if the gun might just jump right into her hand.

Why don't you shoot him?

She started walking. Down the path, toward the hedges and the plots of grass. Toward the fountain spraying up at the far end near the street. *Away*. She heard her flats clap-clapping on the asphalt. She felt her knees wobble, as if she were on high heels. She took three steps. Four. Five. And then . . .

"You won't forget now."

She pulled up short. It was the beggar's screaking whisper behind her.

"Eight o'clock. You won't forget."

Slowly, Nancy turned around. He was still standing there beside the bench, under the bough of the tree. His hand was still out. His knotted yellow-white hair fell around his jowls. He smiled wildly, his eyes bright.

Nancy stared at him. She swallowed hard.

"That's the Animal Hour," he cackled. "You have to be there. That's when he's going to die."

Staring, clutching her purse, Nancy shook her head. "Leave me alone." She couldn't believe the sound of her own voice. The deep, hollow, throaty sound. As if she were dead with fear. "Leave me alone."

The beggar just stood, just smiled, his hand still out, his eyes still on her. Behind him, the other beggars sat, huddled into themselves, paying no attention. The gray-black shapes of them pocked the green benches on either side of the path. The path led away, under the sycamores, toward City Hall. She could see the cops there, both of them, beneath the trees. Both were at the bottom of the Hall steps now. They were standing together, chatting, their hands on their guns.

Call to them. Why don't you just . . .

shoot him?

Call to them?

"Come on, Miss. Come on," said the beggar. His voice seemed to crackle with laughter. His eyes were mocking her.

"Leave me alone," Nancy said, louder now. "I said leave me . . . leave me alone right now or I'll call the police!" Just then, on Broadway, a truck roared. It gunned past with a long explosion of black exhaust into the trees. The noise blew her words away. Even she couldn't hear them.

All the same, the beggar seemed to get the idea. When she mentioned the police, the shape of his grin changed. It corkscrewed up on one side, down on the other. It became a sneer. He dropped his outstretched hand. Waved it at her; a crimped claw. "Ah!" he said, disgusted. And he turned his back. He started to walk away.

You're sure you can't stay now? Nancy thought. In her relief, she had closed her eyes for a moment. She took a deep breath. *Next time, don't be such a stranger.* When she looked again, the beggar had shuffled even farther down the path. The bent shape of his dusty black coat was slowly pushing away from her. The scrape of his footsteps in the leaves was growing softer.

All right. All right, she thought. Another breath. Steady as she goes. *All right now. Everything's fine. Everything's going to be absolutely . . . going to be . . .* She looked down. Her fingertips were white with the effort of holding her purse shut. She could feel droplets of sweat running down her palm. She gave a sickly smile. *Well, maybe not* absolutely *fine,* she thought. Something was going on, that was for sure. There was some kind of glitch in the old brainworks. This fever she had. This flu. Causing some kind of hallucinations or something. That's all. That's all it was. No need to go all hypochondriacal about it or anything. Just because a few funny things start happening, just because you see, hear a few strange things doesn't mean you're . . .

Nuts. Going nuts.

. . . totally certifiable or anything.

Right. She licked her lips. Her lips felt stiff and bloodless. Her stomach felt delicate and weak. She relaxed her hold on her purse. Brought it up, still unzipped, under her arm. She stood where she was another second, waiting for her heart to slow. Waiting for the panic to subside.

It was just a beggar, Nance. Just a beggar in the park.

She watched him going. A smaller figure now. His head hung, his hair dangling. Shuffling slowly past one garbage can after another. Shuffling under the trees, through the intermittent falling of their leaves. He went between the rows of benches that lined the path. Between the homeless men on the benches, their bowed heads, their slumped dark bodies on either side of him. He shuffled away from her, toward City Hall.

Nancy felt her heart wind down as he receded. Felt her breathing ease. Her panic was shrinking. It shrank down to a low burn of fear in the pit of her stomach. She did not think it was going to get much better than that. She couldn't just shrug this off anymore. She was afraid, and she was probably going to stay afraid until she had it all figured out. Something was definitely going screwy here. There was no doubt about it. It wasn't just a question of the people in her office. Or of her driver's license. Or of her elementary school. There was the gun in her purse. The voice she had heard. And this bum, this thing he said about . . . What was it? The Animal Hour.

She had to go home. She had to make an appointment with Dr. Bloom. Get a checkup. Ask some questions. Find out what was happening to her.

After all, she thought, maybe it was something simple. Like a brain tumor. Or a flashback from a previous existence. Or maybe she had just died in her sleep and would be forced to live her worst nightmare over and over throughout eternity. There had to be some kind of reasonable explanation.

Nancy smiled a little to herself, watching the beggar go. She nodded. *Sure. Stay cool. It's going to be all right.*

On a bench not far from her just then, one of the other beggars lifted his head. He was a black man with moldy dreadlocks. He had an eerie, distant smile and those same glaring white eyes as the other. He turned those eyes, that smile, directly on her. He winked.

"You won't forget now. Will you?" he said.

Nancy made a noise in her throat. It was a small, horrible noise. Like a frightened animal. Like a snake's prey. She stood frozen like that—like a mouse in the stare of a snake. Staring at the black man on the bench. Staring into his weird smile, his bright eyes. Her heart had sped right up again. Her pulse was drumming between her ears. She shook her head: no.

But the black man kept smiling from the nearby bench. "Eight o'clock," he said. "He's gonna die then, girl. You've got to be there. That's the Animal Hour."

She shook and shook her head: No. No. She backed away from the laughter in his eyes, from the twisting grin. She clutched her purse against her side. She put the heel of her palm against her forehead. Gritting her teeth. Thinking: *Stop. Stop. Stop.*

Another head popped up. Another beggar looking at her from a bench farther down the line. Another sudden pair of eyes. Another gray face grinning at her.

"Don't forget now. Don't forget the Animal Hour."

"Jesus Christ," Nancy said. Her vision blurred as her eyes filled with tears, as she thudded her forehead with her palm's heel. "Jesus Christ."

"That's when he dies. That's when he's going to die." It was a fourth beggar, one on the other side of the path now. A hulking gray creature with a face of running wet clay. "He's going to die at eight o'clock," he said. "You have to be there."

"Jesus Christ."

And another one lifted his eyes as Nancy backed away. As she shook her head at them, thinking: *Stop. Stop.* Another beggar on the benches by the path raised his grin, his glare. And then another did. And then, one by one, all of them. All the beggars on the two rows of benches lining the path. All the grimy faces under the low boughs of the trees. They were all murmuring at her. Their lips were moving. Their eyes were all bright, white and bright. Their whispers floated up around her like tendrils of smoke, encircled her, enclosed her like wisps of smoke. And their words were like flies, like horseflies, swarming around her, nipping at her face as she swung her hand—*Stop. Stop*—to try and brush them off. The words closed over her:

"Eight o'clock."

"That's the hour."

"That's the Animal Hour."

"That's when he dies."

"You have to be there."

"Eight o'clock."

"The Animal Hour."

"You won't forget now."

"Don't forget."

With a small, frightened cry, she spun away from them. Turned her back on the double row of eyes and faces. Tears spilling down her cheeks, she raised both hands. Brought her purse up in front of her face as she tried to press both hands to her ears. But the whispers were still curling around her, the words still swarming at her ears.

"Don't forget."

"Eight o'clock."

"That's when he dies."

"That's the Animal Hour."

It's a dream, she thought. She felt the panic swelling in her. Swelling out of her stomach, into her chest, into her throat. She felt it was too much. She felt it would explode, that she would explode. *A dream. A nightmare. Got to be. Got to be dreaming. Walking down that old nightmare road, that's all. That nightmare highway.* Her eyes were shut tight. The purse was in front of her face. Her hands were over her ears.

"Don't forget now."

"The Animal Hour."

"Don't forget."

In a second, in a second, I'll be in my bed. My heart'll be bumpety-bumping against the old mattress. Good old Mom'll be in the kitchen. "Time to get up, Nancy. Time for work." The sizzle of a pair of eggs frying. I don't even like eggs, but that Mom, she always makes 'em for me. Good old Mom. Making those eggs. Those stupid, oppressive, insistent eggs. Why didn't I move out? Why didn't I leave home like an adult, for Christ's sake? For Christ's sake, they're driving me crazy. They've driven me crazy!

"That's when he dies, Nancy."

"Don't forget."

"Eight o'clock. Eight o'clock."

Oh, Jesus, wake me up, wake me up, Mom. Make this stop, okay? You can make the damned eggs. Fry me right up a hearty pair of those over-easies, okay? Okay, Mom? Just make this stop. Just please make this . . .

A hand clapped down upon her shoulder. The smell of sulfur went up her nose, down her throat. Her eyes wide, wild, she swung around. She screamed—or tried to scream.

The sound turned to dust in her mouth. It choked her. Made her gag.

The beggar. That first beggar. With his hanging jowls and his knotted hair. He was right there, right in front of her. His clawed hand, his festering hand, was on her shoulder. The chancres on his loose-fleshed cheeks pressed into her face. That thin screak, that mocking cackle:

"You won't forget now."

He grinned and pressed down on her.

She cried out. She tore herself out of his grip. Stumbled backward, away from him.

"Leave me alone!" Her voice was ragged with tears.

The gray-haired beggar grinned. He shuffled toward her. The other beggars hunched on the benches grinned behind him. They murmured at her. They glared at her with white eyes.

"Eight o'clock," said the beggar before her.

Nancy's hands were down now in front of her. Her purse hung open in front of her. She looked down and saw it. *Oh God!* she thought. She jammed her right hand into the open purse.

"Get away from me," she said. Spit flew from her teeth. "Get away from me, I'm telling you."

The beggar came toward her on stiff legs. He reached out for her. His eyes seemed completely white. His grin seemed slack. Drool ran from the sides of his mouth into the purple sores under his stubble.

"Don't forget. Don't forget," he kept repeating.

Nancy felt the cold metal of the gun. She felt the rough grip. Her hand closed around it.

Don't do this!

"I'm warning you," she heard herself scream.

"The Animal Hour," the beggar said. "You have to remember. You have to remember."

"All right!" Nancy cried out. "All right! That's it!" She yanked her hand out of the purse. She held the revolver up in front of her. The muzzle of it wavered wildly. "Get away from me," she screamed. "Get away from me or I'll shoot!"

The beggar's grin grew wider still. His jaws, his jowls, hung slack. His white eyes looked at nothing. He took another step in her direction. His hand reached for her.

"He dies at eight o'clock. That's the time. That's the Animal Hour."

"Get away!" Nancy screamed at him. She waved the revolver in his face. "Get away! Get away!"

And then she pulled the trigger.

ZACHARY

Zachary Perkins awoke peacefully that morning. He had had no dreams. He lay in bed with his eyes closed, his mind a blank at first. Then, as the moments passed, he began to imagine a woman.

A sparrow was singing morning songs in the maple tree at the window. There was a breeze three stories below in the garden of Lancer's café. He could hear leaves tumbling lightly over the flagstones down there. He imagined a woman with sable hair, a mane of sable hair.

She was a regal creature. He had imagined her before. She was nude, but armored in her nudity, arched in it, proud. She stood on a raised platform, glaring down at those below. Her flesh was as smooth as a page in a magazine, her skin was as gleaming. She had large breasts that stood erect. She had her hands on her hips. Her long legs were akimbo.

Zachary stirred. He felt his naked body against the sheets. The cool—the somehow wistful—breeze blew in through the window now. It played over his face and made him long for the woman, ache to have her there with him in the flesh. He moved his hand under the sheets, down to his erection. His erection was very hard. He stroked it, imagining the woman's imperious smile. He moved his hand faster. He threw off the bedsheet with his other hand. Breathing rapidly, he opened his eyes. He looked down at himself . . .

"Christ!" he whispered. "Christ!" His erection shriveled. He stared, saucer-eyed, at the blood.

There were streaks of it—dried blood—on his forearm and the back of his hand. There were brown cakes of it under his fingernails. He rolled his hand over, staring. There were more dried daubs of it on his palm. It looked like paint or chocolate, but he knew what it was. He knew what it was the minute he saw it.

He sat up. His heart thudded in his chest. He couldn't think. He couldn't think of anything. He surveyed his genitals desperately to make sure they weren't damaged. He looked on the floor by his bed and saw his clothes in a pile there. His T-shirt was on top of his jeans and it was soaked in blood, still damp with blood.

"Oh God," he whispered. "What is this? Where am I?" He couldn't think. His stomach was grinding over like a cement mixer.

He gasped. Someone was at the door. There was a knock —three knocks—quickly—one-two-three.

"Mr. Perkins?" A man's voice, but high and mild. No expression in it. The knocks again: one-two-three. "Mr. Perkins? Are you there?"

Zach's lips moved, but he couldn't speak. He stared wildly around the room. White walls with gray gouges where the paint had chipped. Bookshelves made of bricks and boards, stacked with newspapers and magazines. A dirty braid rug. A broad passage into the other room. He was at home, an East Village railroad flat. His own apartment, his and Tiffany's.

"Mr. Perkins?" The voice at the door was still soft and expressionless. "Mr. Perkins, this is Detective Nathaniel Mulligan of the New York City Police Department. If you're there, would you open the door please?"

The mews. It came back to him in a burst of light, like a

camera flash. He remembered what had happened in the mews.

Oh Christ, he thought. He put his fingers to his lips. *Oh Christ. They figure it's me. Oh God. They figure I did it. That would be the first thing they'd think.*

"All right, Mr. Perkins." A poster of Dali's *Crucifixion* hung on the front door. Mulligan's mild voice came right through it. "We're coming in now. We have a key from your landlord. If you're there, please don't do anything foolish. We don't want anyone to get hurt."

All Zachary could do just then was stare at the poster. It was a picture of a modern man, half-naked, his head flung back, his arms pinioned against the sky. All Zach could do was watch fascinated as the detective's voice spoke from it.

"We're coming in."

Then he heard a key scrape in the door lock. He heard men's voices murmuring. The lock began to turn over.

Terror coursed through Zach like blood, like liquid lightning. He jumped out of the bed.

He was a small man, much smaller than his brother Oliver. His strict diet kept him thin almost to the point of emaciation. Still, he was sinewy, muscular. His stomach rippled. His legs were strong. When he burst out of the bed, he went quickly, a blur of limbs and white skin. He tossed the sheet aside. Scooped his clothes up as he hit the floor. He pressed the pile of clothes to his chest, feeling the squish of his blood-soaked shirt against his flesh. He grabbed his sneakers in his other hand . . .

He heard the lock turn over. He froze and gaped at the door. A frightened squeal squeezed through his teeth. "Eeeeee . . ."

But it was only the first lock. The upper lock. There was still the latch below it. He had a few seconds left. Grimacing with fear, he started to lope across the room. He ran on tiptoe, barefoot, trying to make no noise. He heard the key click into that second lock, that last lock. He heard the men's voices again.

". . . ready behind me," one of them said. "Smooth and easy."

Oh God. Oh God, please, Zach thought as he ran. He felt the hard braid rug beneath his soles, then the gritty floor. *Oh Jesus please please please.*

There was a closet against the far wall, the door only half-way closed. There was a poster on that door too. An ink drawing of swirling clouds and mythic mountains; unicorns in the mist, nymphs and centaurs. *Eternity* was the caption. Zach tore bareass for *Eternity.*

Then the second lock turned. The front door opened. Zach slipped through the closet door, slipped inside.

He pulled the closet door toward him as best he could. He stood there, still as stone. He was in among Tiffany's clothes in the close, gray dark. Linen brushed against his nakedness. He could smell Tide detergent, and talcum powder, and the musk of Tiffany's skin. He was huffing, his teeth gritted. His hair was damp with sweat, his eyes were wet with tears.

Oh please, Jesus, he prayed. *Oh please, please, please.*

Just in front of his nose, the closet door was ajar. A line of light fell through it across his eyes. Zach wanted desperately to reach out and shut the door, but he didn't dare. The policemen were already entering. He could hear their voices become louder, their words more clear.

"Steady. It's a railroad flat." This was Mulligan, his high, mild tone.

"Fire escape in the other room."

"Closet over there. Bathroom."

"Burke the closet, Brown the john. I'll move through," said Mulligan.

Now Zach had moved. He could see them. Not Mulligan —he'd stepped too quickly into the other room—but the two others, Burke and Brown. Burke was a black man, broad and muscular in a plaid jacket, a sky blue shirt. Brown was white; round, mustachioed; he wore a green leisure suit. Each man was holding a small revolver in his right hand. Each had it pointed upright. Each held his hand steady, his left hand wrapped around his right wrist.

They'll kill me, Zach thought, clutching the blood-soaked clothes to his chest. *They figure I did it, and they'll shoot me. Oh Jesus, please. What could I do? I just wanted something*

*good. I just wanted something good of my own for me and
Tiff. Just give me a chance to convince them, Jesus. Please.
To get out and convince them. I'll do anything, I swear, I'll
tell everyone what I think about you, I'll explain your words
to everyone, just please . . .*

He watched as the two detectives moved to their places.
They moved stealthily but swiftly, taking long quiet strides.
Brown went to the bathroom across the room. He entered
and was out of sight. Burke was at the closet door in a second.

Please please please please please, thought Zachary. He
clutched his fists around his clothes, around his sneakers. His
whole body shook. He could barely keep his quick breath
silent. He hated himself for this, for praying like this. It wasn't
like him at all. It wasn't the sort of prayer he believed in. But
he was so afraid. Jesus, he was so fucking scared. He clamped
his mouth shut to keep his teeth from chattering.

Burke threw open the closet door.

The detective held his gun high, right beside his cheek. He
reached into the closet with his left hand. He moved Tiffany's
dresses to one side and then the other. He pushed them back
and looked down under them. Then he stepped away again.

By that time, Brown had returned to the bathroom doorway. Burke looked at him and shook his head once. The white
man answered softly, "Not here."

Zachary continued to cower. He was in the secret compartment now. He had managed to slip in there as Mulligan
gave his orders. It was a small chamber at one end of the
closet. He had built it himself: He was an excellent craftsman,
a fine carpenter. The door was pivot hung and molded at the
edges. It looked just like the closet wall when it was closed.
Then, when you put your shoulder to it, it swung around at
the middle like a secret door in an Abbott and Costello movie.
You could slip right into the compartment and the door would
shut silently behind you.

Inside, the compartment was dark and cramped, just big
enough to stand up in. With the bundle of clothes in his arms,
he had to stand very straight, his back against the wall. But
he could jut his head forward and put his eye to the
peephole—that's how he watched the detectives moving.

He had fitted the peephole with a wide-angled lens. He could see the bed through it and much of the room on either side. Out in the room, the peephole was hidden in yet another poster. A sketch of Adam and Eve on this one, and a little verse about how Eve was drawn from Adam's rib in order to stand beside him, not below him or above. The peephole was hidden neatly in Eve's left nipple.

Now, as Zachary watched, Mulligan returned to the bedroom. He was a short guy, Zach saw. He did not look like a cop, not like a very tough cop anyway. He had a round baby face under receding curls of sandy hair. He wore wire-rimmed glasses, and he blinked repeatedly behind the lenses. His pug features were impassive, like his high voice. He was wearing a khaki trench coat.

"Well, he was here," he said mildly. He stood with the other two cops beside the bed. It was a cheap double bed with a metal frame. Its sheets were all tousled. Its gray blanket was pyramided on the floor. Mulligan bent down and laid his palm on the bottom sheet. "He was just here."

Zach's eyes fogged with tears. He licked his lips. *They're going to search the place. They're going to find the red bag under the bed. Then it's over.* He would never be able to explain things now. If they found the red bag, he would never be able to convince them that he was not their man.

"Are the windows open in the other room?" Burke asked.

Mulligan nodded absently. "But Southerland would've seen him if he used the fire escape. He was just here, and he left through the door before we came."

Please Jesus please, Zach thought. He leaned closer to the peephole, almost lifting onto his toes. He really did feel like crying: It was half terror and half frustration. How could he have let this happen? How could he have done this to himself? He had had a perfect plan. A perfect way to present the evidence to the police so they would believe it, so it would convince them. How could he let it all go wrong like this? For God's sake—how could he have *overslept?*

"Maybe he went to breakfast," Brown said. And now, as Zach watched, as he prayed, the little round white man was kneeling down painfully. He was bowing his head down so he could look under the bed.

He's going to find it. He's going to find the red bag. Zach's mouth contorted. One tear ran down his cheek. He blinked it away so he could see out the peephole. With the blackness so close around him, his whole being was concentrated on the other room, on what he saw.

"Maybe he went to work," said Burke. "I mean, he may not even be the guy."

That's right! That's right! thought Zachary desperately. *I may not even be the guy, for Christ's sake.*

He saw Brown straighten. He heard him groan. Brown looked at Mulligan. Mulligan, blinking mildly, turned his head to survey the room.

"Some kind of red overnight bag under there," Brown said. "We oughta toss this whole place."

Mulligan nodded again, as if he hadn't heard. "He might've gone for a bagel. That's true. Southerland can watch half an hour, rope him if he comes back. Burke can go to the magazine, ask around there. That way we don't scare him away. And half an hour, forty-five minutes, we can come back with a warrant too. That way we'll be legal guys. Happy legal guys for all to see." He said this tonelessly, softly, as if to himself.

"Listen . . ." Burke, the big black man, tugged his own earlobe. "Listen, the feds are gonna go nuts. They're *going* nuts now. Aren't we gonna bring 'em in at all here?"

Detective Mulligan just kept nodding, kept looking around. Then he said: "Fuck the fucking feds." Only he said it very mildly. It sounded strange coming out of his blinking, baby face.

With one last nod, he started walking to the door. The other two exchanged a glance and followed him.

Zachary stood amazed. They were leaving! Just leaving! *Yes!* he thought. His whole body was taut and eager as he leaned toward the keyhole, as he watched them go. Detective Mulligan paused at the door, his hand on the knob. Zach peered at him, protected by the dark; feeling well hidden now and powerful—and a little guilty, too, about that sense of secret power. Staring out at Mulligan like that, he thought the detective looked like a pretty decent guy actually. A sweet guy. Zach would have liked to come out and talk to him directly. Explain things to him, person to person.

But he didn't; he didn't move. He stood still, his head jutting forward, his bloody clothes smearing his chest. He held his breath as Mulligan took one last look around. Then the detective pulled the door open. Zach watched as he went out, as the others followed after.

The door shut. Zach started to breathe again. He pulled away from the peephole. Leaned his head back against the wall. He closed his eyes and let all the breath come out of him. For a second, he felt his innards unclutch themselves. Relief washed over him.

But it was only for a second. Then he was thinking: *They'll be coming back*. Half an hour, they'd said. They would search the place and then they'd be sure to find him. He shook his head. He opened his eyes and gazed up at the dim ceiling. Jesus God, he thought. Jesus God. Overslept. The perfect plan, the one way out, and he had overslept. He had blown everything. Now he was trapped. The cops were after him. There was a guard on the street outside so he couldn't escape. And once they had him in custody, once they had the red bag . . . it was over. There would be no way they would ever believe that he was not the guilty guy.

Christ, Christ, Christ, he thought. He hadn't even meant to lie down. He remembered everything now. He had come home and stripped off his bloody clothes. He had just been about to clean up. He hadn't even meant to lie down, and then . . .

The drug. Yes. He remembered that too. He had injected the drug again. That's what had overcome him in the end. He had injected Aquarius. Even though he had sworn to himself he wouldn't. Even though he had promised Ollie; and Nana. Even though he had promised God.

Sorry, he thought up at the ceiling. *Sorry, sorry*. He had never broken a promise to God before. Never once. It was a pretty shitty feeling. Like he'd swallowed a rat and it was trying to gnaw its way out of him. The Giant Rat of Remorse. *Sorry. Sorry.*

For one more moment, he stayed where he was, the wet clothes in his arms, his head tilted back. For one more moment, he appealed to the ceiling with his eyes. *Please, Jesus. Please.*

It was not that terrible a sin, after all. It was not like cutting down the rain forests or spilling oil all over the ocean or anything. He had tried to stay off the stuff. He *had* stayed off it for a long time. Surely God would not let him get arrested now. God would not let the police believe that he was guilty for what had happened in the mews.

No. With a breath of resolution, he straightened up. There had to be a way out. God closes a door, but opens a window. Somehow, Zach had to push on. Even with the guard on the street, even with the search party on the way. Somehow, he had to continue with the original plan. Get cleaned up, get rid of the bloody clothes, get the red bag . . . and get the hell over to the only person who could save him. The one person on earth who had always saved him before.

He smiled a little at that, a goofy, lopsided smile. In a way, it was just like the old days, wasn't it. It was just like after Mom died, after Dad deserted them and went to California. In those days, there was no one in the world who could help or comfort him—no one, except for his older brother. And now it was the same.

Now again—somehow—he had to get to Ollie.

NANCY KINCAID

The day exploded. The revolver bucked in Nancy's hand. Startled pigeons fluttered up from the park path, up from the squares of grass and out of the trees' branches. They rose in a gray mass and tacked off in a body to soar toward the dome of the Hall.

Nancy stood immobile. Her mouth was open. The pistol's handgrip was hot against her palm. *Uh-oh,* she thought. The explosion seemed to go on and on forever.

She stared horrified at the beggar. He stared back, amazed. His slack jowls wobbled. His strings of gray-yellow hair trembled on his brow. She expected him to fall in the next second. To clutch his stomach and drop to his knees on the path. But he just stood there. He just stared at her.

"Jesus, lady," he burst out finally. "All I wanted was a quarter."

Nancy looked down, at the pistol: a squat black monster in her small white hand. The muzzle was pointed off in some wild way, up into the trees. She glanced up there and saw a squirrel crouched in terror on the stout branch of a sycamore. She had missed—missed the beggar at point-blank range. She lowered her eyes to him again with a green, sickly feeling . . .

And she saw the police coming after her.

The two patrolmen who had been chatting together in front of City Hall had leapt into action. They'd jumped the park railing and were jogging across the grass toward her. Their hands were at their holsters, gripping the handles of their guns.

Instinctively, she swung around, looking for a way to escape. Two more cops had entered the park from the far end. A man and a woman. They were running toward her on the paths, one on each side of the grass. The fountain sent a silver plume into the air between them.

Nancy swallowed hard. She turned north to the cops from the Hall, south to the cops from the street, then north again as all four cops closed in on her. She started to prepare her explanation in her mind: *It's all right officers I'm Nancy Kincaid even though everyone says I'm not and I couldn't remember where I went to elementary school so when all these beggars started staring at me I took out this pistol which just appeared out of nowhere in my purse and I . . .*

"I better get out of here," she whispered aloud.

"Crazy bitch," the beggar muttered.

Wildly, she turned her back on him. She took a big step up onto one of the green benches.

"Hey, lady, hold it!"

"Hold it right there!"

"Stop! Police!"

"Drop the gun, drop the gun!"

The cops' shouts were small under the thrum of the city. But she heard them. They were already close.

"Don't move, lady!"

"Police! Freeze!"

She jumped. Leapt over the back of the bench. Down over the metal railing onto the grass. Her flats sank into the soft earth and she stumbled. Then she was steady—running—across the littered grass—her purse over her shoulder—her pistol in her hand.

"Stop!"

"Freeze!"

"Oh my God!" a woman shouted somewhere. "Watch out! She's got a gun!"

There were other screams all around her:

"Jesus!"

"Watch out!"

Nancy ran. The peaceful trees shook their leaves above her, their yellow leaves against the so-blue sky. The Hall stood behind them, stately, shaded, to her left. To her right, the traffic groaned and whooshed along. *This isn't happening,* she thought. *This isn't real.* She ran clumsily, her bare knees breaking from her trench coat. *If this were really happening, it would be seriously bad . . .* Her hoarse breath filled her head. And her fear—she couldn't believe the fear. She couldn't believe she was still moving with so much fear inside her. It was like a vast dark that had yawned in her belly, that would suck her in. Her tam blew off and fell behind her.

"Lady! Lady! Stop! Stop or I'll shoot! Police!"

Another railing loomed ahead. She grabbed the top bar, vaulted over. She was on a path again. She was past City Hall. If she cut to her left, she could duck through the parking lot, duck around the building. She skidded to a stop. Cast a look back over her shoulder.

And, good God, there they came. Four uniforms, four silver badges. Closer now. Two on the grass, climbing over railings, crushing soda cups under heavy black shoes as they thudded toward her. One on the path, one through the parking lot; churning like engines. Pedestrians dodged them, crouched down in terror, swiveled to spot her. Pointed. Screamed.

Me? she thought. It was a high, thin note in her mind, crazy fear. *The police after me? The cutest little thing?* The neighborhood ladies used to call her that when she was little. It came back to her now. And how Daddy used to catch her up in his arms. Hoist her into the air, her legs kicking. "How's my little button?" She stared at the onrushing coppers. *They're going to gun down Daddy's little button?*

There was no doubt about it. Those four stolid faces, their frightened eyes. Each clawed the air with one hand to keep balance. The other hand was at the holster, elbow pistoning. Guns the size of bazookas were circling up into the air. Pointing toward her.

And when she stopped, when she turned to see, one cop braked on his heels. Leveled his .38 right at her, gripping it in both hands.

"Drop it, sister! Drop the rod!"

She bolted. Dashed behind a tree. Broke out, running for the edge of City Hall. With every step, she expected to hear the gunshot. To feel the bullet hit her temple like a mallet blow, knocking her down. *I'm not doing this. This isn't happening.* She was into the lot, around the building. Pressing her purse to her side with her elbow, waving her gun, gasping for air.

She was too exhausted now to jump the railings. She took the short path between plots of grass. She half ran, half stumbled on it. Her flats scraped the pavement. With her hat gone, her curls tumbled down around her face.

She reached the elms that bordered the park. She tumbled through onto the broad sidewalk. She pulled up with a gasp at the edge of the breathless city. The wide highway. The distant towers of the Brooklyn Bridge. The huge winged Municipal Building, hanging over her. Pedestrians clacked past her oblivious. She turned. And there, to her left, against the backdrop of a Parisian courthouse, against its mansard roof, its columned facade: an opening into the ground. A vanishing stairway. An unobtrusive black sign.

A subway station.

The cops rounded the Hall behind her. She glanced back and saw them converge. Four uniforms, shoulder to shoulder. Four pairs of eyes—they surveyed the scene. Got her.

"All right, lady . . ."

She was already staggering away. Reaching for the banister to the subway stairs like a thirsty woman reaching for water. The Beaux-Arts courthouse tilted this way and that as she came near it. The pit into the subway grew bigger.

And now, she heard the running footsteps behind her. Thap thap thap. Getting louder. Closer.

Oh, turn around, she thought. *For God's sake, Nancy. Turn around and surrender. Explain it to them. "My name is Nancy Kincaid . . ."*

"Drop the gun, lady!"

She pushed herself faster. Threaded through the people walking past the entranceway. She grabbed the banister. Pulled herself into the hole. Rapped down the stairs. Faster. Forcing herself to go faster, down into the tunnel. The darkness came up at her from below.

There'll be cops down there.

She stuffed her gun back into her purse. Pulled out her wallet. Never stopped skipping quickly down. She snapped the wallet open, found a token as she hit the landing below. She broke for the turnstiles. Everything was darker here, quieter, close. Lots of glare from the fluorescents overhead. Bright yellow signs, bright silver stiles. Light-washed faces turning to her. The lizard stare of the woman in the glassed-in token booth. The travelers waiting on the token line looking up. People pushing through the turnstiles, glancing back.

Nancy found an open stile, stuck her token in the slot, pushed through. Already, the cops were on the stairs, their footsteps echoing. *Turn around. Stop. Explain. Damn it.* She just wanted the black fear to stop. But she ran. Her vision blurred as her eyes filled with tears. She couldn't stop running. *What is happening to me?*

She ran down the long hall, under the low ceiling, the low fluorescents. She dodged through the sparse, fast-flowing crowd. Past the faces that swung around to see. A wake of cries went up behind her as the cops came into the station, as they took up the chase. A wake of shouts:

"Stop!"

"Watch out!"

"Get down!"

"Hold it!"

There were the tracks, right up ahead. People waited on the platform. They turned at the shouts. A bald businessman lowered his newspaper, stared at her. A broad black in jeans squared, as if to stop her.

She barreled toward them. "Watch out!" she cried. "I've got a gun."

The black guy hesitated and she was past him. Cornering onto the platform. Out of sight of the cops. Running along the platform's edge, her flats skirting the yellow line at the brink of it. There were the tracks below—the empty tracks.

No train.

She was sobbing with exhaustion now. Stumbling on in despair.

No train.

There was no train coming. She could see up the tracks. And there was no place left to run. The concrete platform ended up ahead. She thrashed her way toward it. She wove out over the tracks, wove back toward the filthy yellow tiles of the wall. Ahead of her, frightened faces turned, whitened by the low fluorescents. Behind her, new cries: The cops had rounded the corner. They were coming after her. Their shouts were right at her shoulder.

"Stop!"

"You're under arrest!"

"I'm gonna shoot, sister, put 'em up!"

And she was trapped. Out of room. The platform ended two steps ahead. A metal ladder led down from it onto the tracks and the tracks curved on and out of sight into the unknowable dark.

She flailed toward the edge. Toward a white sign that hung askew where the station wall ended: "All persons forbidden to enter or cross tracks." The red letters blended together as she started to cry, as the tears streamed down her cheeks.

Turn around. Just tell them. Don't shoot. I'm just scared. Just a scared little button.

She was finished. She stopped, her chest heaving painfully. She turned and stumbled backward a few steps toward the brink. Her shoulders sagged. Her breath honked in and out of her. She peered through her tears. It was all a blur. Dragon-toothed lights. Featureless faces. And the four cops like shadowy blue goblins. Big, unfocused blue creatures pulsing toward her. They moved more cautiously now—now that she was cornered. They walked—quickly—their free hands raised, their guns leveled at her.

Jesus Christ. They are going to put me away, she thought. It was true. They would think she was nuts. They would put her in a hospital, in a room, in a white room. Just her and the walls. And the voice inside her head . . .

The Animal Hour. That's when he dies. You have to be there.

They would call her mother. Her mother would come to visit her. She would sit beside her and call her name and cry. But Nancy would only hear . . .

Eight o'clock.

The voices. She would be alone in a padded room with voices.

You have to be there.

The cops were only a few steps away from her now. Two of them were coming on ahead of the others, a man cop and a woman. They had their guns leveled at her. They had their hands raised toward her to keep her steady.

"Easy now, Miss, easy," the woman cop said.

She gazed at them wearily, panting and crying. They were going to put her away and . . .

You have to be there! The Animal Hour! He's going to die!

"I have to," she whispered. "I have to be there."

She swung around suddenly. The shouts flared behind her. She crouched down . . .

"Hey!"

"Wait!"

"Stop!"

She grabbed hold of the top of the ladder. With a single motion, she swung herself over the platform's edge. Out, into the darkness. Down, onto the tracks.

She stumbled. Straightened. Ran.

OLIVER PERKINS

A blonde came toward him from the corner of Sixth. He had just left Nana's to head for the mews. The blonde was beautiful, a student with books propped against her middle. The sight of her broke Perkins's chain of thought.

He watched her as she approached, as he approached her. She was tall and broad. Athletic-looking in a red down vest and jeans. Her skin was white but her cheeks were pink with sun. She glanced at Perkins as she passed. He glanced after her to watch her backside move.

By the time he reached the avenue, he was imagining having sex with her. Not just sex—a whole way of life together— the way of life he figured would go with a girl who looked that way. He pictured them in an A-frame cabin in the Colorado Rockies. She was on her back on a bed of bearskins. Naked, she was spread wide: a naturalist, abandoned. He had dropped a load of freshly hewn wood just inside the door and stripped off his own jeans fast. He was still wearing his sweater as he ploughed into her. There was frost on the windowpanes. Snow on the misty mountains outside.

He was walking down Sixth now, approaching the library on his right. His hands were in his pockets, his shoulders hunched. His chin was on his chest and his straight black hair was bouncing on his brow. He raised his eyes from his sneakers as he thought about the blonde's lusty cries. Before him, the low buildings of stone and glass faded away toward a crisp blue sky. The bright day made him squint. The hangover had made his eyes feel raw.

He riffled his lips as he humped down the avenue. The taste of solitude was in his mouth again, the weight of it was in his belly.

> . . . desolate and sick of an old passion.
> Yea, I was desolate and bowed my head.

Shit, he thought, with a heavy sigh. Julia had been blonde too. She had been big and athletic too with that way of flinging herself open to him. Flinging her head back, letting loose with those abandoned howls. He thought about how he had finally lost her: because he had made it with a boy in the river near their house. The kid was no more than eighteen, nineteen. Frail bodied and white skinned. With faraway, dreamy black eyes. *Yea, I was a moron and shot my wad.* The kid had been sitting on a rock near Perkins's swimming hole. He had been sitting there naked and dripping. He had been reading *Leaves of Grass,* holding it open on the rock. When Julia came down the forest path and found them, they had been locked together in the deep water, turning and turning in the current. Perkins's arm was wrapped around the boy's chest, the boy's head was thrown back on Perkins's shoulder.

"I thought you were trying to save his life!" Julia cried out to him later.

"He was sitting naked on a rock, Jule," Perkins said. "He was reading Whitman, for Christ's sake! What was I supposed to do?"

Somehow this argument had carried exactly no weight with her. She had stood and glared at him, her arms crossed on her breasts. Tears streamed steadily down her sunburnt cheeks. He had never seen her cry before and it razed him inside, turned him to ashes.

"It's just the desperate things you do to keep from loving me, Oliver," she said finally. "I can't stand it, all right? I really can't stand it anymore."

Just now, just as he remembered this, he was passing under the Jefferson Market Library. It was a storybook castle of a place. All red brick towers and battlements rising out of the low-flung Village mini-malls. Stone spires and gray-metal roofs. Turrets and Gothic tracery around stained glass. A peaked clocktower with four faces rising over all. It was an appropriate reproach to him, and he thought: *Look on thy workspace, ye dickhead, and despair.*

He was supposed to write his poems here. It was part of a grant he'd won with *The Animal Hour.* Along with giving him some seven thousand dollars, the state rented him a small workroom in the rear of the library. He even got a key so he could go in after hours. He did go in: every day; and at night, too, sometimes, when he wasn't tending bar in the café. He sat alone at a small metal desk hemmed in by metal book-shelves. Barely a foot of free floor space to pace in. He sat hunched over his notebooks, with his loneliness perched on his shoulder like the Raven. He wrote bad lines of poetry and threw them away. Day after day. Night after night.

He averted his eyes from the building as he passed it. He had been meaning to go in there tonight, but not to write. Just to get a good view of the Halloween parade. The march-ers would go right past the place. Transvestites and monsters and Dixieland bands under the windows. The sidewalks below jammed with spectators. The music bouncing off the Village sky . . .

It made him think of Zach again. Zach was going to be in the parade. He had been all geared up for it the last time Oliver had seen him. That was Friday. Ollie had gone over to Zach's place to return his copy of Schillebeckxx, a philo-sophical enquiry into Jesus Christ that Zach had forced on him. He'd lugged the 800-page doorstop all the way up the brownstone's narrow stairway. Pounded at Zach's peeling door with his fist. The door had just swung in. Pure Zach: it was unlocked—just open in that crackhead-infested hellhole. Anyway, in the door swung and there they were. Sitting opposite each other on the bed by the window. Tiffany was at the foot. Venus-faced but rail-thin. Black T-shirt, black jeans. Long black hair streaked with shiny silver. Her back was propped against the bedrail, her legs stretched out before her. She was smiling with her rich lips and absently shuffling a deck of Tarot cards. And, at the head of the bed: It was like her reflection. Black T-shirt, black jeans, and just as rail-thin because of that stupid macro-whatever vegetarian diet she had them on. Except the face on him was the face of Death. It was Zachie in a pullover latex skull mask.

"Jesus, Zach," Oliver said. "You look like Death."

Zach's happy, boyish laughter sounded hollow inside the mask. He was practically bubbling over with the news. "I'm gonna be in the parade, Ollie. *Downtowner*'s gonna have a contingent and I get to play King Death. Isn't it great?"

Oliver had to smile. Even through the skull's eyeholes, he could see Zach's bright, black eyes. The awestruck excitement in them. *Isn't it great?* The same as when he was seven years old. Shaking his head, Oliver tossed the Schillebeckxx down on the bed between the two of them. Thunk.

"Here's your book back, kid. There's still no God."

Zach let fly with that boy's laugh again. "Oh, Ollie!" The death's head tilted back.

Tiffany, though, smiled her voluptuous smile, cast her eyes heavenward. Launched into her sweet contralto. "Oh, Ollie. If you just kept a more open mind, you wouldn't be so stuck with your poetry in those retro paternalistic modes of yours."

Oliver gave her a long look. Retro paternalistic modes. God, he disliked the woman. A simpering Scarsdale debutante gone mystical fem. He hated the lot of them: mystics; fems. Debutantes. He wasn't too fond of Scarsdale either. Or maybe it was just Tiffany.

He finally simpered back at her. Held his tongue. Zach hated it when the two of them argued. He wanted them to like each other. Zach wanted everyone to like each other under the tender eyes of a loving God. Too bad he lived on Earth . . .

With these thoughts, Perkins was carried away from the library. Down Sixth to the corner of West Eighth Street. He turned there. A broad street lined with shoe stores, T-shirt shops, poster stores. Lots of heavy metal pictures of death in the windows: flaming Death on a motorcycle, drooling Death playing the guitar . . . It was only about 10:35 now, and most of the stores were still closed. The sidewalks were quiet. A line of children in costumes—devils, turtles, ballerinas—trooped toward Sixth, their teacher leading. Perkins went past them, chin down, shoulders hunched, hands in pockets. His mouth was working angrily.

Tiffany. She shouldn't have called Nana. Face of a Botticelli, brain of a midge. She shouldn't have called Nana about Zach. It was stupid. The old woman was sick, for Christ's sake. She wasn't supposed to worry. It was bad for her, bad for her heart. Just because his own phone was temporarily disconnected. Just because he'd tried to steal a few moments of human tenderness and communion with Mindy or Milly or whatever the hell her name was. That was no reason to get all panicked, to get Nana all panicked. Maybe Zach was working. Maybe he'd gone for a walk. Maybe he just wanted to get away from *her*. It was no reason to murder his grandmother.

Perkins crossed to the far sidewalk. Went down MacDougal Street. His thoughts had come full circle now. He was thinking about Nana, about how frail she was. He was thinking about Nana dying—and then about his mother dying and how he had found her. That's just what he'd been thinking about when he left Nana's. When he walked past the blonde: that day when he found his mother, when he was fourteen years old. He remembered how he had come in from playing baseball. They had been in the house on Long Island then. He had strode through the kitchen, his bat on his shoulder. The minute he stepped through the door into the living room, he'd seen his mother on the floor. She was stretched out on her side between the sofa and the coffee table. Her short hair spilled over her cheek. Her thin arm was flung out over her head. The saucer was upside down on the rug and the cup was on its side. There was a small spurt-stain of tea on the white shag.

He remembered how that had bothered him: that stain of tea. His mother had been such a meticulous housewife. Fluttering around with her nervous hands, her frightened smile. Setting everything straight all the time. Flitting from room to room like a household spirit. Oliver had run to her where she lay. After that, after he saw she was dead, he must have gone into shock. He had simply stood up and wandered away, back into the kitchen. He had brought a sponge in from the sink. He had knelt down on the rug and washed that tea stain right out. He had rubbed it away thoroughly, his hand braced against the floor, his mother's soft hair brushing his forearm. Then, very carefully, he had sponged off the coffee table too. He had carried the teacup and saucer in to the sink. He had rinsed them out and put them in the dishwasher. He did not snap out of it until he returned to the living room. Then, he saw his little brother standing in the doorway. That brought him around. The skinny ten-year-old was staring down at their mother with his big, dark eyes. After a while, he lifted those eyes up to Ollie.

"Don't worry, Zach-man," Oliver had said. His voice was toneless. "Go upstairs now, buddy. Don't worry."

Zach had turned away. He had gone upstairs to his room. Oliver had knelt down next to his mother. She was a small woman, but he was only fourteen: he did not think he could lift her onto the sofa in a dignified manner. He turned her onto her back instead, right there on the rug. He arranged her arms by her side. He brushed the hair off her cheeks and forehead. Her mousy little face was turned up to him now, the eyes closed, the lips parted.

"Don't worry, Mom," he told her softly. He stroked her cheek with the back of his fingers. "Don't worry anymore."

And then he had returned to the kitchen to phone for his father and the ambulance . . .

That was what he had been thinking about when he came out of Nana's place, when he saw the blonde come toward him from Sixth Avenue. And he was thinking about it now again as he reached MacDougal Alley.

He paused for a moment there, at the black iron gate that barred the way. He saw the little lane stretched beyond the bars. It was a queer, quaint private alley, sealed at the far end by a high-rise wall. Cottages faced one another over the pavement, ruffled with rose ivy, shaded with red maples and yellowing ash. The sun came through the trees in patches, dappling the cottage walls.

Perkins pulled the black gate open and went in. Nana's mews was on the left. A small one, two low stories. It was brick, painted white, but there were chips in the paint where the red brick showed through. Black shutters and doors. Reddening ivy climbing up one side to the flat roof.

Nana had lived here with her husband when he was alive. And with the two boys after Mom died, after Dad declared he couldn't raise them. She had not moved out to West Twelfth until after Zachie went to college. Then she had decided she could not handle the stairs anymore, and that she wanted a doorman for deliveries and so forth. But she hung on to the mews. She'd let Zach and Oliver stay there when they came to town on visits. And after Zach's first breakdown, she let him move in and live there by himself. She was trying to sell the place now though. She felt certain that Zach was getting better. And she sure enough needed the money, with Zach's expenses and his shrink and all. Too bad the market was so lousy, Perkins thought.

He reached the front door. Knocked with his fist. It made the sidelights rattle. In the silence that followed, he could feel the emptiness of the place. He cursed Tiffany. Why had she insisted Zach was here? She must have known it would scare Nana senseless. He rooted in his pocket for his keys.

Idiot broad, Perkins thought. He brought the key out. Unlocked the door. Pushed it open. Stepped inside.

"Christ!"

The smell hit him first. The shutters were closed downstairs and the place was in shadow. But the smell was thick; like liquid air; miasma. Wet and rotten as a sick old dog. Perkins gasped as it caught him. He took another step, came away from the door. Then the light slanted in from the alley behind him.

"Christ. Oh Christ."

He saw the place, the big room downstairs. He saw the wooden pillars rising to the ceiling beams. The shape of them came out of the dark. Then the rest of it.

"Oh no. Oh man."

It was a shambles. The studded leather chairs lay on their sides. The sofa was upended. The marble coffee table had been knocked off its stand, hammered to pieces on the Mexican rug.

With a curse, Perkins stepped to his left. He felt his way along the wall. Found the light switch, hit it. There was a loud pop. A spray of white sparks shot from a nearby lampstand, drifted to the floor. Only the chandelier went on; only one of its flame-shaped bulbs. The other lamps were all shattered, the jagged necks of the bulbs sticking up out of their sockets. The shattered glass was sprinkled among the broken marble on the rug. The rug beneath, he could see now, was burned. There were round black bits in it. One fringed corner of it had just been torn away.

Zach, he thought. His brain had seized up for just a second, but now he remembered his brother. *Jesus.*

"Zach?" he tried to call. His voice caught in his throat. He cleared it. "Zachie!" He kept walking farther and farther into the room. In past the kitchen alcove. In under the low crossbeams that went from the pillars to the ceiling. Glass crunched under his sneakers. "Hey, Zach!" This time, he managed to raise his voice. "You here? Don't fuck around, man." He stopped to listen for an answer. He heard his heart beating. There was nothing else. The old cottage sat broken and silent. Perkins's eyes trailed over the wreckage. Over the shuttered windows. Over the littered floor to the foot of the stairs and there . . .

"Oh . . . Oh no."

He caught his breath. He lifted his eyes from stair to stair. He gazed up toward the second story, his stomach clutching, his hands balled into fists.

"Zachie?"

It was only a whisper this time. His lips parting, he looked down at the stairs again. He looked down at the worn tan runner. At the stains on it.

The blood.

NANCY KINCAID

She was too exhausted now to think. She drove herself deeper into the subway tunnel. Deeper into the dark. The walls fell away from her. The tunnel fanned out. There were four sets of tracks before her, each curling off in a different direction. Shiny patches of steel gleamed in the light from bare bulbs overhead. Concrete pillars hulked in the shadows like giants, motionless, watching.

She stumbled on, her arms flailing. She couldn't believe herself. Could not believe she was doing this. She felt at any moment she must stop, turn around, turn herself in. The rails, the ties, the white flecks of garbage in the gravel—they blurred and blended under her feet. It all seemed unreal to her. Faraway, foggy. Even the shouts of the officers on the platform behind her seemed part of a dream. They didn't shoot or anything, there were no bullets zinging around her. Their voices just got farther and farther away, fainter and fainter.

Ahead of her now, the tunnel narrowed again. Two of the tracks peeled off to the right. The walls closed in on her. They were cement walls. They were washed in a swirl of graffiti. Writhing signatures and profanities covered every inch of stone; a snake's nest of spray paint colors. She saw it through tears as she staggered on. She saw a glow pass over the face of it, making the letters seem to twist and coil. She panted hoarsely, her tongue hanging out. The glow on the walls spread. A wind began to rise behind her, cold on her neck. It blew her hair over her cheeks.

A train . . .

The tracks began to quake beneath her feet. The tunnel began to rumble. The glow grew brighter now. It glared on the walls. The coiling letters danced frantically.

Train, a train is coming . . .

For another second, she couldn't get her mind to take it in. It was coming. Coming from behind her. Hammering the tracks, making everything shake. Making everything glare and tilt.

My God!

She spun around. It was right on top of her. A world of thunder. A wall of wind. Two lanterns like wild eyes burning her blind. The horn screamed. Screamed in her head. She screamed back. Tried to throw herself to the side, throw herself clear. She fell. Down onto the track. Her shoulder hit the rail. She rolled onto her face, screaming, pissing, covering her head with her hands.

"No no no!"

And then it was on her. As if the sky were on stampede. That long explosion of deafening noise. The track bouncing under her. The hot sting of urine on her legs. The wind like a wave crashing onto her back.

The express.

She could feel it. It was passing. Passing to the side of her, a flashing white line. A blue spark lanced the dark above her head. She felt a sharp, sizzling burn on the back of her hand. She looked up.

And it was past. The express train. The express train on the express track, which was the track next to the local track, which was the track she was lying on. She rolled over in time to see the train's red taillights shivering off into the tunnel. The yellow rectangle of the rear window growing smaller as it pulled out of sight. The rumbling ground subsided beneath her. The noise grew distant. She lay gasping for air, giddy to be alive. The dark was quiet around her.

Gee, kids, don't try this at home.

Now she could hear the footsteps. Hard shoes on gravel. The cops had come in the tunnel. They were moving toward her. She could hear their voices growing closer.

"Jesus Christ!"

"Are you all right in there, lady?"

"They're supposed to stop the trains. These fucking people."

"Lady?"

A moment later, she saw their flashlights. Beams sweeping back and forth, crossing each other. She saw the silhouettes behind the beams, moving forward among the pillars.

She tried to move, to stand up. Her body felt limp. Her face felt numb, as if she'd been shot with novocaine. She moved her legs and felt the damp.

Oh shit!

Oh, mortification! She'd wet herself! The idea that these cops—these men—were going to see . . . Oh, she wanted to shrink down to nothing.

Nancy, you . . . ! Damn it!

She managed to climb to her feet. Stood unsteadily. She hoisted her purse strap over her shoulder. Rubbed the back of her hand. The spark had burned her there; there was a purple line in the flesh.

The cops came closer. Their flashlights picked out portions of brown tracks and white pillars. She looked around herself. She felt dizzy and weak, but her mind was clear.

She saw she was in an abandoned station. A ghost station. A platform above the tracks. Unused coils of electrical wires, bags of plaster. Those graffitied walls. Kids must have climbed in here to spray-paint the place.

"You see her?" one cop called to another. His voice echoed in the distance.

"I don't know. Hold on. I hear something."

Right under the platform, Nancy saw, in the wall down there, at track level, there were alcoves. Low arching entranceways cut into the cement. Lightless nooks beyond them. Hiding places for subway workers, she thought. For when trains came.

Her hand went to the leather purse at her side.

"Come on out now, lady," one of the cops called wearily. "We don't want to hurt you."

"We want to kill you," another cop muttered.

"Shut up."

"Just kidding. Just kidding, lady. Come on out."

One of the silhouettes was moving away from the others now. He was coming toward the ghost station, toward her. His flashlight beam swept the track. It stretched out toward her feet.

If I could hide the gun . . . , she thought.

She touched the leather purse. Stared at the alcove in the wall.

If I could hide my purse and the gun . . .

Then they could not prove anything, she thought vaguely. Then they would have to let her go. She could go home. She could go see Dr. Bloom for a checkup. She could . . .

come back for the gun later.

Yes. She could come back for the gun when she needed it. When the time was right.

At the Animal Hour.

Yes. She started moving. She hardly confessed to herself what she was thinking. She only knew that she had to hide the gun. And, strangely enough, it sent a thrill through her. A coursing bolt of . . . maybe fear, maybe anticipation. She wasn't sure. She didn't want to think. She wanted to hide the purse, the gun.

She moved. The policeman's silhouette came closer. His footsteps sounded loudly on the gravel of the tracks. His flashlight beam stretched out to touch the edge of her shoe. She moved away from it quickly. Stepped over the rail. Ducked under the platform.

"Lady?" The cop was only a few feet away. He must have heard her moving. "Lady, is that you?"

She knelt down next to the alcove. The smell from inside it burned her nostrils. A juicy smell, sour and organic. It brought her stomach up into her throat. Something was in there, giving off that stench. She could see it against the far wall, some dead hump of something.

She swallowed hard. She stripped her purse off her shoulders.

"Lady?" He was almost beside her. Another step and his flashlight would sweep right over her. Pluck her right out of the dark. "Are you there?"

She screwed up her face. She held her breath. Turned half away. With a gasp, she shoved the bag into the alcove, stuck it into the pile of muck at the far end. She felt the clammy goo close over her hand, over her wrist, her sleeve. The stench washed over her. She shoved the purse in deep.

"Take it easy, lady," the cop said tensely.

But then he stopped. She heard the gravel crunch as he pulled up. She heard another sound too: a loud click. A track switch turning over. Nancy pulled her hand free. Looked up over her shoulder. A faint glow was beginning to spread over the swirling graffiti on the walls again. A faint wind was beginning to blow.

"Oh shit," the cop whispered.

And another cop called from the darkness: "Here comes another one! Damn it! The downtown local!"

"Dumb fucks! They're supposed to stop them," came a third voice.

"Goddamn it," muttered the cop standing over her. "I hate this fucking city."

He was backing away from her now. The glow was growing brighter on the walls. The police were shouting to one another, but the rumble of the oncoming train was drowning them out. The ground was shaking under her flats. The wind was whipping her face. The white headlights broke up out of the tunnel as the train pounded toward her. The local train. Her track this time. For another long second, she could only stare as the lights closed in, as they bore into her.

Then she ducked into the alcove. The juicy stench enveloped her. The air shivered and throbbed and roared with the onrushing train. She opened her mouth, strangling on the smell. The entranceway went white with light. She pulled her knees into her chest.

And then the train shot past the arched entrance. The streak of its silver sides, the churn of its flashing wheels. She pulled back, her head to the wall. All she could hear was the roar and blast of it . . .

And then a screech. It knifed through her. And what a screech—intolerably loud—the fingernail of God on the blackboard of heaven. On and on, the sound piercing her until she cried out in pain. She held her ears. She closed her eyes.

The screak tailed off. The shaking ground began to settle. The thunder died away.

She opened her eyes. The train had halted—right in front of her. Shivering, she peered out at it through the archway. She was looking up at the coupling between two cars.

She heard the cops' voices in the distance. "Oh, nice going."

"Fuckheads."

"I hate this city."

She sat still in the cramped alcove. Her legs drawn up, her arms around her knees. Her eyes teared with the stench. The smell of her own urine mingled with it. She was miserably aware of the chafing sting on her bare thighs.

She heard the policemen. Their male voices shouting commands.

"You gotta move it in. Move it in."

"You want it in the station?"

"No, I want it in my living room. Bring it into the fucking station. These dickheads."

"We're bringing it into the station! Right."

And Nancy sat still. Gazing blankly at the haunch of the enormous creature before her. The sharp gleaming wheels, motionless now. The safety chains dangling from the coupling.

They're about to move it into the station, she thought. *They're going to pull the train into the station and the doors will open and passengers will get out.* She gazed up at the coupling between the cars. She thought: *any second now.* She wanted to move. She wanted to climb out of the alcove and up onto the train. She could hide among the passengers. She could get out with them and escape . . .

But she couldn't bring herself to do it. It was too crazy— she would fall—she'd be killed. Still, she kept thinking: *The train will pull into the station any second.* And then she would have to come out of the alcove. With her hands up. And the police would surround her. And the idea that the police—these *men*—would see that she had peed on herself . . . She wanted to curl up like scorched paper and crumble to ashes.

Any second, she thought.

She came out of the alcove. Quickly. Uncurling. Ducking under the arch. She ducked again, down lower, twisted up under the safety chains. There was an iron rung on the side of one car. She took hold of the coupling floor, lifted her foot to fit it to the rung.

The subway jolted. It started to move.

Nancy cried out. She was sliding backward, off the coupling. The subway chugged slowly. She gripped the coupling floor but she was sliding off. Down to the tracks, down beneath the train, the big wheels.

Oh please.

Grunting with the effort, she pulled. Dragged herself up. Poked her toe into the rung. She grunted and struggled to haul her body back onto the coupling. Her arms strained. Her breasts were crushed painfully against the metal. The train bucked and cantered toward the station just ahead.

Then, with a cry, she made it. She was up on the coupling's edge. Rolling onto her side, rolling against the car door. She reached up and seized ahold of its handle. The train whistle shrieked. The tunnel walls gave way to the light of the station. Nancy fought her way to her feet, crying with the effort. With a muscular shove, she pushed the door in. Staggered into the car. And it was . . .

Well, she could hardly believe her eyes. She pulled up short, blinking. It was as if she had come into another world, a world as sweet as harp music. The inside of the subway car was clean. The metal fittings were shiny. The fluorescent lights were bright, making everything soothingly clear. There were handsome businessmen here, natty in their suits, substantial behind their copies of the *Times.* There was a mother cooing to her baby in its carriage. A pair of German tourist boys chuckling thickly.

Nancy stared. *Look at them,* she thought. All these good,

calm, regular people going about their lives. *And look at me!*
What must she look like to them? Her clothing torn, her hair
disheveled. Her face and hands covered with filth. What must
she *smell* like, for God's sake?

Quickly, she tugged her trench coat closed in front of her.
She prayed to the merciful mother of the Lord that the pee
wasn't showing through the front of her skirt.

*I'll become a nun, I swear, just dry that pee, merciful
Mother . . .*

And now, the train was coming to a stop. She could see
the tiled station walls, the waiting faces outside the window.
She thought she spotted some uniforms out there too. Some
granite brows under blue caps. Badges. There was nothing for it now though. She had to brass it out. Go through
with her plan and walk out with the others. She straightened.
Lifted her chin. Clutched that trench coat tightly shut. And
then . . .

> painted lips, painted eyes,
> wearin' a bird of paradise . . .

. . . she paraded—practically sashayed—into the midst of
the other passengers.

No one even looked up at her. They went on, reading their
papers, cooing their coos, chuckling their guttural chuckles.
She took hold of a shiny support beam, as if it were the staff
of Columbia. Her head thrown back, she stood at attention
as the train sailed into the station.

> Oh, it all seems wrong somehow,
> cause you're nobody's sweetheart . . .

"Ladies and gentlemen, your attention please." It was the
voice of the motorman over the intercom.

Nancy swallowed hard. *Don't let him say it.* She tilted her
chin back even farther. *If he announces there's a fugitive . . .
if he says they're looking for someone . . .* She held her breath,
staring straight ahead. *They'll see. Everyone will see. I'm meat,
I'm dead, I'm through . . .*

"Your attention please," the motorman continued. "This train will be sturfing in stazit fif noreen mozens due to a poleaxe on da traz."

Nancy looked up. The other passengers looked up, narrowing their eyebrows. They tried to make out the man's garbled words through the intercom's distortion and static.

"I repeat," said the motorman, "we'll be sturfing fif noreen mozens due to a poleaxe on da traz."

"Well," said one businessman with a shrug, "if there's a poleaxe on da traz, sturf we must."

Nancy closed her eyes. *God bless the Metropolitan Transit Authority!* She opened her eyes, braced herself as the train halted. She really might make this, she thought. She really might just walk right out with the other passengers. Walk right past the cops. Right home. To sleep this off, to get some help. To see her mother . . .

The motorman repeated his announcement once again, just the same as before. *Who says this ride isn't worth a buck and a quarter?* Nancy thought.

And with that, the doors slid open. The passengers came out of their seats. Surged toward the exit. She held back just a second until she was surrounded by a cluster of suits. Then she came forward. Stepped boldly through the door, onto the platform, part of a crowd of passengers, hidden in the crowd.

Instantly, steel hands gripped her. She was slammed back against the wall of the train. One cop grabbed her around the throat. Two others yanked her arms behind her back. They wrestled Daddy's little button into handcuffs while a fourth cop stepped forward with his .38 drawn. He shoved the black muzzle of the gun up under Nancy's right nostril.

"All right, you nutty cunt," he said, "where's the fucking rod?"

Nancy's head fell back. Her coat . . . Oh God, it was falling open, the pee . . . Her eyes rolled up in her head until only the whites were showing. Everything seemed to whirlpool away from her, a black swirl of faces, a dizzying murmur of words.

Well, she'd been right about one thing anyway, she thought,

as she felt her legs folding under her. This *was* turning out to be kind of a lousy day.

OLIVER PERKINS

Cautiously, Perkins moved into the ransacked mews. He slid his feet through the shattered glass and marble. His eyes flicked to the far corners of the room. The corners were deep in shadow. Anyone could have been hiding there. Watching him. Perkins lifted his fist to the side of his chin, to be ready for an attack.

"Zach?" he said again, softly.

He moved slowly to the stairway, his fist cocked.

He reached the foot of the stairs and peered up into the darkness. He saw the gray shape of the newel post on the second-floor landing. Not much else was visible. He found the light switch on the wall beside him, flicked it. Up and down, up and down.

But here there is no light . . .

Nothing. His eyes went down over the runner again. There were stains on every step, all the way up, as far as he could see in the dark. The stains were reddish brown on the tan runner. They might have been chocolate stains or catsup. But Perkins knew they were blood. Someone had come down these stairs—or gone up them—dripping blood.

He stayed where he was, at the foot of the stairs, for a long moment. The mews was quiet. The alley outside was quiet. He could hear his heart beating. He could feel the tightness in his throat. He did not want to go up there. The cops were the thing. He ought to call those cops. But Zach . . .

He had this picture in his mind of Zach on the floor in the bedroom. Their old bedroom upstairs. Zach on his back, reaching up. *Help me, Ollie.* Zach bleeding.

Don't worry, Mom. Don't worry anymore.

He started up the stairs, breathing through his mouth, keeping his fist raised. He kept his back turned to the wall. He kept glancing behind him to fend off a surprise attack.

> But here there is no light,
> save what from heaven is with
> the breezes blown . . .

The shadows on the landing above resolved themselves. The phone table in one corner. The doorway into the dark bathroom. The hallway to right and left.

He came up onto the landing and turned left. He could see dimly down the passage. He could see the bedroom door etched in gray light, as if a window were unshuttered in there. And now the stench hit him again. He had become used to it; he had stopped smelling it. But now, as he rounded the corner, it came over him in a fresh, dark wave.

Like a slaughterhouse.

He had never been in a slaughterhouse, but that was the thought that came to mind. Probably just the stains on the stairway that made him think of it. Something butchered. Torn flesh, spilled blood. He edged down the hallway with his fist pulled back.

I'm coming, Zachie.

Man, but he was scared. He definitely did not want to be doing this. He did not want to see what was in this room, not one little bit. Man oh man.

The dimly lighted door came closer. It had been their bedroom, his and Zach's. After Mom died. After their father had moved to California. *I just can't handle them, Mary.* After Nana had taken them in. The two brothers had lain in the dark in there, on the twin beds. The city had sounded so strange outside, the house had had such a strange old-woman smell. That first night, Oliver had stuffed the sheet in his mouth so Zach wouldn't hear him crying. He had heard Zach though. Zach had made a high-pitched sound—*eee eee eee*—as he fought his sobs in the other bed.

Don't worry, Zach-man, I'm right here.

He pulled his fist back an extra notch as he reached the bedroom doorway. The stench was thick here; it was like walking under stagnant water now. He swung around the door into the room.

The window was unshuttered—the window against the left wall. The red leaves of a maple were there and the bright blue sky behind them. The light came in and the room was gray. In the gray light, Perkins saw the shape on the bed. A dark, human shape lying motionless on the bed to the right. Zach's old bed.

Instinctively, Perkins's hand went out to the side, hit the light switch. He was already remembering the lights were broken—*but here there is no*—when the light in the room went on. The top light went on and Perkins saw what was on the bed.

He threw both hands up before his face and let out a hoarse cry.

The blood . . .

The blood was everywhere. The sheets were sodden, black and scarlet with blood.

Jesus, the blood, Jesus . . .

The shape on the bed was a woman's. But he couldn't comprehend it. He couldn't comprehend what he was seeing.

Her green leggings were torn. Her legs were scratched. The sheet was still white around her legs, but spattered with blood. He couldn't comprehend it. Her arms were at her sides. Her arms were torn. Frayed ropes were around her wrists, her small hands clenched. There were burns on her white skin. Her skirt was soaked with blood. He stared, shaking his head. *Jesus, the blood everywhere . . .* Her skirt was pushed up around her waist. Her leggings were ripped open. Her groin was exposed and her pubic hair was black with blood. Perkins's mouth was open. He stared through his raised hands. Her blouse was soaked with black blood and torn open and her breasts had been torn apart as if by an animal and the blood was everywhere, soaked into everything, the sheets sodden around the lacerated torso, around the neck, the ragged neck, the jagged stump of a neck where the head . . .

Oh Jesus, oh Jesus, oh . . .

The woman's head was gone.

The shock of it pinned the poet to the spot for another endless second. He simply could not take it in. And then he did. He saw the headless body on the bed and the smell coming off it hit him hard. Nausea rose in him with a great gush. He reeled back from the doorway. Stumbled down the dark hall. He had to get to the bathroom. He covered his mouth with his hand. His stomach rolled over.

He charged headlong through the bathroom door. He flung his arm out wildly. Hit the light switch. The light came on, brilliant and blinding on the white porcelain. The toilet was in the corner and . . .

Goddamn it!

The goddamned lid was closed. He would puke over everything. He fell to his knees. Threw himself on top of the toilet. Clawed at the lid. Pulled it open. Stuck his head in.

The woman gaped up at him from the bowl, her eyes an inch from his. Her severed head lay in a pool of black blood. Her hair was half submerged in it. Her slack mouth was filled with it. Her eyes peered out of it. Staring. Vacant. Glassy.

China blue eyes.

PART 2 →

HER PSYCHIATRIST'S TESTICLES

"Oh, let me not be mad.
Not mad, sweet Heaven!"
—*King Lear*

NANCY KINCAID

It was not as bad as she thought it would be. In fact, the hospital looked kind of peaceful through the trees. A castle of red brick. Round towers rising to peaked roofs. Arched windows with stained glass traced in stone. It was not bad at all.

Nancy pressed her face to the window as the police cruiser wound down the long driveway. The building appeared at intervals through the row of cypresses. It stood at the center of gently rolling grounds. Hills of green grass, low hedges, shady trees. White figures glided serenely along the pathways. At this distance, Nancy couldn't tell if they were the patients or the nuns. They looked almost ghostly, floating like that from bench to fountain, from birch to flowering laurel bush.

Still, she felt encouraged. The patrol car rounded the cul-de-sac and stopped before the main doors. The doors swung open and out stepped the hospital's director. He stood on the steps to greet her. He was smiling, holding out his arms. Nancy grew excited as she watched him through the window. His eyes were so kind and sad. His sharp, lined face framed with long black hair—it was so sensitive. There was so much understanding in him.

She got out of the car on her own. She climbed the steps to him as he smiled down at her. It gave her a warm rush—the way he seemed to comprehend her. The way he seemed to know her down to the very bone. It was all going to be all right.

Smiling, he stood aside as she came. He held the heavy door open with one hand to let her enter.

"Maybe there will be deer in the mist at the edge of the meadow," he murmured to her gently as she passed. "Maybe raccoons will waddle down the driveway for the trash. Maybe there will be sightings of bobcats, their yellow gazes reaching from the woods . . ."

She felt reassured by this. She entered the hospital almost expectantly. The door shut behind her with a hollow thud.

She was alone in a white corridor. A corridor of closed doors. Behind the doors, people were whispering, whispering. Reluctantly, she started down the hall. The whispers reached her.

"Nancy. Nancy."

They were whispering her name.

"Oh, Nancy."

A whispered song.

Slowly, she continued down the corridor. At the end of it, a dark figure was sitting on a throne. It was a slender figure draped in a flowing black robe. It held a scepter in its hand. Its hand was white bones. Its head was a grinning skull; Death's head.

"Nancy. Nannnnceeeee."

The whispers came to her through the doors. Frightened now, she turned from side to side, looking for help, looking for a way out. But there were only the voices.

"Nancy. Oh, Nancy . . ."

She did not want to go on. She did not want to go toward the throne, toward the skeleton. But she could not stop herself. She drifted toward it, as if floating above the floor. Her hand reached out to the skull, even as she recoiled from the thought of touching it. Her hand came closer; closer. She looked into the skull's eye sockets. She saw that it had china blue eyes.

Oh no! Oh no!

But she could not stop herself. In another moment, she had clutched the skull. Grabbed a fistful of its rubbery skin. It was a mask. She yanked it up. She saw the face beneath . . .

"Nancy. Oh, Nancy Kincaid."

It was her own face. Towering there above her. Grinning down at her from the throne, the blue eyes gleaming. Pointing at her with one skeletal finger. Whispering:

"You won't forget now. Will you?"

"Oh!"

A car horn blasted and Nancy woke up. Sat up straight, blinking. Her heart was thumping hard in her chest. She did not know where she was. Then she saw: the city streets whipping by at the windows. The stolid napes of two necks in the seat before her. The backs of two police caps. She tried to shift and felt her hands caught behind her. *Oh . . . Oh, Jesus . . .* Panic crawled in her chest like spiders. Wide-eyed, she turned this way and that. Peered out the window. First Avenue. The cop car was humming uptown amidst a cortege of fast yellow cabs. Anonymous buildings, white stone and glass, whipped past under the wide blue sky. And then, up ahead: a humorless brick temple of a place. Hunched wings, tall, frowning windows. It hoisted its walls out of a red cluster of low-grown maples. A grim fence of black iron surrounded it.

Bellevue! she thought. And the truth dropped down on her like a stone.

She remembered the subway platform. Coming awake facedown, her cheek pressed into the grainy concrete. She remembered the weight of the cops on top of her, a hand on her neck, a knee in her back. The bark of their voices: "Where's the gun? Where's the fucking gun?" Hands digging at her waist. Pushing at her thighs as if she were a slab of beef. Someone—a woman—said: "Aw crap, she urinated herself!" She had closed her eyes at this. She had concentrated on the dark, on the cold of the stone against her cheek. She just wanted to lie there and let things happen.

"Do you know where you are?" the woman had shouted in her ear. "Do you know where you are right now?" She had a thick Queens accent: "D'you know wheah you aw right now?"

In deep shit, Nancy thought, lying there. She felt a tear run out from under her eyelid. Snot ran from her nose and pooled on the platform under her mouth. She did not want to move.

She did not want to do anything. "Awright. C'mon!" the woman said finally. Nancy was yanked to her feet.

"Ow!" That roused her a little. Big male hands gripped her forearms tight. Pain stabbed her shoulder. "You don't have to hurt me," she said as fiercely as she could.

No one bothered to answer. The blue uniforms closed in on her. Beyond them, she could see commuters, their faces, white and brown. Gum-chewing mouths. Eyes—lots of dark eyes with the light dancing in them. The people were up on their toes, straining to see her. *Oh, look. A crazy broad getting arrested. Pissed all over herself. Snot all over her face.* Nancy couldn't wipe her nose—her hands were cuffed behind her. She couldn't even get around to rub herself clean on her shoulder. She wished she could stop crying. She wished her head didn't feel so heavy and thick.

The woman from Queens—a policewoman—brought Nancy's attention back by gripping her shoulders, leaning her face in very close. Nancy saw wisps of blonde hair curling out from under her police cap. Big, soft, brown eyes like a deer's. She was wearing blue eyeliner—a big mistake with her coloring. "Lissen to me, okay?" the policewoman said loudly. "D'you know wheah you aw? D'you know woy this is hehppening to you? Hah? Do you?"

Nancy had tried to steady herself on that big face. Okay, she thought; she had to give the right answer here. She sniffled once, hard. Her voice sounded high and strained to her like a little girl's voice. "I went to work this morning," she said slowly. "I went to work, but no one knew who I was. I mean, *I* knew who I was but they said I wasn't. But I was! And then all the beggars started winking at me."

The cops cast long looks at one another.

Good one, Nance, Nancy thought. She hung her heavy head. It all just seemed too hard.

"All right," one cop said with a sigh. "She must've dropped the piece in the tunnel. We'll go take a look."

And the woman cop answered, "We'll take huh ovuh ta Bellevue. Let dem figger it out."

Nancy had looked up when she heard the name. *Bellevue.*

The mental hospital. For people who had gone crazy. Her lips moved over the word: "Bellevue . . ."

And now, here it was. Through the patrol car window she saw the hospital's name etched in its wrought iron gates. Then that was gone, and the car was turning. Gunning down a deserted street. Past another hunkering brick pile. A solemn row of urns on concrete columns.

Nancy licked her dry lips. They must be heading around to the emergency entrance, she thought. And they were going fast. They'd be there any minute now. She tried to swallow but she couldn't. Christ, what were they going to do to her? Were they going to lock her up? Would she have to be in a cell with crazy people? God, she felt if she couldn't get out of these handcuffs, if she couldn't get free, she'd start to scream. The patrol car barreled down the deserted street. It was all happening so fast. And the silence—the way the two cops didn't even talk to her . . . She might have been alone in all the world.

She looked up at the backs of the two immobile heads in the front seat. The one on the passenger side was the woman. Her short blonde hair stopped just below the back of her cap. Her neck was slender and smooth.

"Excuse me . . ." Nancy said. It was a mouse voice. The cops couldn't hear her over the roar of wind at the windows. She cleared her throat. "Excuse me."

The policewoman barely turned. She glanced at the driver.

"Are we going to the hospital?" Nancy asked. "Are you taking me to Bellevue now?"

The policewoman shouted over her shoulder. "Yeah. Wuh right heah."

They had come out of the empty lane. The weight inside Nancy grew heavier as she looked out the window. There was a new building. Flat, broad, white. Columns of windows with strips of white stone between. It looked down deadpanned on a wide parking lot below. The road curved around the lot. The cruiser approached the curve.

"Will I be allowed to call someone?" Nancy had to fight to keep the tears out of her voice. "I'd really like . . . to call my mother. All right?"

The policewoman cocked her head and shrugged. "Shuah. Just take it easy now, okay? Don't get yerself all upset."

"I'm not upset," Nancy said firmly. "I'm fine now. I just wasn't feeling very well before. I got confused but . . . I'm really fine."

The policewoman didn't answer.

"I would just like to call my mother when we get there," said Nancy with some dignity.

"Shuah," the policewoman repeated. "Everything'll be fine."

Nancy could only nod. *I do have the right to a phone call,* she wanted to say. But she didn't have the courage. She looked out the window.

The police car rounded the bend. It headed toward the white building. Nancy watched the building growing larger, coming toward her. Suddenly, she heard herself give a nervous laugh, and she blurted out: "Boy, I am just really scared here. I guess it's silly, huh? But I've just never been in a hospital like this." She fought down her tears. "I am just really, really frightened, I don't know why . . ."

The policewoman glanced at her partner again, but she didn't say anything else. By now, anyway, they had arrived. The car was slipping into a low-ceilinged bay that ran along the building's side, pulling to a stop at the hospital curb. Nancy pressed her forehead to the window. All she could see was a glass door. Then the policewoman was out of the car. Out on the sidewalk, opening Nancy's door. She reached in and took Nancy by the elbow. Drew her out onto the sidewalk.

"Let's just take it easy now," the policewoman was saying. "Everything's gonna be awright."

Nancy pressed her lips together. The policewoman wasn't even talking to her. She was talking to someone else, to some crazy woman she didn't know. Nancy felt alone.

Another cop—a squat black woman—pushed open the glass door from inside. The blonde policewoman gripped Nancy's arm tightly and walked her quickly through the open door. Nancy heard the door swing shut behind her. The sound made her look up. What she saw made her gasp. She cried aloud: "Oh no! Oh God!"

There was a white corridor before her. A corridor of closed doors. Behind the doors, there were whispers. She could hear them.

"Nancy. Oh, Nancy."

She could hear the singsong whispers calling to her.

Her mouth went wide, but she could not scream. She was being pulled along the corridor and there, at the end, was a figure on a throne. A slim figure in black robes, holding a scepter in a bony hand and . . .

Nancy dug in her heels. She would not go. "NO!" She started screaming. Twisting to get free. Struggling to pull her arms free from the cuffs. "Please! Please! No!"

She could hear her own high-pitched shrieks. It was odd. She could hear her wild cries and she could see herself as if from a distance. She could see herself twisting and struggling frantically in the policewoman's grip. Her eyes rolling, white. White froth bubbling over her lips onto her chin. She could see her feet kicking and skidding on the slick linoleum floor as she fought against going. Her head thrown back, her neck taut. Every muscle of her slim body strained backward as if she were a child being dragged to the woodshed.

And it was odd—it was really bizarre—because she could also see now that she was not in the nightmare corridor at all. She was just in the hospital. In a hallway. With a policewoman struggling to hold on to her arm. And two more officers were charging toward her from the far end of the hall. And two women in white uniforms were running at her too, shouting over her crazy screams.

She felt as if she were putting on a performance. In front of them, in front of herself. As if she were just pretending to be insane so she wouldn't be held responsible for everything. She could even hear her real self thinking: *Okay now, this is a bad idea. We are not making a good first impression here at all. So let's stop this right now. All right? Right this minute.*

And yet she couldn't. She couldn't make the performance stop. She went on screaming, kicking. Lashing her head from side to side, snapping with her teeth. And now came a man in a white coat—a slender young doctor with a pointed beard. He strode through a doorway, walking at her quickly, holding

101

up a syringe. A syringe! She could see him squeezing a spurt of juice through the needle, clearing the air bubble. Two nurses waddled out of another door, holding a terrifying contraption of pads and straps.

That's a straitjacket, Nancy! she thought. *They are not kidding, all right? Let's knock this off right now.*

But the performance would not end. The doctor, the straitjacket—these only seemed to crank her hoarse shouts louder. She hurled herself to the floor, her body whipping and bucking even harder in her efforts to get free. Her real self watched helplessly as policemen, orderlies, nurses, and the doctor converged quickly on the shrieking performer. Only once, at the very end—only for a second, with an insinuating little chill of nausea—did it occur to her that this was not a performance at all.

And then they swarmed over her.

OLIVER PERKINS

Perkins managed to vomit on the floor. He flung himself away from the toilet. Away from the glassy eyes, the severed, blood-drenched head. He fell to his hands and knees as his stomach disgorged Avis's scrambled eggs and toast. The loose yellow mess splattered on the white tiles. Perkins could not lose the image of the woman's slack and ghastly face beneath him, and he vomited again. He groaned, his eyes closed. Then, still spitting bits of undigested toast, he started crawling to the door. He wiped his mouth with his hand. He kept crawling. He had to get away from it. He had to get out of there.

The second he was in the hallway, he climbed to his feet. He braced his hand on the phone table and got his wobbly legs under him. He was gasping, out of breath. But he had to get out of the mews, get away from it. He stumbled to the top of the stairs, grabbed the newel post. He could see light below, gray light in the living room. He realized he had left the front door open.

That was the project: Get out that door. Get out of here and back into the sweet, bright, busy city. Get to a telephone. Call the police. Get out of . . .

He was about to start down the stairs when he heard something that made his breath stop. It was the creak of a floorboard. Somewhere in the house: a footstep.

His first crazy thought was to look down the hall. At the gray door, the door to his old bedroom. What if the sound had come from in there? What if the headless thing on the bed was moving? Rising . . . coming into the doorway . . . A silhouette in the rectangle of dim light.

Look, Oliver. Look what they did to me. Let me show you what they did to my head.

Then he heard it again. Another step. He stood absolutely still. He listened. It was coming from downstairs. Someone was moving around down there. Moving stealthily, slowly. Crossing the kitchen. Just out of his view. Coming toward the stairway. He heard a deep murmur, a few low syllables.

Shit, they're still here.

He backed away from the head of the stairs, back into the shadows. Another floorboard creaked. *They're still in the house,* he thought. Whoever they were, whoever had done this. They were still in the mews. The woman's face seemed to appear before him again, her dead stare up from the toilet. They had carried her head from the bedroom down the hall . . . She had been alive just before. She had been a woman. She had had blue eyes. A woman's voice. She must have thought thoughts—*lived*—even as they put the knife against her throat . . .

And they were still here. The people who had done this. They were in the mews. In the kitchen. Creeping quietly toward the stairs.

Perkins dragged his hand across his damp mouth. He looked right, down the dark hall, toward his old bedroom. He looked left. It was the only way to go. The way to Nana's room. The outline of the door was dark. The room was dark, darker than the hall.

With a last glance down the stairs, Perkins moved. He took long strides along the passage. Going quickly, trying to stay quiet. If he could get to the room, get a window open . . . It was only a one-story drop, and even a broken ankle was a lot better than meeting up with these guys.

He reached the doorway and paused. Listened. A stair creaked—one of the bottom stairs. They had started up.

He entered the small room cautiously. The air was musty here, but the smell of butchery was not as thick. He could see the wooden shutters on the windows to his right. Lines of white light between the slats. Then he pulled up short as a movement caught his eye. But it was only a dresser mirror against the far wall. He could make out the dim shape of it. And the queen-sized bed against the wall beside him. A rocking chair . . . He scanned the room slowly. No other shapes. No human silhouettes . . .

Look, Oliver. Look what they've done.

He heard another step on the stairs. Closer to the top now. He moved swiftly around the end of the bed. Crossed the room to the shuttered window.

Come on, come on.

His fingers fumbled with the metal hook that held the shutters closed. He couldn't hear the footsteps anymore. He didn't know where the hell they were. The hook swung up with a little rattle. He folded back the shutters.

The light hit him bright and hard. The white-blue sky over a Tudor cottage. A car parked quietly at the alley curb. A woman walking her corgi turning the corner onto MacDougal . . . Christ, to be out there in the light . . . Perkins pushed open the double casements. The crisp, autumn air sighed in to him. He glanced over his shoulder once, to check the door . . .

Something stopped him. He saw something. On the bed. Frightened, he flicked his eyes over it. There *was* a shape.

No. Just an impression. The imprint of a head on the pillow, of a figure on the spread. Someone had been lying there and . . .

And there was a gleam. He was about to turn away, about to go out through the window when he saw that, that little gleam of light. A thin line of silver. It lay on the pillow where a head had been. A single silver hair.

Perkins hesitated a second, his eyes fixed on it.

Tiffany?

And that was one second too long.

The floor creaked again. At the threshold. Right here. Perkins's stomach dropped as his eyes flashed up from the bed to the doorway. A shadow stepped through into the room.

My head, Oliver.

But it was a man. Or not a man—a kid. A boy, still in his teens it looked like. He came into the light, blinking. A kid with a thin, pimply face. Blond hair in a crewcut. Frightened eyes—he looked almost as scared as Perkins. The two of them stared at each other. Slowly, the kid lifted his hand. The sunlight glinted blackly off the barrel of his gun. His lips worked silently for a moment before he could get the words out.

Then he said: "All right. P-P-P-Put your hands up. NYPD. You're under arrest."

ZACHARY

Zachary remembered how Oliver had found him. That time at the mews. It was over a year ago now. Zach had been lying in the bedroom, on the floor next to his old bed. He had been

ANDREW KLAVAN

naked and the warm night air had felt like water on his sinewy body. There were images floating in that water. Swirling, drifting, dissolving. Memory become vision. He had been gazing at those images and laughing and crying. He had not even heard Ollie arrive.

Then, all at once, Oliver was there. Zach had thought his brother was just part of the vision at first. But Oliver was loud, solid. He did not swirl or dissolve. Oliver was shouting at him, telling him to get up. Zach tried to explain about the teacup. He was laughing; it was so beautiful. It was the same teacup that had lain beside their mother when she died. And he could see it, floating in the liquid air above him: an inexpensive cream-colored teacup with a brown border at the rim. Only it was changed now. Not in appearance, no—it had been metamorphosed from within. It was filled with meaning that seemed to unite it to all the meaning everywhere. It was as if it had gone from being an individual object to a pattern in the greater pattern of an endless tapestry.

Zach had tried to explain this to his older brother. "Look, Ollie," he had said, laughing. "Filled with love. Our love. Brothers. Everyone. In the structure, the molecules. See it? Right there."

"Get up, you stupid prick!" Oliver had shouted. Oliver had not seen it. "Come on! We've gotta get you to the hospital."

Zach remembered this as he pressed against the wall beside his window. He was naked now too. His balls tight with fear, his dick shriveled. He was peeking out at the street, at the detective stationed below him in the street. The detective was a pasty-faced thug in a tartan windbreaker. He leaned against a blue Dodge Dynasty with a long scrape in its front door. He smoked a Camel, glancing up and down the street. Watching for Zach. Waiting to arrest him because of the body in the mews.

This was how the world was without the drug, without Aquarius. Everything grainy with details. The crumpled cigarettes in the gutter at the detective's feet. The rubble in the empty lot across the street. The lightning bolt shape of the crack in the plaster right beside Zachary's nose. How was he supposed to think with all this *stuff* cluttering his mind?

106

He pulled back from the window, rested his head against the wall. He *had* to think. He had to get out of here, get to Ollie. The police would be back any minute. They would search the place. Find him. Open the red overnight bag. Somehow, he had to get past that detective downstairs. Haul his ass over to big brother's.

He slid down the wall, rough plaster scraping his naked back. Down to the floor. On all fours, his bare ass high. Carefully, so he could not be seen from the street, he started crawling. He crawled back through the railroad flat, back to the bedroom. Over the dust balls on the wooden slats. Over the long gray patches where the white paint on the slats had peeled away. *Oh Jesus, please,* he thought. He was so sorry he had taken the drug again last night. He knew that God was punishing him for breaking his promise. But he could not believe that Jesus meant him to feel so alone, so detached from the tapestry.

He did not stand up until he was at the closet door again. Then he slipped back into the closet. Back among Tiffany's clothes. The trace of her smell, her delicate musk. She wore jeans a lot of the time, but sometimes, luckily, she liked skirts too. Long skirts with colorful South American designs. He selected one of these now. An ankle-length with swirls of red and blue, cultic stick figures and rude drawings of sheep. It made him flash back on an argument Ollie and Tiff had had in Lancer's, the café downstairs.

"Ol-i-ver!" Tiffany had said, musically drawing out the syllables as she strained the petals from her chamomile tea. "Are you so invested in your Eurocentric authority that you can't even accept native art's validity as art?"

And Ollie, leaning his head so far back that he was gazing at the ceiling, groaned, "I accept, I accept. Native art is art and native medicine is medicine. But give me a Park Avenue surgeon and Picasso any day."

Zach felt dizzy. He leaned against the wall. Closed his eyes. He remembered the soggy flowers lying on her saucer. The coffee grounds at the bottom of his demitasse. The way the lines of Tiffany's sweet face turned down at Ollie, as if she were more hurt by him than angry. And the way Ollie waved her off. And himself, seated at the table between them, with that feeble grin on his face. "You know, I really do believe that a mystical reading of the New Testament can help us transcend these categories." Blessed are the peacemakers, for they shall be ineffectual.

He sighed. Opened his eyes. There was too much to straighten out. He could never get everything right. The police figured he'd killed the woman in the mews. They were going to put him in jail for it. He might as well give up now.

But he didn't. Moving heavily, he tugged one of Tiffy's sweaters off a hanger. It was a bulky Guatemalan knit, gray with blue zigzag patterns. *Under the Volcano*, the label said. He carried it and the skirt to the dresser in the corner.

The dresser was by the open window. He felt the autumn air on his skin as he stood there. It made him nostalgic and sad. If they put him in prison because of the woman in the mews, he thought, he would kill himself, that's all. Even if they accused him, if they indicted him, he would kill himself. He couldn't stand it. He would throw himself in front of a subway or something.

He opened Tiffany's underwear drawer and then changed his mind. He went for his own briefs and a pair of white socks. Then he moved away from the window. He didn't want anyone to see him from the buildings surrounding Lancer's garden.

He went into the bathroom. Shaved first—super-careful not to nick himself. Then, once he had his underwear and socks on, he stepped into Tiffany's skirt. Pulled on the sweater. He knew he had to hurry but he couldn't focus his mind. At one point, he just stopped, just stared, stupidly. At the beard hairs in the sink. At the smear of toothpaste on the faucet. All this *stuff*, he thought. God! He shook himself out of it. Pulled open the mirror that covered the medicine chest.

Tiffany didn't wear much makeup. She didn't need much, she had that natural cream complexion. But there was a tube of lipstick and some eyebrow guck in there. Zach took the lipstick. Swung the mirror shut. He leaned into the glass and started to paint his lips bright red.

Do it fast, he thought. But then he was lost in the task.

Smearing the stick on carefully. Pressing his lips together the way Tiffy did. He was thinking of Tiff again. Of Tiff and Ollie, arguing. In the churchyard over at St. Mark's this time. Sipping cider, standing on the implanted memorials. Oliver had just given a reading in the church, and Tiffany's friends from the bookstore were pissed. Trish and Joyce, radical fems in studded leather. They stood behind Tiff, at either slim shoulder. Glared at Ollie from the night like specters of revenge. Zach had stood at Ollie's shoulder trying to look husky, just to be fair.

Tiff, though, had only been petulant. She crossed her arms, stamped her foot at him. "I don't know, Oliver. I think you're just being shallow on purpose . . ."

"Right," Oliver had said wearily. "So if we're not biologically determined, Oh Enlightened One, what are we determined by? Little messages from our incorporeal souls?"

Trish and Joyce had snarled like pit bulls. Tiffany's doe eyes had gone wide. For a moment, Zachary thought she was actually near tears. "Damn it, Oliver," she said. "You just do this to alienate people."

"Why don't you two stop?" Zach had said finally, a little desperate. He had put his hand on his big brother's arm. He had hated the small, plaintive sound of his own voice. "Why don't you two ever *stop?*"

He was done. He leaned back from the mirror. He stood on tiptoe to get a look at the length of him. The bulky sweater hiding his shape. The skirt to his ankles, the white socks and clogs covering his feet. The detective was not expecting him to come from inside. It would be enough. It would have to be.

But when he finally stood in the hall outside his apartment, when he stood at the top of the stairs, looking down, the fear almost paralyzed him. It made him feel frantic and sluggish at the same time. He wanted to run. And he wanted to sink down on the top step and burst into tears. *Okay, Jesus. Please,* he thought. He was so sorry he had taken the drug last night.

He took a breath and started walking slowly down the stairs.

He had a bandanna on now. Tiffany's cotton scarf with the elk pattern on it. It covered his head, dipping down over his

109

brow, hiding his nearly crew-cut hair. He was carrying the red canvas overnight bag, his long raincoat draped over it. Trying to think how a woman would carry it, how she would hold her arms. He worked it out as he went down. Bending his arms at the elbow. Placing his feet carefully so that his skirt would sway. *Please Jesus please.*

By the time he got to the ground floor, he was a walking prayer. *Please sorry please sorry sorry please please please.* He thought he might give himself up out of pure terror. And now too, there was a windy, diarrhetic feeling in his belly. His bowels were starting to move. He knew if he turned back now, if he went back upstairs to the bathroom, he would never get away. That was another aftereffect of the drug: It turned your shit to mud. Even if Mulligan's men didn't come back for an hour, they'd still find him in there clutching the crapper rim, straining for dear life. He just had to hold his gut together until he got to Ollie's.

He pushed open the door. Stepped out onto the stoop. The pasty-faced detective was right there, leaning against the car at the curb. He was in the act of dropping yet another cigarette into the gutter. He looked up. A mean square face. Acne-pocked skin. Beady, marbly eyes. He looked right up at Zach. And Zach, frozen in terror, just stood there like an idiot. Returned the stare.

Slowly, the detective smiled.

He's got me! Zach thought. *Oh Jesus, I'm so sorry, help me please!*

And then, with a jaunty little gesture, the detective raised one finger to his brow and saluted him. And Zach understood. The cop was *flirting* with him! Thinking fast, he dropped his eyes shyly, shyly smiled. The detective's grin widened. He straightened against the car, shifting his shoulders manfully in his tartan coat.

Zach held his breath. He knew he was going to make it. His fear was turning to excitement. His groin was hot with it.

Holy shit! he thought. If he had an erection, he was dead.

His heart hammered at his chest as he came tripping sweetly

down the stairs. The detective's eyes were glued to him, following every step.

Zach tossed him one last saucy look. Then, the red bag swinging with casual feminine grace, off he went, his skirt switching behind him.

NANCY KINCAID

Nancy opened her eyes. She took a long, slow look around her. Then she began to cry.

She couldn't hold it in anymore. She let loose; she cried as if she were alone. Her mouth was wide open. Her eyes were shut tight. Her head was thrown back against the thin pad. Her body shook as the tears poured out of her.

Oh Jesus, Jesus, Jesus, is this me? Is this who I am?

She gulped the air, sobbing.

She was strapped to a gurney in the middle of a narrow room. A coarse gray blanket lay on top of her legs. Her coat had been taken away and the sleeve of her cream blouse had been rolled up to bare her arm. An IV bag hung on a hook above her head with a clear tube running from it to the crook of her elbow. The needle had been pushed into the vein there. It was taped down to hold it in place.

Nancy moaned. She opened her eyes. She stared through her tears at the white tiles of the ceiling, the hazy fluorescent light. She sobbed and her chest heaved against the strap that held her. She could not stop crying.

The room she was in was long, more of a corridor than a room. Along the walls were molded plastic seats. Hospital issue, blue, all linked together. Most of the men and women in the seats were black. They sat heavily, chins on their chests, mouths hanging open. Collapsed into themselves as if they'd been plopped down there, pats of dough off some big spoon. One old man with a grizzled beard was drooling. One fat woman was talking to herself. She wore a T-shirt that said: "Life-styles of the Poor and Unknown." Her huge breasts lay on the rolls of her belly flesh. "*I* understand," she kept saying. "*You* don't understand. *I* understand perfectly."

These patients sat on either side of Nancy. She was strapped to the gurney right in the middle of the room, right in front of everyone. The nurses had to turn their bodies when they wanted to get past her. One nurse smiled down at her as she squeezed by. *Poor crazy thing.* Nancy couldn't stand it. She turned her face to the side. Her tears spilled across the bridge of her nose.

Is this really me? Is this really who I am?

The nurses slipped past her and past her again, carrying their folders. One was supporting a scrawny black woman by the elbow. The patient was staring at the floor, shuffling slowly along. Nancy tracked them as they went past the entranceway. She saw a policeman sitting there, a little cluster of blue chairs all to himself. His veiled eyes studied a tall wooden frame: a metal detector. Gotta watch those crazies, Nancy thought. Gotta watch those nut cases every second.

That made her remember: how she had screamed. How she had braced her heels against the floor, throwing her body back, shrieking up at the ceiling. Had that been her? The image of it seemed to swim sluggishly through the murk in her head. *Was that me?* The thought flashed neon out of the murk and vanished. It was all very tiring. That IV—it must have been pumping drugs into her. She was sooo sleepy. Thinking uphill. They must've been dripping some kind of secret drugs into her arm as she lay there strapped down, helpless. Made her want to scream some more. Scream plenty. That they could just do that to her. That they could just do anything to her they wanted. Because she was so goony. So goony as to be moony. So loony she was a loony tuney . . .

She laughed wearily through her tears. Christ, Christ, Christ-ti-Christ, she thought. What if this *was* what she was like? What if she just forgot sometimes, escaped, wandered out into the world . . . ?

Yes, she likes to go into offices and pretend she works there. She can keep the game up for a while, but she's completely insane. Hears voices, sees things. Thank you for bringing her back here, officer . . .

What if what she thought was her life was only a dream of her life, a wish for what her life would be if she weren't . . .

The gaga girl from Booga-booga U.

She smiled, dimly now, her eyes half closed. All that weeping—it sure tired a person out. Made you muddy headed. And that sneaky IV—something was in there for certain. She could hardly keep her eyes from fluttering closed . . .

Then they shot open. Her heart was beating fast. Had she been asleep? She didn't know. She didn't know how much time had gone by. Someone's hand was on her arm. She turned her head. Looked up.

A face hung over her. Round and black. Like a chocolate moon in the white sky above her. A lowering brow of dark, shiny granite. Huge, stern brown eyes.

"Who . . . ?"

"Take it easy," the black woman said. She patted Nancy's arm. Nancy felt the calluses of her palm. She glanced down. All right; a nurse. She could understand that. The black woman was a nurse. Dressed in starched white with maroon piping. Squat and bosomy. With thick meaty arms, bare from the elbow.

"Let's get you out of this," she said.

"Opie's," Nancy said. She was trying to say, "Oh, please."

There was a ripping noise. The nurse had pulled the tape up. Nancy sucked in a breath as the long IV needle was drawn out of her vein.

"How you feelin' now?" the nurse said. "You got your mind in gear? I don't want you biting my head off or anything, I got enough troubles of my own, you understand?"

Nancy tried to nod. Her eyes felt funny—untethered from her head. Her tongue tasted like a can of chili left open overnight.

"I'm Mrs. Anderson," said the nurse. "I'm gonna take you to see the doctor." With a few expert movements, she undid the strap around Nancy's chest. Pulled the blanket off her legs. Undid another strap down there. And more stuff: There were a lot of rattling sounds, gears croaking, metal clanking. God knew what the woman was doing. Nancy didn't care. Her whole body had sagged into the gurney with relief. She was free!

"Come on," said Mrs. Anderson.

Nancy felt the callused black hand take hold of her arm. With an effort, she sat up on the gurney. It was like a storm at sea. The narrow white room tilted up until she thought the dreary patients would be tossed from their blue chairs. Nancy swayed.

"I gotcha," said Mrs. Anderson. One heavy arm went around Nancy's thin shoulders. Nancy leaned against the papery material of the uniform. Felt the soft, solid body underneath. She loved this woman. She was ready to follow Mrs. Anderson into the sulfury pit.

They went down the hall instead. Just another nurse with another shuffling patient. Nancy's neck was bent as they went, her head down, just like the scrawny black woman she had seen before. Her feet—still in her flats—did not come off the floor as she scraped along. They crossed the narrow room into an even narrower hallway: a cinderblock corridor with doors on the left-hand wall.

"Right in here," said Mrs. Anderson. "You sit, and the doctor be right with you."

They had come into a tiny room. A cramped cubicle packed with furniture. A file cabinet in the corner. A desk topped with imitation wood. A table of the same material. Shelves in the wall stacked high with papers, papers overflowing. Two chairs: a cheap black-and-metal swivel for the desk, blue plastic for guests. Hardly a bare strip of scarred linoleum floor visible under it all.

"You sit," said Mrs. Anderson again.

Nancy carefully lowered herself into the plastic chair opposite the desk. Her head felt enormous, but she managed to raise it. She nodded at Mrs. Anderson, smiled her nice-girl smile. *I'm fine now, see? I'm a very nice girl. You'll have no more problems with me, no sir, you betcha.* If they strapped her to that gurney again, she really *would* go out of her mind.

Mrs. Anderson nodded her big head gravely. Then she was gone from the open door.

Alone, Nancy sat in her plastic chair and tried to look docile. Shoulders hunched, hands clasped on her lap. Ready for the doctor. She studied the shiny metal leg of the desk in front of her. *Excuse me, Doctor,* she thought, *would it be possible for me to make a phone call?* She shook her head, tried again. *Excuse me, sir. I don't want to make any trouble or anything, but later, if there's time and I can find a phone free . . .* She took a trembling breath. Maybe she wouldn't even have to ask, she thought. Wouldn't they just let her call her mother at some point? Sure they would. Maybe they'd already called her. It would probably be best to just wait; don't start any trouble.

The phone on the desk gave a soft *breep.* She dared to raise her eyes a little until she saw the phone's light blinking. Papers stacked on the desktop. A manila folder open, forms fanning out of it. Pencils here and there.

"Ah! The new victim."

She turned to the door quickly. A man stood there. An older man in a worn black suit, a loosened red tie. Bent-backed, hands in his jacket pockets. He had straight silver hair pouring down one side of his face. A mottled face with white lips that smiled kindly, small eyes that glistened merrily as they took her in.

Nancy composed her expression: friendly, respectful. The way she'd greeted Dr. Bloom since she was thirteen years old. "Hello, Doctor," she said.

He unpocketed one hand, held it up at her. "No, no. Not a doctor, just a . . . well, a counselor, I think, is the politest word for me. Why not just call me Billy Joe? Billy Joe Campbell. And you are . . ."

She managed a party-manners nod. "Nancy Kincaid."

"Ah," said the old man again. Briskly, he stepped forward. Sat in the desk chair and swiveled around to face her. The phone was still ringing but he paid it no mind. He rolled his chair forward a little, until his knees were nearly touching hers. He leaned toward her, his merry eyes bright. "You," he said slowly, "are afraid."

Nancy pressed her lips together. What was the right answer? "A little, yeah." She had to speak carefully to make the words clear. "A lot actually."

He smiled. He reached out and took her hands off her lap, held them in his. "I don't blame you." His hands were cool and dry and somehow reassuring. "What's happening to you is very frightening," he said. "And the task before you is more frightening still."

He held her gaze with his, no matter how much the phone breeped. Nancy saw its light blinking from the corner of her eyes. "The task?" she said thickly.

"Oh yes!" He leaned back, still holding her hands. To Nancy's relief, the phone stopped finally. "It's a sort of journey really. A journey down into the dark. An adventure— different for every person and yet, for each person, almost exactly the same."

She licked her lips, shook her head a little. She was held by the jolly light dancing in those eyes. She couldn't think of what to say.

"For each person," he went on, "there are . . . talismans that must be found. Trials to overcome. Riddles to answer. And, at the end, in the darkest place of all: a fearsome creature: the Other; the self whom, above everything, you wish not to be. Only if you have the courage to embrace that self can you learn the magic word."

Nancy could still only shake her head. "The magic word?"

And he, with a nod, would only answer her, "The magic word, yes." And then he lowered his chin to his chest. Peered up at her from under bushy brows.

"Well . . . what do I have to do?" Nancy said after a moment. She felt she had to say something. "I mean, what do we do now? Where do we begin?"

"Ah!" He chuckled amiably. "First of all, we have to kill the Jews."

"What?"

116

"And I mean *all* the Jews. We have to kill them and send their bodies to the moon."

Nancy was still gazing into those merry eyes as, very slowly, her mouth began to fall open.

"That will be fun, won't it?" said the man.

Nancy yanked her hands from him. "Why, you're . . . you're crazy."

"OH, LIKE YOUR SHIT DON'T STINK!" he screamed. He jumped to his feet, his arms flying. "What do you think you're here for, sister? Shingles?"

"Billy Joe!"

It was Mrs. Anderson. She came steaming back into the little room, her great chest a prow.

"What're you doin' in here? You quit screaming at that girl! Right now! You hear?"

The man in the worn black suit hunched his shoulders. He pulled his head in like a turtle. "Yes, Mrs. Anderson," he said.

"You go on, get back out there where you belong 'fore I lose my temper. Go on. Right now."

Billy Joe had to make himself the width of a piece of paper to squeeze past the mighty nurse. But he managed it—fast —and slipped out of the room.

"I'm surrounded by goddamned crazy people," Mrs. Anderson said. She shook her head. Turned her big, stern eyes on Nancy—who was pinned to her chair, welded to it, back straight, features frozen in a silent scream, as if an electric shock had gone through her. "Oh, don't you let that one bother you," Mrs. Anderson told her. "He don't do nothin'. Here come the doctor now."

Nancy swiveled as stiffly as a mannequin. Turned her electric eyes on the door, thinking: *Magic Word? Magic Word? Jesus Christ! Get me out of here!*

And then the doctor strolled in, whistling.

OLIVER PERKINS

"*The Animal Hour.*"

Perkins looked up, surprised.

"*The Animal Hour and Other Poems.*"

"Yeah," Perkins said. "How do you know that?"

"It's a book."

"That's right."

"You wrote it."

"How do you know that, man? Come on."

The other blinked, his face impassive. A queer, dangerous little guy, Perkins thought. Short to the point of insignificance. With that mild round face. The pug nose. The curly hair high on his forehead. He kept blinking behind his wire rims but his expression never changed. His high-pitched, airy voice never changed its tone. He never even took off his trench coat.

Nathaniel Mulligan, his name was; detective, NYPD. The two of them were alone together in a room in the Sixth Precinct. It was one of those soulless rooms only governments build. Green cinderblock walls. White linoleum floor. Louvered windows with no view. Papers posted on corkboards everywhere. There were four big desks, all shiny metal with wood finish on top, all unoccupied. Four black swivel chairs and four chairs of black plastic. Perkins was in one of the plastic chairs. Mulligan was standing, his hands in his trench coat pockets. Gazing down at him. Blinking down.

The detective let the silence lengthen. That was a little trick of his apparently. Build up the suspense. And it worked; Perkins hated it. Every time the talking stopped, the girl's face came back to him; her head staring up from the toilet. She had been alive, he kept thinking. She had had a woman's voice. He remembered the TV cameras at the alley gates. The way they had crowded around the patrolman who brought out the white plastic bucket with her head in it. Man, when Nana saw that on the evening news . . . It would kill her. And that brought him back to Zach too. What about Zach? Where the hell was . . . ?

Mulligan drew one hand out of his pocket. He held up the book. It was in a plastic bag, but Perkins recognized it all right. The white cover, the small black letters. Mulligan put it down on the desk next to Perkins. Perkins glanced at it.

The Animal Hour
and Other Poems

by Oliver Perkins

There was a streak of rust brown in the white space under his name. Another across the *r* in *Hour*. Blood. Christ. More blood everywhere. Perkins's tongue felt thick in his mouth.

"Where'd you find that?"

"On the floor next to the bed," said Mulligan. "Next to the body. You don't know how it got there." This was another trick of his. He didn't ask questions. He supplied your answers. It gave the answers sort of a sardonic tone even though his high voice never changed. It made the answers sound like lies.

"No," said Perkins. His elbow on the desk, he pinched his nose with thumb and forefinger. He shut his eyes. It was getting hard to think in here. He had to find Zach. He had to break the news to Nana. It was late; it was after one already. They'd kept him waiting around the mews, and then around the precinct house, for hours. They'd been questioning him for hours. "No. I don't know how it got there."

Mulligan went into his silent routine again. Perkins nearly groaned aloud.

He straightened. Opened his eyes. Avoided Mulligan's gaze. Looked over the cluttered corkboards. Up to the featureless light at the louvered windows. He was feeling better physically, at least. Puking had done the trick there, cleaned him out. Then, later, some detective had brought him a bagel and coffee. He'd managed to get some of it into him before the girl's head bobbed to the surface again. *Look what they did to me, Oliver.* Jesus!

Anyway, his hangover seemed to have ebbed away. So that was on the plus side. On the minus side, he was under arrest for murder. Life, he'd noticed, was like that sometimes.

"This house, this mews," Mulligan said quietly. "You don't own it."

Perkins puffed his cheeks, let out a long breath. "No. No, it's my grandmother's."

"And her name is . . ."

"Mary Flanagan."

The pug-nosed detective blinked a few more times. The fluorescent light flashed off his glasses. "Nice place," he said.

"Yeah."

"But she leaves it empty."

"She's trying to sell it."

"And you have a key."

"That's right."

"And she has a key."

"Yeah, sure."

"And no one else."

Perkins hesitated. Some protective instinct almost made him lie. But the little balding man in the trench coat continued to blink down at him, and he strongly suspected that lying would be a bad idea.

"My brother has a key," he said. "Zachary."

Mulligan inclined his head, the slightest hint of a nod. "Your brother Zachary."

"Yeah. The family. We all have keys. Hell, the realtor must have one too. Anyone could get in."

"You got in this morning."

"Yes."

"Because you were . . ."

Again, Perkins hesitated. Again, Mulligan stood completely impassive, hands in his trench coat, pug features mild, set. *What does he need a trench coat indoors for?* Perkins thought bitterly. "Because I was looking for Zach," he said.

"Your brother."

"Yes."

"He's missing."

"No!" *Shit.* "No, of course not. I just . . . don't know where he is," he finished lamely.

"And he wasn't at the mews."

"That's right."

"Just the woman upstairs."

Perkins shook his head. He was getting sick of this. If the little weirdo wanted an answer, let him ask a goddamned question.

The detective blinked and gazed down at him. Perkins scowled, gazed back. He braced himself for the coming silence.

"The dead woman didn't have a key," Mulligan said at once in his high monotone.

"How should I know?"

"That's right. You didn't know her."

"I told you that before."

"That's right. But there was a copy of your book by her body."

Perkins's eyes flashed. "There was a copy of my book by her body."

"And you can't explain that."

"Maybe she was a fan. After all, she had her head in the toilet."

He felt bad the minute he said it. And even Mulligan's expression seemed to change: his lips might've puckered a little with distaste.

"Look, I told you," Perkins said quietly. "I didn't know her. I never saw her before. I don't know how the book got there."

Which brought them to another suspenseful Mulligan silence. How, Perkins wondered, could he just stand there like that? Hands in his pockets. No expression. No movement. Perkins found himself gazing at him so intently, waiting for him so anxiously, that the little khaki figure seemed to stand out in relief. The light green walls, the scarred white floors, the deserted, paper-covered desks: all this began to seem flat and unreal behind him, like a Hollywood backdrop. Perkins gritted his teeth, his jaw working.

"Last night, Mr. Perkins," Mulligan said at last. "Tell me what you did last night."

"I gave a poetry reading at the café."

"The café where you tend bar."

"Right. I went home around one A.M. I had a girl with me."

"And her name was . . ."

"I don't know. Milly. I don't remember her last name. I can find out. Maybe Molly."

"Milly Molly."

"No, her first name's Molly. Mindy maybe."

"Molly Mindy."

"Never mind. I'll ask at the café."

Mulligan's chin may have inclined a little. "You know people there," he said. "At the café. You knew people at the reading."

"Sure. Yeah. Almost everyone."

"Except Molly."

"Well . . . You know."

"Your brother wasn't there."

"Zach? No."

"Or your grandmother."

"My grandmother is in her eighties. She has a bad heart. She never goes anywhere. Leave her out of this."

"What about Tiffany Bernstein?"

The question came suddenly. It hit Perkins like a blow. He felt the blood drain from his face. The hair—he remembered the single silver hair on the bedspread. "How do you know Tiffany?" he said slowly.

"She's your brother's girlfriend."

"Well, how do you know that? What's going on?"

"When did you see Tiffany Bernstein last, Mr. Perkins?"

Perkins swallowed. His stomach was going sour again. "Friday. Friday—why?"

"And your brother was with her."

"Yeah, yeah sure. But . . ."

"Your brother's a magazine photographer, is that right?"

"All right, hey," said Perkins. "I mean, just wait a minute. What the hell is going on here? Why do you know all this stuff about Zach?" The detective answered with silence and Perkins suddenly punched his own palm. "Come on, Mulligan. Damn it!"

The silence continued another moment. Then Mulligan took a breath: Perkins saw his trench coat rise and fall. Slowly, always watching Perkins, the detective reached inside the coat. He drew out a small manila envelope. He reached into the envelope and pulled out a photograph. Gently, he laid this on top of Perkins's book.

The poet looked at the picture. It was grainy, unclear. Two faces leaning toward each other in the dark.

"Recognize them?" Mulligan said.

Perkins shrugged. He didn't look up at the detective. He studied the face on the right. A jutting, Dick Tracy jaw. Honest, intent, all-observant eyes. He gestured to it vaguely. "That one looks like a cop," he muttered.

Mulligan gave a soft snort. When Perkins looked up, he thought he saw a faint gleam of humor in that remorseless gaze. "Special Agent Gus Stallone," Mulligan said. "Federal Bureau of Investigation, undercover." And then, after a pause: "Clearly a master of disguise."

Perkins managed a faint smile at this. But he knew what was coming.

Mulligan made the slightest gesture: tilted his head at the picture. "The one in the car, Mr. Perkins," he said. "Take a look at the man in the car."

Perkins shrugged again.

"Is that your brother?" said the detective. "Is that Zachary? Would you take a more careful look please?"

Perkins girded himself with a breath. He looked again. He hadn't noticed before that the man on the left was in a car: the photo was too dark. Now he made out the frame of the window. The man was leaning out the window to talk to the agent. The man's face was round like Zach's. He had a crew-cut like Zach did too. It was enough to make Perkins queasy, looking at him. But the features . . .

123

"It's all grainy. Out of focus," he said softly. "Anyway . . ." What would Zach be doing talking to a fed? he was about to say. But he stopped himself. After a moment, he cleared his throat. "I can't tell," he said. "It's too grainy. I'm not sure."

Mulligan blinked at him hotly, but Perkins stood his ground. Well, it was true, he thought; he just couldn't tell. Mulligan stretched the silence a little. But finally, he reached into his envelope again. Brought forth another photo. Laid it down on top of the first.

"Jesus!" Perkins hissed it through his teeth. He felt a brief tingle of excitement in his groin.

It was a picture of a woman being sodomized. She was naked, leaning forward, both hands pressed to a desktop. Only her face was covered—covered completely by a black leather mask that zipped up the back. There was a leather leash around her neck. A naked man was holding it. He was yanking back on it so that the woman arched as he drove into her from behind.

Perkins's tongue came out and touched his lips. *Jee-sus!* The woman was thin, dark-skinned. There was a string of freckles along the trail of her spine. Some of her hair stuck out of the mask. It was black with strands of silver in it. *But maybe I didn't even see that hair on the bedspread,* Perkins thought. *Maybe I imagined it.*

"Is that Tiffany Bernstein, Mr. Perkins?" Mulligan asked. "Is that your brother's . . . ?"

"Christ, I don't know," Perkins said sharply. "I mean, she's wearing a mask, for Christ's sake. I mean, for Christ's sake, Mulligan, how am I supposed . . . ?"

Wham! Mulligan moved so fast that Perkins didn't even see him come. He slapped his hand down hard. Slapped a third photo down on top of the other two.

"How about her, Mr. Perkins?" His voice was still eerily mild. "Do you recognize her?"

Perkins turned and looked. "Oh hell," he said. The woman in the photograph smiled out from under her mortarboard and tassel. Her smile was shy and proud, her cheeks high and round. Her brown hair tumbled to her shoulders in rich waves that caught the photographer's light. Perkins had to close his eyes a moment. Yeah, he recognized her, all right. When he looked again, her china blue eyes were still gazing up at him. Their expression seemed to him indescribably sweet and hopeful and sad.

"I told you," he said hoarsely. He cleared his throat. "I told you I didn't know her, Mulligan."

"Well, that really is a shame," said the detective mildly. Perkins felt his eyes on him. Felt the weight of that impassive gaze. "I think you would have liked her."

The poet nodded wearily.

"She was a sweet kid," the detective went on. "One of those late bloomers. You know? One of those—they stay girls a long time. It's nice. They're very trusting. Like girls. They sort of look up at you . . ." His voice died away.

Perkins glanced at him. The detective's eyes were still expressionless, but he had pressed his lips together tightly. It was a moment before he could go on.

"I had a couple of talks with her, in fact," he said then. "She was gabby; friendly; you know. She'd make jokes out of the corner of her mouth and roll her eyes. Laugh. Like a giggle. Like a girl. She said she wanted to be a dancer. She wanted to meet a guy. Have a family. She was a kid: she wanted a lot of things."

Mulligan's gaze shifted to the photograph. Slowly, Perkins turned to it again. It was true, he thought. She had been alive. She had had a woman's voice and she had giggled and made jokes out of the corner of her mouth. She had been alive when they came toward her with the knife. She had been thinking and alive to the last moment . . .

"What . . . ?" He had to clear his throat. He had to swallow hard. "What was her name?"

And Mulligan answered him almost in a whisper.

"Nancy Kincaid."

NANCY KINCAID

"Nan . . . ceeee . . ." The doctor murmured it as he penciled the name in on his form. "Kinnnn . . . caaaaid . . . Good!" He smiled up at her. "Address?"

"Gramercy Park," she said softly. "I live with my parents on Gramercy Park."

"Gram-er-ceeee . . . Park! And what is your current . . . ? Damn it!"

The phone on the desk had started breeping again, one of its lights blinking. "Excuse me," the doctor said to her. With a sigh, he took up the handset.

Nancy sat in her blue plastic chair opposite his desk. Squeezed, in that tiny room, between the table to her left and the edge of the open door. Nurses with their folders walked by in the hallway. Sometimes patients shuffled by. She felt they could hear every word she said, see everything she did. She kept her hands folded in her lap. Her chin lowered. She kept her eyes trained on a single cigarette burn in the linoleum floor. She was trying very hard to act harmless.

She stared and stared at that burn while the doctor spoke into the phone. She had not lifted her eyes from it since he came in—only briefly, meekly, respectfully, when she answered his questions, then she looked down again. Maybe she was staring at the burn too much, she thought. Maybe the doctor would write in his folder, "Stares at burns too much. Strange. Very strange." She risked glancing up at him. He was leaning forward, elbow on his desk. Massaging his brow with his free hand.

"No. No. They're going to have to keep her on the medication at least three more days. Well, explain it to them. I haven't got time now. No. No. Explain it to them, I haven't got time."

She recognized him as the doctor with the syringe, the one who had pumped her full of stuff when she was screaming. He was a young man, maybe thirty, maybe just. He had shaggy black hair and a black, pointed beard, which didn't stop him from looking bright-eyed and boyish. He wore a tweed jacket with patches at the elbow. A black knit tie on a plaid shirt. Every inch the Young Professor.

"Well, explain it to the family. I'm with a patient right now. Right." He hung up the phone. "Right-right-right-right." He tapped his forehead. "Where were we?"

Dr. Schoenfeld. That was his name. Dr. Thomas Schoenfeld. A decent guy. A concerned, good-hearted guy. His buddies probably called him Tom, Nancy thought, or Tommy. *Yo, Tommy, how about a couple of beers when you're sprung from the loony bin tonight?* His mother maybe still called him Thomas. Shaking her finger at him. *Thomas Schoenfeld, how do you expect to meet any nice girls working in a horrible place like that?*

And he can sign his name, Nancy thought. *He can sign his name to a piece of paper and have me locked away in here. Locked away with that nut case Billy Joe.*

"We're going to have lots of little chats like this, Nancy. We're going to find the Magic Word together."

"Okay," said Dr. Schoenfeld. He swiveled his chair around to face her. Nancy stared hard at that cigarette burn on the floor. "Sorry for the interruption."

"S'all right," she murmured. She wasn't exactly going anywhere, was she.

"No one else can handle anything in this place," he said. He had a gentle smile behind the sharp beard. She dared to smile slightly in return. "So," he said. "We were getting the rundown. Any drugs?"

"What's that?"

"Have you been using any drugs? Any alcohol?"

"Oh. No."

"Cause you were pretty agitated out there a while ago. Drugs'll do that to you."

She shook her head.

"The police say you made quite a fuss downtown too. I mean, you're really lucky they decided to bring you in here. They could've just charged you, then you'd have real problems."

She nodded contritely.

"So?" said the doctor. "You want to tell me what the trouble is?" He lifted his brows, waiting for her. Leaned forward, his hands clasped between his knees.

And Nancy thought, *All right then. This is it.* She figured she had exactly one chance to explain this thing. To tell her story and sound rational doing it. Otherwise, they would put her away. Dr. Tommy would sign his name and she'd be gone for good and . . .

The Animal Hour. Eight o'clock. You have to be there.

Oh, not that again. She forced the thought back into the murk. She had to forget about that. Stay calm. Think calm. *Sound* calm.

She fought off the pressure of the little room. The files and desks and chairs and he and she all crammed together. The nurses with their folders who continued to go past in the hall. Listening. She swallowed, braced herself. "Well—" It was her most reasonable voice, her grown-up voice. "Some very . . . uh . . . very strange things have happened to me today, Doctor." She glanced up at him with a quick smile. "To say the least! I mean, I went to work this morning . . ."

"Goddamn it!" the doctor said. The phone was breeping again. "I'm sorry, Nancy. I'm sorry. Excuse me for one moment here." He grabbed the handset. "What? No. No! I'm with a patient right now. I'll call you back in a few minutes." He put the phone down hard. Shook his head at her. "Sorry. Go ahead."

But now, her heart was racing. The interruption had thrown her off balance. What if she messed it all up? What if she lost control again? Oh Christ, what if they strapped her back down to the gurney? They would never let her out of here, never, and . . .

He's going to die. At eight o'clock. You have to, have to . . .

It was a struggle to control her breath, to keep her voice from shaking. But she raised her eyes to him and went on as steadily as she could. "Well, I got to work this morning . . . Doctor. And, uh . . . Well . . . no one knew who I was." She spread her hands. She gave a small nervous laugh. A nervous glance at the door as a nurse walked by. She lowered her voice. "I mean, I know it sounds . . . crazy. I know that. But no one *recognized* me, Dr. Schoenfeld. And then . . . then, I started hearing these strange things like . . . Oh God, I know this makes me sound so crazy, but I swear this has never happened to me before." She laughed again. "I mean, most days I manage to be pretty much myself. You know?"

Dr. Schoenfeld smiled gently. "It's all right, Nancy. I understand. Go on."

She hesitated. *You understand?* she thought. That simple remark—the kindness of his tone—actually brought tears to her eyes. She regarded him carefully. *You understand?*

And, well, yes: he did seem to. This young Dr. Thomas Schoenfeld. Judging by his face: the soft brown eyes, the boy's mouth hidden in the doctorly black beard. Judging by the concerned way he leaned toward her. The way he nodded encouragingly. He seemed ready to listen anyway, ready to give it his best shot. She wanted to throw her arms around him and tell all. Weep into his tweed shoulder. Move to a cottage where he would be her father and Mrs. Anderson, the fat black nurse outside, would be her mom. God, she thought, to have someone actually understand!

"Well, like I said," she went on—more quickly now, pushing down the tears. "Like I said, I heard a voice, okay? From nowhere. And it was telling me to shoot someone. I mean, I know it sounds so awful but . . . and then later, in the park later, I heard all the beggars there saying things and . . ." She shook her head, trying to find the words.

"Go on," he said—and yes, his voice was gentle, kindly. *Understanding.* Yes. "What were they saying? Go on."

"Jesus. Jesus," Nancy whispered. "They were all saying that someone was going to die. I mean, that's what I heard them say. All right? They said that someone was going to be killed at eight o'clock tonight and that I had to be there. And the thing was . . . the thing was . . ."

It was true! It was all true! They are *going to kill him. At eight o'clock. At the Animal Hour. I do* have *to be there! It's all true, Doctor!*

But no. No, she didn't say that. She couldn't say that. She mustn't. Even if he was the Gandhi, the Schweitzer of psychiatry, it didn't matter. Even he could understand only so much. And yet . . .

And yet, as she sat there, jammed into her little chair, her little space between desk and doorway, between the doctor and the wall, she suddenly felt certain of it. It *was* true. What the beggars had told her. It was all exactly right. Someone *was* going to die. At eight o'clock. At the Animal Hour. And for some reason, for some reason just beyond her reach, she *did* have to be there. It was urgent. It was everything.

"Anything else?" said Dr. Schoenfeld. And he said it so sweetly, so patiently, that she really did hunger to tell him. To tell him everything, unburden everything. She ached up into the pillowy depths of those brown peepers of his, half a doctor's, half a boy's. Maybe he *would* understand, she thought.

But she shook her head quickly. "No. No, that's everything. I just got so scared, I took out the gun. I don't even know where the gun came from. I don't even know what happened to it."

That was a lie, of course, and she felt bad about it. She knew perfectly well where the gun was and that she should tell him, but . . . Well . . . That ol' debil gun. That bad, bad gun. She would need it, wouldn't she? Yes. At eight o'clock.

"Can you remember anything preceding all this?" the doctor asked her now. "I mean, before the subway. Anything that might have set it off? Can you remember what you were doing yesterday, for example?"

"Well, yeah," she started. "I mean, sure, I was . . . I was . . ." *Oh no!* Her jaw hung slack. Her silence poured out of her mouth like dust. What *was* she doing yesterday? She couldn't remember. There was just nothing there. Yesterday, the day before—it was all darkness. "I . . . I . . ."

The doctor waited another moment for her to continue. Then he nodded. He leaned back in his seat. He steepled his fingers, doctorly. He said: "Nancy. I want you to know, first of all, that I understand how frightened you must be."

"Wuh . . . I . . . Jesus," she said. "I mean, you're telling me."

He gave a snort at that. He nodded. "But these things are not . . . entirely inexplicable."

Her next exclamation died aborning. She could only look at him. "They're not?"

"No, absolutely. I mean, what we're dealing with . . . goddamn it!" The phone again. He yanked it to his ear. "Yes? I don't know, I'm with a patient, I can't talk now. Yes." He hung up. "God!" Shook his head. "You want my job?"

"Uh . . . No. No, thanks."

"Good. At least you're not *really* crazy."

Nancy surprised herself with a laugh. She looked at this young doctor of hers with something like wonder. Could he really have some answers for her?

Dr. Schoenfeld rolled his chair to the side a little now. He reached out past her cheek to the edge of the door and swung it shut. Oh, that was good. She liked that. The click of the door. The privacy. She was a human being, after all. She faced him gratefully as he rolled back into place before her. He leaned forward again, elbows on his thighs. He peered deeply—warmly—at her. She peered back, her lips parted. Waiting for him to tell her.

"Nancy," he said slowly. "I want to be totally honest with you. All right? I mean, you are not the usual customer we have coming in here. You understand? You strike me as a very intelligent, very responsible person. I see no reason to jolly you along or sugarcoat things for you or anything like that."

She nodded. Waited.

Dr. Schoenfeld clapped his hands together three times softly: pop, pop, pop. He marshaled his thoughts. Gave her the moment to prepare. And then he let her have it. "I can't

131

make a complete diagnosis after just one interview, obviously. There are tests we have to do and . . . other questions to ask and so on. But right now, I would say it's a pretty damn good bet that what you're experiencing is an episode of schizophrenia."

He waited for her reaction. She had none. She felt nothing. Only her confusion. She was still waiting for the news. "Schizophrenia?" she said—but only because he seemed to expect her to say something. "You mean like . . . a split personality?"

He smiled quickly. "No, no, no. That's . . . you know, that's just a popular misuse of the term. That's something very different. Schizophrenia is a very general term—it's so general, in fact, we don't really like to use it anymore but . . . it's a general term for a series of mental disorders characterized by . . . oh . . . auditory-command hallucinations—which means voices telling you what to do. Fixed delusions, like 'Someone's going to die at eight o'clock.' Memory lapses. Just various other manifestations like the ones you've been experiencing. Do you understand?"

Well . . . no. No, she didn't. A series of mental disorders. It didn't register. She just sat there, feeling nothing. Gazing at him. Waiting for him to tell her what had happened to her, where her life had gotten to.

And then it dawned on her.

Schizophrenia. Sure, she *had* heard of that. Schizophrenia was what street people had, homeless people. People who muttered to themselves on the street. That was, like, mental illness. She started to smile. "Yes, but . . ." Not *me*, she was going to tell him. You don't mean that *I* have this. "But . . . But that's, that would . . ." That would mean *I'm* mentally ill, she wanted to say. As in sick, as in crazy. You don't mean *I'm* schizophrenic? I have a life. I'm a real person. I have friends. I have parents, things . . .

But he did. He did mean her. She could see it in his eyes, in the sympathy in his eyes. He was *pitying* her. He was gazing at her warmly and thinking, *Tough break. Poor kid. Thank God it's not me.* Jesus. Jesus! She couldn't speak finally. Not at all. She could only shake her head at him.

"I know," he cooed. "I know. It's very scary. But things are a lot different now than they used to be. All right? We have new drugs and . . . new methods of dealing with the disease."

The disease! Jesus Christ! Nancy kept shaking her head. New methods of dealing with *the disease?* Listen to him. He was trying to sound optimistic. He was trying to give her hope. But she could see it, right there in his eyes: He had no hope. This was not a hopeful situation.

"Can this . . . I mean, can this just happen?" she said. "I mean, you're walking along and then, poof, you're a schizophrenic. I mean, that doesn't sound . . . I mean . . ."

He nodded. "Yes. Yes, it can just happen. It does just happen. Unfortunately. Right around your age. Ordinary people—oh, shit." *Burreeeep,* went the phone. He deflated. Sank back in his chair. Lifted the handset wearily. "Hello. I'm with a patient now. Uh-huh. Uh-huh. Okay. I can't deal with that now. I'm with a patient." He hung up. "Sorry."

She was silent a moment. Her mind was racing. Darting down every possible avenue, looking for a way out of this. "You mean, this is like . . . You mean there's no cure for this. Is there?" she whispered. "That's what you're telling me. I'm just going to be this way."

He didn't look at her. He looked down at his desk. He gestured at the papers on the imitation wood desktop. "Well . . . Sometimes . . . Listen . . . sometimes there's only one attack. Sometimes it doesn't get any worse at all. There's an incident like this and then . . . nothing. It's very mysterious. You can't really predict . . ."

"Oh . . ." It was a little gasp from her parted lips. She shook her head at the cigarette burn on the floor, her old friend. "Oh . . . Oh . . ." *Sometimes it doesn't get any worse.* That's what he'd said. And that meant that usually it does get worse. Didn't it? Usually the voices became louder, that's what he was saying. The delusions became stronger. The good periods, the clear periods, got shorter and shorter. And then after a while . . . *She just couldn't take care of herself anymore.* That's what her mother would say, crying into her handkerchief. And her friends would shake their heads and say, *She was such a nice person. It's just so awful.* And she—she could see herself. She would scrape along the sidewalk beneath their windows. Her eyes on the middle distance. Her hair in tangles. Her clothes in rags. The handsome men in suits would swerve to avoid her. The women in dresses from Bergdorf's would shake their heads and look away. She would come out at midnight, live from midnight to midnight. Sleeping in doorways. Muttering in the dark, *to* the dark, or shouting suddenly: "The Animal Hour! Someone is going to die! At eight o'clock! At eight o'clock!"

"But it's true," she whispered, clenching her fists, clenching her teeth. "I swear. It's all true. It's all going to happen."

And Dr. Schoenfeld's pity—the way he cocked his head, pursed his lips—it scorched her to her marrow. It was a martyrdom.

"Come on, Nancy," he said after a moment. She heard his chair squeak. She was dimly aware that he was standing over her. With his patched tweed jacket and his black knit tie. And his sanity. And his freedom. He reached down to her and touched her arm. She jerked away—what did he know about it? "It's all right," he said softly. "We have to do some tests on you. It's going to take about three days. All right?"

He took her by the arm again. This time, she let him. He drew her out of the chair. Onto her feet. She stared up at him with pleading eyes. *It's all true. Really. I swear it. Please. Help me.*

"We're gonna get in touch with your family," Dr. Schoenfeld said. "Meantime, we'll get you a nice room. A view of the Empire State Building even. Pretty fancy stuff for a newcomer, but I've got some pull. All right?"

He smiled down at her and she gazed up at him, clinging to the kindness in that smile. She nodded her head.

"Good," he said. He patted her arm. "Now come on. I'll introduce you to the gang."

She nodded again. Then she drove her knee up into his testicles with all the strength she had.

She hadn't known she was going to do this until she did it. She hadn't had the slightest idea. And when she had done it, she could only stand there, waiting, as if she expected him to respond.

There was a long, queer moment when everything was just the same. The doctor continued to smile down at her, his hand on her arm, the kindly little crinkles at the corners of his eyes. Then, very slowly, the crinkles disappeared as his eyes widened. His whole face seemed to slowly expand. His mouth opened. His eyes blew up like balloons. He made sounds: "Uh . . . uh . . ." These little expulsions of air. And very, very slowly, his hands moved to his groin and his body bent forward. He turned—slowly—away from her. Groped for his desk with one hand, holding his groin with the other. He knocked papers off the desktop. They flapped and fluttered to the floor. His hand tipped over a pencil holder and the pencils spilled out with a clatter. "Uh . . . uh . . ." He kept making that soft little noise.

Nancy stood through all this, gaping. *I'm sorry, I'm so sorry, I have to, I have to be there,* she thought. The doctor groped across the surface of his desk, clutching his groin, doubled over.

And she realized he was reaching for the phone.

Oh, don't . . . Quickly, she stepped around behind him. Took up a position just at his back with her feet planted firmly. She clasped her two hands together. Pulled them back—as if she were raising an axe over her head. And then she swung down at him as hard as she could.

She grunted as her clasped hands connected with the back of his head. Dr. Schoenfeld's face was driven down into the desktop. His nose was crushed against the imitation wood. Blood burst from either side of his face, little red sprays on the white papers around him. His body went limp. He slumped onto his desk. He slid backward, hitting the chair as he fell. He dropped to the floor at her feet. The chair tipped over on top of him.

"Shit!" Nancy said. She looked up suddenly.

Bureeep. Burreeep.

It was the goddamned phone again.

OLIVER PERKINS

"Fernando Woodlawn. You never heard that name."

Detective Mulligan was sitting now, tilted back in a swivel chair. His feet were propped on the edge of the desk in front of him, his trench coat hanging down around his seat. His profile was to Perkins, and it seemed to the poet that the cop was suddenly weary. His eyes blinked lethargically, the batteries running down.

Well, the sparring is over anyway, Perkins thought, looking at him. He's made his decision about me.

The thought was not a soothing one.

"I've heard the name," he said after a moment. "I can't place it, but I have heard it somewhere."

Mulligan blinked slowly at the cinderblocks in the far wall. The empty coffee maker there. The skewed, wilted pages tacked to their strip of brown cork. Even the high monotone of his voice seemed to have grown heavier somehow.

"You probably read about him in *Downtowner* magazine. They did a feature on him a while back. Your brother took the photographs."

"Yeah? So Zach took his picture. So what? That's his job. Who is the guy?"

"Woodlawn? Oh, he's . . . a lawyer. A big shot lawyer. A big hoo-ha in the city. Into a lot of real estate deals. The navy port. Times Square development. A lot of deals with a lot of pols. Big, big hoo-ha; one of the back room boys." He seemed to need to gather his strength for a moment before continuing. "He's also the man that Nancy Kincaid worked for. The dead girl; he was her boss. And . . . he's also the man with his Johnson up the masked girl's ass. The one . . ." He gestured toward the photographs.

"I know which masked girl's ass we're talking about," Perkins said glumly. "What does this have to do with my brother?"

Mulligan spared him a tired glance. Showed his profile again. "The people who run this city are Democrats," he said in that flat, mousy voice of his. "Even the Republicans are Democrats; there are no Republicans. If you want to build a building, or win a city contract, or pass a law, or lower your assessment, or park your car in the middle of Fifth Avenue at rush hour, you go to Someone who knows the Democrats. Right? This Someone then tells you what to do: You hire lawyer A because he is the council leader's brother-in-law; you hire accounting firm B because your local rep used to work there. You don't need a PR man? Tough shit: The PR man sucks the borough president's dick so you gotta hire him too. Right? And you make a campaign contribution here and there and finally you get to supply the city with widgets until Jesus comes. Understand?"

Perkins gave a slow nod. Thinking: *Hanh?* He had definitely lost the thread here somewhere. It was a little hard for him to focus on a civics lesson when he couldn't stop obsessing about Zach and the girl in the toilet and what the hell were they asking about Zach for anyway and where was he and was Nana going to have a coronary when she heard about all this and those glassy, china blue eyes staring up at him from the blood-streaked porcelain . . .

Still, he gave his vague nod. Gestured Mulligan on.

And Mulligan wasn't looking at him anyway. He stretched a little. Ran his hand over his receding tide of springy curls.

"Right," he said mildly, always mildly. "Fernando Woodlawn. He's the Someone you go to, the Someone who knows the Democrats. All right?"

"Yeah . . ." said Perkins uncertainly.

"And you go to him and he spreads your money around—but he never does an illegal thing. That's important. He hires you lawyers you don't want, and PR men you don't need, and he contributes to causes you don't believe in; he helps you get a contract you shouldn't get or build a building that shouldn't be there—but not once in any way does he break the law or pass an illegal buck or sidle up to people in the dark or wear sunglasses or anything like that at all. Right? Only greedy people make those mistakes. Not Fernando. All right."

But it was not all right with Perkins. It sounded serious and he wasn't following it and what the hell did it have to do with his brother? He blew a long breath out. Brushed back his long black hair. This was worse than Mulligan's silences. Where the hell was Zach?

"Now." Mulligan just went mildly on. "For the last six months, Fernando Woodlawn has been spreading around an uncountable number of dollar bills. The idea is he and some other people want to build a complex of buildings called Ashley Towers over by the Hudson. So, if he takes all the necessary steps, which he has, and he wins permission for this complex, which he will, he will have enough jobs to hand out and enough money to pass around so that he will be made the Democratic nominee for governor next year, which means he will be automatically elected because there are no Republicans in sight who can run against him. So here's tomorrow's news today: Woodlawn is going to be your next governor. And that's what's with Fernando Woodlawn. Which brings us to the Republicans."

Perkins bent over, held his head. He could just barely keep himself from saying "Argh!" "I thought there were no Republicans," he said. He shook his head at the dirty white tiles of the floor.

"In New York," said Mulligan. He lifted a finger, but not at Perkins. He waggled it at the wall. He continued, with excruciating patience. "There are no Republicans in New York. In Washington, there are lots and lots of Republicans. Passels of Republicans. Republicans everywhere. And some of these Republicans don't want Fernando Woodlawn to become governor because his dishonest plans to milk the state for gain might interfere with their dishonest plans to milk the state for gain. So these Republicans, see, have asked that the

FBI investigate Fernando until they find something that will end his gubernatorial hopes and dreams. So for the past year or so, there have been idiot FBI agents sidling up to people in the dark and wearing sunglasses and finding out exactly nothing because Fernando never breaks the law—not the Laws of Man anyway."

"Jesus, Mulligan," Perkins said. He was still bent over, holding his head in his hands. "I mean, you're killing me here. I give up. I confess. For God's sake, would you get to the point?"

Mulligan dropped his feet to the floor with a clunk. Perkins looked up. Saw the detective standing, his hands slipping into his trench coat pockets again. The round face was blank as the cop walked toward him. Perkins straightened in his plastic chair. Mulligan blinked down at him from behind his wire rims.

"Last week, a young woman came to me," he said. "That was Nancy Kincaid. She didn't want to come to the police, but she was scared and she didn't know where else to go. She was afraid her employer, Fernando Woodlawn, wanted to involve her in something illegal. Something strange anyway, maybe even dangerous. She couldn't tell her parents, because they idolized Woodlawn and wouldn't understand. And no one else could help her. So she came to me."

"Okay. All right," said Perkins. He was all ears now. More than a little wary of the impassive face above him, the slowly blinking eyes. Mulligan had come close, and he remembered how fast the detective had moved when he slammed the photo down on the desk. A dangerous guy, definitely. Not a fun, not a takin'-it-easy kind of guy at all.

"Woodlawn wanted her to pick up a package under mysterious circumstances," Mulligan ploughed on. "At night. In a Chinatown alley. Carry the package straight back to the office without looking at it, he said. If anyone asks, tell 'em you're responding to an anonymous call. Don't involve Fernando . . . On and on. Understand? So it frightened her. It sounded dirty. She thought he might be using her for something dirty because no one would suspect her or follow her. Oh yeah—to add to the mystery, she was supposed to carry a book." The detective nodded toward the table, and Perkins turned to it, his mouth opening. "*The Animal Hour*. She was supposed to carry *The Animal Hour* under her arm for identification."

What could Perkins say? He showed the cop his bewildered gaze; he had no better response. How many people, after all, could possibly own his book? Or even know about his book? The café crowd? The crowd over at St. Mark's church? Even over at St. Mark's, the rads and the fems despised him. But then maybe that was it, he thought. Maybe this was some advanced new form of literary criticism. It was a logical extension of the going thing, after all . . .

He was about to make some sort of crack to this effect, but the detective's expression stopped him. Or not his expression—that would be going too far. Some tension in the impassive face. Some irradiating pain beneath the pasty skin. Something grim anyway that made Perkins wait.

And Mulligan licked his lips once and blinked as his glasses flashed in the fluorescents. And then he said: "I referred her to the feds."

What was this? Perkins didn't have time to figure out the full meaning of the words. But it sounded like a confession of some sort, didn't it? *I referred her to the feds*. Somehow, this strange little man had brought him into this soulless office—with its empty desks and its hanged papers and its unforgiving cinderblock walls—this weird little cop had brought him in here and had then proceeded to beat a confession out of himself.

"The feds," Perkins said.

"It was an interagency courtesy. It sounded like what they were after, right? Something on Fernando. It sounded like it might make them happy and they might make my boss happy about me." His shoulders lifted and fell. He looked down at his shoes. "And so Nancy Kincaid went to the feds. And the feds—who are arrogant and incompetent to the point of being . . . well, feds—the feds went off and sidled around and wore their sunglasses and talked into their walkie-talkies. And they played their bullshit cloak and dagger games, which I am not at liberty to discuss with you. And, in the end, they got the package in the Chinatown alley . . ."

Perkins wasn't even trying to understand anymore, but suddenly it just clicked into place. "And that was the photograph. Fernando up the masked girl's ass. It was a blackmail thing."

Still blinking at his shoes, Mulligan nodded slightly. "The feds thought they finally had Fernando, and instead they had a gang of shmoes trying to extort money from him—twenty-five thousand dollars—nothing."

And Perkins was surprised to find he really *did* get it now. "But that was good, right? Good for the feds."

"Right." The detective raised his blank and yet somehow agonized eyes to him. "Now the feds could bust the extortionists and come off as competent and nonpolitical—and still slip it to the papers that Fernando was doing leather and rectums in his off hours. No governorship and no trail to the Republicans. It was perfect." He turned away, to the louvered windows. Wistfully, Perkins thought. Gazing at them as if he could see something through their thin, filthy panes. "And everyone was happy," he said. "And everything was great. And that was the last I heard about it until this morning. And then the feds called me. And everyone was panicking. And everything had turned to shit. Nancy Kincaid had been abducted right out of her own apartment building. Our federal friends hadn't even thought to put a guard on her. Even her parents weren't at home that night. So zippo, she was just gone."

And you referred her to them, Perkins thought. *You referred her to the feds.* He had the picture now. He understood, in some measure anyway, that pained glow lighting the detective's skin, that phosphor of rage. But the understanding did not improve his day. In fact, it made him feel heavy inside. Weighted down with dread. Oh yes. The Bad News was definitely a-comin'—he could feel it. Little black gibbering Bad News Demons. Crowding in around him to carry him off, like the devils in those apocalypse paintings who drag the sinful souls to Hell.

He had to ask—he couldn't stand the suspense. "What about Zach? What about my brother?" And when the cop let him wait for an answer: "I mean, okay, so he took pictures of this Woodlawn guy for *Downtowner*. He's their photographer, he always does stuff like that. But I mean, he's not in this other stuff. He's just a mystical little guy, Mulligan. He never hurt anybody but himself."

Mulligan lifted a hand from his pocket and pointed—and all Perkins could think of was the Ghost of Christmas Yet to Come pointing at Scrooge's grave. The detective was pointing at the photos on the desk beside him. "The man who delivered the photographs of Woodlawn fit your brother's description. He was driving a car that had been rented in New Jersey in your brother's name. When my people searched your brother's apartment this morning, they found a secret compartment in his closet."

"What?"

"With a peephole and special photographic equipment and sexual paraphernalia inside—all of which was almost definitely used in taking the pictures of Woodlawn and the girl."

Perkins turned slowly again to the photographs lying on his book. The graduation shot of Nancy Kincaid was on top, but it lay askew. The photo of

Tiffany it's Tiffany

the woman in the mask peeked out from under it. Perkins could see only the masked head but he thought of the dark freckled skin.

You don't understand anything, Oliver, not anything.

And then, with a queasy thrill, he thought of a naked ass. Tiffany's compact, glisteningly naked ass. And then not hers. A child's ass. Zach's bare ass, to be exact, his corduroy overalls down around his thighs, his cheeks purple, almost black, with bruises and the heavy brass ruler smashing into the soft flesh again; its almost silent, sickeningly silent, thud . . .

But I broke it. I broke the typewriter, he thought. His stomach turned, his throat thickened with dread.

"There's something else," said Mulligan. Perkins looked up. "We got an anonymous call this morning. Reporting that a man with longish black hair, wearing a sweater and blue jeans, had been seen entering the mews in MacDougal Alley . . ."

"Yeah, so? That was me."

". . . and that terrible screams had been heard . . ."

"What?"

". . . coming out of the place and that we should get someone over there on the double."

"*What?*" Perkins stood up. "An anonymous call? From
who?"

He was a head taller than the detective. Mulligan had to
lift his chin in order to blink up at him.

"Well, you know what I mean," Perkins said. "What did
he sound like?"

"It was a woman."

And again, Perkins thought: *Tiffany. Tiffany!* She had set
him up. He almost said it out loud. She had lured him to the
mews with that desperate call to Nana. Then she had called
the cops so they'd catch him there. He *knew* there was treach-
ery behind that angel puss of hers. She had set him up, and
he was willing to bet anything in this world that she was setting
up Zachary too. That car rented in Zach's name. That stuff
hidden in the closet, the secret compartment or whatever. It
was all Tiffany's doing. She had gotten herself involved in
some sort of mess and now she was trying to pass it off on
Zach, on Zach and him both. I know my brother, Perkins
wanted to tell Mulligan. He's not the least neurotic guy in
the world, and God knows he's had his problems. But blackmail? That girl in the mews? No way, man. It just wasn't him.
He was being set up—they both were. By Tiffany.

He wasn't sure what kept him from speaking out right away.
The instinct to silence was powerful, a physical restraint. She
was Zach's girlfriend, after all—and he had to protect Zach.
In any case, his accusations died in him the way his poems
did. Rising from his belly, dissipating, falling away like dew.

And then what? The detective was still blinking up at him.
His face was still unreadable and dangerous. And they'd found
him, Perkins, right there, right in the mews, with the body.
They could charge him with murder. He'd have to stand trial.
They might even . . .

"Now you can go," Mulligan said.

"I . . . what?"

Mulligan almost sighed—it was something like a sigh anyway. His hands in his trench coat, he turned and walked away. Walked over to the windows. Fed his face up into the dusty sunlight.

"I can go?" said Perkins.

"Right. You didn't do anything." Mulligan seemed to give his answer to the unseen sky over Tenth Street. "The girl'd been dead for hours when you got there. Anyway, I'm talking to you and I know you didn't do anything. Maybe the feds'll see it differently."

Perkins resisted the impulse to run for it. "You think I'll lead you to Zach, don't you?" he said.

Mulligan gazed at the windows. "I think you'll find him. Or that he'll come to you, yeah."

"And you're gonna follow me?"

"No." He shook his head. "You're gonna bring him to me. You're gonna turn him in."

"Oh really?"

"Yeah." Mulligan drew out the syllable wearily. He glanced over at Perkins, just for a moment, then turned wistfully to the light again. "A young woman who came to me for help got herself stuffed into a toilet bowl," he said mildly. "Stuffed into a toilet, just as if she were a piece of shit instead of a girl, instead of a human being." A meditative pause. Perkins closed his eyes a moment to erase the girl's stare from his mind. "If you bring your brother to me," Mulligan continued, "I give you my word that I will personally beat the living shit out of him until he tells me everything he knows about this murder."

The poet let out a mirthless snort. "So why would I bring him to you?"

Mulligan faced him from across the room. His glasses flashed. His face remained impassive. "Because as pissed and humiliated and panicked as I am," he said, "I am only exactly half as pissed and humiliated and panicked as the Federal fucking Bureau of Investigation. Right? And if they get hold of your brother before I do, they are going to gun him down and announce that the case is solved. They are going to kill him, Perkins. I know this for a fact.

"If the feds get to him first, your brother is going to be dead."

NANCY KINCAID

The phone on the desk kept breeping.

This, Nancy thought, *is very bad.*

Dr. Schoenfeld lay at her feet. Curled on his side, half covered by the chair that had fallen on him. Blood was still pulsing from his shattered nose. It stained his mustache. It ran into his mouth. Nancy stared at him.

Bureep. Bureep. The phone shrilled. A voice shrilled in Nancy's mind: *Who did this? What kind of person would do this?* Keen as the phone, just as insistent. *What kind of monster would do this, Nancy?*

Shut up—I don't know—this is so bad—I have to think. She held her hands over her ears. She stared down at Dr. Schoenfeld. She could still hear the phone. She could still hear the voice in her mind: *What kind of psycho . . . ?*

She heard Dr. Schoenfeld now too. He started moaning: "O-o-o-o-oh . . ."

I've got to get out of here.

What kind of vicious . . . ?

Shut up, shut up! We'll take questions later. God!

Desperately, she looked around her. It was like being trapped in a box; in a coffin under the ground. Hemmed in by table, desk, and chairs. Sealed in by the closed door. No room to move. The fallen doctor covered almost the whole floor. His tweed jacket touched her foot.

"O-o-o-o-oh . . ." he moaned. He spit weakly: a bloody tooth fell out of his mouth.

Bureep. Bureep.

"God!" Nancy whispered.

She had to do something. She stepped over the doctor. Into the narrow space between the doctor and the desk. Now she could feel the back of his head resting against her ankles. His soft hair on her skin.

The phone breeped: *What kind of a person are you, Nancy?*

"Shut up," she whispered. God, she *hated* being schizophrenic! She leaned over the desk. Pushed papers aside. Her open folder—*Nancy Kincaid* printed on the top form. Blood spattered over the letters. She pushed the pages away. She needed a weapon. Anything.

The phone shrilled.

The doctor's ballpoint. She picked it up. She could brace it against her palm, she thought. Drive the point into someone's throat.

"O-o-o-o-oh . . ."

What kind of savage . . . ?

"Shut up!" she hissed. She threw the pen aside. A pen was no good. No one would be afraid of a pen. She yanked open the desk drawer.

A letter opener! She seized hold of it. Lightweight. A flat handle. A brass blade.

The doctor's chair fell off him onto the floor.

"Christ. Help me."

Nancy whipped around, looked down. Young Schoenfeld had rolled onto his back. His bearded cheek was pressed to her leg. His shoulder pinned her foot. His smoky eyes appealed to her. He coughed blood.

"Help me . . ."

She might have to give him the old stomperoo, she thought. Really put him out.

The phone shrieked wildly. She pulled her foot free. Grabbed hold of a chair for support as she stepped over him. She was at the door. With one hand on the knob, she palmed the letter opener in the other. Blade up along the wrist, handle hidden in the hand. Then she cracked the door open. Peeked her head out.

The hall was empty for the moment. She could see down it into the narrow room beyond. The slumped figures in the plastic chairs. Three nurses gathered at the far end. The cop—she couldn't see him from here, but she knew he was there: the cop and the metal detector at the entranceway.

"Someone help . . . ," Dr. Schoenfeld murmured. She heard him shift on the floor behind her.

Shit!

She had to get somebody's attention—fast. She peered feverishly at the cluster of nurses.

And a door opened. She brought her head around. It was one of the doors down the hall. It opened and someone came backing out. A broad white wall of a someone.

Mrs. Anderson.

"All right, Doctor," Nancy heard her say. "I'll bring that right to you."

The squat black woman backed into the hall, shutting the door as she came.

"Mrs. Anderson," Nancy hissed.

But the nurse didn't hear her. She turned away from her. Started walking away, down to the end of the hall. Nancy watched helplessly: the wide stride of her elephant legs, the swing of her black-sausage arms.

"Mrs. Anderson!"

The nurse stopped.

The phone in the office breeped again. "Oh Jesus," Dr. Schoenfeld said from the floor. His voice was getting louder.

Mrs. Anderson glanced over her shoulder, puzzled. Had someone called her? Yes: she spotted Nancy. Her big brown face went stony, her eyes narrowed.

"Mrs. Anderson! Hurry!" Nancy gestured toward the office with her head. "It's Dr. Schoenfeld. Hurry. Please."

Mrs. Anderson didn't think twice. She came down the hall like a locomotive, her fat arms pistoning. In a moment, she was at Nancy's side, blotting out everything behind that monumental face.

"What's happening, honey? What's the matter?"

"I don't know. Dr. Schoenfeld . . ."

And right on cue, the doctor moaned loudly: "Oh God, somebody . . ."

Nancy jumped back out of the way as Mrs. Anderson charged across the threshold. The nurse stopped short as she saw the wounded doctor. She stood in all her massiveness, looking down at him.

Behind her, Nancy quietly shut the door.

The phone squealed. Mrs. Anderson knelt down beside Dr. Schoenfeld.

Nancy stepped up in back of her. She grabbed a handful of her hair.

"Ah . . . !" said Mrs. Anderson.

Nancy yanked her head back. She pressed the blade of the opener against her throat.

"I can kill you with this. Don't be stupid." The words sounded strange in her small voice.

"Help me . . ." The doctor had rolled onto his side again. He was lifting his head. Trying to push himself up out of his own blood.

Mrs. Anderson's head was all the way back. Her face was toward the ceiling. Her mouth was forced open. Nancy felt her stiff, lacquered hair tugging against her fist. She was trying to nod, to acquiesce.

"Good," Nancy whispered. The nurse winced as she tightened her grip.

Dr. Schoenfeld shifted again. He lifted his arm, reaching blindly for purchase. His hand fell on the overturned chair. He grabbed hold of it. Started to pull himself up.

"Phone," he gasped. The phone answered shrilly.

"You're going to walk me out of here," Nancy whispered to the nurse.

Mrs. Anderson tried to shake her head. Nancy held her hair tightly. "Can't do it," Mrs. Anderson managed to say. "HP—the hospital police."

"I don't care. You have to do it. You have to do it or you'll die. Now stand up."

She yanked on Mrs. Anderson's hair. The big woman put her arms out for balance. She got hold of the edge of the desk. She braced herself as she worked her legs under her.

Right beside them in the tiny room, Dr. Schoenfeld was now trying to scale the overturned chair. Slowly, he was climbing over it toward his desk. The phone breeped, its light blinking. Schoenfeld forced his eyes open wider at the sound.

Nancy got Mrs. Anderson to her feet. She still had a grip on her hair, still had her head pulled back and the opener at her throat. She pressed her own back against the doctor's desk. Dr. Schoenfeld was next to her, pulling himself onto the desk, dragging himself toward the phone.

"Listen," said Nancy breathlessly. She held her mouth close to Mrs. Anderson's ear. "Listen: I'm sick."

"I know that, honey," Mrs. Anderson said. "But we can help you, truly we can . . ."

"Shut up. Damn it. I don't mean that. I mean, we're going to pretend that I'm sick. You're going to hold me and help me walk. Put your arm around me. You're going to walk me out of here."

"We can't just—"

"Shut up. Just shut up. I mean it."

Bureep. Bureep. Dr. Schoenfeld stretched out his arm. "Phone," he gasped. He stretched his fingers toward the phone. He touched the base of it. "Phone . . ."

With a quick snap, trip-hammer hard, Nancy drove her fist down, drove the handle of the letter opener into Schoenfeld's temple.

Mrs. Anderson cried out. Dr. Schoenfeld dropped—a marionette with cut strings. Hands flailing, legs limp, he collapsed onto the overturned chair. Tumbled off it onto the floor again. He lay still, unconscious, wheezing quietly.

And the letter opener's blade was back at Mrs. Anderson's throat before she could blink. Her whole body had gone rigid. Any notion of escape was gone.

Good, Nancy thought. "All right," she said softly. She brought the opener down from Mrs. Anderson's throat to her side. She dug the point into her ribs. "There's your heart. You're a nurse. You know."

"I know," said Mrs. Anderson.

"I go in and twist and you're dead before you hit the floor."

"Okay. I hear ya."

Is this any way for Daddy's little button to . . . ?

"*Shut. Up!*" Nancy barked.

"I didn't say anything!"

"I'm not talking to you!"

"Oh. Okay." Mrs. Anderson did not seem reassured.

Nancy shut her eyes, tried to steady herself. The phone—couldn't they call back later?—it sliced into her. She was busy, for Christ's sake!

Her voice came out in whispered spurts. "All right. You hold me. Okay? Hold me like this." She let go of Mrs. Anderson's hair. She squeezed around in front of her, between her and the doctor's body. She pressed herself against the nurse's front, against her breasts. Clutched her uniform with her free hand. She kept the opener to Mrs. Anderson's ribs, hidden under her own body. "Hold me against you. Now!"

Slowly, cautiously, the nurse put her big right arm around Nancy's shoulder. She pressed Nancy's head into her bosom.

"Remember the knife," Nancy said.

"It won't slip my mind, honey, believe me."

"Good. Now we go out the door, down the hall to the exit. Right past the cop."

"I gotcha."

Mrs. Anderson started walking, holding Nancy to her breast. A step to the door.

"Open it."

Nancy felt the nurse hesitate, only for a moment. Then she felt her shift, reach. Heard the door click open. She clung to the front of the big woman, held there securely by the powerful brown arm. They moved together out into the hall.

"Close the door."

She heard the door click shut.

"Now move," she said.

They started toward the narrow waiting room. Mrs. Anderson was no fool. She moved at a swift but stately pace. Nancy moaned into her shirtfront for effect.

"O-o-o-oh . . ."

"There, there, honey," Mrs. Anderson said. She played it

just right. Patted Nancy's shoulder. "We gonna get you up to the ER, you gonna be just fine." It was perfect.

They came out of the corridor into the waiting room. A row of distorted faces stared from the white walls. Nancy pressed against the big nurse. She smelled her smell; a musty Negro smell. Sweat and laundry detergent and some smooth, flowery skin lotion—Jergens, possibly. Nancy closed her eyes. Such a deep liquid pool of breasts under the cool linen. She moaned again.

"There, there, honey," Mrs. Anderson murmured. Her voice was warm and deep, like bathwater. Nancy gave a little whisper of pleasure as she pressed deeper into her softness. *I'm sorry,* she thought. *I was a teenager and I was angry and crazy and I'm so sorry.* It made no sense but the words came to her anyway. *So sorry, sorry . . .*

"You got a problem there?"

A man's baritone, right beside them. Nancy's eyes snapped open. They had reached the wooden gateway, the metal detector. Nancy could see only the white field of the nurse's uniform. Blurry stares from the maniacs' gallery just beyond. But she sensed the cop was standing behind her. She dug the blade into Mama Anderson's side.

"Everything's fine," the nurse said. Casual but authoritative. "Doctor wants her upstairs for tests."

And the baritone of the cop: "You want me to call for escort?"

Nancy moaned.

"Yes, yes, there, there," said Mrs. Anderson, patting her. "No thanks," she said to the officer, "we'll be fine."

And that was it. They were moving again. Under the wooden canopy. Into the . . .

The metal detector! Nancy tensed against the great bosom. The metal detector: Would it pick up the opener, the brass blade?

But they were already through. The metal detector had not made a sound and they were already out the doorway. Twisting her head a little, Nancy saw the white hall. They were in the long white entrance hall where she had been brought in. Dragged in, screaming.

Mrs. Anderson released her. "All right," she said. "Go on then, if you're going."

There was a pause—a moment before Nancy pulled herself away from the nurse's musty depths. Then she straightened. Looked down the corridor toward the door at the end. The door had a glass pane. She could see the daylight through it. The concrete bay where the cop car had parked. Oh, she could almost smell the cool, the free, the open autumn air.

She glanced back gratefully at Mrs. Anderson. At the granite dignity of the round brown face. "Go on," the nurse said.

I'm not really like this! Nancy wanted to cry it out to her. To fling herself back into her arms, back against her breast. *This is not who I am, Mrs. Anderson. I'm really nice! Really! Nice!*

As if she had heard, Mrs. Anderson said quietly: "You sure you don't want to just come back in now? No one's gonna hurt you. I'll just walk you right back in."

Nancy's lips parted. "I can't," she whispered. "There's someplace I have to . . ." She shook her head. "I'm sorry. I can't."

Quickly, she pivoted away from her. Without another glance, she started running down the hall, toward the door. Toward the light. Her hands moved at her side, right fist clutching the letter opener. She heard her feet flapping faster and faster against the floor.

What kind of person . . . ? She heard it in the rhythm of her own steps. *What kind of monster does these things?*

Not me, she thought as she ran. Not me. Not really. Not really me.

Behind her, far away it seemed, she heard Mrs. Anderson shouting. The door ahead came closer to her. The light at its window brightened. The car bay—its concrete columns—loomed.

And then a police officer moved into the square of glass. The light went out. And it occurred to Nancy as she ran toward that square of shadow that Mrs. Anderson was shouting very loudly. She was sounding the alarm—to everyone—at the top of her lungs:

A madwoman has escaped!

OLIVER PERKINS

Before Zach was born, Oliver and his dad had taken walks
together. Hand in hand down tortuous streets. Mysterious
jazzy Manhattan streets with slanted brownstones lowering.
There had been the smell of garbage, he remembered, and
no sun—the sun too low by three P.M. to crest the building
tops. There had been old women leaning out of windows.
Negroes at the corners slouched into question marks.

His father had been a graduate student then, at NYU.
Reedy and somehow elegant in his rumpled black suits. He
had chatted as they walked and then murmured and then
fallen silent after a time. He had gazed off into the distance,
absently holding Oliver's small hand. He had still been happy
then. Before Zach was born.

They are going to kill him, Perkins. I know this for a fact.

Perkins glanced back over his shoulder. He was at the corner of Bleecker now. He glanced back down Tenth at the cop
house, a concrete bunker hunkered amid quaint brick apartments. No one was following him; no one he could see anyway. He had to get away from here before they changed their
minds. He had to find Zach. Before Mulligan did. Before the
fucking feds . . .

Your brother is going to be dead.

He hurried away down Bleecker. Hands in pockets. Shoulders hunched. Heavy with his thoughts, with his solitude. Tons
of solitude now. Worse than before. Traffic steamed past him,
past parked cars. He strode under green gingkos and yellow
elms. The leafy autumn wind curled down out of the blue

sky. A T-shirted girl leaned in the laundromat doorway, arms crossed on her chest, a wry twist to her lips. But for Perkins, inside Perkins, it was all a lunar landscape. Cratered vales of emptiness; the black sky; no help from anyone. Had to find Zach. He had to.

And Nancy Kincaid's severed head floated along beside him.

Look what they did to me, Oliver. I wanted to be a dancer. I had a woman's thoughts . . .

He hunched his shoulders higher to ward her off. He stared at the pavement as he walked. What could he do about it anyway? What did he know about any of this? New York City politics? Democrats, Republicans, the FBI? He wanted no part of any of them.

But the blue eyes stared him down, and he thought of the woman in the leather mask. *Was it Tiffany?* He thought about standing there in front of Mulligan, unable to speak out. Silence like a wall of glass. Words like moths beating themselves to death against it. Everything felt dead now as the moon inside him.

Man oh man, am I depressed or what?

He was depressed, all right. Even the panic of his thoughts—*got to find Zach, call Nana, got to*—even this was smothered under a powerful nostalgic yearning. Oh, but he longed for the people he had loved. Just to see a familiar face on the interior moonscape.

So his thoughts went back to the house on Long Island. They had lived in Port Jefferson after Zach was born. They had had a small white house with jolly dormers and gingerbread trim. There had been a steep hill behind it. Straight down from the Hartigans' picket fence to their own cellar door. The slope glistened with snow in the winter. The gray, naked trees all around it were bright with snow. That's how he hankered for it now. He remembered tugging Zach to the top on his Flexible Flyer. Kid brother swathed to the eyes in scarves. His earmuff hat pulled down to his brows. His eyes, lamplit with fear and excitement, beaming out at the slit between. And his legs in his huge buckle boots sprawled out before him on the sled.

"Mom says I shouldn't get too wet, Ollie."

Ollie trudging upward, tugging the rope.

"We're not gonna go over the bump, right, Ollie? You're gonna ride with me, right?"

Puff, puff, puff—cottony blasts of frost as Ollie panted. "Yeah, Zach, I told you already."

"Cause I don't like it when it gets too fast, okay?"

"Okay, Zach-man. Jesus."

"Mom says it's because of my inner ear."

Perkins smiled grimly now as he edged by a troop of school-children. Trick-or-treaters in black nylon capes, plastic masks. A harried woman shepherded them past.

His inner ear, Perkins thought, shaking his head. Christ, he had to find the guy, inner ear and all. Little Zach, in the playroom with his carpentry kit between his legs, his hammer going. Or down in the cellar like Dr. Frankenstein with his chemistry set—he had known more about science at seven than Oliver knew now. He had known more about everything. He could take apart their father's typewriter and put it back together. Ollie had tried to do it himself once, just to prove he was at least as smart as his baby brother . . .

Oh, if the feds hurt him, Perkins thought . . . if the cops got hold of him . . . Jesus . . .

He could remember standing at the top of that wintry hill. Breathless. Zach sitting on the sled by his feet. Both of them looking down over the slope of snow. The stretch of darkling sky over the housetops. The lighted windows in the house below. Their mother's anxious face at the kitchen window, the fluttery spirit of the house. And upstairs in the northern dormer, their father. Seated at his desk. Turning from his work to the round window. Turning as if to glare at an intruder. Turning like a wolf from the innards of a deer.

Jesus, where had *that* look come from? That snouty rage? Zach and Oliver had debated the question endlessly. Back and forth from bed to bed in their little room upstairs in Nana's mews. Dad was gone by then, of course. Off to California with one of his students: a chirpy twenty-year-old brunette who called Zach and Oliver "the boys." Dad hardly even wrote them anymore, but "the boys" couldn't let the matter rest. They wanted to understand it: Why had he become such an angry man?

"When you were a kid, he was a promising young grad student," Zach would say mildly. And the fact that he said it mildly made Perkins feel guiltier still. "When I was a kid, it was all failure already, it was all disappointment."

Dad had been an associate history professor at the university when Zach was a kid. He was popular with the students. A favorite lecturer; all that reedy, abstracted charm. Everyone talked about how much they loved him. "And they hold that against you," he often said—grumbling at the dinner table, snapping his mashed potatoes off the fork. "According to academia, you can either be popular or scholarly. They won't let you be both. If the kids like you, then your work is looked down on. How can it be any good? You're *popular*. You must be shallow. That's that."

Perkins came to a stop on the corner of his block. Ran his fingers up through his hair. Looked down the narrow lane of brownstones and slender trees. Yellow leaves blowing in the gutter past the closed windows of the café. Only a few cars parked way down at the far end, near Sixth. A few pedestrians. Two older men, a couple, carrying groceries. A sheepdog dragging its dumpy matron for a walk. They could be cops, he thought. Any one of them could be watching him. Could be feds even. He stood, feeling obvious and exposed. Feeling guilty.

Look what they did to my head, Oliver.

Yeah, yeah, but for God's sake, what did he know about it?

And again, he thought of the woman in the leather mask. Her strands of black and silver hair. The curve of her naked spine. The man—this Fernando Woodlawn—was drawn back from her a little so you could see most of her ass.

And all at once, he felt a chemical change. His loneliness, this bittersweet nostalgia, thickened into real sadness. *Oh. Oh. Oh.* He shuddered. *For many a time I have been half in love with easeful Death.*

Little Zachie, man. His father had grabbed him by the back of his neck. Pinned him facedown to the big writing desk, his cheek crushed against it. The little boy's legs were dangling over the side. His corduroy overalls were dangling around his thighs. "*Daddy! Daddy! Daddy!*" he kept screaming. But Daddy kept lifting that heavy brass ruler. "This—will—teach—you—to stay—away—from my—things!" Bringing it down on the child's bare ass till the flesh turned purple and then practically black. While Zachie screamed till he was hoarse. And Mom stood to the side, her fingers fluttering helplessly at her lips. Staring with blank eyes. Smiling a dazed smile. And Oliver stood in the doorway. Drawn from his homework by his brother's shrieks. Stood with his hands out from his sides and his fists clenched. And he couldn't speak then either. His throat felt bunged with excitement and terror and he could only stand there, thinking, *But I broke it. I broke the typewriter.*

A breath riffled out of him. He shook his head. "Fuck," he said aloud. He started toward his building, head down. And fuck Mulligan too, he thought. And the NYPD, and the fucking Republican FBI, all of them. He'd get a lawyer, that's all. He'd go to the newspapers, break this thing wide open. Kill his brother, would they?

God, he was depressed.

He reached his stoop. Paused there for a last narrow-eyed look around. A bald man in a red dress strutted past the end of the block, his high heels clicking. *And Christ, you can't tell if you're being watched or not. The entire Village is in disguise.* He waved off the world. Fuck it. He jogged up the steps to his door and pushed inside.

He went quickly up the stairs to the third floor, to his door. Fumbled in his pocket for his keys. Maybe Avis was still upstairs, he thought. It would be a relief to talk to her, lay all this out. She was not going to believe it, that was for sure. He found the key. Unlocked the door. Stepped in.

The door swung shut behind him. He snapped on the light. And he froze where he stood.

Hey. Somebody moved Goethe.

Perkins's hand went around behind him. Felt for the door-knob. Seized it. He stood stock-still there, his chest rising and falling. His ears pricked. He was ready to bolt at the slightest motion, the slightest sound. His head stationary, his eyes panned from one end of the apartment to the other.

The place had been cleaned. All the empty brown bottles of Sam Adams beer had been picked up. Dumped into shopping bags in the kitchenette for recycling. That was Avis. It had to be. There was no stopping the little dope once she got started. She'd done the goddamn dishes too. Picked up his clothes. Straightened the bedcovers on his mattress. Had she polished his writing desk even? He thought he remembered a few bottle rings that now seemed to have been wiped away.

But his books. The dust-gray piles of books against the wall from floor to ceiling. In tilted stacks between bed and table and chair. Wedged under the windowsill . . . Avis knew better than to rearrange his books. They were all carefully in place. He knew the location of each by heart. Avis was too sweet to send that kind of shockwave through his universe, but somebody . . .

Somebody had moved the Goethe.

Right there. That short stack right at the foot of the mattress. Poe's *Tales* at the bottom. Which, of course, had reminded him of Lacan, and so of Freud, so that Otto Rank's *Myth of the Birth of the Hero* came next. Which led him to think of Rank's *Will Therapy*, so that Schopenhauer's *The World As Will and Representation* was on top of it. Which brought to mind *Buddenbrooks*, so that Mann's *Dr. Faustus* was on top of that. Which had led him by a far more direct line to Heinrich's *Mephisto* and so finally to the two volumes of Goethe, *Faust II* and then *Faust I*. At least that's how he'd left it: the second part under the first. But now—now, someone had obviously slipped the second part out. Glanced at it maybe, then casually tossed it back on *top* of the pile, as if he wouldn't notice.

He was sure of it. Someone other than Avis had been in his apartment.

Slowly, he released the doorknob. Came away from the door, looking this way and that. He stood in the center of the room finally. Listening. Hearing nothing, but the faint whoosh of traffic over on Sixth. Once again, tense, poised, he surveyed the room. Passed his gaze over the books, from window to mattress to lamp to bathroom . . .

He stopped there. The bathroom door. It was closed.

Oh no. Not again.

What the hell was it closed for? Had he closed it himself? He couldn't remember. Maybe that was Avis too. Sure. And maybe Avis was still in there . . .

Don't think it.

Right. Right, don't think it. Only maybe she *was* right in there, right through that door. In that toilet. Staring up at him from behind her big square glasses. Her lips gray, parted. The curls in her blonde hair straightening as they became soaked in the puddle of her own . . .

Just don't even think it, man.

He gritted his teeth. Shit. Shit. It was just a door, just a closed door. No reason to just stand there staring at it like this. Confronting it like an adversary, head jutting, fists clenched. He ought to go right over there and open it, that's what. Open that door right up. Yessireebob.

He took a slow, slow sliding step toward the bathroom.

And the bathroom doorknob turned. The latch clicked. The door began to swing open . . .

I'm here, Oliver. I came to your house. To show you my head, what they did to my head.

Stopped in his tracks, Perkins watched the door come squeaking out little by little. He watched—as a human head did, in fact, come squeezing through it. Peeking around the edge of the door. Big, dark eyes sneaking a look at him around the wood.

"Ollie? Is that you?"

And Perkins rushed toward him. He had not even realized how worried he'd been until now, when it all drained out of him. And he shouted: "Zach!" He strode toward him with his fist over his head as if to club him down. Crying: "Zach, where the hell have you been, you idiot? You *stupid* son of a bitch!"

NANCY KINCAID

Running. The long corridor. The distant door. Its square pane of glass dark with the shadow of the cop.

The shouts behind her were growing louder. Nancy held on to her letter opener as she ran, hiding the blade against her wrist. Her head was swimming.

Not me, she was thinking, almost dreamily. *I'm really nice. This isn't really me.*

"Careful now, she's got a knife!" That was the nurse, Mrs. Anderson.

"Hold it!" The cop behind her.

The cop ahead of her, behind the glass, was the same black policewoman who had held the door open for her when she had come in. She pulled the door open now.

I may have to kill her, Nancy thought.

But the woman just nodded her head at her. She even smiled a little. And Nancy realized: She was holding the door open for her again!

Nancy plunged toward the opening.

"Grab her!" came the shout from the corridor.

"She's got a knife. Watch out."

Nancy saw a flicker of comprehension in the policewoman's eyes. But it was too late. Before the cop could sort it out, Nancy was through. Steaming around the corner, down the length of the car bay. The concrete columns blurring at her sides. The East River out there somewhere. And the end of the bay ahead, the asphalt of the parking lot through the links of a fence.

"Hold it!"

"Stop!"

The cool air was on her cheeks, on her throat. The shouts behind her seemed to fall away. The end of the bay was just ahead. She felt that she was almost free—and yet she had to force herself on. She felt logy, like she was running under water. Churning the air with her arms, clutching the letter opener. She was gasping, slowing down, almost as if there was a force inside her urging her to stop. Urging her back the other way. She could feel it: She didn't want to go through with this. She wanted to give herself up. To go back. To lie on a bed with white sheets and see Dr. Schoenfeld's kindly face above her. To feel Mrs. Anderson's strong black hand upon her brow. What had she done to them? What kind of person does those things?

Who was she? Who the hell was she?

She broke out from under the bay, thinking, *No. Go back, go back.* The parking lot was wide. The sky was wide above it. The glum brick piles of Bellevue surrounded the near horizon. The Empire State Building speared up from behind them into the blue. It was a strange blue, she thought as she squinted in the sudden brightness. Strange light everywhere.

Then she understood: It was afternoon. She had been in the hospital for hours. The morning was gone. It was getting late . . .

She stumbled forward. Coughing, dizzy. She glanced back over her shoulder. Saw two cops standing back there at the hospital door, under the roof of the bay. One—the man—was talking into his walkie-talkie. But they weren't following her. They were holding their posts. They were letting her go.

A road ran around the edge of the parking lot fence. She took this, trying to keep up her speed. She was afraid if she slowed down she would be drawn backward. That she would give in to her urge to surrender . . .

But the road sloped upward. She just couldn't keep running. She fell to a walk, her head heavy, her shoulders heaving as she sucked in air. Below her, by the river, cars were racing by on the FDR Highway. She thought she could hear the distant keen of sirens under the noise. She wasn't sure. She just didn't care.

She raised her eyes. She saw the narrow lane ahead, the end of Twenty-ninth Street. Hemmed in by the old hospital's glowering brick walls. The row of solemn urns on one side perched atop their columns.

She had no idea where she was going, she just headed on. All that urgency, those voices inside her: Eight o'clock. The Animal Hour. Someone is going to die. Where the hell were they now when she needed them? It was all quiet in the old cranium. Nancy laughed bitterly at that, still panting. She dragged herself into the alley, into the shadow of a column, under the blank face of a concrete urn.

She leaned against the pillar and slid to the ground. She sat there slumped at the foot of the rising lane. She shook her head, trying to fight off the full understanding of what she'd done. But the images, the words—even the physical sensations—came back to her, crowded in on her. Dr. Schoenfeld's gentle, furry smile and the way his eyes widened when the pain hit him. The way the soft tissue between his legs flattened with the force of her driving knee. *(What you're experiencing is an episode of schizophrenia.)* The feel of Mrs. Anderson's hair in her grip. Her scared face yanked back. *(I can kill you with this.)* She let the letter opener slip out of her hand now. She let it fall with a clink to the sidewalk.

And she sat slumped on the pavement there beneath the brick walls, the dark, arched windows of the hospital complex. She leaned her forehead against the cold pillar, her legs bent under her. The urn stood stolid above her head like an indifferent owl.

Those sirens, though—getting nearer. A lot of them too, it sounded like. She tried to laugh again, but it came out like crying. *I'm nice!* she thought. *I'm really a nice person!*

"*Oh,*" her mother used to say, "*you look so nice.*"

(It's a general term for a series of mental disorders characterized by auditory-command hallucinations, fixed delusions, memory lapses . . .)

When she was little, her mother would tie a ribbon in her hair and tell her she was beautiful. And that was all she needed. She believed she was beautiful then. She felt beautiful.

I go in and twist and you're dead before you hit the floor.

Oh, had she really said that? In her own little voice? She could still hear her own little nice voice saying that. *I go in and twist . . .* What kind of monster, for Christ's sake, was she? *Who* was she? How on earth could she begin to find out? What do you have to know in order to know who you are? Your past? Your face in the mirror? What you believe in? Your name? What did she start with?

The Animal Hour.

Oh, the Animal Hour. Swell. Nancy groaned. She lifted her head, her eyes closed. She clenched her teeth as if she were holding herself together by will alone. All this—this breaking out of a mental institution—this kneeing doctors in their nasties—this threatening nurses with letter opener blades—had she done all this for a voice in her head, for words she didn't even understand: the Animal Hour?

The sirens were louder now. By the sound of them, the cop cars were coming from all directions. From behind her on the FDR down by the river. From north and south up and down First Avenue. They would converge, she imagined, above at the mouth of the lane. They would come speeding up the curving road around the parking lot below. They would race between the brick walls from either direction and pin her between their grinning grilles.

Good, she thought. *Let them. I'm armed, I'm dangerous, I'm out of my mind. I belong behind bars. Let them come and get me.*

But even now, she was gathering her legs in under her. She was surveying the road ahead for the first sign of the cops. Her fingers, meanwhile, were trailing over the sidewalk— touching on the letter opener—wrapping around the handle.

Don't do it, Nancy, she wanted to scream at herself. But she knew she would do it. She knew she had to.

She looked down at her wrist. Her watch was gone. They had taken it away from her in the hospital. The fact sent a little bolt of panic through her, a little white lightning bolt through the torpid zone. She didn't know what time it was.

And it was getting late. It was afternoon. Late afternoon by the look of it.

How much time left before it happens?

She didn't know. That made it urgent. She had to get going again. She braced her hand against the pillar. Grunted as she worked her way to her feet. The sirens were loud enough to send another current of electricity through her. She was being jolted out of her groggy dream. Her head was clearing.

She had to be there. She was sure of it. She didn't know how, but she was sure it was real. Someone was going to be killed tonight. Someone somewhere. At eight o'clock . . .

What you're experiencing is an episode of schizophrenia. Auditory-command hallucinations. Fixed delusions.

Leave me alone, she thought wearily. And she saw the doctor's face again. The doctor's warm eyes widening in agony just after she had driven her knee up.

What kind of maniac . . . ?

She started up toward First Avenue. The sirens whooped like Indians. Closing in. They would be here in a minute. She walked faster, keeping her head down, keeping the letter opener hidden against her arm . . .

What kind of monster . . . ? You were going to kill that woman.

She thought of Nurse Anderson. Her head jerked back. Her wide frightened eyes.

Is that any way to behave? Why, I've never heard of such a thing.

I have to be there, Mother, she thought pettishly. She went by the long iron fence that fronted the brick building. Up toward First Avenue. Glancing back over her shoulders as the sirens screamed. She could see one now. The spinning red flashers coming around the bend, up the road behind her by the parking lot.

And she thought of Nurse Anderson's soft breasts, the blade against her ribs.

Dead before you hit the floor.

The images, the thoughts, swarmed around her like crows, picked at her like crows. Under the heavy shadow of the building, she came to the corner of First. She could see them here too. Just as she'd imagined. One car racing down from the north, flashing red, weaving through the swift traffic. Another under the broad blue sky to the south, bearing straight up as cabs and cars jumped out of its way.

It's for me! Really for me! Something screamed it in her suddenly. *They're coming for me! Because I'm like this! Because I do these things! This is really who I am.*

And all the images—all the crows—seemed to sweep down on her at once. All at once, it made terrible sense to her. The Animal Hour. The blood flying as the doctor's nose shattered on the desk. The blade at Mrs. Anderson's throat. These oncoming sirens . . .

She ran. The light was hers, the traffic idling uncertainly as it waited for the cop cars to come on. She ran across the street. Ran to get away from those swooping crows, those images. Those police cars bearing down on her from either side because this was who she was, this was what she was really like. This was the kind of monster that she was.

She reached the far sidewalk. The traffic started to cough forward. Pull sharply to the side to make way for the cops. She ran wildly. Because she had to be there. The Animal Hour. Eight o'clock. Someone was going to die tonight and, of course, of course, she had to be there.

Because she was the one who was going to kill him.

PART 3

LULLABY

"I don't want harmony . . . I want harmony."
—Dutch Shultz on his deathbed

OLIVER PERKINS

"So then I had to take a shit."

Oliver had the beer bottle tipped to his lips. It just stopped there, hovering. He stared across it at his kid brother. "What?"

"I had to take a dump. I had diarrhea."

"Zachie. You had every cop in the city after you. You were dressed like a girl, for Christ's sake."

"Well, that was the thing. And, you know, they're getting ready for the parade out there so there are all these policemen around the square and around Sixth Avenue. They're everywhere."

Oliver could only marvel at him. Sitting all gangly on the mattress, his knees up around his ears. His eyes wide and dark and goofy. His smile like a goofy child's. He was not wearing Tiffany's clothes anymore. He was in faded jeans, torn at the knees, and some sort of bulky, patchwork shirt. Each square a different color and design; looked like it had been made at a quilting bee for psychopaths.

"So you know, I went into that place—Mom's or Mama's—it's that ice cream parlor . . ."

Oliver, sitting on the desk chair, still holding the beer bottle up around his mouth, shook his head in wonder. "Papa's something . . ."

"Right. And I ask the cashier, you know, can I use the bathroom. And he can see I'm dying, I'm all doubled over. And he says sure. So I run to the back and I slam myself into this little room and I'm wrestling—you know, you have to sort of get your skirt all bunched up around your waist with one hand and then pull down your underwear with the other and I feel like some sort of contortionist or something and then all of a sudden there's this pounding on the door—bang, bang, bang, you know—and I'm desperate and I shout: 'What?' And it's the cashier. He's yelling, 'Miss! Miss! You've got the wrong room! You're in the men's room! Miss!' "

Oliver laughed. He lowered his beer to his lap. He nodded.

"And I had to shout back in this high-pitched, this falsetto voice, you know, 'Oh, thank you, sir, it's all right, thank you very much.' But he just kept on *pounding*. What could I do? I'd finally gotten my skirt over my head so I could hold it up, but I couldn't see. And my jockey shorts are down around my ankles—and I mean, my gut is exploding, there's no turning back. And he keeps calling me: 'Miss! Miss!' I was in there for, like, forty-five minutes. He kept coming back and shouting at me the whole time."

Oliver looked at Zachie, at his bright, black eyes. Saw him nod his goofy head, smile his goofy smile. And he laughed some more.

If the feds get to him first, your brother is going to be dead.

He pinched the bridge of his nose and laughed harder. "You idiot. Christ!" His black hair trembled on his forehead as he laughed.

Zach shrugged. "What was I gonna do?"

"Stop. Jesus," Oliver said. He couldn't stop laughing.

Zachary watched him from the bed. Big smile. Nodding his head up and down. Sipping from a glass of water. In an unspoken agreement, they had turned the apartment lights out. The light of afternoon was fading from the room as well. The mounds and rows of books all around them were melting into a comfortable brown dusk.

"Oh! You asshole." Oliver took a gulp of breath. Wiped the tears of laughter from his face with his open hand. Shook his head into his beer again. Took a sip of it. Then he just sat for a moment, staring at his little brother.

They are going to kill him, Perkins. I know this for a fact.

"So?" he said, as solemnly as he could. "Were you there?"

Zach, still grinning, puffed his cheeks. "Whew! The mews, you mean? Yeah."

Both men nodded somberly. A long moment passed in reflection.

"So did you puke?" Oliver finally asked. "I puked. Did you puke?"

"I don't think so. I was pretty upset though."

"I just puked. Christ, when I saw her head right there in the toilet like that, Jesus . . ."

"Oh, so that's where it was."

Oliver just exploded with laughter, beer spraying from his mouth. He had to put the bottle down. Bow his head into both hands. Oh, so that's where it was! He couldn't stand it! He closed his eyes. He could see the woman's face staring up at him from the toilet, but he didn't care. He laughed until his voice became a thin squeak: eee eee eee. Zach laughed too, just watching him.

"Oh, man!" said Oliver finally. "That's where it was, all right. Jesus. Right there in the toilet. I went in to throw up . . ."

"Oh no! You didn't . . . !"

"No, but I just missed, man."

"Oh no."

"Jesus. Oh God." He kept on laughing. "Wait'll Nana finds out about this. She's gonna flatline."

Zach gripped his chest and stuck his tongue out: Nana having a coronary. That set Oliver off again and he actually stood up, he was laughing so hard, stamping his feet against the floor, shaking his head. When he finished, he sagged wearily against the wall. He looked down at Zach, who still sat on the mattress, all knees. Smiling. Nodding his head up and down. The same stupid Zach he'd pulled up the hill on that sled.

We're not gonna go over the bump, right, Ollie? You're gonna ride with me, right?

Oliver had to fight the urge to cross the room and just lift him off the mattress in his arms. Just kiss him smack on the forehead. The two of them didn't do things like that.

"Oh God!" he said instead. He tilted his head so far back

he was staring up at the ceiling. "Oh God, what is *happening* here? I can not believe this is happening."

"I know. It's insane."

"Well, what went on with you, Zach-man. All this blood-stained clothes shit and Detective Mulligan and everything? Christ!" Oliver kicked the floor with his heel. "I can't believe we're even having this conversation. I mean, the FB-fucking-I . . . What's *happening,* man?"

"Nothing!" Zach exclaimed. He put his skinny arms out, showed his empty hands. He was wide-eyed. "I had a fight with Tiffany. That's all. That's how it all got started. I don't know: something's the matter with her. She's been acting weird for weeks. I don't know. We had this quarrel and she got all pissed off and . . . she told me to leave. 'Go back to your stupid mews and live there,' that's what she said. What was I gonna do? It was, like, four in the morning or something, I don't know. And I came in—to the mews, I mean—I went to the mews and the place was all messed up and everything. So I figured it was robbed, right? And I went upstairs to check things out and . . . that's when I saw the body. You know? And I got all messed up. This is the stupid part. Cause I . . . don't know what I did. I ran over to it. You know, I didn't even notice about the head. Well, I mean I noticed it, but I just . . . I wasn't thinking or something, you know, because I ran over to it—the body—and I took hold of it, you know? To see if I could help or something . . . I took hold of it by the shoulders. I don't know. I wasn't thinking. So I got all covered in blood. And then I saw, you know, what happened to the head. And I thought, Oh shit. Oh shit, now I'm all covered with blood, you know, they're going to think it was me. And I just . . . I . . . ran out. I ran home, back to Tiffany. I didn't know what I was doing." He sighed; sagged. "Then, when I got home, you know, I told Tiffany everything that had happened, right? And she just went all—pale, like, just the red going out of her cheeks, just all gray, and I said, 'Tiff, what's wrong,' but she wouldn't tell me. And then she said, she said, 'Just wait. Just wait here, okay?' She said she had to go out for a little while and then . . . then she said she'd come back and explain everything." He gave a slow baffled shrug. "Only she never did. She never came back at all. I haven't seen her since." And he just sat there, gazing at the floor. That was the end of it.

The smile was gone entirely from Oliver's face now. He grimaced, snatched his beer bottle up by the neck. Carried it over to the window, stepping around the books. Dread—his old friend Uncle Dread—was back. In spades. Mr. Relief had moved away and good old Uncle Dread had set up camp in his stomach. Building quite a little bonfire in there too by the feel of it.

He was on the drugs, Ollie thought. He swigged the beer. Looked out the window, through the grillwork of the fire escape. Down on the little Village bystreet going shadowy in the afternoon. Two children in store-bought masks danced through the shadows behind their mother—impossible to tell which TV characters they were supposed to be. And a gay couple in studded leather and motorcycle caps followed after them, hand in hand. Oliver, watching them all, felt so alone, felt such a lonesome hankering for childhood days, that he almost spoke aloud in his bitterness: *You went back on the drugs, you stupid shit. No wonder you couldn't think straight.*

He glanced over his shoulder. There was Zach, knees around his ears. Gazing off stupidly. Sort of waggling his head. *We're not gonna go over the bump, right, Ollie?*

Oliver didn't say anything. He turned to the window again. He sighed. Thank God the window was open, he thought. Zach had come up the fire escape and climbed in and thank God the window was open for him. If Mulligan got his hands on the Zach-man now, if Zach told his story—trying to revive a headless body, hugging it, getting covered with blood . . .

I give you my word that I will personally beat the living shit out of him until he tells me everything he knows.

Zach had been on drugs. That was the only explanation. The way he acted, the things he did. The way his stomach was all messed up. He was on drugs and Tiffany knew it and threw him out. Go back to your stupid mews and take your drugs there. That's what she must have said. Go back to the mews like you used to.

He sent a long breath echoing into the neck of the beer bottle. Go back to your stupid mews . . . he thought.

Or had she known? Had she known he'd go there and find the body? Had she sent him there to find it, to set him up, just like she sent Oliver himself there later in the day—sent him there and then called the cops to report a woman screaming?

She said she'd come back and explain everything. She's been acting weird for weeks.

She was the key to it, all right. Oliver was sure of that. She had the answers. But how were they going to convince Mulligan? Especially now with his brother on drugs again. On drugs and all bloody, his fingerprints probably all over. His idiot brother. How could they convince Mulligan to talk to Tiffany before he kicked Zach half to death?

Oliver gazed down at the crowns of the gingkos, which were slipping into the street's shadows too. He pulled at his beer angrily. Thought of the first time Zachie had broken down. Up at SUNY. In New Paltz. Brilliant guy like Zachie killing time in a bogus little state school like that. Goofball U, Oliver used to call it to himself. People majored in tans there; rock-scrambling through the Shawangunks. Ollie himself had just finished up at Bennington. He was bartending his way down the White River. Writing bad poems and some good poems too. When Nana called him, he was living in a tent, in a campground near Gaysville. Laura, the waitress at Hemingway's, had come to fetch him. "It's your grandmother. She says there's a catastrophe."

Oh, and it was a catastrophe, all right. Zach had been curled up in a corner of his dorm room for four days. Arms around his knees. Wouldn't move. Wouldn't talk to anyone. Even when Ollie got there, he would only lift his solemn little face and pronounce grimly, "This is not what God wants me to do, Oliver."

Not what God wants me to do. Oliver sneered down at the gingkos. Hissed through his teeth. An old man stood under one of the trees, belly in his T-shirt like a medicine ball. Gabbing forcefully across a shopping cart with an old lady in a housedress.

Or maybe they're cops, Oliver thought. Maybe they're FBI and they're watching the place and any minute they'll come bursting in here, guns blazing.

If the feds get to him first, your brother is going to be dead.

Oh boy. Oh yes. Uncle Dread was cooking up a storm in the old breadbasket now. Oliver brought the bottle to his mouth again. Tasted the bottom suds. Wished the alcohol would take hold a little. Calm him down. Blunt the edge of this depression. This fear.

After SUNY, Zach had come home to the mews again. Nana had gotten him a psychiatrist that time too, paid all his expenses, everything. And Zach had lain in there, in the mews, in the dark. Reading Augustine and C. S. Lewis and Hans Kung, days on end. Thomas à Kempis, for Christ's sweet sake, days on end. And finally, one day, he just took off. Joined some sort of Christian religious retreat somewhere in Pennsylvania. And wrote joyful, pious letters home for a year and a half until he broke down again and Ollie had to go fetch him . . .

Oliver tilted the bottle back. Drained the beer. To no avail, like the man said. His heart was still lead. His mind wouldn't stop working. Mulligan:

I will personally beat the living shit out of him until he tells me everything he knows.

That prick. The pug-nosed detective without a trace of emotion in his voice or his face. Blinking down at him from behind the round wire rims. Laying his photographs down like playing cards, blank-eyed, poker-mugged. And those photographs. That picture of the girl with the leather mask over her head and the politician up her ass. Damn it, Ollie thought. Goddamned Tiffany. What the hell was she up to here?

She said she'd come back and explain everything.

"Ach!" He waved it all away. Turned around.

There was Zach, perched on the mattress. Arms flung over his raised knees, hands dangling. Looking up at Oliver with his big eyes and waiting for him to speak. *What're we gonna do now, Ollie?* Just like after Mom died. What're we gonna do now?

"Oh hell, Zachie. You gotta turn yourself in," Oliver said. "You got to. There's no other way. We'll get you a lawyer first. Nana must know somebody. Mulligan won't be able to touch you if you've got a lawyer . . ."

"Oh Jeeze, Ollie, I don't know . . ."

"Look, man, they knew this girl, this dead girl. The cops, I mean. They knew her and they're pissed off. If they catch you, if you run and they catch you, they're gonna teach you new meanings of the word 'excruciating.' You gotta do it. You gotta turn yourself in."

The two brothers were quiet then in the dusky room. Oliver, ashamed, shuffled at the window. Gripped his empty beer bottle, studied the floor. On the mattress, Zach considered things, his eyes moving. Glancing from one skewed stack of books to another. Lingering on the cover of *The Wasteland*.

Goddamned Tiffany, Oliver thought. Where the hell was she?

"Okay, Ollie," Zach said then. "Okay." He lifted his shoulders. "Jeeze. And I was gonna be King Death in the parade tonight and everything."

"Yeah. Well. Next year," Oliver said. He couldn't meet Zachie's eyes.

Zach tilted his chin up a little. "There's just one thing, Ollie . . ."

"What's that?"

"Well . . . Tiffany."

Oliver looked at him. "Yeah? What about her?"

"Well, I mean, I think I know where she is now."

"What?"

"I mean, she's supposed to work at the bookstore today. I mean, there's no place else she could go except to Trish and Joyce at the bookstore. Or maybe home to Scarsdale. But I think she's at the bookstore. I'm almost sure of it. I'd have gone there myself except . . . the cops, you know, and I was so sick and all."

Oliver said nothing. He looked away, trying to think. Running his hand up through his hair. Zach had to turn himself in. He had to. But what if . . . what if Oliver *could* find Tiffany? What if she did have some of the answers? Enough

176

to convince Mulligan Zach was innocent, enough, at least, to keep him at bay?

"Shit," he said aloud. He was a poet, not a cop. It was impossible to work this out.

"Maybe we could call her," Zach said.

"No," said Oliver at once. If they gave her warning, she might run off. "The bookstore's right around the corner. Maybe I could go over there."

"I sure would like to talk to her," said Zach. His head swung back and forth slowly. He studied the empty air. "I mean, I'm really worried about her, Ollie."

Oliver drew a long breath. He nodded, let it out. "Yeah," he said after a moment. "So the fuck am I."

BEVERLY TILDEN

Beverly Tilden was on her way to the NYU Medical Center to visit her father, who had recently had his gallbladder removed. Mrs. Tilden had asked the taxi driver to leave her off on Second Avenue because there was a good Korean grocery there, on the corner of Thirtieth, across from the shopping center. Mrs. Tilden had popped in to the grocery and bought her dad some pink carnations and some strawberry Crumblies. He would sneer at the flowers, she knew, because he was an old-school tough guy. But he'd like them secretly. And though he probably couldn't stomach the cookies yet, he would be able to offer them to visitors. That would make him feel more like a host, more in control.

Mrs. Tilden, tall and trim, strode down Thirtieth then in her fashionable, ankle-length black coat. The flowers, wrapped in foil, were in one gloved hand. The cookies were in a white plastic bag over her forearm. Her purse was strapped over her shoulder. She glanced at her watch as she walked and made a face. It was three-thirty already. She had to make this visit and get home by five at the latest. The Halloween party was at six, and every girl in Melissa's class had accepted her invitation. That meant eleven six-year-olds in a two-bedroom apartment. Bobbing for apples, OD'ing on sugar. Giggling, shrieking . . . Even with the caterer and the hired magician, there was going to be plenty of hysteria left over for her.

She walked a little faster. She was about halfway between Second and First. A police car came speeding up behind her, sped past her, its siren howling. Mrs. Tilden wrinkled her nose a little at the noise. After the police car turned onto First, there was no other traffic on the street. There were no other pedestrians either. Mrs. Tilden was alone on Thirtieth. But she did not notice that.

Not until the dark figure stepped out into her path.

Mrs. Tilden was on the south sidewalk, passing a row of brownstones. Thin sycamores with yellowing leaves spread sun-flecked shade. A breeze from the river made the elms sway. The light and shadow played and danced. Mrs. Tilden slowed. Her eyes flashed over the strange figure before her, dark and dappled beneath the trees. Mrs. Tilden didn't like what she saw. Not a bit.

It was a woman. She had appeared suddenly. Slipping out from behind a brownstone stoop as if she had been hiding there. She was a bedraggled creature. Brown hair in tangles to her shoulder. Mascara on her wide, pale cheeks. Lipstick smudging her chin. Her cream-colored blouse was splashed with grime, torn at the shoulder, revealing a bra strap. Her dark skirt was streaked with dust. Her feet, in flats, showed filthy, nearly black. But it wasn't this that scared Mrs. Tilden. Homeless people were all over the city; they rarely hurt anyone. No, there was something else about this woman. Her slumped, sullen, determined look. Her eyes—they were foggy—were veiled like the eyes of a snake Mrs. Tilden had once seen on a PBS nature special. Well, whatever it was, it set the alarms off, all right.

On the other hand, the alarms were always going off in this city, and Mrs. Tilden was in a hurry. She kept walking right toward the strange woman. After all, it was broad daylight. The busy corner of First Avenue was just a few steps off. There was even another police car passing by down there, its siren wild. And there had to be other people . . .

Mrs. Tilden glanced around nervously. No. There were no other people. The block was empty. She was alone.

And at that moment, the woman stepped toward her. Mrs. Tilden, suddenly terrified, swerved to get past. Swerved the wrong way, toward the buildings. *Oh, damn it!* she thought. The woman cut her off, backed her up under the stoop's balustrade.

Good God, thought Beverly Tilden, *this is it, this is the real thing, it's really happening!*

The woman stared up at her dully with those glazed eyes. "I just escaped from Bellevue," she said in a harsh whisper. "I have a knife. Give me bus fare."

Mrs. Tilden was surprised to find she could still think clearly, almost calmly, though she was now icy with fear. She would just give the woman her money, that's all. Just cooperate, that was what everyone told you.

"All right," she said. "Just a minute."

She fumbled for her purse, trying to open it with the flowers still in her hand. As always when she felt threatened, a New York tabloid headline screamed in her mind. MURRAY HILL MOM STABBED FOR BUS FARE! She fought the thought off. It would be all right if she just cooperated. With a quick curse, she dropped the carnations to the sidewalk. Let the bag of cookies slide off her arm as well. She snapped her purse open.

"I'll give you whatever I have."

"I just want bus fare," the woman hissed. "Bus fare. I have a knife." She held a brass letter opener up before Mrs. Tilden's eyes. Mrs. Tilden would not have thought that would be a very scary thing to see, but it was. She fumbled her wallet open. Picked through it frantically with her gloved fingers.

"I have a token," she said. "Is a token all right?"

"Fine. Yes. Hurry!"

"I'm trying to get it out."

"Hurry! They're all after me."

Mrs. Tilden bit her lip as she hunted the token out of the wallet's cloth folds. They're all after me? she thought. The woman must be some sort of paranoid.

BLUESTOCKING HOUSEWIFE SLASHED BY MADWOMAN!

But she was aware of the sirens now too. All those sirens, lots of them, baying like hounds, like a pack of hounds gathering down on First. Oh God, this really *was* the real thing. This was really serious.

SICK DAD'S DAUGHTER EVISCERATED IN KILL SPREE!

"Here it is!"

She held the token up, pinched in her fingers. The woman snatched it.

"Thank you."

She kept standing there. Glaring up at her. Mrs. Tilden hardly dared to look her in the face, but she sensed her youth. Her young, hot misery and desperation.

"I really appreciate it," the woman said.

"All right."

"I'm really a very nice person."

"I—I'm sure you are."

"Maybe I better take a five too."

"For God's sake, take everything."

"I haven't eaten."

"Here!" She snatched a fistful of bills out of her wallet. Held it out to her.

"Just a five," said the snake woman. "I'm nice. I mean it."

"Please," said Mrs. Tilden. "Don't hurt me. I have children. Just take whatever you want."

The woman pulled a bill out of Mrs. Tilden's clenched fist. She was still holding up the letter opener. "Thank you," she said. "I appreciate it. Really. I'm nice."

Mrs. Tilden nodded, trying not to steal glances at the blade, trying to look nowhere.

At long last, the woman lowered the opener. She began backing away. Staring at Mrs. Tilden, but backing away. Mrs. Tilden cringed by the balustrade. Didn't move a muscle. She was excruciatingly aware of how quickly the woman could change her mind. Change her direction and leap at her, hurt her. On First, the sirens kept gathering, siren upon howling siren, growing louder, more numerous. But not one car came this way. Not one other person appeared on the sun-dappled block.

Mrs. Tilden huddled into herself as the woman sidled off. And the woman still eyed her. Still studied her crazily with those creepy, baleful, Nature Special eyes. And then, she stopped.

Oh please, Mrs. Tilden thought. *For God's sake, please.*

The snake woman leaned toward her. Whispered to her in a voice like a sizzling fry pan. "I wish I were you, lady. Watching me go." Mrs. Tilden stared. The snake woman's eyes filled with tears. She turned away, her shoulders hunched. "But I'm myself," she muttered dismally, "whoever I am."

And with that, she shuffled off toward Second.

AVIS BEST

Avis was thinking about going outside when Perkins came through the window. She hadn't really been outside all day. She had been stuck in this stupid apartment all day, ever since she got back from Perkins's. She had been reading—a 750-page manuscript called *A World of Women*. Which "might be something for Julia Roberts," according to the cover letter from Victory Pictures. The cover letter also said she had to finish the book and get her report in by tomorrow. Because

Julia was waiting with baited breath to find out what Avis thought, har har har.

Anyway, the novel was garbage; she could hardly follow it closely enough to write the synopsis. And, of course, the baby had to be nursed and changed and played with and kept out of trouble. So by three-thirty, when Perkins came up the fire escape, Avis was only on page 400. The brilliant blue of the autumn sky was starting to fade to violet. She could see this happening above the brownstone cornices and it filled her with a growing sense of claustrophobic despair. She would never get out, she thought. The novel's prose had turned her mind to tar—it would take forever to finish it. And the baby was sitting under the folding card table, making a funny noise by putting his hand in his mouth, so she had to stop and smile at him every two minutes to let him know what a wonderful thing he was doing. And the sky was growing darker by the minute and soon the crowds would gather for the parade and there would be no point to going out anyway and she'd be stuck here for the rest of the night and she hated her life and she glanced up from manuscript to baby to window for maybe the seventieth time—and there was Perkins. Arms spread, face pressed to the pane. Well, her little heart just went pitty-pat.

She waved him in. Perkins ducked down under the sill and jumped to the floor.

"Pa!" said the baby. And he stuck his arm into his mouth up to about the elbow and added, "Arrragherageraggah . . ."

"Whoa, nice going," said Perkins, smiling at him. And then his smile vanished. "I need you, Ave."

"Jesus." She stood up. Her head was so heavy with *A World of Women* it felt like a cinderblock. She stared at the poet through her huge, square glasses. "You're all pale, Ollie. Have you eaten?"

"No, I don't need to eat."

"I have cold chicken in the refrigerator."

"Avis! My baby brother is wanted for a murder he didn't commit."

"What? Holy shit! Let me get the chicken."

"Avis . . ."

But she hurried into the kitchenette: getting him fed would help her to think. She bent into the refrigerator while he, trying to follow her, was waylaid by the baby. The baby had crawled out to him from under the card table. Perkins gave a quick flinch of annoyance, but the kid loved him; he couldn't just walk away. When Avis brought her aluminum foil-wrapped plate to the counter, Perkins was there with the baby on his hip. The baby pulled at his hair, crying "Pa! Pa! Pa!" and farting happily.

"He's hiding in my apartment," Perkins said. "The cops'll kill him if they hunt him down."

"Oh my God," Avis said. "Dark meat or white?"

"I gotta go out. I gotta see if I can find his girlfriend."

"Give me the baby. Here, take this."

She traded a drumstick for the baby. The baby complained as Perkins handed him over.

"Zach's not feeling well. He's gonna catch some z's," Perkins said. He wagged the drumstick at her. "Just do me a favor, okay? If the cops come, call down there. Two rings then hang up, then call back, that's our signal. And watch what you say on the phone."

"Okay, okay," she said quickly. She blinked across the counter at the poet's haggard, angular face. She felt worried and excited and warm for him all at once. Already, racing through her mind, were half-acknowledged, jumbled scenarios. Handsome Zachary. Persecuted. Brave. Or frightened. Loved her, his head buried in her breast, and she was prettier. She was Jessica Lange in *Country*. Or Oliver loved her for helping Zach . . . Avis was eager to be more involved in this. "I'll go down when he wakes up," she said. "I'll check on him."

"I should be back by then," said Perkins. He tore into the drumstick as he headed back toward the window. "Thanks, Avis."

"The baby goes down for an hour at six," Avis called after him, working it out. "I'll come down then and bring you guys some food."

"Yeah, forget the food." Perkins had one leg out the window. "He's got the quickstep."

"Ooh, poor guy," said Avis. (Zach was lying in bed, gazing up at her weakly. She was hovering over him wearing a nurse's cap.) "I'll bring chicken soup with rice then. That's good for that."

"Avis . . ." said Perkins. But then he only shook his head. He blew her a kiss and was gone, the fire escape rattling behind him.

Avis stood alone, watching after him, her baby wriggling in her arms.

NANCY KINCAID

The bus pulled away from the curb. The police sirens whooped and bayed. The sound seemed to spread out over the low-flung avenues. Dart up over the sidestreets. Echo down off the blue sky. The hounds seemed to be everywhere.

Then the bus gave a roar of its own. It rumbled downtown, smaller cars clinging to its wheels. Nancy looked out the rear window at the traffic scuttling along behind. She saw the shopping center falling away. And not a police car in sight. The sirens grew fainter under the bus's grumble. They grew fainter still as the bus gunned and picked up speed. Nancy faced front in her seat, the corner seat against the rear wall. She leaned her head back, her crown to the window. She gazed up dully at the emergency exit in the bus's ceiling. "Push up to open for ventilation."

I'm the one who's going to kill him, she thought blankly. She closed her eyes. *I'm going to kill someone. I'm a*

Murderer! Murderer! And you said you were nice!

But her inner voices were growing dim too, as if the bus were also leaving them behind. After a few moments, she became aware that her mouth was open. She ought to close it, she thought. But she just sat there, head back, eyes shut. Not even hearing the engine anymore. Not knowing what to think about or daydream. She felt herself floating in a strange, pulpy element: the blackness of not knowing who she was—or really, not knowing what she was *like.* Because she was still sure she was Nancy Kincaid. She just didn't know what that meant anymore. She didn't know what Nancy Kincaid was going to *do* from one moment to the next. What decisions she would make. What cruelties she was capable of, what kindnesses. How were you supposed to know that? How were you supposed to find it out?

I'm twenty-two years old. I work for Fernando Woodlawn. I live on Gramercy Park with my mom and dad . . .

The words dropped away, down into this pliant interior mass. Down and down and down, as if into a well, and she waited for the splash and it didn't come. And she slumped now in the corner, her mouth hanging open. The bus jostled her gently. *So sorry,* she thought. She felt the soft mother breasts against her. White sheets. Soft mother lips against her cheek and the smell of dishwater. *I was a teenager and I was angry and crazy and I'm so sorry.* The reassuring weight of her mother sitting on the end of her bed as she lay with the covers pulled up to her chin. The reassuring rhythm of her mother's voice, like lapping water. Storybook in her frail, red hands. White cover, black letters. *The Animal Hour. And Other Poems.*

What if we went off together into the hills
and on into the hills beyond the hills where the
    leaves are changing?
Where the first remark of gray among the branches
is insinuated in me now like something one
    learned before youth
and has, in consciousness, forgotten.

Her mother's voice like water. Water bearing Nancy away. Carrying her away in waves from the night bedroom. From the shadowed, half-visible hall threatening beyond the door. From the half-open closet and the monster's eye pressed to the crack. From the mutterings in the street and all the chill emptiness around her since her father fell in . . . fell in . . . Wait—there he was. *Oh, I was so angry about it.* She could see him falling. Down into the dark well where the words had gone. Daddy . . . Daddy fell in . . . Tumbling backward, his arms pinwheeling, his mouth agape . . .

Daddy!

Nancy started in her seat, her eyes coming open. She lifted her head and looked around her. Licked her dry lips. Tasted her dry mouth. A woman in a nearby seat cocked an apathetic eye at her. The other passengers—there weren't many—huddled over themselves, backs to her. Without thinking, she glanced at her wrist. No watch. Right. She remembered. They had taken her watch.

What you're experiencing is an episode of schizophrenia.

She glanced out the window. A suggestion of dark coming on over a low, drab, brick landscape. It got dark early this time of year, but still . . . She did not know how much time she had left.

Eight o'clock. Eight o'clock.

The bus pulled to the curb. The doors gave a whoosh and opened. Nancy got up quickly. Grabbed seat backs, went hand over hand up the aisle to the rear door. She pushed out, tumbled down the steps to the sidewalk. With a blast of exhaust behind her, the bus pulled away, left her alone.

She was standing on the shore of a desolate territory. Low buildings. Curtained windows. The first slate-blue of evening in the air. A few cars moving back and forth but no other pedestrians. Just a cluster of unshaven men at a tavern a few doors down. Black and white men, five of them, all smashed beyond comprehension. Gesturing at one another with great conviction. "Anudder ting: fauben at bish in sunight. Ha!" one of them said.

They turned when Nancy got off the bus: She was something to look at anyway.

"Hey, mama," one muttered.

She walked by them quickly, her back primly erect. When she figured she was safely past, she stole a quick look at them. They had gone back to their conversation, but a ghostly figure was watching her now from inside the tavern. A disheveled specter under the neon sign for Coors. A woman. Just as seedy as the men. Clothes torn, hair in tangles. Nancy met her eyes a moment. And then her guts plummeted as she realized it was . . .

Murderer!

Herself. Reflected in the dark tavern window.

Oh boy. Terrific.

It brought the whole muddle crashing back on top of her. *It's me! I'm the one. Look at me. I'm the one who's going to kill him! Jesus, just look!* She was past the tavern now. Facing forward again. Walking on. But that spectral stare, that glassy, baleful stare from the window . . . It walked with her, beside her. *I'm you. I'm who you are.* She was beginning to take a sort of grim satisfaction in torturing herself with it. Remembering the sweet doctor staring at her as the pain flooded up from his crushed testicles. The terror in Nurse Anderson's eyes as she yanked her head back. And then that poor rich lady—whom she had mugged, for Christ's sake. *Mugged! That's what you're like, Nancy,* she told herself, hurting herself, glad to hurt herself. *That's the sort of thing you do. You're bad, you're not nice, you're bad. Bad Nancy.*

The next thing she knew, she was heading downstairs. Moving down through the dank concrete of a subway entrance. She hadn't even been thinking about it. It had just taken care of itself. Now, she was slipping her stolen bill out of the waistband of her skirt. Out from under her famous letter opener. She was buying a token, pushing through the turnstile. And, she realized, she knew exactly where she was headed. She had known all along, in fact: that was part of the hurt, part of the misery of it. She knew where she was going and she hated it but it didn't matter. She couldn't make it stop.

I wanted to be a dancer! she thought, waiting for the train. But she had taken the job with Fernando. She had stopped looking for an apartment, even though she had wanted a place of her own. Her own actions had seemed to just happen to her. She had not seemed to do them herself. She made fatalistic little wisecracks and she complained to her friends—and then she went ahead and did exactly what she didn't want to do. She was not in control of things.

I wanted to be a dancer.

But somehow—she could not even remember how—she had turned into this instead.

Now, she was on the subway. Sitting in her corner seat, pressed into the corner, almost cowering there. There were nine or ten other passengers in the car, and they were all sort of ignoring her and keeping tabs on her at the same time. Just another bum on the train. Nothing dangerous, but peep over there now and then to make sure. She peeped back at them sullenly. The subway was getting closer to her destination. With every stop, she felt heavier inside. Sicker with herself. And the others just sat there. Reading newspapers. Stroking their children's hair. Why didn't they stop her? Why didn't anyone stop her?

City Hall. Her heart was beating harder now. Her tongue kept going to her lips to keep them wet. She couldn't be doing this again. It was crazy. She couldn't. But when the doors slid open—sure enough, she got out of her seat. She joined the small crowd exiting. She stepped out onto the platform. She couldn't make it stop.

A thin line of passengers were on the platform, waiting for the train, pressing in on it as the doors opened. She slipped through the line to the center of the station. She scouted out the long cavern. Scoped its pillars, behind its stairways. Two black men lounged on a bench. A woman hugged her briefcase to her chest, gazing off dreamily. No cops. Not a cop in sight. She started moving. Casually as she could. Sidling away from the exiting crowd toward the far end of the platform.

Nobody watched her go. She swallowed hard, turned and walked faster. She saw the station wall ahead. The white sign with its red lettering. "All persons forbidden to enter or cross tracks." And there the concrete ended and the blackness began. Blackness like the sludge inside her, and she thought: *Not again. I can't. Really.*

And then she had reached the end of the platform, the metal ladder there. She looked back once. Saw a beatnik-type near the stairs, watching her with wan interest. She ignored him. Took hold of the ladder. And lowered herself down onto the tracks.

She did not look back again. She walked quickly into the tunnel, hanging between the track and the wall. She tried to keep her eyes straight ahead, her mind straight ahead, like a laser, narrowed to a beam. But boy oh boy was her heart going now. Her pulse at her temple was like one of those small steel hammers: In case of emergency, take hammer and break glass. Her senses were heightened. Every aspect of the tunnel grew sharper as she went in deeper. The underground pillars loomed out of the murk. Bare bulbs burned like eyes amid pipes and wiring. The click of switches in the distance sounded like rifle shots. And every time she thought she had the mind-laser going, something scuttled suddenly: a rat? Something worse? Her eyes flicked swiftly over the four tracks as they fanned off into nothingness. Her breath trembled. But she kept walking. Fast. Straight ahead.

And there it was. A few yards away. That spot where the tunnel narrowed. Oh, she thought. Oh no. But she kept walking. And then the walls were rising up around her. The high corridor of snaking graffiti. Coiling letters. Tendrils of sprayed paint. She could hardly breathe at all now with her heart in her throat this way. She was in the ghost station again. The platform took shape, and the shapes of the abandoned bags and wiring on it. The smoky shapes of the graffiti on the wall above. And the shape, the silhouette, under the platform's ledge, of the little arched alcoves. The place where she had hidden her purse. Her gun.

I'm the one. I'm the one who is going to kill him.

She stopped. She felt her throat tighten as the smell wafted up to her. It stung her nostrils: that damp, living tang of decay. She glanced up: She'd heard a snap. Another switch on the tracks going over. She felt the first faint breeze. Saw the first creeping glow in the far tunnel. A train was coming. She had to get to work.

She ducked under the edge of the platform. Knelt down at the entrance to the alcove. Already, she could feel the ground shivering as the train came on. And that stench grew denser. It was a cloud around her. She swallowed thickly. Her stomach began to churn.

She felt the air stir on her neck. Glanced back over her shoulder. Saw the glow of the train's headlights spreading up over the tunnel walls. She held her breath and ducked her head into the alcove. She could see it as the tunnel grew brighter: the humped gray thing in there. The soft rotting thing.

She had to breathe. She turned her head and gasped and the stench swarmed into her mouth, into her lungs. She groaned and her stomach went all the way over. She held her breath again. Narrowed her eyes to slits. Reached out and shoved her hand into the mound at the back of the alcove.

The juicy mass closed around her hand, squeezed between her fingers. She gagged, her tongue coming out between her teeth. The ground was really bouncing under her knees now. The tunnel was beginning to fill with the rattle of the train, with the light. She worked her hand deeper into the muck and when she had to breathe this time it was like swallowing vomit. She dug around in the mound as the racket of the train grew louder, as the wind of it pushed at her and the glow spread.

And it wasn't there. The gun: It was gone. The cops must have gotten it. They must've searched the place and found it.

"Ah . . ." She gave an inarticulate cry. Pulled her hand free of the mound's suction. She worked her way to her feet. Staggered back from the platform until her heels touched the track rail. She gasped for breath. Her hair blew across her eyes. The train's rumble seemed to shake her from the inside.

She looked up to the platform. She was going to climb up there to get out of the train's way. She looked up and saw the spreading outglow play over the walls. As before, the graffiti seemed to come to life in the spreading light. The letters seemed to move. Great brown boas of paint seemed to squirm and wriggle. Slashes of green coiled and turned. Maroon swaths twisted.

And then one large black shape writhed violently amidst the others. It curled away from the rest and began to come toward her.

Nancy's lips parted. Even as the train's lights broke out of the tunnel, two circles of glaring light growing larger by the second, she could only stand, she could only stare. The shape that had broken from the wall was shambling toward her. It was hunched and enormous. It was leering at her, glaring at her from two marble eyes that caught the oncoming subway's light.

A man. It was a man. Jesus Christ. He lumbered toward her. Lumbered to the edge of the platform. Rose above her like a behemoth. Rose to the dark heights from which his eyes burned down at her. From which his gray grin gleamed.

His shoulders shook as if he were laughing, but she could not hear him above the roar of the train. He opened his mouth and lifted his arm as if he were laughing, and his mouth gaped wider.

And then he pointed something down at her face. And she saw it was the barrel of her gun.

OLIVER PERKINS

The light of the late October afternoon was dying over Sheridan Square. The sun was touching the flat roofs of the cafés, and the last rays of it were going golden on the fenced-in flora of the Viewing Garden. Long shadows spilled onto Seventh

Avenue. They fanned the flames of Perkins's dread: Time, he thought, was a-wasting.

He came into the square from West Fourth Street. Passed through to the corner and stood at the red light, absently wiping chicken grease off his fingers onto his jeans. He could feel the time passing, minute by minute. And it was only a matter of time before Mulligan tracked down his brother. When the traffic light changed, he charged across Seventh. His arms swinging, his shoulders hunched. He was thinking about Tiffany now. About how she would resist him. *I don't want to talk to you, Oliver. You know how you are. I'm not talking to you at all.* Then she would smile at him, that superior, ethereal smile of hers. His mouth worked as he thought of how he'd tell her off. He was itching to shove her back against a wall and shout the truth out of her.

The bookstore where she worked was called The Womyn's Room. It was on the ground floor of a yellowing brick building on Bleecker Street. Perkins barreled down Grove, just off the open square, deeper into shadow. Bleecker, at the next corner, was more shadowy still. Perkins was bent forward urgently, pushing forward with long, urgent strides as he reached the intersection.

And there he stopped. Pulled up like a reined-in horse. The bookstore was just across the street, a little to his right. A new red brick facade under the yellow brick. There were two large display windows full of books, framed by black metal. The front door was set in between them, forming an entrance alcove. The door within the alcove was swinging out.

And out, under the alcove, to the sidewalk's edge, stepped Detective Mulligan.

"Fuck me," was Perkins's comment.

He pulled back around the corner. Clung to the wall of the apartment building at the end of Grove. Peeked around the edge of it, feeling like Peter Lorre in some old spy film. Curly-haired, baby-faced Mulligan just stood there. Hands in his trench coat pockets. Eyelids batting behind the round wire rims. Perkins had to yank his head back as the lenses turned his way in a slow scan.

"I can't believe this," he said to the cold bricks against his cheek. He waited a full minute before he dared to peek his head out again.

Mulligan was moving by then. Walking to the black Dodge parked alone—illegally—at the curb. He slid in on the passenger side. Perkins could not see the driver, but he heard the engine fire up at once. The car pulled out. Perkins had to draw in again, like a turtle, as the Dodge sped past the corner.

The second the car was out of sight, Perkins resumed his charge. Strode across the street to the bookstore. In past the windows with their prim displays: clusters of an author's books, huddled together as if for warmth. Those photographs, the severe women, their grim intellects in their eyes.

He pulled the glass door back. Stepped into a small shop. The door hissed shut behind him. The warm amber of the wall-to-wall shelves embraced him; the smell of books, the stillness of them.

Trisha—or Leatherhead, as Perkins called her—was behind the counter, an octagon of low shelves in the middle of the room. Perkins stomped over to her impressively. Trish did not so much as look up. She was a woman in her twenties, pole thin. Even her head was a thin cylinder, topped with spiked white hair. Only the broad shoulders of her studded leather jacket gave her any bulk at all. She was leaning over an inventory list. She was chewing gum.

Perkins leaned in toward her, his fists pressed into two stacks of lesbian poetry.

"What'd you tell him, Trish?"

"Fuck off, Ollie."

"What'd you tell Mulligan?"

"Eat me."

"Where's Tiffany?"

She flipped him the finger. She chewed her gum.

"Look, Trish," Perkins said. "I know how you feel about me, okay? But try to understand. There are your feminist theories and feelings and opinions. And then there's reality. See? Reality's important. Your theories and feelings are meaningless. Now we're dealing with reality. Have you got that?"

She glanced up long enough to sneer around her spearmint. Perkins saw the five gold rings through her right nostril. He sniffed—they always made him want to sneeze. "It amazes me that you would just come in here and be so phallic," she drawled.

"Oh Christ."

"Do you really think I'm just going to accord you your masculine privileges?"

Oliver hung his head.

"We shouldn't even let you in here," said Trish, "the way you objectify women."

"Hey. Hey. I haven't objectified a woman in over a week. Can't a man change?"

"Lethal misogynist."

"Not lethal enough for you, baby."

"Your poems should be hung in effigy."

Perkins's face went red. His arms, braced against the books, trembled. "You can't make an effigy of a poem, Trish. It doesn't make sense. Now who do you want Tiffany to deal with, me or the fucking police?"

Something sparked in Trisha's eyes at that. She made a show of casually reviewing her inventory, mashing her gum with pistoning jaws. Finally, and without looking up, she said sullenly, "The cop said there'd been a murder." She raised her eyes to him. "That true?"

He nodded. "There's been a murder, yeah."

"Great. That's just great." Her lips twisted. "You bastards. You and your brother. What did you get her into?"

"Did you tell Mulligan where she is?"

"I don't know where she is. I didn't tell him anything. All right? Now why don't you just get out of here, semen-breath."

"It's me or the cops, Trish," Perkins said again. "She's gonna have to talk to one of us."

"Yeah? Which is worse?"

Perkins didn't answer. He wasn't sure.

"Shit," said Trisha. "Why don't you just fuck off, you macho shit. Damn you. You and your brother. Damn the two of you."

He was surprised by the red flood of rage in him. He wanted

to drag her over the counter by her leather jacket front, mash that sneering face a little. He backed away from her instead.

"I told her there was nothing in men," Trish muttered.

"Yeah," Perkins snapped. "I'll just bet you did, you jealous bitch."

Now it was Trisha's turn: She flushed scarlet. Her eyes grew damp. "Go suck some little boys, creep-o," she nearly shouted at him. "You do anyway."

"Yeah, yeah, yeah," he said.

And that's intellectual discourse in the Village, he thought, as he turned his back on her, waved her off.

He stomped to the door. He had his flattened palm braced against the metal frame.

"Hey!" Her bark stopped him but he didn't turn. "Hey," she said again. "Testicle-head. Hold on."

He glanced back over his shoulder. "What?"

There was a pause. A breath, a long breath; forlorn. "Are you actually telling me they're gonna arrest her?" Trish said.

"That's my guess, yeah."

"And what're you gonna do to her? Fuck her over somehow, I'll bet."

Perkins didn't say anything. He sensed he had her and he didn't want to muck it up. He came around slowly until he was facing her and, sure enough, she was wrestling with it, her mouth working, her chin lowered. He waited in silence; let her come to it on her own.

"Fucking pig cop," she said finally. "He'll go there eventually anyway." Still, Perkins kept quiet. She glanced up at him angrily. "All right," she said. "All right, you shithead, but you better not fuck with this. You better not fuck her up anymore."

"At least I'll give her a chance to explain," Oliver said. That was true enough, at least.

Trisha made a short, nasty gesture. She had pulled something from a pocket. A small rectangle of paper. She tossed it onto the countertop. She looked away.

Perkins decided she had gone as far as she would. He walked back to her, his tread heavy. The paper on the counter was white with blue markings. It was a schedule for the Metro-north trains out of Grand Central. He picked it up. It was the schedule for the trains to Scarsdale.

"I found it in her desk," the woman said. "This morning, when she didn't show up for work. I called her there. A couple of times. But there's no answer."

The schedule was marked. Perkins could see two small scratches that seemed to have been made by a pen that had run out of ink. One scratch was near the 12:03 out of New York; the other was by the 4:35 return, which arrived in the city just a few minutes after five.

"I don't even know if it's for today," Trisha said. "It's just she hasn't gone home like that in ages and I . . ." She hardened at once. "If you give it to the cops, Oliver, so help me God, I'll kill you dead."

He nodded at her. "Thanks, Trish."

"I swear it, Ollie."

But he had already turned away again. He was already heading back toward the door.

NANCY KINCAID

"*Bang!*"

The man waved the gun barrel in Nancy's face. She heard him shout the word above the wind and rattle of the onrushing train.

"Bang! Bang!"

The train's lights beat down on her from the right. Her peripheral vision was wiped out by the glare. The deep, black bore of the gun swallowed the rest of her sight, and all her thoughts, every thought but of the instant death in there, the coming flash of fire. She breathed hoarsely. Stood frozen in that black thought. The man on the platform kept waving the gun. Nancy's mouth opened. She put her hands up.

"Put your hands up!" the man screamed.

She put her hands up higher. She felt the ground bouncing under her feet. The rail hot with vibrations against her heel. Her body had turned to liquid, her will was empty air. She couldn't move. She stared, her whole heart pleading.

"Bang!" The man waved the gun in her eyes. He leaned down at her so that his face caught the glare of the train. It was an intelligent, cultivated face. Sandy-haired, sad-eyed, full-lipped. Etched with a grin of inner agony. "I know who you are!" he shouted—and he really had to shout now. The roar of the train seemed to be expanding, filling the place. The light was blinding. The wind blew Nancy's hair across her wide eyes, her open mouth. "FBI!" the man screamed. "Extraterrestrial FBI! Trying to get into my brain, aren't you? Trying to take over my brain! EXTRATERRESTRIAL MOTHERFUCKERS EVERYWHERE! You can't fool me, you federal space fucker!"

Nancy stared.

He's experiencing an episode of schizophrenia . . .

The madman took another step toward her. She whimpered and leaned away from that deep black bore. He jabbed it toward her nose, about a foot above her nose. She could see all the way into it, into the dark of it, and everything else was white and roaring. The train shrieked—its horn stabbed her ear—a wild animal shriek of warning.

"Please!" she screamed.

"I know who you are, you federal fucker!" She felt the barrel pressing down at her. She felt the heat of it. It was ready to explode.

"Die!" he shouted and the train's horn shrieked again.

Nancy's hand shot out—her right hand—slapping the man's gun arm away to the side. He pulled the trigger. Nancy screamed once more as the pistol snapped into the shivering thunder. Flame and smoke blew from the barrel into the white glare. But she had already dodged away from it. She did not know—could not think—what she was doing, but she had dodged to the right and toward the platform. She had seized the madman's wrist in her left hand. She was spinning in the small space with her right hand balled into a fist. The train was an avalanche of noise and light, filling everything, moments away.

She yanked hard at the madman's arm. Yanked him down with her left hand and slugged him in the jaw with her right. Too crazed for pain, she still felt the shock in her elbow and shoulder. Felt her knuckles popping against his gristly chin. The pull and the blow brought the madman over the platform's edge. Screaming, he fell, arms pinwheeling . . .

Daddy?

Down into the white light. Down onto the track. She gaped at him, horrified, as the massive silver front of the engine ramrodded toward them both. The crazy man lay pinned to the track in the icy white light. There was no time even for him to look afraid. He just stared up into the light in dull amazement. And Nancy had no time to help him. She had to get up on the platform, or under it. She had to get out of the way or she'd be crushed between steel and concrete.

The crazy man lifted his arm before his face as the train rushed at him.

Murderer! Murderer! Nancy thought.

And she leapt onto the track. She straddled the madman. Grabbed his shirtfront and hauled up on him. He was too big, too heavy for her. He wouldn't budge. The train ploughed at them. She felt it at her back. She felt her ears would burst from the thunder, the insane harpie shrieking of the horn. The crazy man stared stupidly past her at the train. He still had his arm up for protection.

Nancy shouted. She hauled him up. She dragged him to one side, over the rail, off the tracks. She tossed him under the platform as if he were a doll. Threw herself after him, on top of him. Clung to him as the lights flashed past her, as the knife-sharp wheels of the train churned past her over the tracks at a distance of inches. She clung to the madman and sucked in his sour smell, the smell of his urine and filth, and the electric smoke of the train. The engine flashed by and then a car and then another and another, flash, flash, flash.

The train howled once more, as if in triumph. And then it was rattling away, the thunder fading, the dark returning. It was past them. It was gone. The clatter retreated. Faded away.

In the sudden quiet, Nancy groaned. She leaned over the side of her crazy pal and vomited. A thin green gruel burned out over her teeth.

"Eagh," the crazy man muttered. "How humiliating."

"Shut up," said Nancy. She rolled off him onto the ground. Rolled over onto her back, her arm flung out over the ties. Her fingers brushed the handle of the gun, which lay discarded now at the center of the tracks. She stared up stupidly into the darkness above her. "Just shut the fuck up," she whispered hoarsely.

OLIVER PERKINS

Twenty to five.

Perkins stood at the marble balustrade overlooking the main concourse of Grand Central Terminal. He felt harassed by the time.

He was at the café on the balcony. Hemmed in by suits at either shoulder, men and women drinking at the tables around him and the bar behind him. He leaned over the balustrade, gripping a mug of Sam Adams beer.

Below, on the floor of the huge concourse, streams of commuters flowed in all directions. They flowed into the concourse from the long hallways on every side, and out through the marble archways that led to the tracks. Under the vast cerulean vault above, where the zodiac was painted on ass-backward with weak light bulbs twinkling here and there for stars, the people swirled and intertwisted. They eddied and turned around the information kiosk at the center of the place.

The kiosk was a brass gazebo with an archaic clock atop it. The hands on the clock read twenty to five. Perkins sipped the foam off his beer.

He should've gone home, he thought. He should've gone back to check on Zach. The dread was climbing into his throat, almost nausea now. It was getting harder and harder to think. He should've just headed the fuck on home.

But what then? What could he do then besides stand by and watch while Zach turned himself in? While Mulligan and the feds tore him limb from limb?

The lacy black hands on the clock atop the gazebo swept around slowly. Four forty-five. A whirr of wordless voices rose up steadily toward the backward stars. He thought about Tiffany. He thought about finding her, questioning her about the body in the mews, about the photograph of her with Fernando Woodlawn. He had phoned her mother's house in Scarsdale, but there was no answer. He had decided to come here to wait for the 5:02, the train she had marked on the schedule. He had come reluctantly. He kept telling himself that he ought to go home.

The man in the information kiosk had told him that the train would come in on track 28. Perkins could see the number painted over one of the marble archways below. He watched the arch and sipped his beer. He hoped the beer would cut through the gel of dread that clogged him now from belly to brain. But no, it was going to take a lot more beers than one to do that. He drank more deeply. He thought about Tiffany. He shuddered. Grimaced on the streaming rush below.

He remembered the first time he had seen her. She was already living with Zach by then. Oliver had never even heard of her and then one day he went to visit Zach at home and she was just there, just living with him. They had met at the Pennsylvania retreat apparently. The Christian place Ollie had yanked Zach out of after his second crack-up. She had stayed on there alone for a while after Zach left. But apparently she missed her snookum's mystic brilliance. She had to be with him.

"He was operating about three astro-levels above everyone else there," she explained to Ollie, when he met her. "That's why his aura got so clouded over. It was the effort of trying to shine through their misunderstandings."

"Yeah," Oliver said. "Yeah, that must've been it."

Zach and Tiff had looped their arms over each other and beamed at him. Two cosmic goofballs in love.

Perkins shook his head as he remembered. Even the thought of her made his tongue go sour. The thought of her treacherous, deep, doe eyes. He glanced up a moment at the stars painted on the ceiling. The April constellations rolling eastward into winter. She believed in astrology. She believed that dreams were messages from God. She believed that Jesus had a white aura because Mary had conceived from the divine energy radiated by the star of Bethlehem. "You know," she told him once, "it's just so hard for me to get it into my head that you're actually Zach's brother." She had that Venus face, that voice like music. She tilted her head at him when she spoke. "I mean, his astro-level is so high, you know, his aura is so pure and he understands so much and, I mean, you . . ."

Perkins snorted. He tilted back his mug and let the beer ripple into him. The suit standing on his right had moved off toward the bar. Now, when he set his mug down on the balustrade, he saw a woman in a green dress seated at one of the café tables nearby. She had one leg crossed over her knee, the black shoe swinging out and back, out and back. She was sipping a soda water and lime. She looked up at Perkins and he looked away. He scanned the concourse grimly. Leaned against the flat cold stone and gazed down at the steadily rising flood of rushing people under the man-made heavens. The hands on the kiosk clock had moved closer to five.

You don't understand anything, Oliver, not anything. That's what Tiffany had said to him. That night. That night a year ago. It made his guts curdle to remember it, and he detested her and he detested himself and he was sick of it. Full of dread and sick of it. *You don't understand anything.*

This time, when he glanced down, the woman in the green dress held his gaze. She considered him; she let her lips soften. Perkins had the almost overwhelming urge to hurl himself onto his knees before her. Wrap his arms around her, bury his nose in her groin. Nuzzle her like a puppy dog, sniffing for sex and comfort and a little respite from his loneliness.

Probably unwise, he thought, all in all. He offered her a sad smile, then turned back to the balustrade, back to the view below.

The hands on the kiosk clock touched five.

That night, he thought. That night when he had found Zachie drugged out of his mind. Lying on the floor of the mews bedroom, mumbling about the goddamned teacup and brotherly love. Where was Tiffany then with her fucking astro-levels? She should have taken care of him a little bit. She should have opened her eyes and seen what was happening to him. No. She showed herself that night. She showed herself in her true colors . . .

He grimaced again, an expression of pain. His stomach was sour and his heart was lead. He thought of this afternoon: finding Zach at his apartment; Zach and him together. When they'd been kidding around, laughing like that—it was the first time since he could remember that his loneliness had lifted a little. That pall of loneliness.

Jesus Christ, he thought. *Jesus Christ, what have we done?*

Just then, out of the corner of his eye, he caught the movement at track 28. He turned and saw the staggered flow of commuters break through the marble archway, spread out across the grand concourse. He straightened. His eyes picked over each person who stepped under the arch, followed each figure as it entered the surrounding currents. The flow through the archway stalled a second, then began again in a fresh gout.

And Perkins reared up at the balustrade, stunned for a second by what he saw.

Out through the arch, there had come a small, slim figure. Its head was bowed, its face obscured by the brim of an oversized baseball cap. But he recognized the outfit right away. That crazy quilt shirt, the coat of many colors: How could he miss it? The jeans, torn at the knees. The red canvas bag the figure was carrying . . .

"What the hell?" he said. "Zachie?"

The figure moved across the concourse toward a corridor of lighted food concessions. There was a subway entrance there, just across from a magazine stand. As the figure moved to the center of the concourse, it turned. Looked up at the information kiosk, at the antique clock that now read 5:09.

Perkins saw the profile in that moment, and said nothing. His lips parted and the air came out of him silently.

The figure hurried on across the concourse toward the subways. And it was not Zach. It was Tiffany.

NANCY KINCAID

The gray-haired man with the folded *Times* would go home tonight and tell his wife that he had seen a monster. He was a stocky, staunch old Wall Street crusader. Florid skin, pulpy nose. Planted on the subway platform like an oak, waiting for the next train. He would chuckle as he said it: "So I'm just standing there waiting for my train when this . . . this *creature* came crawling up onto the platform. The way it looked, it must've been living in the tunnels for years! I've read about that sort of thing . . ."

That's how Nancy imagined it anyway as she climbed up the ladder off the tracks. The way the old guy was staring at her made her want to shrivel up to nothing. She was painfully aware of what a mess she was. Her blouse in shreds, her bra sticking out of it. Her face and arms streaked with dirt and blood. And then, when she got a whiff of herself . . . Climbing onto the platform on her hands and knees, her head hung down. She smelled her urine and her vomit. Her rank sweat. The traces of that juicy garbage in the alcove. This guy, this Wall Street guy, made a face at the very sight of her; and who could blame him?

She pushed herself to her feet. Felt the weight shifting at her groin and smoothed her skirt down nervously. She had the gun hidden in the front of her panties now. She'd lost the letter opener in her fight with the madman, and she couldn't find her purse, but she had hung on to the gun. She could feel it, heavy against her pubic hair, warm and somehow vital against her flesh. She looked around to see if anyone noticed it bulging through her skirt. But only the stalwart businessman was looking at her at all, and he was staring at her grimy cleavage. The rest of the crowd was gazing off to the left, watching the oncoming lights of the next train.

She turned her profile to the businessman, ignored him. She shuffled to the edge of the platform. She was on the uptown side now. She had crossed over in the tunnel. As she was limping back toward the light, she had seen the train— the one that had nearly crushed her. It had been stopped before the downtown platform. She had seen the transit police pouring into the station there. Blue uniforms weaving between the gray suits and the tweed skirts and jackets. They were searching for her. They had seen her and the madman on the tracks. She had scurried away from them, across the tunnel, between the columns, to the other side. She was going uptown anyway. She was going to Gramercy Park.

She had decided to head for home. To see her mother. She didn't know where else to go. Her address was the only clue to her life that she had. And if her mother didn't know her, if her mother didn't know who she was, *what* she was . . . Well, then she was lost for sure, forever.

The uptown train sliced smoothly into the station. Clean silver cars flashing by, slowing to a stop. The doors slid open and Nancy limped wearily into the car. Several of the passengers glanced up at her. When she sat down, the woman in the seat next to her got up, moved away.

The train took off. Nancy stared straight ahead. Clasped her hands between her knees, hunched her shoulders. Clutched her misery to herself. She felt like crying. Her mind kept showing her a movie of the subway tunnel. The glare of the train lights. The glare in the wild, agonized eyes above her. The bore of that gun, the sudden death ready to explode out of that gun . . .

That man, she thought, shuddering. That madman. She began to tremble as she remembered his dull face caught in the subway lights, pinned on the tracks. His arm raised uselessly before the onrushing train.

You are experiencing an episode of schizophrenia . . .

She had to hug herself to get the trembling to stop. That's what he was, she thought. That man. He was a schizophrenic. Just like me.

At the end, in the darkest place of all . . . She remembered the merry gaze, the quiet, merry voice of Billy Joe Campbell, the crazy man who had accosted her at Bellevue. *In the darkest place of all, there is a fearsome creature,* he had said. *The Other; the self whom, above everything, you wish not to be.*

Well, that was him, all right, she thought. That nut case with the gun. That was definitely a self she would prefer to avoid. Living in the dark like that. Drooling in the dark. Screaming out fantasies about federal agents from Mars; extraterrestrial brain snatchers; murder at eight o'clock; at the Animal Hour . . . Oh yes, she too could have a career as a Crazy Subway Guy.

Only if you have the courage to embrace that self can you learn the magic word . . .

"Ugh." She let out a little moan, shivering. And then caught herself. Huddled into her stink. Muttering. Shuddering. She stole a glance around the crowded subway car. All those faces against the wall. The people standing at their silver poles. Why, to them, she already *was* the Horrid Thing. The Creature from the Subway Tunnel. They were probably all staring at her really, secretly. Peeking secretly at the bulge

of the gun in her panties. They were probably all just waiting
for the next stop to start shouting for the police . . .

Suspicious, her eyes traveled over the crowd. The Black
Secretary. The Warehouseman in the plaid shirt. The two
Businesswomen. And then, also, here and there, mingled with
the others, strange beasts. The white-skinned Vampire between the secretary and a clerk. A furry Wolfman behind the
businesswomen. A ghoulish Monk at the warehouseman's
shoulder. *Hey, wait a minute,* she thought. What was going
on here, anyway? Everyone was secretly watching *her* but did
anyone else even *see* these monstrosities?

She had forgotten it was Halloween.

Twenty-third Street. She saw it with a start, as if coming
awake. This was her station. She stood up quickly and joined
the small gush through the doors to the platform. She kept
her eyes turned down as she shuffled behind the crowd. A
policeman stood at the stairs, scanning faces. She looked away
as she shuffled past him.

She came up onto Park Avenue South. She was surprised
to see how dark it was. It must be after five already. At least.
The clear autumn blue of the sky was gone. A violet dusk
hung over the broad double avenue. The string of traffic lights
at each corner to the north burned green in the darkling air,
all the way up to the bright facade of Grand Central. Then
the lights changed and burned bright yellow; then bright red.
The thick rush hour traffic halted. Great buses grumbled, and
white headlights glowed in the deep blue air.

Three hours left, she thought. She stood on the corner,
looking around, looking for a clock. But something else
caught her eye. She turned and found herself peering into the
broad display window of an electronics store. A Newmark
and Lewis right there on the corner. "Halloween Deals!"
declared orange cardboard letters pasted to the glass.

Oh, she thought dully. That explained the monsters in the
subway car. There were monsters here too. A nearly life-sized
cardboard Frankenstein, his arms outstretched. A witch stirring her brew. A cardboard skeleton on the glass door with
yellow eyes and an evil grin and worms and rats squirming in
his rib cage.

But that's not what had caught her attention. What had made her turn was something in the display itself. Nine television sets glowing in the center of the window. Twenty-inch Sonys, stacked together on shelves, three on top of three on top of three. Each had the same picture. A pretty coffee-skinned newswoman peering out earnestly. Must be the five o'clock news, Nancy thought.

She gazed at the TVs absently. Hadn't there been something else? Something on the screen just a moment ago? She had caught a glimpse of it out of the corner of her eye, hadn't she? Something familiar, something that had stirred her memory . . .

For another moment, she gazed through the window at the nine newswomen. All the same, all surrounded by cardboard bats and ghoulies, draped with Halloween crepe. Then she shook her head. No. It had just been a sensation. A glitch. Like déjà vu. She began to turn away.

And the picture changed. She hesitated. She stood there on the sidewalk, this ragamuffin in her tattered blouse. She forgot, for a moment, her filth-streaked skin. The weight in her underpants. The rank smells coming off her. And she gazed through the store window at the nine television sets, the nine pictures. They were pictures now of a young woman's face.

Do I know her?

She was a pretty girl, wearing one of those graduation hats with the tassel. High rosy cheeks and a shy smile. Glistening brown hair to her shoulders. Blue eyes.

I know her . . .

The sight of her made Nancy's stomach contract with fear. *The Other; the self whom, above all, you wish not to be.*

And now the picture—all nine pictures—had changed again. There was a video shot of a house now. A small house. White brick fringed with red ivy. Shaded by a maple tree on a small tree-lined lane. And it made the fear worsen: It was like a memory, a threatening memory, just out of reach. The ragged, smelly young woman stood there, gazing at it, licking her lips. *What. What is it?*

And again, the picture changed. A quick cut, almost simultaneous on all nine sets. On all nine sets, men carried a stretcher out of the house. A stretcher with a black shape on it. A black body bag.

I know this. I know this. Damn it. Her stomach was sloshing around now like a washing machine. Her breath was quickening, her pulse was like a drum. And yet she felt at the same time as if she were floating away. Drifting off above her own body, this physical cauldron, its weird, unthinking fear.

She watched the TVs as if hypnotized. Another cut. More people in the narrow lane outside the little house. Policemen striding purposefully past the cameras. The camera shakily panning down to a plastic bucket in one cop's hand. The camera zoomed in. The bucket—nine times the bucket—filled the screen—one bucket on every screen. And Nancy's hand rose slowly, her dirty hand. She pressed it to her throat. She felt like she was strangling. She was so frightened . . .

"Oh!"

She gasped. Her hand flew from her throat to her mouth. A man was walking toward her, nine times, on nine screens. A man in jeans. Black hair, almost to his shoulders. Weary eyes. She knew him, yes. Those weary, lonesome, lovelorn eyes.

But I . . . I made him up!

She couldn't mistake him. The sharp planes of his face, the lived-in lines. It was her poet! The poet she had dreamed about. The suffering artist who had put his naked arms around her. She had fantasized him! She had wished for those sad eyes to turn to her. To look up from the pages on his desk to where she lay naked beneath the sheet in his garret . . . And there he was! Walking down the alley, his shoulders hunched. Holding up his hand to ward off the reporters' microphones. The microphones converging on him. Policemen flanking him, escorting him to their car. Nancy's fear had spread all through her, and yet she wondered at it too: She had fantasized him and there he was, right there, he was . . .

The pedestrians heard her cry out. There were a lot of pedestrians on the sidewalk around her—it was rush hour now. The pavement was rhythmic with their homeward footsteps. The darkening air was alive with their vital eyes. She cried out and they heard her and glanced her way. Glanced at this pitiful, slack-jawed, staring thing, this filthy, muttering rag of a girl. They veered to go around her safely as she stood there, oblivious to them, gaping at the nine televisions in the Newmark and Lewis window. Gaping at the nine faces on the nine sets, all the same.

And no one—none of the pedestrians—noticed that the face she was staring at—the nine faces on the nine TVs—was her own.

But it was. Nancy shook her head for a moment, unable to take it in. There she was, nine times, three on three on three, staring back out at herself. Another second and the truth of it got through to her. She broke from her trance. She bolted forward. She ran forward to the glass door with the worm-eaten skeleton. Pushed through into the store.

And now, she was surrounded by herself. Everywhere—on both long side walls of the store—in the center shelves that ran from front to back—everywhere, her own face stared from screens of various sizes. It was a still photo, a color picture faintly out of focus. But she saw the broad cheeks, the strong jaw softened by the fall of curling hair. The direct, strong, honest eyes.

There I am! she thought, turning from set to set, drinking in her old self. *There I am! I found me! There . . .*

From somewhere, some speaker somewhere, a newsman's voice was telling his story in short hammer strokes. She tried to concentrate, tried to listen, but then . . .

"Miss?"

At first she did not know where the voice was coming from. Soon enough, though, she saw. A store clerk. A tubby Indian in a sweat-stained white shirt, his red tie loosened at his throat. He was hurrying toward her down the aisle. Waddling between all her faces as they rose up the wall, as they ran along the shelves.

"Miss . . ." He was shaking his finger at her angrily. "You cannot come here. Dressed like that. You must go."

". . . as outraged law officers promise to work relentlessly," the newsman was saying.

209

The store clerk waddled toward her, belly first. "Excuse me. Excuse me, Miss."

". . . sifting clues around the clock . . ."

I have to listen to this, she thought.

"You are not buying something," said the store clerk like an angry hen.

". . . trying to solve the savage murder . . ."

"Out, out, out, out."

". . . of Nancy Kincaid . . ."

"What?" said Nancy.

But the store clerk was upon her. His round belly pushing her toward the door. His finger waggling in her face. "You are not buying something dressed in this way. You must go."

She staggered back from him. Staring, open-mouthed, as her face—as all her faces—flicked away to nothing on the walls and the shelves. The coffee-skinned anchorwoman returned.

"Elsewhere in the city tonight," she said, "firefighters in Brooklyn are working to contain a blaze that . . ."

"Brooklyn?" said Nancy. "But what . . . ?"

The savage murder of Nancy Kincaid?

"You must go!" the store clerk screeched in his high-pitched Indian accent.

You mean I'm not the murderer? I'm the goddamned victim?

"What's happening?" Nancy cried out.

"I will call the police!" said the store clerk.

He came on hard, driving her back, sending her staggering back until she was at the door. She wanted to throw her hands up at him. She wanted to scream: For God's sake! Leave me alone! Can't you see I'm dead!

But the store clerk reached out past her head. Shoved the door open behind her.

"Out, out, out," he said, bellying her backward.

The pedestrians passing on the sidewalk glanced up briefly as Nancy was forced out among them. She stood still in their scurrying midst, staring at the store door as it swung shut with a pneumatic hiss.

But what the hell . . . ? she thought. *What the hell is happening?*

She stared at the glass door; at the new evening reflected there; the televisions glowing and flickering within; the skeleton hanging before her. That skeleton, worm-infested, crawling with rats: It was staring out at her. Grinning and staring with his yellow eyes, out from behind the reflection of her own terrified face.

OLIVER PERKINS

Perkins bolted from the balustrade. Shouldered his way through the bar crowd, then short-stepped down the sweep of marble stairs to the concourse. His first thought was to run straight across the floor. To grab her arm. Spin her toward him, shouting in her face. *Tiffany, what the fuck is going on?*

But he hung back. He watched as she ran ahead of him. Weaving her way through the streams of commuters. Across the vaulted canyon, by the marble arches along the walls. She clutched her red bag tightly. Kept her head ducked down, her face hidden by the baseball cap, her hair tucked up under it. She ploughed grimly through the gaps in the crowd. Moving urgently, by all the looks of it. Heading toward some definite destination.

Why did she come back? Perkins thought. He slipped through the lines and crowds behind her. Moved after her steadily, keeping her in view. His whole body seemed to be pulsing and tightening, anxiety and excitement making him jittery, breathless. His thoughts pulsed too, little electric bursts of them: *Where did she go? What was she doing? Why did she come back? Damn her, why did she have to come back?* "Excuse me," he said softly, as he worked his way around the shoulders of a rushing businessman. He was not even trying to get close to Tiffany anymore. He was following her, plain and simple.

He slid around an elderly woman, pushed between a pair of backpacking kids. He watched her over the heads of the crowd, through the spaces between their bodies. He kept moving after her. Tiffany had now reached a subway entrance. She stopped there. Perkins pulled up short, about fifteen yards behind. He let the crowd converge in front of him. Ducked down, hoping to hide behind them, but catching glimpses of her still. He saw her turn, slowly; turn her head to scan the vast terminal with big, hunted eyes. Did she know she was being followed? Could she pick him out? He couldn't tell. He saw her ashen cheeks, the thin line of her white lips.

You don't understand anything, Oliver.

And then he saw her take a breath—and she darted into the entranceway.

He moved forward quickly, afraid of losing her in the crowd. But when he came into the entrance, he spotted her at once. That colorful quilt shirt was easy to see. He tailed it down the stairs into the station. Through the turnstiles. Across the low-ceilinged underground plain of columns and signs and stairwells. She moved with the other travelers, with their quick, synchronized steps. He kept her in view: the movement of her hips, the way her arm went out at the elbow as she hurried down another flight of stairs to the train platform . . .

She had worn black that night, he remembered. *The night he had found Zach drugged and loony at the mews. He had taken his brother to St. Vincent's Hospital and called Tiffany from there and she had shown up wearing black. Black jeans, a black turtleneck. Her black hair pulled tight behind her with the silver streak woven into the ponytail. Her face had been drawn and very pinched and white. She had looked tired to Perkins, cross and unattractive.*

She got on a number 7 train now, crosstown, and he got on, one car behind her. He worked his way to the storm door, where he could see through the glass panels from his car into hers. He leaned his shoulder against the door and watched her. Sitting there with the red bag on her lap. Staring into space, miserable and pale. Perkins wiped his mouth nervously.

The doctors had kept Zach at the hospital overnight. Perkins had taken Tiffany back to her apartment: the railroad flat in the East Village, hers and Zach's. She had sat on her bed with her hands hanging down between her knees. Looking straight ahead of her. He had seen her in the dresser mirror as he turned to go. He had wanted to scream at her. He had wanted to grab her by the shoulders and shake her. All her mystical horseshit. Why hadn't she taken better care of his brother?

The train pulled to a stop at Forty-second Street. She got off there, and so did he. Once again, he followed her through the wide, low underground caverns. She was going faster now. Casting little glances side to side at the men and women walking around her. Did she sense him there? Did she know somehow he was behind her? His nerves throbbed in him to the rhythm of his footsteps. His footsteps echoed in the broad underground passage, the echo lost in the echoing footsteps of the crowd.

"Well . . ." he had said, and moved toward the door.

"Don't go." Tiffany had not even looked up at him. She had sat on the bed, stared straight ahead, and her pale face had begun to tremble. And then she buckled forward, covering her face with her hand. He had gone to her, sat next to her on the bed. Put his arm around her, thinking, Well, why didn't you watch out for him, damn it? But he hated to see a woman cry. She had pressed her cheek against his shoulder. He had felt her tears dampening his shirt and stroked her hair. She had looked up at him desperately. "Oh God, Oliver, oh God," she'd said. And then he had kissed her.

He swallowed the bitter taste in his mouth as he watched her moving ahead of him. Why the hell had he had to kiss her? Why the hell did it have to happen at all? He watched her vanish and reappear in the hurrying crowd. Caught glimpses of her hips switching and remembered Mulligan's photograph and her white, naked ass. The nape of her neck looked bare and delicate with her hair all piled up under the baseball cap . . . Christ. Christ, he had known Zach loved her. Even when it was happening, he had known she was the only woman Zach had ever loved. He had told himself that it was nothing; just this one urgent moment with her. He had told himself that they both just needed comfort on a rotten, lonesome night when things had gone wrong. And then, oh Jesus, how he had ploughed into her. How he had pistoned into her, crying out as she cried out, as she tore at his shoulders with her frantic fingers. Her body had felt soft under the cotton turtleneck, but when she stripped the shirt away she was sinewy and hard. Her skin was dark, her breasts were small and sharp, her thighs clamped him and he could not stop touching her, nipping at her, driving into her soft mouth with his tongue. He had come with his powerful arms wrapped around her, holding her tightly to him and moaning her name in a way he did not like to remember.

Tiffany boarded the West Side train. Perkins pulled up a second, still trying to swallow that taste that would not go down. Then he went in, one car behind her. Dashed through the doors as they were sliding closed. Snaked swiftly through the jam of workers, secretaries, execs. Pushed to the storm door, so as not to lose her as the train pulled out, as it picked up speed.

He pressed against the door and peered through its glass panel into Tiffany's car. He saw her, sitting against the right wall around the center. And then the undulating movement in the car caught his eye and he saw the rest of it. He saw the celebration.

It was a party of freaks. All through the car. Human hybrids, mutant beasts. Dancing in the aisle, arms raised, hips swaying. Standing on the seats, their heads thrown back, their chests forward: howling at the ceiling till they lost their balance and tumbled into the arms of the creatures below. Cowled, chalk-faced ghouls; zombies in pinstripe suits; cadavers in lacy slips dry-humping top-hatted Mr. Hydes. And every centaurlike combination of the sexes—women with padded jockstraps, bearded men with padded bras, indefinable assemblages of curves and bulges and body hair—fandangoing with one another, bottom to bottom, crotch to crotch, in the swaying, jam-packed car.

Perkins peered through the glass. Turned and glanced at

his own car: the sedate gathering of workers crushed against one another, wriggling to find space to read their evening tabloids. He turned back to the glass panel and peered through at the bizarre celebration. And then he noticed Tiffany again, and caught his breath. She was gazing right at him.

She was gazing desperately up at the glass panel from her seat. Smiling an unhappy, mendicant, despairing little smile. Gazing right at him. Or was she? A second later, she had turned away again and was staring blankly into the wild scene before her. He wasn't sure if she had seen him or not.

The train pulled into the West Fourth Street station. The creatures in the next car howled in unison: "Halloweeeeen!" They poured out the doors. Perkins pressed his face to the glass, his view obscured by the mob of them.

Then the car was clear. He could see again. Tiffany was gone. And the subway doors were closing.

He leapt to them. Caught them as they shut. Grunted as he forced them ajar. They retracted a moment and he slipped through. He stood on the platform, looking this way and that until he caught sight of her quilted shirt again. She was in the midst of a huddle of monstrosities, moving toward the stairs. He followed, rising up after them into the blue evening.

As he stepped out into the chill air, he checked his watch. It was nearly six. The parade wouldn't start for an hour, but Sixth Avenue was already lined with spectators. Some were in costumes, some in street clothes. Some had taken up their viewing posts by the police barricades along the sidewalks. Others, most, strolled in a heavy flow past the broad display windows of the low malls. Vendors were setting up their tables before the windows. They were hawking noisemakers to the passersby, and domino masks bordered with flashing colored lights.

The avenue itself was cleared of traffic. Policemen patrolled freely on it, pacing up and down. Perkins clutched a little at the sight of so many of them, so close to home, so close to Zach. But he couldn't do anything about it now. Tiffany was getting away from him. Heading uptown, quicksilver, slipping through the dense crowd, zig and zag. Perkins had to lift up on tiptoe to watch her Mets cap weaving ahead of him.

He followed her—and he wanted to stop following her. He felt she was leading him on now, taking him somewhere he did not want to go. He wanted to let her disappear, let the whole thing disappear . . . "Excuse me, excuse me," he murmured as he worked his way around the strolling people. He could not stop himself. He felt powerless, as in a dream. As in a dream, he had a horrible sense of premonition. And it was building . . .

He looked up. Ahead of him, darkening against the dusk, the spires and turrets, the brick and tracery of the Jefferson Market Library rose up out of its surrounding cluster of trees.

"Oh hell, sister, that was wrong." That's what he'd said to her when they were finished. He had sat on the edge of the bed, his head in his hands. Wishing he could wriggle out of his own skin. Get away from his own remorse.

"Oliver. Don't say that." She had sat up, the sheet falling from her breasts. She had put her hand on his shoulder. He turned away from her. "I needed you," she said softly. "I needed you. Really." He wanted to tell her to shut up. He wanted to get the hell away from her. She leaned her head against his back, her soft cheek against his skin. "This has been getting me all so confused," she said. "The way he's been. What he's been talking about." He heard her sniff. He felt one of her tears roll down his spine. "I mean, he's so wise, he sees so much, I don't understand what . . . I mean, the things he makes me do now . . ." His skin crawled. Damn her. He felt like such a shit for doing this; goddamn her. He sat where he was, hunched and silent. And she said: "I just sometimes feel like I can't stand it anymore, that's all. I mean, I try to understand, but he's, like, on such a whole other plain from me, from everyone . . . it's just these things . . ."

"Stop it," he said. It came out a growl, harsher than he'd wanted. "What're you talking about? Just stop it. Don't put it all on him."

She pulled away. He glanced over his shoulder and saw her looking at him, baffled, teary eyed. "I didn't . . . I didn't mean . . . Well, you saw what he was . . ."

216

"Stop." Goddamn it. He ripped himself free of the sheets, stood naked off the bed. "The man's on drugs, that's all, that's what I saw. He needs some help, for Christ's sake. That's all. A little less of your airy-fairy bullshit."

"Oliver, don't you understand what . . . ?"

"I mean, he wasn't taking that garbage before he met you, Tiffany." He only muttered it, but her face went slack, as if he'd stunned her with a blow. He felt bad; it made him angrier still. "All that—cosmic crap. All that expand your mind, purify your aura, raise your astro-level. What'd you expect?"

"But I'm not the one . . ."

"I mean, isn't this what you wanted? Isn't this what you wanted him to be like?"

She stared at him. Slowly, she shook her head. Her chin began to quiver. "God, Oliver! God, why are you being so mean to me?" Then her face buckled and she began to cry in earnest. "Oh God!" She flung herself back on the bed. Buried her face in her arms, sobbing. "You don't understand! You don't understand anything, Oliver, not anything. Just get out, damn it. Just get out of here. Please."

Then he lost her. Right in the shadow of the library. He had looked up for only a second at the blackened patterns on its stained glass windows. He had thought, only for a second, about how he had planned to go up there tonight. Up to his workspace. To try to write a little, to watch the parade. And he had thought, without meaning to, without expecting to, without understanding why, he had thought suddenly that he could never go back. He could never write a poem again. He must keep silent. Must . . .

And when he looked down over the thick currents of people going to and fro in the gloaming, the blue baseball cap was gone. Tiffany was gone.

Perkins ran forward. Pushed forward through the crowd. He slid and shouldered his way up to the corner of West Twelfth. That's where she'd been standing. That's where he'd seen her last. He looked down the sidestreet. Along the brick facades, beneath the yellowing trees. Traffic had been stopped here too. People walked in the street, and along the sidewalk under street lamps and shadows. But there was no sign of

Tiffany. Perkins stood there, looking for her, his heart pounding hard, his thoughts jumbling.

And then, with a little coppery spurt of fear on the back of his tongue, he realized this was Nana's block. There was Nana's building right in front of him. She must have gone in there. She must have gone up to see Nana . . .

He punched his fist into his palm as he charged forward again.

"Bitch!" he whispered. He started running. "The bitch!"

NANCY KINCAID

The building rose up over Nancy into the twilight sky. A broad brick facade with alabaster ledges and balconies. Shouldering the ledges, flanking the balconies, gargoyles stared out over Gramercy Park. They were grinning homunculi, squatting, gibbering. Wagging their tongues lasciviously. Rolling wild eyes.

Nancy stood on the sidewalk below them. She shivered, cold in her rags. Her eyes moved over the stone monsters overhead, over to the corner window, *her* window. It was dark up there. Nobody home. She gazed up at it until her vision blurred. She swayed where she stood. Faintly, behind her, she heard children's laughter. Two mothers were herding their costumed trick-or-treaters around the iron gates of the little park. Nancy listened to their voices wistfully. Closed her eyes. Feeling woozy again. And tired, so tired. If she could get upstairs, if she could get into her own home, onto her own bed . . . Oh, she would sleep for a year. The cool sheets around her body, the cool pillow under her head. The weight of her mother sitting at the foot of the mattress. Her mother singing.

She swayed backward. Nearly toppled over before she jacked her eyes open wide and steadied herself. She had to hold it together. She had to hang on if she was ever going to get inside.

The building was on the corner of Twenty-first and Lexington. The entrance was on Twenty-first, facing the park. The heavy wooden doors were open, but the doorman was there. A hard-looking Irishman. Face like a hammer, body like a fireplug. He was sitting on a three-legged stool just within the entrance. He had not moved for fifteen minutes.

Nancy lowered her eyes to him, blinking to stay awake. Maybe she should just walk up to him, she thought dreamily. Maybe she should just say, "Hi, I'm Nancy Kincaid. I was savagely murdered today and I'd really like to change my clothes. Are my folks home?"

Well, maybe not. If he didn't recognize her—if he called the police . . . She did not have the heart for that anymore. She did not have the energy to escape again. Most of all, she did not have anyplace else to go.

Anyway, the doorman was going to move soon. She was almost sure of it. He had to work the elevator too. She remembered that—or at least she thought she did. If she could just stay on her feet long enough, someone would ring for him upstairs. He would have to leave his post and go fetch them.

So she waited, swaying. She could almost feel the passing time. The dark falling all around her like rain. Getting late, she thought. Getting to be eight. Can't wait. Got a date. Got to be there for the Animal Hour, woo, woo. The flood of darkness closed around her. She could feel herself going under. Jesus, was it really only this morning that she had vanished from the face of the earth? All that running through subway tunnels, getting arrested, kneeing shrinks in the balls. Fighting with insane gunmen beneath the sidewalks. And then to realize that she was a murderer—and then to find out that she had *been* murdered—*I mean, what a day,* she thought. Her eyes fell shut again. She smiled, swaying comfortably on

219

her feet. Feeling the goose pimples tickle her bare arms as the chill October dusk wove through the tatters of her blouse . . .

Then her eyes shot open. She had heard the bell inside: the elevator. She saw the doorman sigh and push off his stool to his feet. He shut the doors to the building. Through the doors' glass panels, through their filigreed glaze, she saw him humping away across the lobby. She waited another moment, breathing heavily. Then she looked around. The children were gone. Only a vampire and his girlfriend were strolling arm in arm by the park, pausing under the old iron street lamps. She moved toward the building.

At the door, through the glass, she could see the elevator across the way. The doorman had shut himself in the old-fashioned cage, and now the door slid shut and he rose out of sight. Quickly, Nancy hiked her skirt up. Reached into her panties and pulled out the .38. She struck the thick glass panel with the gun butt. Struck it again, down at the left-hand corner. A small triangle of glass burst from the pane. She heard it fall and shatter on the lobby floor. With another glance over her shoulder, she reached through the hole and seized the doorknob. In another moment, she was inside.

Imitation gas lamps burned low, threw yellow light on the dark oak paneling around the walls. Nancy's shadow danced on the marble tiles of the floor as she crept forward swiftly. She heard the elevator stop above somewhere. The arrow over the door pointed to the fourth floor. She heard the cage slide open. She went around the corner into a small mailroom.

Brass mailboxes lined three walls. On the fourth there was a solid metal door. Nancy pointed the gun at the doorknob. Her finger tightened on the trigger. On second thought, she reached out and tried the knob with her hand. The door opened easily. Inside there was a wooden pegboard with keys hanging from hook bolts. She lifted the key to 3K. Shut the door. Hurried back into the lobby.

She had not heard the elevator cage slide shut, but she could hear the car in motion now, descending. The arrow pointed to three, then two. Then light showed around the edges of the box. But Nancy had already crossed the lobby to the stairwell door. She pulled it open and slipped inside. As it shut behind her, she heard the elevator cage rattling open.

The adrenaline pumped through her and she climbed quickly. The rags of her blouse trailed behind her like white streamers. She gripped the key in her left hand, the gun in her right. On the third floor, she pushed the door open gingerly. She peeked out to make sure the hall was clear. Then she stepped into the hall, went with long strides toward the door at the end.

The hall lights were dim and she moved from shadow to shadow. The plush paisley carpet muffled her footsteps. She prayed that no one would open his door and spot her there. A beggar with a gun. This stench around her like a cloud.

When she reached 3K, she rang the doorbell. But she didn't wait for an answer. She unlocked the door with her key and went in. Shut the door behind her. She leaned back heavily against the wood. Her mouth hung open with weariness. She peered into the darkened foyer, seeing nothing but a blur. She brought her hand up quickly to brush tears from the corners of her eyes. Hi, Mom, she thought. I'm home.

It was several minutes before she could move away from the door. When she did, her heart was beating rapidly. She was eager—she had not known how eager she was—to see a familiar thing. Some room she had been in. Something she had touched. A face; her mother's face. Anything she remembered. The newsman's sonorous drone played in her head as she came through the small foyer. It taunted her: *The savage murder of Nancy Kincaid* . . . It was ridiculous. Obviously. She was not dead. It was crazy. And yet she was, in fact, beginning to feel like a ghost. Unseen. Unknown by anyone. She ached to exist again.

She moved into the living room, the gun held down at her side. She peered steadfastly into the shadows. She could make out an aging, respectable place. A thinning rug on a wooden floor. A stolid sofa. Stalwart club chairs that looked as if they would smell of pipe smoke. Nancy's eyes darted anxiously from one thing to another as she passed through. But it all seemed two-dimensional in the dark. It did not seem real.

She did not seem real moving through it. Her heart began to beat harder. With every step she took, she felt she was growing more ghostly, more transparent. *The savage murder* . . . *The savage murder of Nancy Kincaid* . . . Her head felt light. Christ, she was fading away, wasn't she? None of this was familiar. She could not remember it at all.

She crossed the room and came into a hallway. Doors opened on either side and there was one door at the far end. She moved down the corridor, peeking in the rooms. Looking at the pictures and photographs on the wall. Recognizing none of it.

The savage murder of Nancy Kincaid . . .

"Who am I then?" she whispered into the shadows. "Who the fuck am I?"

She felt like no one as she reached the end of the hall. She felt she was fading away.

Then she looked in through that last doorway. "Oh!" she whispered. She turned on the light.

It was her room. She had found her room. The lace curtains stirring over the partly opened windows. The Degas posters on the flowery walls. The ballerina jewel box on the white dresser, reflected in the mirror there. And snapshots wedged in the mirror's frame. The bed was a sweet four-poster with a frilled canopy over a thick white quilt. A huge stuffed panda was propped against the headboard. She moved among all this with her lips parted, her eyes swimming. Did she remember it? Was it hers? Well, wasn't it? Of course it was. She knew it was. A young woman's room that looked like a teenager's. That looked like a little girl's, in fact. Yes. That was just her. Because she hadn't wanted to grow up. Because she hadn't wanted to move away. She should have found her own apartment, her own job, a job she wanted, her own life . . . But she didn't care about that now. She tossed her gun down on the quilt. She took hold of one of the bedposts in her hands. She pressed against it. Rubbed her cheek against the warm curve of the wood. That was it for the outside world as far as she was concerned. She was going to live in this room for the rest of her life. Forever. She never wanted to leave. She closed her eyes and the tears overflowed them. Olly olly oxen free, she thought. Home.

It was a long while before she opened her eyes again. She gave a little laugh and sniffled. Looked around her. She let go of the bedpost and moved over to the dresser, to the mirror. She ran her eyes over the photos there. They were photos of girls mostly. Teenaged girls standing together, laughing. Arms thrown around each other's shoulders. Girls in evening gowns with boys in tuxedos beside them. Girls making faces, clowning in costumes and thrown-together outfits: the rich dame, the motorcycle bandit, the New Orleans whore. Her eyes moved from face to smiling face and she ached, she was so hungry, to remember any of them, one of them.

But there were only phrases. Words rising to the surface of her mind like bubbles in a pond. *Would you stop worrying? You look fantastic . . . Well, you ask him out. Guys love that . . . Let's just hit Columbus Avenue and shop until we die . . .* Phrases, words, but no voices. She just could not hear the voices. She could not remember them.

Her eyes began to fill again. She glanced up at her own reflection. *Whoa.* She snorted. What a sight she was. Jesus. Her skin looked like the side of a submarine. Her hair . . . *Well, I just had it dipped in shit and I can't do a thing with it.* There were scratches and streaks of black filth on her cheeks that made her lips look ashen like the lips of . . . well, of a corpse. She studied herself. She was almost fascinated by the disaster. And then, slowly, she smiled a little.

Ooh, she thought. *Do you know what I'm going to do?*

Moments later, she was stripped naked in the bathroom down the hall. She was in the shower. Catching the hot spray on her chest, letting the water run down between her breasts, over her belly. Her sense of rushing time was gone. Her sense was gone of everything except that water. On her back. In her hair. The shampoo in her hair. The foaming soap on her face, on her breasts, in the crack of her ass. The satisfaction of the black water running off her, running down the drain.

She dressed again in the bedroom, gleefully stuffing her old clothes in a little pink waste can by the window. She found fresh panties in the dresser. Wonderfully dry panties—soft where her thighs had been chafed by the others. She found a full-length mirror on the inside of the closet door, and she watched herself as she fastened her bra. She was half in love with the sheen of her own skin, pink from the heat of the water.

She pulled on some loose-fitting black jeans and a bulky gray turtleneck. She slipped her pistol into the jeans' waist, covered the handle with the sweater. She turned this way and that, studying herself in the mirror. *Dressed for travel, armed for hunting,* she thought. And the reflection of herself in her clean clothes made her feel more awake, more clearheaded, than she had all day.

She pulled on a pair of sneakers and she was finished. She stood in the center of the room. She felt satisfied with herself, but she was a little at a loss as to what to do next. She had to fight back that sense of urgency that was creeping back on her now. She glanced over at the dresser. Noticed a lipstick beside the ballerina box. *Ooh,* she thought. She went to it. Uncapped it. A pink gloss, good for her pale skin. She leaned in close to the mirror and spread it on.

Oh, it was a luxury. She would never take makeup for granted again. Wonderful makeup. She would build a shrine to it. Lipstickhenge. She would sacrifice a lamb. Just to feel it on her lips now, to see the color come, as if she were drawing it out of herself, drawing herself out of the ashes, becoming more distinct, more real . . .

Her hand stopped moving. Absently, she pressed her lips together to even out the color. But her eyes had moved away from her reflection now. She had noticed something—another reflection in the glass.

It was a clock. On a table on the far side of the canopy bed. Right under the shade of a bedside lamp. She had not noticed it before. It was a small digital clock with red-light numbers. 6:27. She stood there, with the lipstick in her hand, staring at the numbers reversed in the mirror. An hour and a half, she thought. And she thought of voices down a hallway. *Eight o'clock.* She narrowed her eyes. Trying to remember. That long hall . . .

But now she noticed something else, something in front of the clock. And she thought:

We'll have to draw him there. Bring him there at just the right time. Voices down a hallway. The hard carpet under her hands, against her cheek. The low voice at the hallway's end. *You won't forget now. You have to be there. Eight o'clock.*

She hadn't realized she was holding her breath until the air came shuddering out of her. She put the lipstick down on the dresser. She turned around, away from the mirror. *What is it?* she thought.

She could see it more clearly now. Lying right in front of the clock, a faint glow of red on the shiny white cover.

Oliver Perkins.

Ollie. The name murmured at the end of the hall. The name on the shiny white cover.

She moved quickly away from the dresser. Moved around the bed to the side table. The book was lying face up, the title clear in black letters. *The Animal Hour and Other Poems* by Oliver Perkins.

That's him, she thought. *Good God, that's him.* She picked the book up. Her hand was shaking. She began to turn the book over and she knew what she would see. The voice from down the hall was murmuring, murmuring to her. Whispering in her ear. *He's got to die at just that point, so don't forget. Eight o'clock.* The hall seemed to telescope, grow shorter and longer. The voice was in her ear, then far away, down the hall. And she turned the book . . .

She saw the face she knew she would. *His* face. Angular and sardonic. Wanting her from deep in the eyes: lonesome without knowing how lonesome, needing her love, her comfort. It was her poet: the one she had imagined. A face to turn to her in the dark, to press against her skin in the dark, against her breast . . .

And he's the one, she thought. She shook her head at the photograph, thinking: *He's the one who's going to be murdered tonight.* The low voice whispering down the hall, whispering in her ear. *Oliver Perkins. He's going to be killed. He's going to be killed at eight o'clock.*

You have to be there.

She gazed down into the lovelorn face a long moment. Then she jerked back suddenly, the book falling from her hand, fluttering to the floor. She gasped, covered her mouth to keep herself from crying out.

There had been a loud, jolting noise from down the hall. The front door was opening.

Someone was coming into the apartment.

AVIS BEST

Avis was sitting in the blue dark. The rocker was gently moving. The baby was taking a few last sleepy tugs at her breast. The balloon-pattern curtains were drawn against the evening light. But around her, in the pearly outglow of a street lamp, the shapes of mobiles were visible as they swung and dangled. The shapes of stuffed animals, of cardboard mice and birds and frogs, sank into the gathering gloaming. All the colors of the room sank slowly into blue. Avis held the warm weight of her baby against herself and stared into space.

In her daydreams, she was sitting at Zachary's bedside. He was lying there ill, gazing up at her weakly. She was running her cool fingers over his hot, damp brow. She imagined his grateful face.

She knew what he looked like. She had seen his picture. Oliver had once shown her an old Polaroid of the two brothers together. Arms around each other's shoulders. Zach's smaller, slender body pulled to Ollie's. His broad, shy, silly smile. She knew he had taken drugs for a while and that he had had breakdowns. And she knew he had a girlfriend whom Oliver didn't like. In her daydreams, Zach's girlfriend was in prison for the murder that Zachary didn't commit. When he was acquitted at the dramatic trial (at which Avis had been the key witness) he collapsed into Avis's arms . . .

Avis took a deep breath and then let it come streaming out of her. She rocked gently back and forth. The baby was slack in her arms, asleep. It was after six, maybe close to six-thirty.

The baby would sleep for at least half an hour now. She could run downstairs, Avis thought, and check on the Perkins brothers. If the baby woke up and cried, she would hear him through the window. She did not want to take the baby downstairs.

She thought about that now. Oliver would be there, she figured. He would introduce her to Zach. She had made some chicken soup with rice for Zach's bad stomach. She would heat it up for them. "It's no trouble," she would say. After Oliver told her what was going on, she would say she had been too agitated to finish the horrible book she was reading. So she had made the soup instead. The soup was in a plastic container now on the counter in the kitchenette.

She stood up out of the rocking chair, cradling the baby. She stepped forward in the dark, ducking through the mobiles. She moved to the rail of the crib. Lay the baby down among his stuffed animals. She tiptoed out of the room, closing the door behind her.

She stood for a moment in the living room. The empty room with its canvas chair and its folding card table. Its undecorated white walls and the bare white bulb in the ceiling above. Voices came in through the window. The crowd murmur from the street, and the sound of footsteps on the lane: people hurrying to see the parade. She stood for a moment, thinking. And then she decided: yes. She would go downstairs. Definitely.

And she moved to the kitchenette to get the chicken soup.

ZACHARY

Downstairs, around three hours earlier, just around three-thirty, just after Oliver had left to find Tiffany, Zachary had opened the red bag. The minute he saw Oliver heading off toward West Fourth Street, he had hurried into the bathroom for it. That's where the bag was, stowed under the sink in there. He had pulled it out and he had told himself: he had to move fast.

He had kept telling himself that. He had knelt on the floor in front of the bag and thought: *I have to move fast.* Over and over. But it wasn't so easy. He really was sick. The aftermath of the drug. Dizziness. Flashes of light. Occasional goblins crouching at the corners of his eyes. And that diarrhea. That's what had stopped him from dealing with the bag when he first got here. He had just finished hanging his raincoat in the closet when he was hit with yet another attack of the shits. He'd been pinned to the toilet for nearly an hour. Then, after he'd finally stashed Tiffany's dresses in the bag and gotten out his real clothes, Oliver had come home. Nearly caught him too before he could get the bag closed again. Nearly ruined everything. All relieved and glad to see him. Pumping his hand, slapping him on the back. Zach thought he'd never be able to get him out of the apartment again.

And, now that Ollie *was* gone, he was sure to be back in a big hurry. Tiffany's bookstore was only ten minutes away. Which gave Zach less than half an hour to do what he had to do.

I have to move fast, he kept thinking. He knelt in front of the red bag. His fingers moved to the bag's zipper. But still, they just hovered there. His mind . . . It felt like a great balloon, massive and wobbly. Weighted down with details, sluggish with them. *Fast*, he kept thinking. *Fast!* But he was distracted by the feel of the cold tiles through the holes in his jeans. Mesmerized by the spots of brown rust on the silver pipe beneath the sink. The sting of his asshole, the liquid chill in his intestines. All of it was magnified. All of it crowded into the mind-balloon and kept it anchored soddenly to the earth.

Finally, he unzipped the bag. But it was only more of the same. More clutter. Tiffany's skirt, the one he'd worn here. Her sweater. Her scarf. Things, things, things. He pulled all these aside. There was the skull mask underneath. The syringe. The vial of blood. The butcher knife. The stag-handled Colt automatic. He gazed at them—these *things* in their solidity. He couldn't quite take them in, they seemed so meaningless and real.

He swayed on his knees. He thought: *Oh Jesus.* He closed his eyes and sent up yet another quick prayer for forgiveness. Could it really have been so wrong? he thought. Breaking his promise to God, taking the drug? Did he really deserve all this sickness: the oversleeping, the diarrhea, this heaviness of mind? He had only been trying to recapture the old vision, after all. To become part of the great tapestry again. And the living truth was that if he had another needleful of Aquarius right this second, he would pump it into his arm without thinking twice. Christ forgive him, but he would. Just to clear all this *crap* out of his system. Just to be free again, the way he was last night.

Looking down at the objects in the bag reminded him. Last night. How beautiful it had been. These very same objects— how beautiful *they* had been. The knife, the blood, the silver-handled gun. Now, strewn at random in the bottom of the red bag, they were just things, just *it*s. Like the rust on the pipe. Like the little blue patch of mildew in the corner near the tub. Like his own slim fingers . . . So much of their magic, their truth, had seeped away.

But last night. Last night, when he had been on Aquarius

. . . oh, he thought, the vision! Things were not only things then. Each was interwoven with them all, with everything. Like the teacup in the tapestry, each object was the center of a web of being that had stretched out from itself into the universal. And he had been part of it. Everything he touched, everything he saw, drew him from the prison of his own flesh, connected him to a vast Oneness. How could that be wrong? To be so full of joy, so full of knowing. To be, for moments on end, within the very mind of the eternal God.

That's how it had felt, anyway. Especially when he decapitated the woman.

It had been beautiful. It had been so beautiful then. Not like now, when he could only remember it. Now, when the inner experience was gone. When he could only call up images, details, the exterior actions. All morning, all afternoon, he had kept these images at bay. He had tried to preserve the beauty of the true event intact. But now, the sight of the knife and the gun and the blood in the red bag forced it all into his mind again. He had to close his eyes again, shake his head to clear it. He had to remind himself—force himself to remember—that it had been beautiful.

She had been beautiful. Tied to the bed. His own old bed. Struggling as he approached her. Her white limbs straining, her eyes wide: the sensuality of her terror. Right there. In the mews. In the ever-strange house that was never quite home to him, that still smelled of old lady and desertion. Right there in his old room, on his old bed: the woman. Only he could see more than that. He could see the Truth within the Woman, the Woman in her Victimhood. Pleading with him for mercy: *Have mercy. Please, God.* Weeping—just as he had wept so often on that bed. It was like looking at himself, in fact: that was part of the Meaning of it. It was like looking at his Other Self in the past that was always present. Oh, but he had driven the great knife into her throat so slowly, with a sort of childlike fascination. And what an electric connection it was! Like a lightning bolt that touched off her orgasmic thrashing, that loosed the burbling blood, erased the words from her cries and made them nothing but choking and the whistling of air through her severed esophagus. He had felt her pulse beating against the blade, beating through the knife handle and into him, her Life into his, One Life, the Man in his Power connected to the Woman, her Martyrdom his, and he had felt like his own father with his own son's cheek crushed down against the rough desktop and the boy's naked ass lifted like a flirty girl's and the father's ruler whacking and whacking him while his mother's face went hectic with excitement . . . It was all One Thing. This and that, past and present, each and all. He could *see* the connections. And he had leaned down to press his lips against the dying woman's ear—and she was just shivering now, her eyes going glassy —he had leaned down, knowing she would understand him, this Great Secret, and he had whispered to her breathlessly: "*He* broke the typewriter."

She had only stared at him. Her and her empty eyes.

Tears rolled down Zachie's cheeks now. Fell on his hands as they hovered above the red bag. Sure, he thought. Sure. Her eyes. That image of her eyes. He was being punished for breaking his promise to God, even though he had only been trying to become one with the eternal. Jesus was making him forget how beautiful it had been. Was forcing him to remember only the emptiness of those eyes. How lonely they had made him feel. How furious. And the way he'd attacked her then, savagely slashing at her. The way he'd cursed her crazily, slobbering, crying out. Clutching her hair in his blood-soaked hand. Raging at her severed head . . . Oh, sure, from the outside, it was all ugliness.

Well, I'm sorry, okay? he thought. He let out one long, last shuddering sob. Bowed his head. *I said I was sorry, didn't I?* It was just one broken promise, after all. There was no need to torture him about it forever.

It was another few moments before he got control of himself. Breathing in little blasts, his cheeks puffed. He wiped his face dry with his palms. Tightened his lips with determination. God closes a door, but opens a window. Right? It was time, he thought, to get to work.

He forced himself to move with businesslike precision. He removed the pistol first. Stuffed it into his belt. Tugged the quilted shirt down over it. Then, he took out the vial of blood.

He had drawn this from the woman's headless corpse with his syringe. He brought the syringe out and snapped the vial back into it. His hand threw frantic shadows in the light from the bare bulb above him.

He got up. Went into the living room, holding the blood-filled syringe. The lights were still off in here, but he could see his way well enough. He wove quickly and surely through the stalagmitic stacks of books. He went to the dresser. It stood by the window in a wedge of fading daylight. There were two small piles of books on top of it, a framed drawing of Whitman in between. Whitman watched as Zach opened his brother's top drawer.

This was the underwear drawer. Zach gazed down into it, holding the syringe up in his right hand. Oliver's Hanes briefs lay neatly folded in there, next to his balled socks. The red and white waistbands. The crotch panels. Crowding Zach's brain. Too neat, he thought. It was all too neat—one of Ollie's "babes" must have done it for him. The idea made Zach shiver, his stomach coiling. Goose pimples rose on his arm. He stood there, gazing, swaying, for another long moment. Then he shut the drawer hard with his left hand. Blinked. He mustn't let himself get lost in the details. He forced himself to pull open the drawer below.

The sweater drawer. That was the one he wanted. He pulled out one of the burly woolen sweaters Nana was always knitting for Oliver. He knelt on the floor with the sweater lying between two mounds of slanting books. Carefully, he held the syringe over the sleeve. He pressed the plunger down, feeding the dead woman's blood onto the wool. Weird, he thought dreamily. This was all too weird. He gazed at the growing bloodstain on the sweater sleeve . . .

And then he came to himself. *Careful. Not too much,* he thought. He stopped the stream of blood from the syringe. *Just enough. Just like that.* It looked perfect. As if Oliver had stained himself without noticing. He stood and stuffed the sweater roughly into the back of the drawer. He left the drawer ajar slightly, so that a careful investigator would notice it on his own.

He tried to create the same natural effect with the butcher

knife. It was the knife that he had used to kill the girl. He had it in the red bag also. It was all covered in Glad wrap. He had swabbed the blade clean last night, but not too thoroughly. Just enough to remove his own fingerprints and yet leave a trail of blood and fabric for the cops to find and analyze. He brought the knife into the kitchenette now. Unwrapped it carefully, keeping his fingers on the plastic. Then he placed it in the drainer, down among the clean dishes there. That would look as if Ollie had brought the knife home and washed it, but hadn't cleaned it quite well enough.

Like the parables of Christ, he thought, as he set the knife just right. Always a little left to the imagination. Let the cops make their own discoveries, their own deductions. Make them feel like participants, as if they were re-creating the chain of events in their minds. That would bring the whole story to life for them. It would help them convince themselves that he was innocent. Just suddenly, without knowing why, they would think: *Oliver!* With that pleasant shock of understanding, they would think: *It was Oliver all along.*

A loud fart escaped him. His stomach was finally starting to settle down a little. He blinked to keep his mind right. Then he crumpled the plastic wrap in his hand and stepped back from the kitchenette. He regarded the drainer scene. Was it all right? He couldn't think. He couldn't be sure. He found he was studying an opalescent water droplet on the rim of the sink. He had to concentrate. He turned away. He surveyed the entire apartment. Gray with dusk. Jagged in outline with its stacks and swarms of books. He licked his lips and smiled weakly. It was so much like Oliver, this place. He laughed a little. *Oliver,* he thought. The only one who could ever help him. When their mother died. When their father deserted them. When he had broken down in college. When he had collapsed at the Christian retreat in P.A. And that night—that night in the mews, when he was drugged to the gills with Aquarius . . . *Oliver,* he thought. So much history between them. He felt his love for his big brother surging up inside.

So weird, he thought. He returned to the bathroom, to the red bag. It was all just so weird. Him and Oliver. Coming to this point, reaching this stage of life together. It was hard to believe they had grown so old. There was always someplace inside Zach, someplace in his mind, where Ollie and he were still just kids. Still little children in the Long Island house with Mom and Dad around them. He knelt on the tiles, re-packing the bag. Putting in the syringe and the plastic wrap. Burying the skull mask under Tiffany's clothing. It was so weird that Oliver was thirty-one. That his hairline was starting to recede. That he himself had to shave felt strange some-times. And then, sometimes the two of them would have these arguments, these grown-up conversations. About politics or art or religion. And Zach would say something like, "The soul could be a product, a sort of radiance, of the body, and still survive it the way a gas survives the two chemicals mixed to create it." And Ollie would throw up his hands and cry, "It could all be illusion, man! Even self-consciousness could just be the place where the electric function of the brain can't perceive itself anymore!" And right in the middle of the dis-cussion, Zach would suddenly realize that all they were really saying to each other was: *"You are so!" "I am not!" "You are so, ya big doody!"* It was exactly the same as ever between them. That was the truth of it. Nothing really had ever changed.

Zach zipped up the red bag slowly. His neck felt limp, his head heavy. He let out a long breath. Boy, he really was tired now. His arms felt like lead. His eyes were practically falling shut. All right, he thought. The business was done. With an effort, he shoved the bag back under the kitchen sink. He worked himself to his feet. He clumped back into the living room again.

He gave a weary groan and dropped down on the mattress. He gazed up at the ceiling, which was now in gray shadow. Oliver would be home soon, he thought. Any second now. And then, all he had to do was wait it out. Wait for the right time. Good, good, good. He closed his eyes. He crossed his hands on his thin chest. He lay on his back, his feet slanting off the bed so his sneakers wouldn't dirty the bedcovers. Noth-ing really *had* ever changed, he thought. And with his eyes still closed, he thought about Tiffany. He imagined her there.

Naked. Sitting above him. Straddling him with her muscular legs. Nailing his outstretched arms to the bed with her knees. Cooing down at him. *He fucked me, Zach. That night you were in the hospital.* With her sweet face, dripping the words down onto his flesh like hot wax. *He fucked me so hard. I screamed when I came.* Zach's jeans slowly grew tight as he lay there. *He was so big I could hardly take him.* Zach's breathing grew heavier. Oliver and Tiff. He imagined them now. He imagined her bent over the desk with her bare ass lifted. Oliver behind her, thrusting with his hips. Zach's tears started again. They slipped, cool, down over his temples. They dampened the pillow underneath his head. His jeans were very tight, his erection very hard.

Later, Tiffany had tried to tell him she had made the whole thing up. *Isn't that what I'm supposed to do?* She had tried to pretend it was just part of what they did together, part of what they called his Martyrdom. *I mean, you told me to say things like that. Isn't that what you wanted?* But Zach knew it was the truth from the moment he heard it. They *had* been together that night he was in the hospital. He imagined Oliver's hips circling obscenely as his cock slid in and out of her. He imagined watching them from a secret place. Hidden in the dark in a secret place, watching them. Deep in the dark. Far away . . .

His tears had ceased. His erection was fading. He was hidden. Farther and farther away in the dark. The street sough at the window was growing distant. He was deep in the closet dark. In his secret compartment there. With the fish-eye lens in the peephole. With the camera hooked up to the lens.

Are you serious? Tiffany was all wide-eyed over it. *Isn't that blackmail? Zach, that can't be right. It isn't right.*

You know, you look at these actions, Tiffany, and you just see actions, he explained to her. *But the symbolism of an act is just as important to the mind of God as the act itself. Otherwise, why would Christ have killed the fig tree, or attacked the moneylenders. So, when you say blackmail, I mean, you're not operating on the level where you understand the parable. The parable of my life, of our lives. I mean, when we talk about how Nana controls us with her money—and how she's just going to put Oliver in charge of her money when she dies—I mean, that's not just . . . I mean, that's a parable of our slavery to Mammon in the world. You see? And to be free from that requires an act of martyrdom that will redeem sin.*

Oh, Zachie. Oh Zach, please don't start talking about martyrdom again. I mean, it just doesn't make sense to me why—

Hey. Whose astro-level is higher? Yours or mine?

Well . . . I mean . . . blackmail. How can we blackmail someone? Who are we going to blackmail?

Our little friend Fernando Woodlawn.

The lawyer? But he's been so nice to us. Ever since you took that picture of him for the magazine, he's been so sweet. He took us out to dinner and everything . . .

He's perfect. He wants to be governor, he has lots of money. And he wants you.

Zachie! I'm not just going to . . . go to bed with him.

Why not? You did it with Oliver.

She went quiet at that. She frowned, her eyes glistening with tears. Then slowly, in the soft, rhythmic, persuasive voice he often had to use with her, he had begun to explain. The symbolism. The idea. The concept of Martyrdom: the death on which life depends. It would be her Martyrdom this time, he said. It would redeem her from the sins she had been committing against his, Zach's, flesh, which was, through his spiritual knowledge, the body that contained all things. Symbolically speaking. And she had said that she felt bad about the pain she had caused him, hadn't she? Well, when this was over, he told her, the purpose of it would be clear to her. Then she would not feel bad about it anymore.

Still, even when she had agreed to it—as he knew she would, as she always agreed to everything—the tears were streaming down her face. *How do you even know he'll do it?* she asked him softly.

Woodlawn? Oh, he'll do it. He wants you. He told me so. And anyway, Zach had added with a shrug, *he's a New York City politician: he'll fuck anybody.*

Tiffany's frown deepened. Tears spilled down her scarlet cheeks. She stamped her feet, her wrists pressed to her hips. Her face had changed. It was a child's face. She was a crying child. She was crying because Oliver had stolen her soldiers. Oliver had stolen the soldiers and no one would believe it. *Stop shrieking,* her father said, *you sound like a little girl.* And Oliver was laughing at her, standing next to her father and laughing at her as she cried because she was a little girl.

Zach's eyes jerked open. His heart was pounding. He sat up. The apartment was almost dark. The dark was spinning around him. There was noise outside. Voices, coming in through the window, coming up from the street. Were the police here? Jesus! What time was it? Had he overslept again? Where the hell was Oliver? He felt nauseous as the dark went round and round.

"You awake?"

"Hanh!" Zach cried out as the voice came out of the shadows. He turned and saw the shadowy figure there.

"I'm sorry." It was a woman's voice, thin but very warm. "Did I wake you up?"

A light snapped on. The standing lamp, rising out of the books on the floor. Zach squinted in its sudden glare. Slowly, the room began to settle down. "What time?" he said.

"Half past six, I think. I was trying to be so quiet. I didn't want to wake you up. I'm really sorry."

"No. No. It's all right." Zach brought his hand to his head. Massaged his brow. *Oliver.* "Where's . . . where's Ollie? Is he here?"

"No. I was sure he'd be back by now. I just came down to see if I could make you guys some dinner."

"Dinner . . ." Zach stared at the floor.

"Ollie said your stomach was upset, so I made some chicken soup with rice."

The hammering of Zach's heart was now beginning to subside. He ran his hands up over his short hair. The room was still. He could look up, get his bearings. There was the dresser. The kitchenette. The books everywhere. Half past six. Still time, he thought. Still plenty of time.

Finally then, letting out another breath, he turned to look at the woman. She was standing in the middle of the room. She was small with a pert, pretty face. Big glasses with square frames. Short dirty-blonde hair curling around her ears.

She had a slim, cute figure in her white sweater and jeans and . . .

Zachary's breath stopped short. He stared at her. His lips parted.

She was holding the sweater.

She was holding it in both hands. Oliver's sweater—the one he'd just stained with the woman's blood. Was this another dream? She had it draped over one hand and was holding out the stained sleeve in the other. She was looking at Zach, but she was absently rubbing the bloodstain between her forefinger and her thumb.

Zach shook his head. He *must* be dreaming. He must still be dreaming.

But then the woman smiled, very naturally. "Hi, by the way," she said, "I'm Avis Best from upstairs. I was just straightening up a little."

NANCY KINCAID

It could be anyone, Nancy thought.

On hands and knees, she climbed across the bed. She reached out to the light switch from beneath the canopy. Flipped it down. The room—her room—snapped back into the dusk shadows.

She could hear the newcomers in the foyer, talking low. The doorman was sure to have found the broken glass from the door panel by now, she thought. He might have checked his keys and seen which one was missing. He might have come up to check on the apartment. Or he might have phoned the cops. It could be anyone out there.

A light went on in the hall. Nancy rolled back off the bed, away from the door. She heard footsteps. They were coming down the hall, coming toward her. Had she left tracks? Disturbed anything? Would they notice the shower steam in the bathroom? She glanced across the darkened room at the window, the lace curtain dancing in the breeze. There was a ledge out there. The alabaster ledge with the gargoyles under it. She could climb out, try to escape . . .

She hesitated. What if it was her mother? What if she could see her mother again? She glanced over her shoulder at the closet, its open door. She stepped back. She stepped into the closet. She pulled the door closed only slightly, so she could still see out. She sank back into the wafting dark of soft blouses. The scent of talcum powder. Lingering perfume. She held her breath. The footsteps came closer. The sharp click of a woman's heels on the wooden floor. A man's heavy and muffled tread.

And then the man's voice, just outside the door. "Don't, Nora. Don't go in there. Don't torture yourself."

Nancy covered her mouth with her hand. Nora. Her mother's name.

And then the woman's voice. Heavy. Weary. "Just leave me alone, Tom. Just leave me alone with her for a little while."

Nancy did not move. *They think I'm dead,* she thought. She could hear it in their sad, tired voices. They were mourning her. They really believed she was dead. *Maybe I am.* Her head felt light. She felt like she was floating. *Maybe I really am.*

Now the woman came into the room. She shut the door behind her. She did not turn on the light. A moment later, she was moving deeper into the room and Nancy could see her dimly. Nancy blinked, trying to keep steady. She peered out through the closet door.

The woman moved about the room slowly. To the dresser first. Looking into the mirror. Lifting her hand to it. Running her fingers lightly over the pictures wedged into the frame. In the darkness, Nancy could only make out the woman's outline. Her small, plump shape. Her round head. The wedge of her long skirt. The skirt swayed as she moved away from the mirror.

Nancy lifted her other hand to her mouth. She began to cry. *Mom?*

The woman moved to the bed. She stood at the foot of it, looking down at the quilt under the lacy canopy. She reached down and touched the quilt with her fingers. Slowly, she came around the newel post, trailing her hand wistfully over the wood. She passed right by the closet door, right by Nancy. Nancy pressed both her hands to her mouth tightly. She was crying so hard her whole body shook. The woman in the room sat on the edge of the bed.

Oh, Mom, Nancy thought. *I am so sorry.*

She could hardly think for weeping—and for the sudden rush of images. The collage of memories—if they were memories—and half impressions and spoken phrases, flashing on and off and overlapping. There was her own angry face. And her mother's features sagging with hurt and sorrow. And the face of herself as a child. And her mother's shape at the foot of her bed. The weight of her mother on the end of the bed. The empty hallway. The terrifying dark. *Because your father's gone, because your father fell . . .* Her mother's lullaby. *He fell into . . .* And her own face, her face as it was now, twisted in rage. *You leave my friends out of this, Mother. It's a little late for you to be worried about people's friends.*

Your father fell . . .

Now, the woman in the dark, sitting at the foot of the bed, began to sing. Very softly. Nancy couldn't even be sure at first if it was real, if it was only another of the jumbled impressions in her mind. But no. It was true. Very softly, in a whispered croon, she was stroking the coverlet and singing: "Lullaby . . . and good night . . . little baby, sleep tight . . . bright angels up above . . . will send you . . ."

And then, on that "you," the woman faltered. Her hand left the quilt. Rose to her face. She bowed her head. "Oh God," she said, her voice squeaking with tears. "Oh God, please don't. Please. Not my little girl."

Nancy couldn't stand it anymore. She sobbed. The woman

on the bed gave a little gasp and spun around. Aching for her, Nancy stepped out of the closet.

"Mom?" she said.

At first, the woman on the bed didn't answer. Nancy heard her shuddering breath, saw her hand go to her chest. But she said nothing.

"Mom?" she tried to say again, but she was crying too hard.

"Who's there? Who is it?"

"It's me," Nancy managed, her voice trembling. "It's me. I'm all right. I'm here."

"Oh God." The woman slowly rose from the bed, both hands pressed to her chest now. "Oh God."

"I'm sick, Mommy," Nancy heard herself say. She was crying so hard, wanting so much. She reached both hands out toward the older woman. "I'm so sick. I don't know what's happening to me. If you could help me . . . If you could just let me stay here a little while, I don't know . . . Talk to me. If you could talk to me. Mama."

"Who are you?" the woman in the shadows whispered. She moved away. Sidled along the bed toward the wall. "Please. Who are you?"

"It's me. I'm all right. It's me." Nancy took another step toward her, reaching out.

The woman made an inarticulate sound, a little cry of hope, a groan of pain, it was hard to tell which. She was at the head of the bed now. She was pressed up against the end table. The clock glowed red beside her. Her hand went out, trembling, toward the little bedside lamp.

And Nancy kept moving toward her. Crying. Confused. Her hands out. Her mind flashing and melding half memories, half phrases.

Your father fell into . . .

It should have been me . . .

You're not Nancy Kincaid.

Step by step, she moved toward the woman in the shadows. "Please," she whispered. "I'm sick. Help me. I don't know where else to go. I don't have anyone else . . . I'm sorry. Please . . ." She choked on her sobs.

"Who . . . ?" The woman fumbled with the bedside lamp. "Oh God. Oh please God."

"Mom?"

The light flicked on. It cast a pale yellow circle of light around the table. The two women stood in that circle, the older pressed to the wall, the younger reaching out for her. Nancy saw the older woman's haggard face, the pinched mouth, the down-drawn cheeks, the frightened gray eyes. She knew that face. She recognized it. The face of the picture in her wallet. And yet, even as her hands went out to her, she was uncertain. She felt that floating sensation return. She felt cut adrift, like a spacewalker from his ship, whirling away, the cord severed, the infinite, engulfing black of night . . . She thought she was going to faint. She reached out. Her fingers brushed the older woman's soft cheek.

And the woman recoiled, violently. Her arm flew up before her face, knocking Nancy's hand away. Her pale eyes went wide in horror.

"You!"

Nancy tried to call to her, but her voice was slurred, her mind reeling.

"You!" And the older woman's fingers bent like claws, her hands rose up alongside her head. "You . . . you murderer!"

Nancy mouthed the word: Mom?

"Murderer!" the older woman shouted. "What have you done? Look at you. All of you! Murderers!" She struck out wildly, one hand slashing, then the other, driving Nancy back. "Murderer! Murderer!"

"Nora!" It was the man's voice. Coming from outside the room, from down the hall. "Nora! Are you all right?"

Nancy fell back, her arms up in front of her. Back from the hatred that contorted the woman's face.

"Murderer!" The woman stalked her. Pressing her back.

"Nora! Jesus!" And there were his footsteps now. Running down the hall outside. Running toward the door.

The woman took another step forward. Nancy fell back another step. The woman's eyes were white hot, her mouth twisted. "Murderer!"

The door flew open.

Nancy cried out. She was pressed against the wall now, the lace curtains dancing out around her. She covered her ears with her hands.

She could barely hear herself shrieking: "Mother!"

AVIS BEST

"I mean, look at this sweater," Avis said. She shrugged shakily; it was almost a shudder. Meeting new men always made her nervous. "I mean I was just . . . I didn't want to wake you. I'm from the apartment upstairs, Ollie asked me to come down and see if you were all right, and I was just kind of walking around wondering if I should stay and I noticed . . . I mean, that ker-azy, crazy brother of yours . . ." She launched into an imitation of an Ohio housewife on TV. "He cain't keep this place clean for ten minutes in a row. No. Seriously. I cleaned this whole place up for him just this morning . . . I mean, I was just doing him a favor cause he had to . . . um, run out and, anyway, I come back and I just noticed his sweater drawer is all messed up and this one, I don't know what he did to it, it's got some kind of stain or something." *Jesus,* she thought, *stop babbling! You sound like an idiot.*

Zachary blinked up at her from Oliver's mattress. He nodded as she spoke, but he said nothing. He looked like a man who did not know what had hit him. Avis stole glances at his dark, sensitive eyes. His silence made her more jumpy still.

"I wish he'd take better care of his clothes." She just had to go on. "I mean, it's not like he's rich and this sweater, I think your grandmother made it for him, it's so beautiful, she

243

does such wonderful work, doesn't she? I'll take it up and give it a wash tonight, but I think I may have to reknit the end of the sleeve. I wonder if Nana still has the wool, maybe I can match it, I don't know." She shrugged again, wishing she could shut up. "Well . . . As you can see, I'm compulsive."

Zachary nodded at her another moment. Then he smiled; it rose over him like the sun. That broad, boyish smile she had seen in his photograph. It made him look lost and appealing, like an orphan at the side of the road. *Like Dondi,* she thought. *A good role for David Kory.* His baggy, crazy-quilt shirt and his torn jeans added to the effect.

"So . . ." she said, because these long pauses just made her twitch.

"You sure are nice," Zach blurted out then. "I mean, wow. All this stuff you do. You sure are much too nice for Ollie, that's for sure."

"Oh, much!" Avis laughed and rolled her eyes. She flushed and felt herself relax a little. Zach was nodding up and down, goofy as a puppy dog. Looking down at the sweater in her hands, as if he were afraid to look up and meet her gaze. Here was a man definitely in need of being taken care of, she thought. *And, hey, nurture is my life, right?* "And while we're on the subject of how nice I am . . ."

Zach laughed. "Ye-es?"

"I, uh, made you some soup. Genuine Jewish-mother chicken soup. Vit rrrice, dahlink. Oliver said you weren't feeling well so . . . I'll heat it up for you, okay?"

"Oh no! Oh gee!" He was sitting up on the edge of the bed now, his arms wrapped around his knees. He gave a pained grimace. "That really is really, really nice of you. But the thing is—I'm a vegetarian."

"Agh!" said Avis.

"I know, I know. But it's okay."

"Oh—no it's not, damn it. I think I knew that." Avis popped herself on the forehead with the palm of her hand. "I think Ollie told me that and I forgot. Damn it. I must be losing my Jewish-mother touch."

"No, really. Listen," Zach said. He pushed himself off the mattress, got to his feet. "Listen. The thing is"—he held both hands before him as if he were shaping the thought in the air—"the thing is: Ollie will probably be back any minute now . . ."

"You know what I could do?" said Avis—the thought had just come to her. "I could make you a vegetable omelette. Ollie always has enough stuff for an omelette."

"Listen . . ."

"No, no, it's all right." She was figuring it out. Green peppers. Mushrooms. Cheese. Ollie always had cheese. And she wouldn't need onions if Zach's stomach was off. She was laying the sweater down carefully as she thought. Draping it over the Catullus atop a tall stack of books.

Zachary stepped toward her, his hand out as if to stop her. "It's really too much trouble." He kicked over a small pile of paperback mysteries.

Avis was already moving away from him. Stepping over books to reach the kitchenette. Plotting out the omelette in her mind. "Are you kidding?" she called back at him. "I mean, you can't just *be* a Jewish mother if you're a Presbyterian from Cleveland. This is how I earn credits." She moved to the refrigerator, talking over her shoulder. "When I have enough, I send them in and they send me a faded flower-print dress, big breasts, and steel gray hair. Usually I have to practice on Ollie or my . . ." Baby, she almost said. She was about to make a joke about her baby. But she stopped. She wasn't sure why.

She pulled open the refrigerator door. She bent over to look in the crisper, aware that she was showing him her backside in her sleek jeans. Well, she had worked hard to get her figure back after the baby came; someone might as well admire it. She picked out plastic bags holding green peppers and mushrooms. She straightened and turned to him, the bags in her fist.

Zachary, she saw, was now standing over the white sweater she had draped atop the books. He had lifted the sleeve in his two hands. He seemed to be examining the stain on the sleeve as she had. When she turned, he glanced up at her quickly. He flashed that big smile again. "Look, I'm really not hungry," he said. "And the thing is . . ."

"Sorry. You have to eat something. Otherwise, I cease to exist. I am what you eat. It's been in *Science Times* and everything." She turned back to the counter. She set the veggie bags before her, shaking her head. Why is it, she wondered, that a guy like Randall beat the shit out of you if you didn't squeeze his orange juice by hand while these Perkins brothers, from whom something seemed to cry out to the very soul of maternity . . . "Anyway, you know, you *have* been sick all day," she heard herself say, with even a slight touch of exasperation. She found the cutting board leaning behind the drainer. "And you're probably going to need your strength if you have to deal with the police and . . ." *Oops*, she thought. She was setting the board on the counter with the bags. *Dumb, dumb, dumb,* she thought. She glanced at Zach over her shoulder. "Sorry. You probably don't want to talk about that. I was just . . . Oh, hey, don't do that."

Zach, she found, had taken the stained sweater off the books. He had moved to Ollie's dresser. He was stuffing the sweater back into the drawer.

"No, leave it, okay?" said Avis. "It needs to be hand washed."

But Zach didn't seem to hear her. He pushed the drawer in, leaving it a little ajar, as it was when she found it. He faced her, scratching his head dopily. "Uh . . . Look . . . Avis was it? Look, the thing is . . ."

"Mm-hm?" She had turned instinctively back to her work. Corralling the green pepper bag. Twisting off the wire tie.

"The thing is," Zachary said behind her, "Oliver should be back any second now. And, uh, I really need to kind of talk to him kind of personally. Okay?"

"Oh, sure. Okay," Avis said. "No problem. I'll take off the second he gets here." She had her hand in the bag. She squeezed first one pepper, then the other. "I'll probably have to leave soon anyway cause my . . . cause, uh, I have stuff to do." And again, she didn't mention the baby. And why not, psychology fans? Yeah, yeah, she thought; she knew why not, all right. Because if you tell a guy you have a baby right at the beginning, his eyes go sort of flat on you, don't they? You get one of those pained smiles. Like he's wondering how soon he can call for a cab. And she just had to have her little fantasy, didn't she? Her little flirtation. She pressed her lips together, squeezing her peppers. As if she were really going to be ready for another relationship anytime this millennium. And a relationship with a psychological basket case who already had a girlfriend, a drug problem, and a warrant out for his arrest? And a brother she was secretly in love with? Hey, a computer dating service couldn't have made a better choice.

Self-destructive girl seeks emotional cripple for anguish, co-dependency, and moonlight walks . . .

Pepper Number One seemed firmer all around. She drew it out and set it on the cutting board. *Knife,* she thought. *Knife, knife, knife.* She pulled open the silverware drawer.

She heard Zach's footstep behind her—and another stack of books falling over. And he might've started to say something too, but he stopped. Avis found herself babbling on again in the silence.

"It's really nice that you guys are so close, you know, you and Oliver. You can talk to each other and everything when there's trouble like this. I've got, like, four sisters and they all still live in Cleveland? We never talk. I go out there for Christmas or something, and it's like all we say is 'How're you? How's the swim team? How's . . . this and that?' We even joke about it, we call it 'News of the Day.' " She had selected a little steak knife from the drawer. She had lifted it out. But now she spotted the butcher's knife. A monster of a knife, a horror movie special. In the drainer, wedged down among the dishes she'd washed this morning. "Huh!" she said aloud.

"What," said Zachary behind her.

"Oh. Nothing. Just this knife I never saw before." She put the steak knife back in the drawer. Shoved the drawer shut with her hip. "The thing is," she went on, "to them I'm like this big shot New York movie person, you know, I'm like too far out of their lives at this point to even, you know, comprehend their trials and troubles. I mean, if they only knew . . ." She reached into the drainer. The dishes rattled as she drew out the big knife. "Look at this. Where the hell did he get this?" she murmured.

"Listen, uh, Avis?" Zach said quickly. "Ollie's gonna be back any second. Really. And the thing is . . . Um. Um . . ." He really sounded a little nervous now.

"It's okay. Really," she said over her shoulder. "I promise I'll do this so fast I'll be out of here before you know it. It'll lose some of my customary brilliance but . . ." She decided to try this monster out. She steadied the green pepper in one hand. Held the butcher knife in the other. "What I was saying, though, is that if they knew this job I had. This reader's job. I mean, you write these reports." She let the pepper go then. She had noticed some kind of goo on the edge of the knife's blade. She reached out and turned on the faucet. Water hissed loudly into the sink. She had to raise her voice to go on. "No one ever reads them. It's like sending them into a black hole."

"What are you doing?" Zach said with a little laugh.

"You begin to wonder if you even exist," Avis called. "There's just some weird . . . yuch on this knife. I gotta wash it off." She lifted a yellow sponge from the sink counter and held it under the running water. "I mean, I sometimes think I'm a daydream in the mind of some movie executive, you know?"

Zach said something, but she didn't catch it over the hiss of the water. "What?" She examined the blade of the knife in the light. "I swear your Nana spoiled you boys," she said.

"I said, can I see that for a second?" Zach repeated, more loudly.

She glanced back at him. "What?"

He was standing in the center of the room. Standing as if he were frozen there, surrounded by Ollie's piles of classics, the pinnacles and steeps. He had his legs akimbo, his hand out to her, one hand. He was smiling eagerly. There was a bright light winking in his black eyes. "The knife," he said. "Could I just see that knife for one second?"

"Oh," said Avis, "sure, let me just wash it off."

"No, I meant before."

"What?" She squeezed the excess water from the sponge.

"Before you wash it off."

"Wait, I can't hear you over the water. Hold on." Avis brought the sponge to the blade of the butcher knife.

"Could you put the sponge down?" Zach said.

"What? Hold on just a . . ."

"Would you put the sponge . . ."

"I just want to . . ."

"DROP THE FUCKING SPONGE, YOU STUPID BITCH!" Zach screamed.

Avis looked around quickly and saw the gun. She spun then, her back against the counter. Zach was standing straight as a steel rod. He was clasping the pistol clumsily in both hands. Sticking it out at her. Waving it back and forth so that the bore crossed and recrossed her forehead.

Avis gave a bewildered laugh. "Uh, wha . . . ?" she said. The water hissed into the sink behind her. She stared at the gun. "Oh God, Zachary . . ."

Zachary's eyes were wide. He waved the pistol at her. "I said drop the sponge, drop the sponge, damn it."

Avis nodded quickly and dropped the knife. It clattered loudly on the floor.

"The sponge, the fucking sponge!" Zach shouted. "Oh Christ, it doesn't matter now."

All the same, she let the yellow sponge fall from her other hand. She heard it squish as it hit the floor. Avis stared into the wavering bore of the gun.

He is *a murderer,* she thought. She could see it when she glanced up at his wide, bright, frightened eyes. That's why the police were after him. They were no fools. He really *was* a killer. "Oh Jesus," she whispered. "Oh Jesus Christ." On the instant, she was thinking about the baby. The little lump of him asleep in his crib upstairs, his cheek against the mattress. The thought was like an ice bath. A painful, paralyzing chill over her whole body at once. What would he do without her? "Please," she said. "Just don't hurt me, all right?"

"Well, I mean, shit!" said Zach. His cheeks were getting very red, apple red. He looked from side to side once, as if he were trapped, as if he were searching for the way out. "I mean, I'm telling you to get out, I'm telling you to give me the knife. I mean, what the fuck's the matter with you? What if I have to kill you too now?"

"Please . . ." Avis couldn't get the word out of her throat.

She knew Zach couldn't hear it over the hiss of the water. *Please, God,* she thought, *please, Jesus, don't let him. Don't let him. Think about the baby, God, my sweet baby . . .* She felt as if her legs would not support her. As if her whole body had gone soft inside.

"Huh?" said Zach, and Avis jumped. "You see what I'm saying?"

"I'll do anything you want," she managed to stutter. "Really. Please. Don't hurt me, don't kill me, it's important, I'll do anything at all . . ."

Zach's hands trembled violently. He let go of the gun with his left and ran the palm up over his short hair. "Oh Jesus, it must be close to seven now. Oliver'll be *back* any minute," he said softly, almost to himself. "Now what am I supposed to do?"

"Please," Avis whispered. Her eyes filled with tears. *Please, God.* What would happen to her baby? Who would take care of her baby? *Please. Please.*

"All right," said Zach. His voice was suddenly like a tinker's hammer: a finite and decisive sound. Avis looked into his distorted, terrified, and still somehow boyish face. She was unable to speak. Too weak to do anything but pray and wait. She waited, praying, *Please, God, please . . .*

And Zach said again: "All right." And then he said: "We're going up to your place."

NANCY KINCAID

They were still screaming at her when Nancy threw herself out the window. Her mother was screaming: "Murderer! Mur-

derer!" Her father was screaming: "You! Get out of here!
I'm calling the police! I'm reporting this to the police right
now!" And in her mind: chaos. Flashes of memory beyond
knowing. Faces flashing at her. Half phrases. Evocative, vanishing smells. She had her ears covered with her hands. She
was shrieking wildly for her mother. She was watching herself
shriek as if from a distance and thinking: *This family visit is
not going very well.* And meanwhile, these two people, the
woman and the man, were closing in on her. Stalking her,
shoulders hunched, faces jutting at her. Screaming and
screaming. And, well, the window happened to be right beside
her, already half open. And the lace curtains were rising
in a cool fresh evening autumn breeze. And she had to get
out . . . !

She threw the window up, threw it wide. Her mother
wailed. Her father cried out, "What are you doing?"

Without thinking, Nancy ducked under the sill. She set her
two feet on the thin, alabaster ledge. She stood up, facing
the building, holding on to the raised stone around the window
recess, clutching it with her nails.

And in that moment, everything became suddenly quiet,
suddenly cool. A stream of autumn air trailed along the building's brickwork. Traffic hushed and grumbled in the distance
somewhere, three stories below. The lights of Lexington Avenue ran uptown, brilliant and still in the dark. She tasted
the faint tang of exhaust fumes. And heard no voices. No
human voices.

Nancy clung to the building. Leaned her face against the
cold stone, panting, staring along the brick facade. The stone
gargoyles squatted under the ledge on the floor above her.
Squatted with their hairy thighs splayed, their horny heads
protruding, their arms lifted and their armpits to the world.
All gaping grins, all teeth, all saucery eyes . . .

Whoa! Nancy thought, breathless, clinging to that wall.
Whoa-de-yo-do!

"What the hell are you doing?"

The sudden bark of her father's voice nearly sent her over
the edge. She tilted backward. Her hands fluttered off the
stone. Then she fell forward. Got her grip again. Her father

must have stuck his head out the window, but she couldn't turn her head to look down at him. She just leaned her cheek on the stone and panted, wide-eyed.

"Did you hear me? What're you doing?"

What am I doing? Nancy thought. *What am I doing? What the fuck are you asking me for?*

"I've called the police. Do you hear me?" the man barked. "They're coming now."

Nancy stared along the face of the building. About ten yards ahead of her it ended, just disappeared. No, wait. There was a small, one-story structure after that. A connecting structure with a flat roof. It linked one wing of the building with another. *Oliver,* Nancy thought, mouthing the word. *Oliver Perkins. I have to be there.*

"You might as well come in from there. You're going to fall," said her father. If he was her father. Wasn't her father dead? Didn't he fall into something and leave her with that empty hallway. Her mother's lullaby. The scary dark at night.

A horn honked somewhere below. People shouted laughter from a car window. The voices faded as the car whisked past. Nancy lightly thumped her head against the stone, closing her eyes. *Oliver, Oliver Perkins,* she thought. That was all she knew. Oliver Perkins was going to die. The lonely-eyed poet. With those descriptions of twilight that made her feel sexy and melancholy like a schoolgirl. Someone was going to murder him at eight o'clock. In just about an hour from now.

She had to be there.

She started to sidle along the ledge.

"Wait a minute! Where are you going? What the hell are you doing?"

Don't know. Don't know. Don't know, thought Nancy. She slid her right foot along the narrow edge. Her left foot inched up after her. Her fingertips danced over the rough brick. Clung to the lines of mortar. In the whisper of air around her, in the whisper of traffic that rose and fell below, she heard her own breath. Harsh pants. Huff, huff, huff.

"Goddamn it!" she heard her father yell. And then he must have pulled his head in because his voice grew fainter. She heard him talking to her mother inside. She couldn't make out the words. She slid forward. Right foot out again. Left foot following. Fingertips like spiders on the brickwork. Huff, huff, huff. Her lips parted. Spittle on her chin, cold in the wind.

"Nancy . . ."

The harsh sound of her breathing stopped then, stopped cold. She stopped cold on the ledge over Lexington Avenue. Her name.

"Nancy . . ."

Someone was calling her name!

Her fingernails bit into the mortar lines. Her breasts flattened against the brick. Her sweater buckled around her in the breeze. She cocked her ear.

"Nancy, Nancy . . ."

It was not her father's voice. It was too high, too thin. Whispery, like silk sliding over silk. Like breezes in the night forest; something she remembered . . . Beckoning voices, voices in corridors, voices behind doors . . .

Afraid, she lifted her head. She had to raise it by increments to keep steady. Bringing her chin up inch by inch. Bringing her eyes up.

"Nancy . . ."

The gargoyle just above her grinned down. His hands hung before him like an ape's. His tongue darted out between his gaping lips.

"Nancy," he whispered.

"Oh . . . !" She looked down so fast she scraped her cheek on the brick. Her arms and legs had turned to water. She was going to lose her balance. Her heart was beating so hard against the brick that she felt it might knock her off . . .

But she managed to keep her place there, her eyes closed, her mouth open. Her panting breaths coming again, little cries in them.

"Nancy . . ."

"Oh, for Christ's sake," she whispered.

She opened her eyes. She braced herself. She began to sidle forward again. More quickly. Toward the end of the wall. Right foot, inch by inch. Left foot after.

"Nancy. Naaaanceeeeee . . ."

She had reached the next window. Stepped into its recess. Resecured her grip on the decorative stone. She had to stop there, catch her breath. Steady her head. Close her eyes and tell herself: *I don't hear those voices. I do not hear them. I do not.*

But she did. Wheedling, airy, ghostly whispers. Beckoning to her. Taunting her. Slipping her name into the wind, blowing it to her like a kiss. And something else now. Another sound. Starting, stopping. *Chiggachiggachiggachigga . . .* A sort of scratching noise. Scrabbling. Like a cat clawing for purchase.

I do not . . . she thought. And then her will broke: She had to look up. She craned her neck recklessly, swiveling her head back and forth until she caught sight of something. Another gargoyle. A horn-headed devil with a cocked eye. But this one was upside down. Showing his ass to heaven. His fingers reaching below him, right over Nancy's head, clutching the brick. And then, suddenly . . . *he was moving!* Like a cockroach on the wall. Scrabbling down over the bricks suddenly. Just a foot or two toward him, closer to her. Pausing there. Grinning at her, bright-eyed. Then—again—*chigga-chiggachiggachigga*—spindly arms and hairy feet quick as an insect's on the brick. Closer. Scrabbling toward her.

"Hello, Nancy," he whispered.

Nancy screamed. Twisted her head around even farther. Yes, the other one, the one who had waggled his tongue at her before. He was also upside down now. He was also pausing like a wary bug. And then—quick!—he started crawling down the brick face. Coming at her on the diagonal. Pausing. Lifting his head up to grin and wink.

"Nancy!" And he laughed and stuck out his tongue.

Nancy burst out laughing. *Great, just great,* she thought. She closed her eyes and giggled. She rested in the window nook, holding on to the stone. Her shoulders shook with laughter. Tears squeezed out from under her lashes and rolled down her cheeks. *Simply terrific.*

She opened her eyes and saw the others. The ones up ahead. Two more of the white stone creatures angling down at her in fits and starts. Their lancet nails, their simian feet, made that insidious scratching noise on the brick. Their twisted lips shaped her name. Their whispers were in the wind all around her.

This is not, is not happening. You are experiencing an episode of . . . of weird . . . gargoylemania . . . But she had stopped laughing. She was all heartbeat and nausea and tears. The wall was undulating beneath her fingers. She was ready to let herself fall—to throw herself to the street below—just to stop them, just to make them disappear. The bastards. Terrifying her, crawling down at her.

"Nancy. Oh, Nancy." Calling to her.

She gritted her teeth in defiance. *Oliver,* she told herself. *Oliver Perkins.*

The wind lifted a moment. It played at her hair. She forced herself to squint into it. To look forward along the wall toward the place where the wall ended. She could jump down to the connecting building from there, to the flat roof. From there, she could probably climb down to the street. She made an angry noise, shaking her head. Trying to get those giggling whispers out of her ears. The scrabbling of those nails . . .

But they were getting louder. Closer. She had to move—she had to move right away. She didn't care if she fell. She hoped she *did* fall, it would serve the little stone shitheads right. Her right foot darted forward—she really was careless now. Her lead foot was moving again even as her left foot trailed to keep up. Her fingers danced over the brick. Her nipples dragged chillingly, painfully over the stone. Her eyes were tearing in the wind.

And they kept calling her. She could hear them. Their voices were trapped in her head. Their whispers were like tendrils of smoke twisting and coiling around each other. Their scrabbling on the brick seemed so loud to her now it almost drowned out the soft honks and distant rumbles of the cars below on Lexington.

Mewling, she forced herself to keep sliding along the ledge. The end was coming closer: the wall's sharp corner, the curl of the ledge. She could see the flat roof of the connecting building one story below. The gray asphalt lifted up to her out of the dark. She watched her foot, her sneaker as it stretched out to the curve. And she was there. She was coming around the bend. One hand around the corner now. Her cheek against the sharp edge of the wall. She ignored everything else. The whickering sounds. The high, soft, insinuating voices. She looked down at her sneaker.

And from down there by her foot, there came a deep chuckle. Heh heh heh. A low voice said:

"Nancy."

And a gargoyle rocketed up at her from underneath the ledge. Its white hand of chipped stone shot into sight and grabbed her ankle. Its wildly grinning face, cracked jaggedly down the center, gaped and gibbered at her. It shrieked with laughter.

Nancy screamed. She clutched her hair in terror. Tried to pull her leg free of the rock-hard clammy grip.

For another second, she seemed to hang there like that, reeling backward on the ledge. And then she lost her footing. Reached out for purchase—but too late. Toppled over, pitched backward.

Tumbled down into the night.

ZACHARY AND AVIS
→

So he was not going to be spared this either. Everything, Zach thought, everything was going to be taken away.

He had the girl—this Avis—pressed against the wall beside the door. Her face flat against the plaster, her arms raised. He noticed the way her hands trembled. The way the shiny nail of her right middle finger just touched a long crack in the plaster. Her red knuckles. The open pores on the back of her hand. The downy white hair just beneath her wrist . . .

Damn it! he thought.

He shoved the stag-handled pistol into her back hard, making her whimper. He blinked—once, twice—to clear his head of all this garbage, all this *stuff*. He grabbed the doorknob. Pulled the door open. Peeked out into the corridor. Light bulbs on the wall etched every line of grain on the mahogany balusters . . .

"All right!" he whispered. "Go."

"Please," said the girl. She moved reluctantly, her hands over her head. She was crying now. Clear tearstains on her cheeks, no mascara. Water pooling at the bottom of her big glasses. "Please."

"Go, would you! Make another noise and I'll kill you."

He grabbed her by one slender arm and flung her out into the hall. He went after her quickly, closing the door behind him.

His teeth were gritted, his eyes burned angrily into her back as he marched her to the stairs. He was not going to be spared this, damn her. Damn her! He was going to have to kill her without the drug, without the vision. It was going to be all these details. All this *stuff* crammed into his eyes. Blood spattering. Whining for mercy. All the beauty of last night ruined. Just ruined. This finally was his punishment from God.

His eyes burned angrily into the back of her hair. Her hair curled above the collar of her sweater. There was a mole on her neck. Her neck looked thin and fragile. *She just had to clean up,* he thought, *she just had to cook for me, had to this, that . . . Jesus! The idiot.* Well, now she knew everything. Now he had no choice. He had to kill her.

The woman sobbed, her body buckling, as he shoved the Colt in her back to force her up the stairs. He grabbed her shoulder, marched her up quickly.

The baby oh God my baby . . . she thought. She was crying hysterically now. She could hardly see through her fogged glasses. Her mind was swimming. How could he be like this? How could this be happening? She couldn't think of anything else . . .

have to think my baby think

Zach was gripping her shoulder hard. It hurt, his fingers digging through her sweater, into her flesh. The steel-hard gun was pressed against her spine. And she felt his hot eyes.

How can he how can he my baby . . .

He shoved her against the wall outside her apartment. The impact jolted her. She coughed, bent over, helpless with crying. How could anyone be like this, do this?

Think!

"Open it," said Zach.

"No," whimpered Avis. But she was already obeying him. Going into her pockets for the keys. And she thought of her baby stirring in the crib. And his first soft cranking noise as he awakened. What would he do? What would he do when he saw the baby? How could this be happening?

Zach snatched the keys from her hand as she brought them out of her pocket. He held the automatic on her—she stared into its bore. He unlocked the door. He glanced furtively up and down the empty hall.

Scream, she thought. *Maybe if I just scream . . .*

But he grabbed her shoulder again. Threw her into her own apartment. She stumbled toward the center of the room. She heard the door shut behind her, trapping her inside. Her whole body shook with crying. Zachary snapped the light on.

Avis blinked. She ran her hand under her nose, wiping away the snot. She tried to force down her sobs.

Look! she thought. *Look! Think!*

She looked around through her tear-fogged lenses. She lifted her eyes to the bare walls. Those white walls with their spiraling water stains. With their plaster cracks like bolts of jagged lightning. The Spartan card table. The canvas chair . . .

Look! Look!

There was no sign of him! She hadn't thought of that. There was no sign of the baby anywhere. Every single thing the baby owned was in the nursery and the nursery door was closed. And she hadn't mentioned him either. Downstairs, when they'd been talking, she hadn't mentioned the baby once. Zach didn't even know there *was* a baby.

Think

If she could keep him out of the nursery, if she could distract him . . .

think think think!

Oh, if she could think! If she could just think!

Zachary grabbed the canvas chair with one hand. Swung it around into the center of the room. He was squinting. His head was swimming. The room. Every little detail of the room. All the bits and pieces of it . . . Jesus, they swarmed on him like maggots on a corpse. They crawled into his eyes, they ate at his brain. The walls, the whiteness of the walls. The rectangular window with the blue of evening there. Water stains like fingerprints. Parquet blocks set in puzzle patterns on the floor.

All empty. Why is it all so empty?

He felt dizzy. He couldn't think. "Sit, sit down . . ." he said quickly. He jabbed the gun at her urgently. His eyes kept darting from place to place. *So empty.* He forced himself to look at the girl.

She was backing away from him toward the chair. He really did have to force himself to look. Her face . . . God, it was in his eyes, it filled his vision. The yellow mucus above her lips. The creases at the corners of her eyes, behind her glasses. Lavender framed glasses. Big pores on her nose. Everything seemed enlarged before him. He could barely look at her. *All right, Jesus, please.*

He would have sold his soul for one injection of the drug.

"Sit down, would you?" he said. He was really annoyed with her. He was annoyed that he was going to have to kill her and see her face and hear her cries. That she would twist and shake her head and call for her mother, just like the other one did at the end, when she finally realized it was really happening, that there was no escape and she started babbling please mommy mommy mommy . . . A grown woman. He could not stand to look at it, to hear it. Not without the vision, not without the drug. Damn her. *I'm sorry already!* his mind cried out to heaven. "Look," he said aloud, "this isn't easy for anyone, okay? Just do what I tell you and it'll work out much better." Avis nodded quickly, that giant, magnified face

259

going up and down. The square glasses, pooling with tears. The mottled skin. She lowered herself into the chair. Her hands came slowly down. Her fingers fidgeted on her knees.

All right, thought Zach. All right. He had to think this through. It wouldn't all just fall into place like last time. Last time, after it was over, he had sort of blacked out. Gone into some sort of visionary mode of self-preservation. Drawing the blood with the syringe. Cleaning the knife. Making the phone call: *Eight o'clock. You have to be there.* It would not be so easy this time. This time, he had to plot out the details. Like where the hell was Ollie? It was practically seven o'clock. Like what if he didn't fucking come home in time . . .

You can't worry about that now, damn it. Just think! Think it through!

He was getting frantic. He couldn't keep still. He moved deeper into the room, his heart pounding. He kept the gun trained on the woman as he went around behind her. Her head swiveled to watch him. That face—following him. A pimple on one cheek. The ridges in her orange lipstick.

"Don't hurt me please," she said. "Okay?"

"Just. Face. Front," he growled at her. He was trying hard to keep from losing control. "All right? Just face front. I can't . . . I don't . . ."

Flinching, she turned around. Sniveling. Lifting her shoulders. Crying. He ought to just shoot her. Blow that face into a blank mask of blood. But he had to plan this out, he had to pin this on Oliver too.

Think!

And what if he couldn't, what if Oliver didn't come back in time? How could he work it all out now, for Christ's sake, with all this shit in his head? All this face of hers and everything . . . He felt like he was going crazy.

"Would you face front *please!*" he squealed as Avis stole another glance at him. "Please! Jesus, I'm asking you. I mean, this is hard for me too, you know."

"Just please . . ." she said. But she forced herself to turn away from him. "Don't hurt me."

Think! he thought.

He was in the kitchenette now. The gun trained on the girl's back. He had to keep swiveling his head, taking peeks at the kitchen. The white cabinets. Silver sink. Knives—there they were. Hanging from hooks under one of the cabinets. He grabbed hold of a black-handled cook's knife. Wrestled it from its hook. Moved back into the living room quickly. Turned the blade in the light. Good. He would cut her throat with that. Quiet. Then the neighbors wouldn't know when it happened.

He wondered what that much blood would look like now. Without the vision. Without the drug.

She wondered what a woman would do in a movie. A heroine in a movie—trapped in a chair with a gun in her back—how would she get out of this?

Think. If I could just . . .

She strained backward in her chair, both her fists in her teeth. Biting her knuckles. The tears were drying on her cheeks. Her glasses clearing. She was shuddering with every breath. She kept glancing, wide-eyed, across the room, at the door to the nursery.

He'll check in there. To make sure we're alone. He'll check. He'll find the baby. Think . . .

Like the girls in the movies.

It's a good part for Debra Winger.

No, no, no, she thought. *Think, think, think!*

But these images crowded her mind. Of sharp-eyed brunettes with their hands tied. Of open-mouthed blondes running down hallways. She read these books all day. These screenplays, treatments for would-be films. All these resourceful women, these smart heroines, thinking, always thinking . . .

And here she was . . . and what fear had done to her, what it did to you really! She just felt sapped of will. All dazed, trembly and passive as a piece of paper. Her mind was full of static and half images. Why didn't somebody come? Somebody had to come. Ollie would come. God would bring Ollie. She imagined God: a sort of St. Bernard made of wind, whooshing off to get Ollie. He would come through the door now! Now! He would save her. This couldn't happen.

Avis! Think!

She kept staring at the nursery door. Biting her knuckles. Turning to catch quick glances of Zach. Where was he? At the window now. Perched on the windowsill. Peering out the window. Then back at her.

"Face front. Goddamn it," he whined at her. "You're making everything harder on me."

She faced front, trembling. Looked at the nursery door. Thought of the baby in there. Turning his head on the mattress maybe. Sleeping under the elephant mobile. Working his lips as if sucking her breast. Starting to wake up. That first soft crank. She had hung over the crib rail sometimes, watching him. Watching him wake up slowly to find her there. To smile up at her his big hello baby grin.

Oh God. Oh God please. Let him sleep. Let him stay asleep. Ollie would come before he woke up. Ollie would have to come. God would not let Ollie not come to save them, to save the baby. If the baby could just stay asleep till then. If she could just stay alive . . .

Avis glanced around quickly. Zach was still at the window. Peering out. His lips working, as if he were talking to himself. He glanced at her angrily and she faced front at once. Trembling. Looking at the nursery door. She wanted to talk. She wanted to plead with him to let her be. To . . .

Stall him!

That's what they'd do in the movies, she thought. Stall him. Distract him till the hero showed up . . .

Her lips parted. But no words came. Her mind was blank. Heavy. As if it were too much of an effort for her to make words. She felt she had no will to speak, to think. There was only fear. She was only a piece of thin paper. Just trembling, just sitting there . . .

Zach glanced out the window, looking for Ollie. The little lane was crowded now. Demons under street lamps, their tails curling behind them. Phantoms in black capes going arm in arm, reflected in the plate-glass window of the café. A man in leather hot pants walked with a man in a blonde wig. They all moved together, a single flow toward Sixth Avenue. Toward the Halloween parade.

And where was Oliver? Zach thought. Where the hell was he? He rubbed his forehead. He couldn't think. His brain was so cluttered . . . The burnt wood letters on the café sign . . . The lampblack under a vampire's eyes . . . The white web netting in the part of the blonde wig . . .

He shook his head. Turned away. Caught the woman in the chair sneaking a glance at him. He saw the blackheads at her nostrils. The pink splotches on her cheeks from crying. It was driving him crazy.

"Look," he said, getting off the windowsill. "Look. Look. Just face front, okay? I can't stand it anymore. Just face front."

She turned around. She let out a sob. Her shoulders sagged. "I'm sorry," she said. "I'm just afraid. Are you going to hurt me?"

He looked at her. Flyaway strands of her yellow hair caught the light. Her head was bent forward and her fragile neck was bared. The slope of her shoulders struck him as particularly womanish . . .

"Do you fuck Oliver?" he asked her. The words came out before he could stop them. He didn't even think them, he just said them.

The woman's head came up. "What?"

"Never mind," said Zachary quickly. He waved his gun hand in front of him, as if to erase the thought. "Nothing, I . . . It was stupid . . . I mean, everybody fucks him, right? All the girls just love old Ol."

"No . . ." she said. "No. I never . . . I wouldn't . . . Really. I'm serious."

"Ssh," he said. He knew she did. They all did. He slipped the pistol into his belt again. He put the knife in his right hand. All the girls just loved that crazy old Oliver. He started walking toward her.

He might as well get it over with, he thought. He might as well do it now. He couldn't stand that face of hers anymore. And the suspense, the anticipation of what would happen when he cut her throat. All right, he thought. All right. It was his punishment. It was his fate. He sighed with resignation as he moved toward her. His stomach was churning. How could you tell, he thought, what was fate and what was your own decision? How could you know the difference between what God demanded and what you wanted? And who was going to clean up all that omelette shit downstairs?

Christ, what if Ollie is back already?

He couldn't think. He couldn't think of anything. There was too much clutter. Too much of her stray hairs. The crescent glimpses of her cheek as she tried to steal a glance at him. And now: He saw his own hand. He was reaching out to grab her. He had never noticed before how the blue veins on the back of his hand looked like rivers running from the mountains of his knuckles . . .

Avis turned in her chair. He saw the lavender frames of glasses. He saw one brown eye. The almond shape.

And then the eye went wide, circular with terror. She had seen the knife.

She gasped. Her hand came up.

"Face front!" he hissed.

"Please!"

"Now! Or I'll kill you. Face front!"

She did it. She had to. Reluctantly, she turned her back on him. That was better. Much better. He breathed a little easier, although he could still hear her sobby little voice.

"Are you going to kill me now? Are you going to cut me with that? Please don't, okay? I won't tell anybody anything. I swear. I swear I won't."

He reached out. He felt her hair soft on his fingertips. He was going to grab her hair, pull her head back and plunge the knife into her throat. He could do that. He knew he could do that. His fingers curled around the hair to grab it . . .

And then something . . . a noise . . . somewhere.

Zach looked up. Across the room. The door. Behind that door, there'd been a noise. It sounded like a voice almost. Like a human voice.

Zach stood still, bent over, reaching out. He listened. The

sound didn't come again. But he had heard it. He was sure of it.

Someone was in there!

The baby! Avis felt the strength flow out of her like blood. The baby was waking up! That was his first soft sound. His little head turning on the mattress. His tiny fist rubbing at his eye. The noise went through her like a lance. Pierced her through. All the strength flooded out of her.

Go to sleep, baby! Stay asleep!

By some powerful act of mind, she managed not to turn in her chair. She forced herself not to look at the door.

Stay asleep!

She forced herself not to gasp. She held herself rigid. She faced front, the way he wanted her. She kept her hands down on her knees. Maybe he hadn't heard . . .

"What was that?" he said behind her.

"What?" Avis said—she felt as if someone were inside her, doing the talking for her. All she did was move her lips. "Wh-Wh-What was what?"

"That noise. That sound. Didn't you hear it?"

She allowed herself to turn slightly, to look up at him. He was crouched behind her, the knife in his hand. His eyes, hot and white, were fixed on the nursery door.

"I didn't hear anything," Avis whispered.

"Someone's in there." He turned on her angrily, his teeth showing. "Is someone in there?"

Avis shook her head. *Think!* But she couldn't think. She spoke automatically. "No. In there? That's my bedroom. I live alone."

"Damn it!" said Zach. And he started marching to the door.

He went with long strides, his hand reaching for the doorknob even as he moved. The seconds it took him to cross the room seemed longer than forever. Avis stared at him.

Scream. The baby! Scream.

But she opened her mouth and the scream stuck in her throat. If she screamed she would wake him up for sure. That would be the end of it. He would kill them both. She knew it. She had to stop him and she couldn't think and now he was there. He was at the door. He was reaching for the knob in the long, long quarter-seconds. His hand was on the knob.

Do you fuck Ollie? she thought.

The seconds were almost frozen now, so slow they were almost still. And yet he was turning the knob. She heard the latch clicking. The nursery door was coming open.

All the girls just love him.

"Don't go in there," she said. "I do fuck Ollie. I do fuck him."

"What?" Zachary's head came around toward her. The moments broke into full speed. It was as if time, like a carny ride, had reached the top of the loop, stopped for an instant, and now swooped down. The nursery door opened a crack. She could see the shapes of a Muppets mobile. Kermit the Frog, Miss Piggy. Just their dangling silhouettes through the opening, in the dark.

But Zachary had turned away from them. He was looking back at her with a sidelong glance. His eyes were so white, so wide. His hand, his left hand, slipped from the doorknob. In his right hand, he held the knife. He pointed the knife at her. Its blade glinted in the top light.

Stay asleep, baby, Avis thought. *Just stay asleep.*

"What did you say?" said Zachary.

"That's my bedroom," she blurted out, thinking *Stay . . .* "I fuck Ollie in there. Don't go in there. He says things in there. You shouldn't go in. He says things about . . . about you . . . about, uh . . . about your penis."

"What?" He looked at her as if she were crazy.

Avis thought she was crazy too. She didn't even know what she was saying. She was blabbering without thought, going on instinct. She was thinking, *Don't wake up now, baby. Lull-a-by. Lull-a-by and good night, little baby.* And she said, "That's right. He always says these things, he tells me things about your penis and he fucks me. He fucks me and we laugh about your limp dick, what a girl, he says, what a girl you are in bed . . ."

The words tasted like dirt in her mouth but she ignored it. She kept talking and she kept thinking, *Lull-a-by and good night, little ba-by, sleep ti-ight . . .*

"What a limp dick and he fucks me," she babbled.

Zach took a step closer to her. He cocked his head. "Are you shitting me? Are you . . . ? What else did he say? Really. I'm just curious. Is this for real?"

"Real?" Avis's eyes darted to the open nursery door. Kermit and Miss Piggy and Gonzo bear turned softly in a cool breeze in the dark. "Real. Yes. Every day and he fucks me. And we laugh." *Bright angels up above will send you down their love,* she thought.

Zachary frowned. He looked like a little boy about to cry. "Goddamn it," he said. "I knew it. I *knew* it." He took another step toward her. "What did he tell you? What else? Did he say anything about Tiffany, about me and Tiffany?"

Avis clung to the wooden frame of her chair. She leaned back, away from him as he came closer. "Tiffany?" she said, her voice cracking. "Tiffany yeah. He told me about her and that was, yeah, we really laughed and he fucked me a lot . . ."

Zach took another step and he was standing right over her. He was hanging over her like a vulture and yet she was hardly aware of him. Her eyes, fixed on the nursery door, had glazed over. The whole force of her mind was concentrated on keeping her baby asleep. *Lull-a-by* . . . The whory words kept pouring out of her.

"I fucked him and his big dick, his big hard dick, you can't even with that knife but he laughed about Tiffany . . ."

"All right!" Zach barked suddenly. "Shut up!"

Go to sleep, go to sleep . . . Little baby, good night . . .

"You can't even get it up but he fucks me and he laughs . . ."

"You bitch! I can't believe this! Goddamned Oliver! I didn't ask to live, you know. I didn't ask him to save me! I'm the one who suffers with it . . ."

"Laughing fucking dick . . ."

"Stop it!"

"Laughing at you, girl, girl . . ."

"Stop!"

"Laughing."

"*Stop!*"

He gave a wild cry and leapt at her. The movement brought her from her trance. At the last second, she tried to roll away from him, to roll off the chair. But he got her. He grabbed her hair in his fist. She fell to the floor, her knees cracking on the wood. He ripped her backward, ripped her head back over the chair arm, baring her throat.

Avis bit back her scream. She saw his face looming above her, filling her vision, his eyes black. She heard his hoarse panting and saw the flash of the knife as he lifted it in the air. She clutched at his arm, staring up at him.

Lull-a-by, lull-a-by . . .

Zach, holding her hair in his fist, hissed down at her in triumph. Just as he had hissed at the woman last night. Just as he had hissed into the glazed eyes of her severed head when finally in his rage he had stuffed it into the toilet. It was the same sound of triumph. They were the same words.

"You're not alive!" he told her.

Bright angels up above, she thought, *will send you down their love!*

PART 4

KING DEATH

"The soul shrinks from all that
it is about to remember . . ."
—Richard Wilbur

OLIVER PERKINS

Perkins was scared. It wasn't just dread now. It was real fear, beating in his throat like a trapped butterfly. He had left Zach alone too long. He had lost track of Tiffany outside Nana's apartment. And now . . .

He hurried down the hall to Nana's door. He was thinking: *If Tiffany's here, if she's brought Nana into this . . .* He was thinking about Nana, about her weak heart. He was thinking: *She won't be able to stand it.*

He pounded on the door with his fist.

"Nana?" he called loudly. "It's me." He was already fumbling for the keys in his jeans. "Nana?" He had the key. He fit it into the lock. Took hold of the knob.

But the knob turned in his hand. It was pulled away from him. The door swung in. Swung open.

She stood before him in the doorway, peering out at him with frightened eyes.

"Hello, Oliver," she said.

His own fear beat harder at his throat. He spat her name out between his teeth. "Tiffany."

Tiffany pushed her black and silver hair away from her face. She braced herself, took a breath. Then she pulled the door all the way open. Perkins could see his grandmother now. There by the coffee table near the windows. Her shapeless old self was slumped comfortably in the satin bergère, propped by her hand-embroidered pillows. She looked up when he came in. Her sagging, melted face lifted in a smile.

"Why, Oliver!" she said. Her frail voice quavered. "I've

been hoping and hoping you would turn up. You're just in time for tea."

"Yes, Oliver," Tiffany said nervously. She forced a smile of her own, one corner of her mouth lifting. She swallowed hard. "Chamomile or Earl Grey?"

Perkins looked helplessly from the young woman to the old one; back and forth again. He felt sweat beading under his hairline. What could he say? How much did Nana know? He felt the fear beating harder at his throat.

Tiffany shut the door behind him. Perkins started at the sound. He looked at her quickly. A grandfather clock in the foyer struck the hour: six o'clock.

Zach, Perkins thought. *I have to get back to Zach.* "I can't stay long," he said hoarsely.

"Oh," Nana called from her chair. "Stay. Tiffany can put another cup on for you. I'm sure it's no trouble, is it, dear?"

"No trouble at all, Nana," said Tiffany. She did not take her eyes off Perkins. "Well? What'll it be, Ollie?"

He glared at her, his teeth gritted. He wanted to seize her right then and there. He wanted to shake the truth out of her. In fact, he wanted to tear her in half like a piece of paper. "Chamomile," he snarled.

And Tiffany managed to sing out brightly: "Back in a mo." She turned her back on him. Walked away unsteadily. Even in the quilted shirt, even in the baggy jeans, he saw the movement of her figure as she left the room.

Still helpless, still silent, he looked at Nana. The old lady's quivery smile was expectant. Her eyes were expectant and damp. The light was gone from the tall windows beside her. Only one standing lamp cast a pale yellow glow over the nude Venus in its stand. The rest—the carved chairs, the fireplace, the dark pattern on the rug—was fading into the dusk shadows. Nana seemed tiny and dim at the fringe of the circle of light.

Perkins forced himself to return her smile. "Back in a mo, Nana," he croaked. And he dashed after Tiffany. The knick-knacks in the room rattled as he stomped out of the room.

He found her in the kitchen around the corner. It was a narrow corridor of a room but gleaming. Copper pots and kettles hung from the tiled walls and reflected the light. Butcher block counters shone between the black iron stove and the white refrigerator. Tiffany was setting blue willow china on a silver tray. A copper kettle steamed cheerfully over a blue flame on the stove top behind her. Tiffany's mouth was a thin line. Her eyes were fixed on her work. She did not look up, but Perkins could tell she was aware that he had come into the room.

He glanced cautiously toward the living room, toward Nana. Then he bore in on Tiffany fiercely. His voice dropped to a whisper. "What the hell are you doing here?"

She looked up at him. Her eyes were enormous. "You have to stop following me. You have to stop following me *now*."

"What's that got to do with it? Why the hell did you come here?" He was whispering so hard he sounded as if he were strangling.

She turned back to her tray. The china clinked merrily as she arranged the cups and saucers. "How else was I supposed to get rid of you?" Her voice was low. "I know you won't start a scene here. Not around Nana. Especially not . . . well, I could tell her things, Oliver." When she looked up this time, her gentle, pale face was set. Their eyes met, hard. "And I will tell her too. If you don't leave me alone, I'll tell her anything I have to. It'll upset her, Oliver. It'll make her sick, you know that."

"You goddamned—"

"Shut up, just shut up," she said. "You don't know what's going on. It's all crazy. You don't know. Now we're just . . . we're just going to have a cup of tea. You and me and Nana. We're going to have a cup of tea and then—then, after a while, I'll excuse myself. All right? I'll leave—and you'll just let me go. Do you understand? That's all I want. Just let me go. You can't follow me now. All right?"

Perkins rushed at her. The rage seemed to explode from the core of him: molten, white, liquid rage that spread all through him. He grabbed her by the shoulders. Twisted her around to face him, lifting her until she was on tiptoe, until his eyes were inches from hers. "What have you done?" The whisper hissed out between his teeth. "What have you done to my brother?"

"Let me go." Tiffany's eyes filled with tears. "You bastard. You idiot. You don't know anything. Let me go."

"You set him up, didn't you?" He shook her. "You set him up to take the rap for this murder. Didn't you?"

Her hair spilled over her face. She looked up at him through the strands as he gripped her. She said nothing. Their faces were so close he could smell not just her toilet water but the scent of her skin beneath. He stared down at her, searched her eyes, searched in the aching depths of her eyes. He was aware of the sinewy strength of her shoulders under the quilted fabric. He remembered the feel of her flesh in his hands.

His lips parted as if he were about to speak again.

"The water's boiling," Tiffany said softly.

And Perkins, his mouth open, let her go—he practically dropped her to her feet. He turned away from her as she went to fetch the kettle. He stood there, slumped. He looked down at the silver tray. His gaze fixed on one of the teacups, on the creamy white bottom of it. He gazed down into it until his vision blurred.

It was me, he thought. *I broke the typewriter.*

And it occurred to him—in an odd, dreamy way—that his father had always known that somehow, that he had known the truth of it all along. The bitter old man had pounded Zach's ass again and again with that heavy ruler. He had beat him black with it. Black. And all the time he had known, he had known it was really him.

Perkins felt sick to his stomach. He felt that fluttering fear; larger; filling him; beating against the walls of his entire body now.

"Now watch out," said Tiffany.

Perkins stepped aside as she brought the steaming kettle to the tray. She stood at the counter with her head bowed, her hair spilling forward. She poured the boiling water into the china teapot. A tear fell from her cheek onto the side of the copper kettle. The tear sizzled and evaporated in a little burst of steam.

"You know who killed that girl in the mews," Perkins said to her. "Don't you?" He spoke weakly now, his shoulders raised. He did not look at her. "Whoever helped you with your blackmail racket—he's the one, isn't he? God, Tiffany. I mean, blackmail? You just fucked that guy, didn't you? That Fernando guy. You just fucked him and your partner took the pictures, right? Oh, man, oh, baby, that was cold. Jesus." He heard Tiffany let out a broken sob. He grimaced but he didn't look at her. "So then what? Huh? Woodlawn used the Kincaid girl for a courier so he could keep clear of it, and she got scared and brought in the FBI. And you panicked, right? You panicked and your partner killed her because she was innocent. She wasn't like Woodlawn, she was innocent and she had nothing to lose by giving evidence against you." Perkins's breath came faster, as if he were walking uphill. It was hard: working it out, trying to put it together. It seemed like nothing quite fit. Everything was just a little out of joint. "Then you tried to set me up for it, me and Zach. You got us both to go to the mews. You called the cops while I was there and told them you'd heard screaming . . ." He brought both hands to his forehead. He felt like it was full of sludge. Out of joint, out of whack. He couldn't make it all work. He lifted his eyes to her, confused. "He's your lover, isn't he?" he said slowly. "This partner of yours. That explains it. He's your lover and you do what he says. All this mystical feminist shit and you do whatever he says and you just fucked this Woodlawn guy and now you're in on a murder and you don't care who takes the fall, as long as lover boy gets away, is that it? You don't . . ." He stopped. He couldn't make it all fit. His breath hissed out of him like steam. He was silent and looked at her.

But Tiffany said nothing. She sniffed back her tears as she finished filling the teapot. She turned away to set the kettle on the stove again. Then she turned back to the tray. She shuddered once. She wiped the tears from her cheeks with the side of her hand. Finally, she lifted the tray off the counter.

"Okay," she said. "Now we're going to have tea." She straightened, faced him. "And you won't make a scene. You won't make a scene or I'll tell Nana everything. About you and me and the woman in the mews and everything. It could kill her, Oliver, and I'll do it, I swear." Their eyes met again for a moment. "Now we're going to have tea," she repeated. She moved toward him. For a second, he opposed her, he just stood there in her way. But then his eyes dropped and he stepped aside. Tiffany carried the tray out of the kitchen, into the living room.

They had tea with Nana around the white marble table. In the pale outglow of the standing lamp. In the shadows of evening. Each of them sat in a fading embroidered chair with clawed feet and scrolled arms. Tiffany perched on the edge of her seat and did the honors. She poured the yellow brew into the teacups, first for Nana, then for Perkins, finally for herself. She had prepared a plate of Pepperidge Farm Brussels cookies too and she set one on each saucer. She handed the cups around and sat back with her own, averting her eyes from Perkins. With thin, trembling hands, Nana dipped her cookie delicately in her tea. Tiffany sipped the steam from her cup and gazed into the middle distance. Perkins gripped his saucer and stared Black Death at her.

I'll tell. I'll tell everything.

He could not just let her go, he thought. He would hold her here by force if he had to. He would haul her down to the Sixth Precinct himself. He had to get her to tell Mulligan the truth before she disappeared again.

I'll tell.

He had to get her to clear Zach before the cops got ahold of him. And if she tried to start trouble with Nana . . . Perkins's chest heaved as he slumped heavily in his chair. He gripped his cup and saucer tightly. If she tried to upset Nana, or tell her things . . . With her weak heart . . . His jaw worked slowly. The vein in his temple throbbed. Well, he did not know what he would do. But somehow, he had to keep hold of her. He couldn't let her get away.

"Well!" Nana said. "Isn't this pleasant!" She smiled with tremulous benevolence on them: her grandson and her ersatz granddaughter-in-law. "The three of us together for once."

Perkins tried to nod. Tiffany smiled vaguely. Both of them brought their teacups up to their lips, hiding their mouths.

Nana set the crescent of her cookie carefully on the edge of her saucer. "So," she said, "let's talk about the murder."

Perkins choked on his tea. He coughed and sputtered. Tea splashed over the rim of his cup, off his saucer, onto his sweater. "What?" he finally managed to say.

"Well, it's *such* a catastrophe, isn't it!" said Nana. For a moment, there was a wicked little gleam in her damp eyes.

Open-mouthed, Perkins stared at Tiffany. She looked . . . thunderstruck, was the only word for it. Her cheeks had gone gray as slate. Her eyes were hollow and haunted. She cast an unhappy gaze at the old woman.

"How . . . ?" Perkins coughed again before he could speak. "How did you find out about it, Nana?"

"Find out? Oh now. Ollie." Nana looked down her nose at him reproachfully. Strands of gray hair played on her brow. She looked almost ephemeral in the shadows. As if she might dissipate and vanish, a wisp of smoke. "You didn't think you could keep it from me, did you?"

"I . . . I just . . ."

Tiffany sipped her tea carefully. Watched him. Watched them both.

"I own the place after all," Nana went on. "The police called me early this afternoon. A very nice man named Nathaniel something. Mulligan. Nathaniel Mulligan."

Perkins swallowed. He closed his eyes. Mulligan must have called her just before he started questioning him. She probably knew more than he did. "I didn't want you to worry," Perkins said. He tried to capture his usual tone. "You know what a horrible old crone you are when you worry."

"Well, and I *do* worry," said Nana. "I *am* worried. Of course I am. Look at me. I'm coming apart at the seams, anyone can see that. I called you right away and again this afternoon but you weren't in. Where *were* you? I finally had to take a pill! Oh, Oliver!" The full appeal of her damp old eyes was on him. "I knew I should have sold that place the minute you boys moved away. Now *look* what's happened! I won't ever be able to survive it."

At this, Perkins and Tiffany exchanged a long glance across the tea table. Tiffany's sweet face was all terror now. Her big eyes seemed to glow in the semidarkness like lamps. She doesn't know, Perkins thought. She doesn't know what I'll say. She doesn't know how far I'm willing to go.

I'll tell. I'll tell everything.

But if Nana knows, if Nana already knows the worst . . . He bit his lip. Maybe he should just make his play. Maybe he should just call the police right here and now and hand Tiffany over . . .

"Mr. Mulligan said I had to call him right away if I heard anything," Nana rattled on, almost picking up his thought. "It was so strange. He said I had to call him if I found out where Zach is. And I said, 'Zach? Why do you have to talk to Zach? Zach doesn't know anything about this.' And he said, well, yes, he knew that, but he did need to talk to him, that it was part of his routine. But I don't know, Ollie. What sort of routine is that? I told him, I said, you know, 'I have a very bad heart, Mr. Mulligan, and I am very easily upset and you are making me very frightened.' And he said, well, no, I shouldn't worry about anything. But, of course, that isn't possible at all, now is it?"

Perkins swallowed hard. He was still looking at Tiffany. She was still looking at him, trying to gauge his reactions.

"Just don't get all crazy," Perkins said thickly. He looked at Tiffany as he said it. Then he cleared his throat, willed himself to look at the old lady. Her shapeless body trembled. Her teacup clattered on its saucer in her hand. At any moment, it seemed to Perkins, she would keel over. Spill to the floor. And yet he still thought he saw that gleam. "Zach is fine," he said. "I talked to Zach and he's okay. Okay? Don't worry about Zach."

Nana's hand moved to her chest. Perkins couldn't tell if it was a gesture of relief or if this was the Big One. "Zach is all right?" she said.

Perkins hesitated. His blood seemed to have turned to acid. He could taste the burn when he licked his lips. *No,* he thought. *No, Zach's not all right. Zach's in bad trouble and Tiffany here knows why. We've got to turn her in, Grandma. There's gonna be police and ugliness and you'll hear about what I did with Tiff and Zach will hear. But they're going to kill him otherwise* . . . His mouth opened, as if he were about to speak. But he didn't speak. Nana waited for him eagerly, fingers at her breast. The teacup chattered in her other hand. Perkins stared at it.

"I have to go," Tiffany sang out suddenly. She stood up. She looked from one to the other of them. "I'm sorry, Nana. I have an appointment. I have to go."

Quickly, she set her saucer down on the marble table. She smoothed her quilted shirt. Even in the half-dark, the quilt looked bold and colorful against the fading antiques around the room. *Why are they dressed alike?* Perkins thought. *Why are they always dressed alike?*

"Oh, but Tiffany, dear," Nana said. "You just got here. And you mustn't leave me to worry about this by myself. I can't possibly handle it."

Tiffany looked at her. Looked at Perkins. Looked at her. Her lips moved a moment before she could force out the words. "I'm . . . I'm sorry, Nana, really. I have an appointment. I really have to, I . . . I'm sorry."

And with that, she rushed from the room. Hurried down the hall.

The back door! Perkins thought at once. The back door was down there, across from the bedroom. Tiffany could duck out there, take the fire stairs or the freight elevator.

"Excuse me just a minute, Nana," Perkins said. He spilled tea again as he set the cup down. He was on his feet and following Tiffany.

"What on earth is happening?" said Nana.

But Perkins was already on his way down the hall.

At first, he thought she must have gotten away. He saw the rear exit to his right, the heavy metal door with the bolt across it. He saw the dark bedroom doorway to his left. He thought: She's gone, she's already gone. Then he reached the bedroom doorway. He saw her.

She was bent over in the dark, lifting something from beside Nana's bed. She straightened and he saw it was an overnight bag. A red overnight bag just like Zachie's. She turned with it gripped in her hand. She took a step toward the door before she saw Perkins there.

She was breathless, her voice low. "Let me go, Oliver."

He stepped toward her. "Not until you tell me the truth."

"You know the truth. You don't want to know the truth. Just let me go."

She charged him. Stormed toward the door, lugging the suitcase, her head down as if to butt him out of the way.

This time, Perkins stood his ground. He braced himself in the doorway, his heart pounding, the fear coursing in him. Tiffany pulled up, flung her head back. The silver streak in her hair flashed in the light from the hall. Her teeth flashed. Her eyes flashed.

"Let me go, damn you! It's too late to stop it now. It's too late to stop anything. Oh God!" she cried. "Why is this happening to me? Oh God!"

"I'm calling the police, Tiffany." He couldn't think of anything else to say, anything else to do. With the pounding fear in him, he couldn't think of anything except: *I broke the typewriter. Me!* "I'm calling Mulligan."

For a moment, she could only shake her head at him. He could hear the hoarse rasp of her breath, the choked-back tears. "Go on then," she said through her teeth. "For the love of Christ, for the love of sweet Christ, go on."

And for another moment—another interminable moment —they faced each other in the bedroom doorway. Perkins couldn't move. He did not want to move. He wanted to reach out and grab her. He wanted to shake her again and make her tell him. Make her say that Zach was innocent. Zach was innocent! She had to say it! His hands clenched and unclenched at his sides, but he couldn't lift them. He did not want to touch her again. He did not want to feel her shoulders in his hands.

He turned away from her. There was a phone by the bed. An old-fashioned Princess on the bowlegged nightstand. Perkins knew it was there. But somehow, it did not occur to him to use it. He just didn't think of it. He went back down the hall instead. He crossed through the living room.

"Ollie?" said Nana from her chair.

He went right past her, back into the kitchen. There was a phone in there too. It was hung on the wall beside the refrigerator. He lifted it—lifted the handset to his ear. He stood there, staring at the number pad. He raised his hand to the numbers.

But he did not press the buttons. He just stared. He held the handset to his ear. He listened to the dial tone. He saw the kitchen in his peripheral vision. The gleaming copper cookware. The green linoleum floor. He stared at the phone and listened until the dial tone broke. A recorded voice came on: "If you'd like to make a call, please hang up and dial again . . ."

Then, slowly, Perkins lowered the handset into the cradle. He stared at the phone. He felt black and sick inside and the oddest thought came to him suddenly. Suddenly, he thought: *I'm going to die tonight.* Just like that. All at once, he was absolutely certain of it. *They're going to kill me.* It wasn't just a premonition. It made sense in a way, after all. If Tiffany and her partner were setting him up, they would *have* to kill him, wouldn't they? Otherwise, he might be able to clear himself. He might be able to convince the police of the truth. If they could kill him, if they could make it look like an accident or a suicide . . . Well, that way, they could pin the whole thing on him.

And Zach too.

Zach too, he thought. That's right. They would have to kill Zach too . . .

He stared at the phone. His hands began to tremble at his sides. His fear was no mere butterfly anymore. It was a great batlike thing. Squatting there in his stomach. Squatting with its wings furled. Waiting to spread those wings. Waiting to rise . . .

You know the truth. You don't want to know the truth.

Perkins stared at the telephone and trembled. Why hadn't he called the police? he wondered.

I'll tell everything.

And why—it occurred to him now—why hadn't he used the phone in the bedroom? Why had he come in here instead?

Perkins closed his eyes, his heart sinking. The bat-thing inside him tested its wings, beating them against him, yearning to rise. It *would* rise too, if he let it. He knew that. If he

281

relaxed for a single moment, it would tear its way to the surface. Grinning, shrieking. If he let himself go. If he let himself think. If he let himself stay sober too long. If he let himself love someone. If he let himself write his poems, it would rise . . .

It would rise, and it would ruin everything. It would destroy everything—everyone—that he loved.

You don't want to know.

With an effort, he lifted his head. He turned and looked down the hallway. He already knew what he would see.

The door across from the bedroom stood ajar. The rear exit. The bolt was thrown back and a dark sliver of hallway showed between the jamb and the door's heavy edge. Perkins stood where he was and looked at it, and the black thing squatted down deep in his belly, its wings furled again, its eyes red and eager. It was waiting for the right moment . . .

"Ollie?" It was his grandmother's voice. Frail and tremulous. Calling to him from the living room. "Ollie? What's going on?"

Perkins said nothing. He took a breath. He held on to himself, held himself together. He stood in front of the telephone and he looked down the hallway at the open door.

She's gone, he thought dully. *Tiffany's gone.*

And it was true. He had let her get away.

NANCY KINCAID

Nancy woke up to the sound of sirens. Sirens in the air above her head. Red demons, flitting here and there, howling. The flash of them: red lights, white lights . . . She rolled onto her back and groaned. Her eyes fluttered open. She saw the sky. The washed-out black of the Manhattan sky with no stars. A gibbous moon in rainbow wisps of clouds. The jagged city skyline: half-lighted towers reaching up like fingers, clawing up the purple wall of the night.

"Oh God," she grunted. There was so much pain. And the sirens were screaming at her. Swooping and diving at her head. Whoop, whoop, whoop. Louder and louder. *They're here*, she thought hazily. *They're here to get me.* She lifted up a little. The pain! It made her throw her head back, open her mouth in a silent scream. The muscles in her back felt torn in two. The wind seemed to have been pounded out of her belly with a baseball bat. Her head—it was ringing—throbbing—Jesus! She put her hand to her brow to keep her brains from spilling out. The screams of the sirens were intolerably loud. The red lights danced in the sky.

She felt something damp in her hair. Something warm and sticky just above her temple. She brought her fingers away and looked at them.

Blood?

It was. Blood. What the hell had happened? Where the hell was she? She looked up. It made her neck hurt. Her vision went blurry. She squinted into the dark. There was a dwarf up there. Just hanging up there. Squatting lewdly above her head, as if pinned to the brick wall behind him. He was grinning, his legs spread wide, his eyes malicious and bright. He was lifting an alabaster ledge in his two upraised hands. He seemed about to hurl it down on her.

Gargoyles, she thought. Right. She remembered now. The stone gargoyles had come to life. They had chased her, scrabbling right down the side of the building. Oh yeah. It had been that kind of day. She shifted, grunting with the flash of agony through her back. She lifted herself into a sitting position. The sirens now seemed to be a solid dome of sound, ear-hammering sound, surrounding her, pressing down on her. She blinked a little. Peered at the asphalt around her. She remembered that too. She had been at the corner of the ledge when she fell. Lexington Avenue on her left, the flat roof of the connecting building to her right. She had fallen to the roof. If she had fallen the other way, if she had fallen toward the street, it wouldn't be the cops coming for her now, it would be the Sanitation Department.

She almost laughed—and then she grimaced instead as she felt something like a punch in the pit of her stomach. She was working herself over onto her hands and knees now, trying to push her way to her feet. The asphalt roof, the flashing sky around her, tipped and swayed. The sirens throbbed inside her head. She jacked her eyes open wider, fighting down nausea. Other things were also coming back to her. Coming to her in flashes, bathed in the red light all around. Her mother. Her mother's face. Pressing in on her. Her voice. *Murderer! Murderer!*

"Uh!" She let out a syllable of pain as she got her feet under her.

Murderer!

And the newsman's voice: *The brutal killing of Nancy Kincaid.*

Murderer!

Who the hell am I? she thought.

And with a great effort, she stood. Her knees felt raw, bone scraping against bone as she straightened. She groaned and looked down at herself. Her jeans were torn at one knee. Her skin was torn and bloody. Her gray turtleneck was ripped at the sleeve, stained with blood, streaked with dirt in front.

And I just changed my goddamn clothes five minutes ago and now my lipstick's probably smeared and . . .

The sirens stopped. Just like that, they went off like a light bulb, that suddenly. They reached a peak of sound, they filled the sky, the flashing lights danced and sparkled around the moon—and then the sirens died. The lights flashed silently. Nancy stood swaying in the eerie quiet, the whoosh of wind and traffic. Her head felt loose on her neck. Her thoughts were blurred and slow, as if they were underwater. She heard doors opening and clunking shut on the street below. Half-staggering on stiff legs, she moved toward the sound. She moved to the edge of the roof. There was a low parapet there. She leaned her hands against it. She looked down over it onto Lexington Avenue.

The cars had halted to her right. They were strewn around the corner, near Gramercy Park. There were six of them that she could see. More, probably, out of sight. God, you'd think she was Public Enemy Number One or something, the way they were clustered down there. Their red and white flashers spun swiftly. They threw light off onto the wall of the building. The underside of the leaves. The trees and statues and iron gates of the little park. Red and white light everywhere. Nancy leaned against the parapet and watched. The cops were now piling out of their cars. Two cops from one car. One from another. Two from a third. They were all running toward the building's front entrance. Their faces set, their hands to their gun butts. And now, on Twenty-first Street, a huge blue and white truck was pulling up too. A whole truck! It looked about a block long and a story tall. Nancy watched, amazed, as the truck's back doors opened and an army of policemen poured out. Cops with body armor, Plexiglas visors, and metal shields. They rushed toward the building's doors as well.

"Whoa," Nancy murmured. She shook her head. It made her feel tired. All those cops. Coming to get her. She hurt so much. Too much to run for it. And what would happen, anyway, if they caught her now? What would be so bad about it, really? They'd probably just take her back to the hospital. Pump her full of tranquilizers again. Maybe they'd even let her have more therapy sessions with what's-his-name. Dr. Schweitzer, whatever. That sweet man she'd kneed in the balls. Then, of an evening, she could sit around with Billy Joe. Chat about her heroic journey to find the magic word, about sending dead Jews to the moon . . .

Nancy's eyes drooped closed. She swayed back and forth, her mouth open. What would be so bad? she thought. She was tired. So tired . . .

Oliver . . .

She snapped awake. She straightened at the parapet, her fingernails scraping the concrete. Her heart beat fast as her eyes came wide open, as she stared down at the police below. The blue men, gripping their holsters, ran toward the building under the flashing red lights.

And she thought: Oliver. Oliver Perkins. She had to find

him. That was the thing. The urgent thing. The one thing she really knew. She remembered him. No. She remembered the feel of his book. The slick feel of his book's white cover in her fingers.

He gave it to me. He said I had to carry it for identification.

She remembered the rough texture of the pages, their corners between her finger and her thumb. And the black print of the words beneath her eyes.

What if we went off together into the hills
and on into the hills beyond the hills where the
    leaves are changing?
Where the first remark of gray among the branches
is insinuated in me now like something one
    learned before youth
and has, in consciousness, forgotten . . .

She remembered the rhythm, the music of the words. She had not even understood them all exactly. Poetry. Christ. What did she know about poetry? But the *feel* of it. She had gotten that, she remembered that. The sweet-natured melancholy. The sense of life and death creeping down out of the woods at night to the lonesome man watching. She remembered his eyes, his lonesome eyes: the picture of the poet on the back cover. She had sat there, hadn't she? All girlish and dreamy for a few minutes. Her feet up on her desk, the book against her thighs. Thinking back to what it was like when a boy said things to you, so-deep things, leaning toward you with his earnest eyes and you still believed him. She had sat dreaming about the garret where she'd lie, her uptight Catholic body skinny and naked under the single sheet. And him hunched grimly at his desk, his pen moving over the pad in the lamplight . . .

This is the Animal Hour.

She swayed, gripping the parapet, nauseous, weak. The Animal Hour. Yes. Yes. She had to be there. She had to. It could already be too late. She did not even know what time it was anymore. It could already have happened.

Oliver.

They were going to kill him. She had to get there. She had to get to him in time.

Without thinking, she began to climb onto the parapet. She cried out with the effort, cried out in pain. Her back, her knees, her head—the ache everywhere blended into a single hot sting through her entire body. Still, she worked her leg over the concrete parapet. Looked down. A long drop to the sidewalk. She could break her legs easily. She could break her neck . . .

But there was a window below her, halfway between her and the sidewalk. If she could lower herself to the window ledge, if she could get her feet on it . . .

She glanced up. Looked to the corner. More cops were rushing toward the entrance now. Others stood poised at their cars, standing at the open doors, their radio mikes in their hands. None of them was looking her way. She brought her other leg over the parapet, grunting with the pain. Slowly, she lowered herself. Clinging to the parapet with her hands, she let her legs hang down.

She dangled there. Her face tapped against the brick. Her muscles burned as her arms stretched above her. Her head pounded. Her feet sought for purchase on the ledge below. A car horn blasted. Nancy gasped. Her fingers began to slip away. Someone yelled at her from a passing car. She heard their laughter fading as the car went by.

Panting, she lowered her feet to the windowsill. Tears of pain made her nearly blind. Red pain, all through her. The tips of her sneakers touched the sill. Her fingers slipped to the edge of the parapet.

And then they slipped off. She dropped to the window ledge. She clutched at the face of the building. For an instant, she balanced there. But only for an instant. Then, twisting, she half-fell half-jumped to the sidewalk below.

It was a light landing. Not that far to fall. She came down on her feet, but her legs gave under her. She collapsed to her knees. The sidewalk slapped against her raw knees. She gave a muted cry and pitched forward. Sprawled on her face on the concrete.

She tasted grime. Felt the gritty stone against cheek and

nose. "I hope you appreciate this, Oliver," she muttered. Then she pushed herself to her hands and knees.

"You okay, lady?"

She cried out. Her head snapped back. She saw a werewolf. A werewolf was standing over her. A werewolf wearing a high school letter jacket.

He bared his fangs. His red eyes peered through a mask of bristling fur. His hairy paw was reaching down at her. "Need a hand?"

"Aaah!" she said. She stared at him. "Aaa-aaa-ah!" She scrambled away from him on her hands and knees, ignoring the pain. She found the wall and clawed her way quickly to her feet, her breath rasping. The wolfman stood where he was and stared at her with his red-streaked eyes. She staggered away from him. Staggered up Lexington, toward Twenty-second Street. She cast looks back over her shoulder at him. Held her hands up to ward him off.

The werewolf shrugged, finally. Stuck his hands in the pockets of his jeans and ambled off toward Twenty-first Street, where the cops were gathered. Nancy stopped to watch him go. She stood at the corner. Her head throbbed, her heart pounded hard. She watched as the wolfman joined a mummy and Frankenstein monster. All of them walked off together under the canopy of flashing lights.

Nancy let out her breath. She lifted her head. She looked up at the building above her. She saw the open window through which she had come. The lace curtains blowing out through it, fluttering in the cool October breeze. Her father had his head poking out. She saw his silver hair. He had his arm raised and was pointing along the ledge where she had gone. He pointed along the face of the building toward the connecting roof where she had fallen.

Only he's not my father, Nancy thought. *My father is dead. My father died when I was little.*

Now there was a policeman too. A young patrolman with a thin mustache. He was sticking his head out the window also. Leaning out next to the silver-haired man. He was looking along the ledge where the silver-haired man was pointing. Nancy stood on the sidewalk below and gazed up at them. In another moment, she thought, the policeman would look down. He would look down and spot her standing there. Still, she did not move. She did not want to move. She stood there, looking at the window, thinking of the bedroom inside. The soft, frilly canopy bed. The mirror. The photographs of laughing girls who were all friends together. She did not want to leave . . .

She shivered. Shook herself. *Oliver,* she thought. *Come on. Come on. The time* . . . She had to go.

The silver-haired man was pointing and pointing. And the cop beside him was starting to look down, scanning the face of the building with his sharp cop's eyes. He would look down at the sidewalk. He would see her.

Nancy hesitated only another second. *Well,* she thought. *Good-bye. Good-bye.*

And then she turned. She hobbled off. As fast as she could. Around the corner. Into the night. To find Oliver.

OLIVER AND ZACHARY

Now the parade was about to begin. The thick crowd of people on Sixth Avenue had congealed into a solid mass. They packed the sidewalks. They pressed against the blue police barricades. Masked and hooded, smeared with makeup, sucking at sack-covered bottles of beer, they watched the street. They waited for the marchers. Behind them, on whatever thin strip of sidewalk was left, another crush of people pushed uptown: a gelatinous flow between the spectators on one side, and the vendors on the other. The vendors shouted above the shouts and murmurs of the crowd. They hawked their battery-powered domino masks fringed with blinking lights. They blew paper trumpets into the night air.

Perkins came out of Nana's building and saw what was happening. He stopped under the awning. He cursed under his breath. It had taken him several minutes to free himself from his grandmother's anxious hands. It was almost seven o'clock now. And that crowd—he was going to have to fight his way downtown.

But it didn't matter. He had to get back to Zach. He had left his brother alone too long. The police could have found him already. The FBI. Or Nancy Kincaid's murderer . . .

He started toward the avenue. He joined the rapid stream of costumed spectators as they flowed into the muddy human river. *They're going to kill him,* he thought, his mouth set, his eyes fixed. *They're going to kill him and set him up for the Kincaid murder.* He shouldered his way into the mass of people. He ignored the weight of blackness in his belly; the premonition floating around his mind like haze. He kept moving as the heavy tide of flesh closed over him.

He had to get back to his brother.

In the darkened room, amidst the mounds of books, the slanting towers and shelves of books, Zachary knelt on a spot of bare floor. The small, sinewy man was in deep shadow there, his hands clasped beneath his chin. His head was bowed. His eyes were closed. His lips were moving. Silently, he prayed to Jesus.

Let Ollie come home in time, he prayed. It would all come apart if Ollie didn't come home and save him. He would never take drugs again, if Ollie came. He swore it. He knew he'd promised before, but he really swore it now. Really. *Please,* he prayed, *don't let me go to prison. Dear God, please, not that. Just give me a chance to convince the police that I'm innocent. That it wasn't me. It wasn't me. Please . . .*

He shut his eyes tighter. He peered into the blackness beneath his lids. He tried to clear his mind, even of supplication. He tried to go blank, to go empty. He wanted God to come into him. He wanted the power of God to fill him. He wanted to be one with God, a single force of desire.

But his mind . . . He couldn't get it clear. Even in the dark, even with his eyes closed, so many *little* things . . . They invaded him. They ate like termites at his concentration. The sound of voices through the open window. The touch of air, the fresh October air that smelled of leaves. Shouts and laughter from the street . . . And music now too: the music from the parade.

"Damn it!" Zachary whispered harshly.

And a baby crying. Somewhere. Eating at him, buzzing in his brain. Giving him no peace: a baby, somewhere, crying and crying.

The library's castlelike spires were silhouetted against the purple sky. Their silver steeples glistened in the city light and the white light of the gibbous moon. Below, the huge crowd pressed in from either side on the empty, waiting avenue. Masses of humanity coursed sluggishly: uptown on the east sidewalk, downtown on the west by some unspoken agreement. In the street, the police ambled back and forth along the barricades. Under the barricades, children sat on the curb. The children's faces were blackened by makeup or hidden by masks. Their eyes were big as they stared up at the passing cops.

Perkins had crossed over at Twelfth. He was on the west sidewalk now, directly beneath the library. He had shouldered his way into the downtown tide and the flowing mass had sucked him in. Bodies were pressed against him, back and front. Shoulders were pressed against his shoulders. The heat of breath, the smell of sweat, the stink of beer, swept up into his nostrils. He elbowed and twisted, trying to edge his way deeper into the flow. But the mass was unyielding. It carried him along. Under the library's lowering facade. Under a stand of yellowing sycamores. Under the awnings of stores and their dark windows with paper skulls and pumpkins and witches grinning out at him. He made his way downtown yard by sludgy yard. He felt the time passing, felt it like a pulse in the world outside him. Inside him, the black batlike thing crouched with its wings furled, waiting to rise.

Maybe he would find the apartment empty when he got

there, he thought. Or maybe he would find Zach dead. His body sprawled on the bed. The blood everywhere. His head . . .

Look what they did to my head, Oliver.

With a grunt, he forced his way between two women. Forced himself to stop imagining things. He pushed against the mass. He craned his neck, looked over the solid carpet of heads leading downtown. There was his street. Cornelia Street. Just up ahead.

And there was the parade.

It was coming up the avenue. A high-stepping Dixieland band led the way. He could hear the mournful horns playing "St. James Infirmary." He could see a cornet's bell as it caught the streetlight, as it slashed the air, leaving green and golden traces in its wake. Behind and above the band, dancing to the music against the sky, were skeletal dinosaurs. Enormous fossils made of papier-mâché, swaying over the heads of the people who carried them. Clowns and spangled transvestites skipped along the edges of the march, along the curbs, throwing confetti at the onlookers. A cheer went up from the crowd as they passed. It rose up toward Perkins like a wave. Paper trumpets honked loudly. Noisemakers rattled. The crowd seemed to tighten around him.

Then he broke free. He twisted away from the muddy flow. He went stumbling down Cornelia Street, toward his brownstone.

Zach.

Breathing hard, forcing down his premonitions of disaster, he ran for home.

Zachary was on his feet by the time Oliver got there. He was pacing back and forth in the little floor lanes between the books. The sound of the key in the latch made him stop short, spin to the door. The door swung open. Zach saw Oliver there, leaning against the jamb, slumped, panting.

Thank you, Jesus, Zachary thought.

It was quarter past seven. There was still time.

"You all right?" Oliver said, breathless. He peeled off the jamb, staggered into the room. He pushed the door shut behind him. Neither of them moved to turn on the lights. They faced each other in the blue shadows. For some reason, the dark made them speak low, almost in whispers.

Zachary already knew what he had to say. He had it all worked out. Still, the words came shakily. "She . . . she was here, Ollie. She came here."

Oliver coughed, tried to catch his breath. He leaned back against the wall, holding his chest. "Who . . . ? Who did?"

"Tiffany."

"What?"

Oliver straightened. Zach couldn't make out his expression. He didn't want to meet his eyes. He paced back and forth a little in the dark. He ran his hand up over his bristly crew cut. "That's right. That's right. I was on the bed . . ."

"She came here?" Oliver whispered. He shook his head. "When? I just saw her. I just saw her at Nana's. She left, like, ten minutes before me."

At Nana's? Zachary stopped pacing. His heart seemed to ball itself into a fist, expand like a balloon, and then contract again. What the hell was she doing at Nana's, for Christ's sake? She wasn't supposed to be at Nana's. She wasn't supposed to be anywhere! No one was supposed to see her. She was supposed to stay out of town, stay out of the way at her mother's until the time was right. That was the plan. *EVERYTHING'S GETTING FUCKED UP, JESUS, HEEELP!*

"Uh, that's right, that's right," he went on quickly. He paced again in front of his brother. His brother peered at him, watched him going back and forth in the shadows. Zach massaged his forehead. The sound of Dixie brass was at the window. Under that, he could hear the baby crying louder: Aaah. Aaah. Aaah. It was hard to think. "That's right," he pressed on. "She was here, uh, just about ten minutes ago, that's just about right. I was . . . I was on the bed . . ." He went back to the story he'd planned. Oliver, panting, gaping, watched him. "Just lying there and I heard a knock. A knock at the window and I looked up. God, Ollie, it was like she was floating there in the night, floating right outside the window."

Oliver turned toward the window, as if he expected to see her there. "She came up the fire escape."

"Yes. Yes. So I went—"

"How? How did she know you were here?"

"What?"

"How the hell did she know you were here, Zach?"

"I don't know. I don't know," Zach answered quickly. He watched the floor as he paced. His black eyes shifted back and forth. He had to think. "I mean, that's why . . . that's why I was so surprised to see her and . . . And I got up, I . . . I went to the window. I said, 'Tiffany . . .' You know, like: 'What the hell is going on?' And she said—she said she knew everything, Ollie. About the murder. The girl in the mews. She said she knew the whole story."

"Damn her, damn her." Oliver's voice cracked. His eyes were suddenly gleaming eagerly in the darkness. Zach turned his face to the side to hide his smile. *Yes!* he thought. *I've got him.* "Did she tell you?" Ollie asked.

"Um . . . um . . . um . . . ," Zach said. A drum echoed him outside: Bum, bum, bum. And that goddamned baby. The thin wail, spiraling higher now with frustration, fear. Why didn't somebody pick the fucking kid up? "Well, she said, she said she wouldn't talk here," Zach stammered. "She wanted . . . she wanted to meet me. Somewhere private, she said. She said she'd tell everything, but it had to be . . . it had to be somewhere private."

"No." Oliver shook his head. "No. No. No. This is a setup, man."

Zach thought his heart would blow right through his ribs. He halted in midstride. He swallowed hard and turned his head to stare at his brother. "What-What-What . . . What-What . . . do you mean, a setup?" he said.

Oliver did not answer right away. He just shook his head again. "I don't know, I . . . I have this feeling . . . It's just . . . It's all wrong. I can't work it out, it's all wrong." Then: "Where is this? Where does she want to meet?"

Again, Zach buried a smile in the shadows. "At your room."

"My room?"

"In the library. It was my idea. The library is closed during the parade and you're the only one who has a key. You see?

It's totally private, no one can get in but you. Tiffy said she'd meet us there at eight. She said she'd tell us everything. She said if we weren't there by eight, she'd leave." It was a good story. Oliver would go for it; Zach was sure. But he added: "I'm really worried about her, Ollie. This isn't like Tiff at all. She's in some kind of terrible trouble." It sounded bogus even to him, but Oliver didn't notice.

Oliver just made a noise of frustration. He ran both hands through his long hair. "No," he said. "No. Something's wrong. Something's wrong with this. I gotta think. We gotta figure this out. Call a lawyer. Call the cops." He squeezed his eyes shut. His hands gripped his hair.

Zach could only stare at him, stare at his silhouette, holding his breath. He was thinking, *Please. Please, Jesus. Please.*

Oliver opened his eyes. He looked around the room. "Do you hear a baby crying?" he asked.

The sound—the thin wail punctuated by screeches of anguish—vanished for a moment under the sound of the parade. An old-fashioned marching band was passing by the corner of Cornelia and Sixth. "Halls of Montezuma" came in through the window. Oliver wasn't sure he'd heard the baby's cry at all. He held his head. He tried to think. His mind was empty except for the consciousness of blackness: that heavy weight, that hunkering thing inside him . . . For a moment, strangely, he thought of the sledding hill again. The snowy hill outside his home on Long Island when he was a boy. He thought of riding down the hill on the Flexible Flyer, he and Zach. *Don't let go, Ollie, don't let go!*

Suddenly, Zach stepped toward him out of the shadows. His face was clear. His large, dark eyes appealed to him. His voice was tremulous and youthful. "I've gotta go to her, Oliver. You don't have to come, but I've got to. Okay? I love her. Nothing else matters to me. I don't care about the police or anything. I've just got to go."

Oliver looked down at him. The band was marching by. He could hear the baby again. Aaah. Aaah. Aaah. It couldn't be Avis's, he thought vaguely. She'd never let him cry like that. Christ, she'd never let him off her tit long enough.

"I'm going, Oliver," Zach said with boyish determination.

Oliver stood silent. What could he say? That he suspected her? That he'd had a premonition? That he knew she was faithless because he'd done her his own damned self? He stood silent, his lips moving.

"I'm going," Zach said again. "With that crowd out there, I may not make it in time as it is. I've got to go."

He turned and marched away, into the room, into the dark. He went into the bathroom. Oliver knew there was no stopping him. There never was when he got like this.

In a moment, Zach came out again. He was gripping his bag, his red overnight bag. *Just like hers,* Ollie thought. *Everything the same.*

"There are a million cops out there tonight," Oliver told him. "You'll be nailed in a minute."

Zach was at the closet now. He pulled out a long gray raincoat, shrugged it on and buttoned it. He pulled a cap from its pocket and tugged it down over his eyes. "I'll be okay," he said.

Oliver snorted. Zach hardly seemed to be there anymore, hidden under all those clothes. He was like the Invisible Man.

Zach stepped to him and held out his hand. "I've got to see her, bro. I've got to go. Give me the key to the library."

The two brothers stood silent in the darkened room. The crowd cheered outside. The baby cried.

"All right," Oliver said after another moment. "All right. I'm coming with you."

Awright! Awright! I say, Hallelujah, Lord! Zach went high-stepping down the brownstone stairs, Oliver behind him. The younger brother was practically giggling with glee. *Praise Jesus!* he thought. It was all coming true. Ollie had played right into his wicked hands. *Nya-ha-ha!* He clutched the handle of his red bag. He pranced to the entrance hall, to the foyer door. It was going to be easy now, he thought. There was still plenty of time to get to the library. Plenty of time to get the thing done, to make the switch with Tiffany and be off, the twenty-five thousand dollars in their pockets. Even if Nana had seen her, they could still make up some alibi or other.

Besides, when Nana found out Oliver was dead—well, there probably wouldn't even *be* a Nana anymore. *Snark-snark-snark-snark-snark.* Yes! God still loved him. All was forgiven. He could feel it in his crazy bones.

He gripped the door. Pulled it open. Glanced back to urge his brother on.

Oliver wasn't there.

Zach did a double take. His eyes shifted this way and that, as if he thought Ollie had disappeared. Then he looked up. His lips parted. He moved back to the foot of the stairs. He peered up from under his cap, through the harsh light and dark shadows cast by the hallway bulbs.

Oliver still stood on the second-floor landing. He had his hand on the newel post, as if he were about to come down. But he did not move. His head was lifted, cocked, as if he were listening. His face was turned away. He was looking up the stairs.

"Ollie! Ollie!" Zach called up to him. "Come on! Come on! We've got to go. Now! Or we'll be late."

"That *is* coming from upstairs," Oliver murmured.

"What?" said Zach. "What is? Come on! Come on!"

Oliver still hesitated. He shook his head. "That's Avis's baby," he said.

"*Ollie!* Come on! Would you hurry? Would you . . ."

Zachary stopped. The words died in his mouth. They turned to dust in his mouth. He could taste them, taste the dust.

Avis's baby.

His stomach went soft. For a moment, he thought the shit would just stream out of him where he stood. He tightened his ass. He gaped up the stairs at Oliver.

She had a baby. A fucking baby.

He knew it was true. The minute Ollie said it he knew. Jesus! Jesus Christ! If he hadn't been in such a goddamned hurry to get out of her apartment! He should've *checked* that door. He'd meant to. That closed door. That other room. He should've checked in there! There had been a baby!

Zachary felt his face go hot, go red. He felt a helpless wailing rage well up inside him. It seemed echoed by the baby's frantic screams. She had tricked him! Damn her! The bitch! That's why she had started cursing at him like that, he thought. That's why she'd said all those ugly things to him. She just wanted to make him mad. To draw him away from the door. To draw him away so he wouldn't find the baby. So he wouldn't kill her goddamned motherfucking baby!

Zach snorted in his rage. He licked his lips. He tasted the dust in his mouth, the bitter dust. Oh. Oh, he thought. He would've done it too. Oh yes. Oh yes. He would've pinned the wailing snot-nosed little shit to his crib cushion with a single stab. He wouldn't have let him wake up like this, after all. He wouldn't have let him start screaming like this. Drawing Oliver's attention away, drawing him upstairs to find what had happened . . .

Zach peered up the stairs, red-faced. His bowels churned like a cement mixer. This was exactly what he hadn't wanted.

"Oliver," he said again—but his voice was so weak that Ollie probably didn't even hear it. "Ollie . . ."

"Hold on a minute, Zach," Oliver said. He let go of the newel post. Moved away from the top of the stairs. "Hold on. I've got to go up there."

Zach followed his brother up the stairs. He went heavily, miserably, like a prisoner to his doom. His head was hung. His footsteps thudded on the stairs. Why did God hate him so? Why would God not forgive him?

As he trudged up the second flight, he heard the pounding above him. Oliver's fist on Avis's door. Thump, thump, thump. The baby shrieked in answer. Oliver shouted: "Avis! Ave! You in there? You all right?"

Zach reached the landing. He saw his brother at the door, his fist still raised. There was a woman in the hall too, standing in the neighboring doorway. She was a thin woman with a waxy face and bug eyes. Her hands were clasped before her, fingers working, as if she were a mantis.

"She never lets that baby cry like that. Not ever," she whispered. She had an English accent.

Zachary watched sullenly, his shoulders hunched inside his coat. His eyes had sunk deep beneath his brows. *Damn her! Damn her!*

Oliver was reaching in his pocket for his key. He would have a key, wouldn't he? He was muttering to himself. "If her fucking ex is in there . . . if this is you, Randall, if it's you, you just don't know, you can't imagine the hurt I'll put on you, pal, no one can . . ."

He was slipping the key in the door. Zach just watched him sulkily. He could think of no way to stop him. He was out of ideas. *Damn her!* he thought helplessly. His mouth worked bitterly. *Damn, damn, damn her!* She had tricked him. Tricked.

Oliver pushed the door open. The baby's cries were suddenly loud. The hoarse, choking sobs washed out over them in waves. Oliver stepped into the apartment.

Zach sighed miserably. *Shit*, he thought. He shook his head. He did not bother to follow his brother into the apartment until he heard Oliver's wild cry rising up to mingle with the baby's. Then, sagging, he humped to the doorway. The bug-woman frittered along behind him.

"Oh God!" Zach heard her gasp.

Oliver stood just within the threshold. His head was thrown back. His hands were clutching at his sweater. He was tearing at his sweater, tearing it open. Frowning, Zach watched as his older brother cried out wildly again.

Zach thought: *Oh come on, Oliver. Don't overdo it, for Christ's sake.*

Oliver sobbed and looked down at Avis Best. She lay still and silent on the floor where Zach had left her. She lay on her back near the canvas chair. One arm was resting on the seat, the other was flung outward. Her blonde hair was fanned out, turning black at the edges where it had sunk into the pool of blood that surrounded her head like a scarlet corona.

Her face was tilted back, her chin was lifted. Her glasses were askew on her nose. Her eyes were shut.

Her throat was slashed open.

In the other room, the baby cried and cried for her to come. But she was surely dead.

NANCY KINCAID

"Oliver Perkins!" she said into the phone. *My father is dead,* she thought. She had to shout to be heard above the drunken teenagers. There were three of them, white boys, on the sidewalk. Dressed in black rags, their faces blackened. They were spraying each other with some sort of green slime from aerosol cans. They were laughing and screaming. Staggering back and forth on the sidewalk behind her. They were screaming, "Hallloweeeen! Halllooooweeeeeen!"

"No: Perkins," Nancy shouted into the phone. "That's right. I need his address too."

There was a pause. A truck rumbled downtown on the far side of Park Avenue. Sparse traffic zigzagged uptown at a lick. The drunk boys' hilarity was momentarily washed away by the sound of sirens. More sirens: two more cop cars howled down Park. Screeched around the corner toward Gramercy, right by Nancy's phone booth.

My God, she thought, am I the only thing they have to do tonight?

A recording came on the phone line. Nancy stuck her finger in her free ear. The boys were skipping in a circle now, as in a war dance by Hollywood Injuns. They were shrieking the words to "Bad Moon Rising."

"The number is . . . ," the recorded voice said distantly.

Nancy listened with her eyes closed. She repeated the numbers in a whisper. With her eyes closed, she waited for the live operator to return.

My father's dead, she thought. And, with her eyes closed,

she saw the empty hallway outside her childhood bedroom. It was so dark now—now that he was gone. It was so full of the old, half-feared phantoms. The fanged monsters and snakes and red-eyed ghosts. They were crawling out of their closets now, rising in wisps from under the baseboard. The house was big and empty all around her. It was unprotected; no longer patrolled by her father's aura of strength. Her father was dead. He had fallen. He had fallen into something bad . . .

Company. Yes. Bad company.

He had fallen into bad company. She leaned against the phone booth, the receiver to her ear, her eyes closed. She remembered her mother's voice. *They were very, very bad men. They were gamblers. Gangsters. They wanted his money, you see, and . . . and, well, he didn't have enough, he didn't have enough to give them . . .*

"It's bound to take your liiife!" the drunken boys screamed behind her.

Nancy leaned against the phone booth, her eyes closed. She had to press her lips together to keep from crying. Even now, at this moment, she could feel the rage in her stomach. The boiling, tarry rage; the nausea of rage. It was rage at *her:* at her mother. It was a burbling fury at the weary-eyed woman who sat, night after night, at the edge of her bed. Weak comfort against her fear of the dark. All she could do was *sit* there? Just sit there and *tell* her that about her father, and *say* those horrible things about him. How could she just have let it happen? Why didn't she *do* something?

"Can I help you?"

Nancy's eyes came open. Park Avenue stretched uptown under bright green traffic lights. The night breeze rattled the bushes and trees in the center islands. The traffic hissed by pleasantly. The drunken boys were staggering downtown, their voices fading.

"I need his address," she said hoarsely. "Oliver Perkins. I need his address too."

"Cornelia Street," the woman answered.

The words touched Nancy like ice and she shivered. *Cor-*

301

nelia Street, she thought. *He lives on Cornelia Street. He lives. He's real. Something is real. Something.*

She hung up and dialed again at once, repeating Perkins's phone number under her breath. She could not hear her own whispers, because now another flashing police car was speeding down the avenue. Wailing, howling. Dimly, she heard Perkins's phone begin to ring.

Hi, Mr. Perkins, she thought. *I'm a schizophrenic murder victim and I'm coming to kill you tonight. Love your work, by the way. Run for your life, okay?*

The phone rang and then rang again. The siren grew louder. It deafened her as the police car reached the corner. She could not hear whether the phone was ringing anymore or not. The cop car's flasher bathed her face in red and white as its tires screeched, as it took the corner full speed.

Then the sound of the siren softened. Then it stopped. She could hear now: The phone was still ringing. There had been no answer. She laid the handset down. She stood for another moment, gazing up the avenue. There was a hardware store there, just a few feet in front of her. Her eyes lit on its window, on the clock in its window.

It was 7:25.

"Cornelia Street," she whispered aloud.

She started limping for the subway.

OLIVER PERKINS

Perkins sat on the floor next to Avis's body. His hand, dripping with her fresh blood, cradled her nearly severed head against his knee. He patted her cheek with a bloody palm as if to comfort her. Her cheek still felt soft and lifelike to him. Her skin was still warm.

Perkins stared across the empty room. He stared at the stained white walls; at the window; at the night; all without seeing, without hearing anything. It was funny, he thought, how dull-hearted you felt at first. He remembered that from when his mother died. At first, you did not really feel anything. You could not cry. You only wished you could cry. He hung his head. He did wish it. He wished he could feel for Avis right now because she had been his friend and he was going to miss her day after day. He looked down at her, to see her face; hoping to connect with her, to the idea of her at least so he would feel something. But she lay there like a broken thing. Her face was smeared and sticky with the blood from his hand. Her mouth was slack. The gash in her neck was like a second mouth, scarlet, gaping like a fish's: hideous. When he patted her cheek again, a gout of new blood dribbled from the opening. Her head wobbled strangely on its torn stem.

Perkins looked away from her. He stared at the white walls.

Then, after a while, he heard the baby. The baby was making noises in the nursery. Little coughs of complaint. Perkins turned his face toward the room. He heard Mrs. Philippa Wallabee, the Englishwoman from next door. She was in there with the baby now, talking and cooing to him. She had marched in there for him right away, sturdy as stone after her first gasp. She had marched past Avis's body even as Perkins was dropping to his knees beside it . . .

"He must . . ." Perkins had to clear his throat. "He must be hungry," he called in to her. "There's formula in the fridge, Philippa."

"Yes," Mrs. Wallabee called back. "But I don't think I should bring him out there, Oliver. Maybe you could bring it in for me when you're all right."

Mrs. Wallabee owned a candle and pottery store on Sixth Avenue. Perkins had always found her kind of sniffy, a stuck-up prig. It did not seem to matter very much now, though, what he had thought of her. What he had thought of anyone or anything. Nothing seemed to matter to him very much.

"All right," he said. "I'll get it."

He let Avis's body go. He got to his feet. That did bring tears to his eyes for a moment. Avis lay there on the floor beneath him, and she was a piece of clay now and the Avis whom he'd known was nowhere. That did bring the tears. There was a hint, a whiff, of a feeling that was nearly unbearable. He forced it down.

He walked away from the body with his back hunched over, his arms hanging heavily. Shock had slackened the sharp planes and deep lines of his face. He stared straight ahead as he walked. He did not know that his mouth was open.

He found a can of baby formula in the refrigerator. He poured some into a plastic bottle. Screwed a nipple on. Without looking at the body again (or at his brother, who had been standing in the room with him all this time, who was standing now near the front door), he walked heavily into the nursery.

Mrs. Wallabee was there, in the middle of the room. She had the baby on her narrow hip and was bouncing him up and down. She was trying to entertain him by waggling a stuffed walrus in his face. They stood under dangling airplanes. Surrounded by hanging Kermits and elephants, and cardboard cutouts of Mickey Mouse and Goofy. The room looked horrible to Perkins; nightmarish. All the cartoon characters were smiling crazily. What the hell did they have to smile about now? Slack-mouthed, he approached Mrs. Wallabee and handed her the bottle. The baby reached for it at once with both hands. Mrs. Wallabee helped him plug the nipple into his mouth. He sucked hungrily, but his eyes turned. He looked at Perkins. Perkins forced himself to give him a big smile, just like one of the cartoon characters. The baby let the bottle go and drew breath.

"Pah!" he said, and he laughed with delight. He twisted in Mrs. Wallabee's arms. He reached for Perkins now with those two small hands. Perkins took the kid, lifted him up against his shoulder and held him there. "Pah!" murmured the baby into his ear. The small hands clutched Perkins's torn sweater. The little face nestled in his neck.

Perkins thought: *Well, the father will probably get him.* He pressed the baby to himself with his bloody hands. *That shit-head Randall will probably take custody of him,* he thought. There was nothing he could do about it. The father would probably get the baby and then destroy him. Slowly. Abuse him. Every day. A little bit, every day. Some days a lot . . .

"Pah! Pah!" The baby wriggled and squeaked in his arms. Perkins's face crumpled. His whole body shuddered and a tear spilled from each eye. He felt the soft baby in his arms; saw the blood on his hands; the cartoons grinning crazily all around, in the air, on the wall. "Oh man!" he whispered.

He became more dull-hearted than ever. He did not care what happened anymore.

The baby wriggled away from him, looking back over his shoulder. He wanted his bottle again. Perkins handed him to Mrs. Wallabee. She took him into the crook of her arm and fed him the bottle. The baby sucked and looked at Perkins. He extended a hand to Perkins. Perkins turned his eyes away.

He looked at the woman. "Listen, Philippa," he said tonelessly. He swallowed. "You have to listen to me carefully, all right?"

"Just go ahead, Oliver," she said. She was all business.

"I want you to take the baby next door, okay? Don't let him see . . . you know: his mother. Just get him out of here. Get him next door to your place—and then call the police."

"Yes, of course," Mrs. Wallabee said briskly. She blinked her big eyes.

"Tell the police what's happened. And then ask to talk to Nathaniel Mulligan. Detective Nathaniel Mulligan. Can you remember that?"

"Yes, yes, of course," she said. She jogged the baby gently in her elbow as she fed him.

Perkins did not look at the baby. "Give Mulligan my name," he said. "Tell him to get to the Jefferson Market Library as fast as he can. Tell him there's a woman there who has all the answers, who knows what's going on. All right? Tell him I'm going to meet her there at eight and keep her there for him as long as I can. But I don't know how long I can keep her. I don't know how long before . . ." He swallowed the rest of the sentence. He did not know himself what he meant to say. He did not know what to think anymore and he did not care. He shook his head wearily. His eyes filled with tears again, and again one fell, ran down his cheek. "Just tell him that, all right? Tell him he has to hurry."

The woman jogged the baby. The baby sucked his bottle and caressed its plastic side. Mrs. Wallabee looked at Perkins earnestly. She tightened her lips, but there was nothing she could do for him. "All right, Oliver," she said. "I'll do it straight off."

"Thank you." Perkins nodded at her. He turned away.

The baby pulled from his bottle. "Pah!" he called. "Pah!"

But Perkins could not bear to look back at him. He ducked under the mobiles, brushing them aside with his hand. He felt the black, batlike thing sitting heavily in his stomach. He felt the whole world had become the black, batlike thing. He walked into the living room.

Zachary turned to face him as he came in. He was still at the far end of the room, by the door. He smiled nervously at his older brother. The red bag was at his feet, and his hands were deep in his raincoat pockets.

Oliver regarded him from the nursery doorway. For some reason, Zach looked strange to him, almost like a stranger. His gangly figure hidden by the long coat, his boyish face shadowed by the cap brim—he looked odd, out of whack. Oliver felt distant from him. A confused, floating feeling.

For a long moment, the two brothers regarded each other like that; silently across the room. Avis lay sprawled on the floor between them.

Finally, Oliver nodded. He spoke in a near whisper. "All right, Zach," he said. He hardly knew what he was saying. "All right. I'm ready. Let's go."

NANCY KINCAID

The subway car was packed with monsters. A scaly sea thing. A pimple-beaked hag. A green cadaver with blood on its chin. And not a goddamned place to sit anywhere and she was so tired, so tired. She stood in the midst of them, clutching the hand strap. Swaying weakly into their malformed faces. There were spasms of pain running across her lower back. Sharp blades of it pierced her wounded head. She dangled from the strap with her eyes closed, her lips parted. *Oh, Oliver . . .* she thought dreamily. The thin bed in his garret was so soft as she waited naked for him . . .

The train stopped at West Fourth Street. Cackling, the creatures stormed the door. She was carried along with them before she knew it. Pushed out onto the platform. Surrounded by fangy grins and red-streaked eyes. She was jostled toward the stairs; stumbling with the pack, trying not to fall. They carried her upward toward a violet square of October night. She blinked, shaking her head, fighting to stay on her feet. Vaguely, she heard the harsh jangle of music above her. She crested the stairs, supported by the crush of goblins . . .

And then she was swept away.

An aspic tide of human beings washed her into darkness and noise. Harsh notes of music rained down on her like hailstones. A tangy human stench—hot breath and sweat and beer—enveloped her. The night sky whirled above her, alive with indigo and strobic light.

What the hell . . . ? What the hell is happening?

She turned desperately this way and that. Eyes veiled in

dominoes darted by her. Grinning rubber masks bore in on her, then swept away. Distorted faces, twisted bodies, spread out around her as far as she could see. Above her, somewhere, on a platform somewhere rimmed with purple neon, a hairy beast was dancing. He was the size of two men. He was gyrating to the rocking brass rhythms. Two women in leotards bent and swayed and slithered upward worshipfully at his sides. She stared at them. She was pushed on, stumbling, step by step, by the inexorable crowd.

A parade, she thought, breathlessly. *It's the Halloween Parade.*

She closed her eyes hard and opened them. She fought to come awake, to come out of her confusion. The float with the dancing beast rolled past her. The crowd moved after it, traveling more slowly in the same direction. Uptown. They were going uptown.

No! she thought. *No!*

Cornelia Street was right near here. It was just across the avenue.

Eight o'clock. Eight o'clock.

She struggled, twisted, in the grip of the tide. It would not release her. Step by step, it carried her uptown. Farther and farther away from Cornelia. Away from Oliver.

"Let me through. Please!" she heard herself cry.

But everyone was laughing. All around her people were laughing. Paper horns were honking. Music blared. Her high, thin voice was blown away by it.

"Please," she said.

She shouldered hard against the press of bodies. She tried to squeeze through the spaces between them. It was no good. She could hardly move except to trudge along, step by step, amid the mass. She ducked her head, trying to see where she was. The movement sent cold pain snaking down her spine. Her vision blurred for a moment. But vaguely, in glimpses, over people's shoulders, around their heads, she saw the marchers, she saw the parade on the avenue. Screeching demons capered by with upraised arms. Wild-eyed androgynes rushed past, their silk capes flying. Dancers ground their hips. Clowns hurled confetti into the night sky. A zombie slowly hunkered along the curb, munching on a severed arm and slavering down at the children.

She felt her mouth go dry as she watched it. She felt her stomach sink. Everywhere, interspersed with the creatures in the giddy dance, mingling with them all up and down the block, there were stolid men: uniformed men with pale, expressionless faces. With heavy arms. With stares like ball bearings.

Cops.

They patrolled the edges of the crowd. They gazed, watchful, from under their black-brimmed caps. They scanned the screaming, laughing faces that pushed in at them over the barricades.

Jesus. So many cops, she thought. She felt dizzy, dreamy. Her knees were going weak. If she broke out toward the parade, would they spot her? Would they know who she was? Were *all* of them after her?

She twisted to the right. She craned her neck. Fought for a glimpse of the rest of the sidewalk.

But the police were there too. Lined up like staunch pickets, shoulder to shoulder. Cowled in shadow but shaped that cop-like shape. Unmistakable.

She let out a noise, a sob of frustration. She clutched her hair with one hand, trying to think. *Oh, Oliver.* She imagined him, stretched on his back, his mouth open, his sad eyes gaping blindly into space.

Eight o'clock! Eight o'clock!

She sank down heavily in the viscous tide. Step by step, she was forced along.

And then, the crowd reached the corner. She was carried right over the curb. She was dropped down into the street. There, finally, between one sidewalk and the next, the mass spread out and thinned a little.

Without thinking, she wriggled free of it. Elbowing between one person and another. Twisting into the spaces. Gasping for breath.

She fell out of the crowd, onto the sidestreet. She stumbled into the swift traffic of people heading to and from the avenue. Someone whacked her in the shoulder and she reeled back.

Steadied herself. Crouched, braced, staring around her like an animal.

Cops.

There were two of them. On the southern sidewalk, leaning back against a diamond-link fence. They seemed to be watching her with their ball bearing stares. Breathless, she turned her back on them. Another cop strolled toward her, wandering along the edge of the sidestreet, through the sparser crowd.

She stood where she was, jostled by the passersby. The cop on the sidestreet came closer. The cops by the fence leaned their heads together and murmured through tight lips. Was *everyone* after her?

A shout rose to her over the noise of the crowd:

"Masks! Electric, blinking masks! Get your Halloween masks right here!"

She swiveled toward the voice, her knees screaming. There was a panther-man. He was standing at the corner of the sidestreet, where it met the avenue. The spangles in his black vest glittered out of the shadow of a brownstone wall. He was waving a domino mask above his head. It was edged with green and red and yellow lights, all of them blinking on and off.

"Get your Halloween masks right here!" he cried.

With a gasp, she limped through the crowd toward the masked panther. She reached into her pocket as she came, bringing out all the bills she had left.

"Here!" She had to shout. Another brass band was passing. The notes of the "Funeral March for a Marionette" were pounding at her, drowning her out.

The panther-man snatched the bills from her and handed her a blinking domino in return. She held it to her eyes, fixed its strap behind her head.

Masked then, she turned around.

The cop who had been strolling up the sidestreet strolled right past her. He pushed his way through the crowd, onto the avenue; he was swallowed up by the onlookers. The cops against the fence had now averted their gazes from her too.

All right, she thought, woozily. *All right. Downtown. Downtown to Oliver. All right. What first?*

The avenue. She would have to cross the avenue. Slip through the parade. Then she could head over to Sheridan Square. Angle in to Cornelia without hitting the mob . . .

Squinting through the domino's eyeholes, she staggered wearily back toward the crowd. The current caught her. It nearly toppled her as it tried to carry her back onto the sidewalk, back into the gelatinous uptown flow. But she turned her shoulder against it and fought her way through to the intersection. She stopped there. She tilted her head back, her mouth agape.

Look, she thought. She was mesmerized. *Look, Oliver. A big pumpkin.*

A jack-o'-lantern the size of a house was rolling past her, up the avenue. Its grin flickered down at her as if aflame. Flames danced in the triangular eyes and up through the cap. And up through the cap came a beauty queen, grinning broadly, waving happily through the paper flames.

A very . . . very . . . big . . .

She swayed on her feet. The pumpkin rolled on, uptown, as the crowds cheered and threw confetti in its wake. There was a break in the parade. The cops moved in to fill the intersection. They walked back and forth, their hands clasped behind them. A small cluster of people started out of the current to cross the avenue.

She almost let them go without her. Then she blinked herself to life. Staggered along with them. She ducked down to hide below their shoulders. Passed right under a patrolman's nose. The little group hid her as she moved out into the center of the avenue. She was halfway across when she turned . . .

Good-bye, Mr. Pumpkin, good-bye . . .

She turned and looked up to watch the pumpkin roll away. And she halted in her tracks. She straightened. She stared. *What . . . ?*

The cluster of people moved on to the far curb. Only she stood there, alone, exposed, gaping. She shook her head slowly.

There, against the purple sky, a castle of red brick rose up before her. Round towers rose to peaked roofs. Arched windows with stained glass traced in stone. A gray roof in jagged hips and valleys . . . She stared and stared and the music seemed to fade away from her. The cheering faded from her and the lights swam off into a dim periphery. She stared—and a cocoon of smoky silence seemed to twine itself around her . . .

I know that place. I've seen that place before.

It was the building from her dream. It was the asylum she had dreamed when they were taking her to Bellevue in the squad car. Her mouth hung open. A thin stream of drool hung down from it to her chin. She swayed. She stared. She remembered the long, green, empty corridor inside. The whispers coming to her from behind the doors.

"Naaancy. Naaaancy." A chorus of whispers. "Nancy Kincaid . . ."

Where had she first heard that name? Who had first told it to her?

My name is Nancy Kincaid.

Who was it? Who had said that to her first?

She stood where she was in the middle of the avenue. Swaying. Staring at the silhouetted library through the domino's eyeholes. Her stomach roiled, but even her nausea seemed far away. She remembered her dream: the asylum, the long corridor, full of whispers. The granite throne with King Death seated on it. Waiting for her.

That's him, she thought. *King Death. That's who I have to find.* But whose face was behind the mask? Whose voice had said to her:

My name is Nancy Kincaid. I'm twenty-two years old.

Oh, she could almost remember. Someone had sat there before her and told her that. Someone with the face of King Death. A person with a skull for a face had told her:

I work for Fernando Woodlawn. I'm his personal assistant. I live on Gramercy Park with my mom and dad . . .

Me, she thought dimly, *it was supposed to be me.* Oh, if she could just remember.

She stood there, staring. She heard nothing of the noise around her. The parade. The cheering crowd. She did not see the policeman who had spotted her now. Who was moving toward her now with his face set, his hand resting on his holster. If she could just pull the mask away, she thought. If she could just see the face behind the face of Death. Her fingers coiled at her side. She could feel the rubbery skin of the Death's head as if it were in her hands.

My name is Nancy Kincaid, the skull's voice whispered to her.

And then, in her mind, the mask of Death seemed suddenly to come away and she saw:

There was no head behind it. King Death had no head. Severed arteries and veins sprouted from the jagged neck like wires. Gore spewed in coughing gouts up from the ragged hole. The blood poured down over the front of the creature's robes. The voice burbled out with the blood, like the blood, thick and liquid:

My name is Nancy Kincaid . . .

She felt the pavement tip beneath her feet. Darkness closed over her. Her eyes rolled up in her head.

Me. It was supposed to be me. IT WAS SUPPOSED TO BE ME!

A frantic skirl of music flew up around her. A shout rose from the crowd. Her eyes went wide and faces—grinning, calling faces—rose and fell like waves on every side of her. She turned, stumbling. A street lamp's bulb swung overhead. She tipped backward. She let out a terrified scream.

A Death's head blotted out the sky above her.

"All hail!" A shout blew over her like wind. "All hail King Death!"

She staggered back. She held her head. She stared up at the huge skull that bore down on her out of the night, as if the moon itself had descended.

"Whoa," she whispered.

The thing was just enormous. A human skeleton a city block long. Its grinning skull hovered just above her. Its spine undulated and wavered. Its bony arms waved in the air. Below, on the street, puppeteers in skull masks and black skeleton pajamas held the paper creature aloft on poles. They danced around in circles, making the arms spin, the legs kick crazily. They were heading toward her.

"All hail!" they shouted, their voices muffled in their masks. "All hail King Death!"

And the crowd took up the chant. They hurled confetti up under the streetlights. They pumped their fists over the blue barricades.

"All hail! All hail King Death!"

She saw him then. He was at the center of the puppeteers. He was right under the great paper icon that rolled and floated over them. He was not at all as he had been in her vision. He was not stately. He was not enthroned. He was a clown. He was capering. Prancing and skipping back and forth, waving the scepter in his hand like a baton. He was dressed in a colored quilt shirt and torn jeans, like a waif, like a vagabond. His head was covered with a skull mask and there was a paper crown wrapped around his brow. He tilted his head from side to side as he galloped up and down under the gigantic skeleton. He waved gleefully to the crowd.

That's him, she thought. She staggered again, uncertain on her feet. She felt her stomach roll over, and a lifeless cold radiated out from the center of her. It came into her arms, into her legs, her fingers. She was going under . . .

It's too late, she thought. She grabbed a handful of her own hair, as if to hold herself up. *It's too late . . .*

"That's him," she whispered.

She stared at the masked, capering little waif. Her other hand rose up again. She pointed at him.

"That's him!" she called. Tears blurred her vision. "Look."

"All hail!" The crowd's happy roar drowned her out. "All hail the King of Death!"

She called louder. "That's him! That's him! Oh Christ, it's already happening." She jabbed her finger at him. "That's him! Please! Somebody!"

The giant skeleton was passing above her now. The puppeteers were all around her, dancing, holding their poles. King Death was capering toward her, spinning, his arms flung wide. She could see the light through his eyeholes when he turned to her. She could see the glint in his dark eyes. He waved to the crowd on either side of her. They shouted out to him.

"All hail!"

She covered her mouth. "Oh God! Oliver . . ."

And suddenly, an iron hand gripped her. Fingers dug into her upper arm. She looked up. A pale, steel-eyed face glared down at her. The cop's black cap brim jutted toward her eyes. She pointed at King Death.

"*Officer,*" she shrieked. *"Officer, arrest that skull!"*

"Come on, lady," said the cop. "Move out of the way, willya."

But with an enormous effort, she wrenched her arm free. She staggered forward a step toward the prancing king. She clutched her hair.

"Won't anybody listen to me? That's him! It's happening! That's the one!"

King Death spun full circle, his arms stretched wide, his knees rising high. He came full around and faced her.

And he pulled up short.

His hands were still out from his sides. His head was slightly forward. The eyes in the eyeholes were staring out at her where she stood not three yards away from him.

Everything else went on. The rapid rhythms of *Danse Macabre* pattered into the night. The crowd's shouts rose and fell and rose again. Confetti burst and sparkled overhead. And the great skeleton passed over the sky like a storm cloud. But King Death stood and stared and she stood and stared back at him. The scepter fell from Death's hand and clattered on the pavement.

And then King Death broke and ran.

He dashed between two puppeteers and lit for the western intersection. Confused, the crowd laughed and applauded. There was another chant of "Hail!" but it fell away. A few more scattered voices raised an ironic cheer. King Death lowered his white skull and charged the crowd, running like blazes. In another moment, he had slipped through a break in the current of human traffic. He was vanishing behind the closing masses.

For a second, the woman in the domino mask could only stand and watch him. She felt a black pool of sweet sleep spreading at her feet, widening all around her. She wanted more than anything to sink down into it, to drift away.

King Death rushed off, down the sidestreet, toward Sheridan Square.

The woman in the domino mask gave a single hoarse cry of pain, and took off after him.

OLIVER PERKINS

On Seventh Avenue, the traffic was jammed. Car horns sounded again and again in the night air. Costumed strollers went slowly along the sidewalk under a pall of exhaust. Some paused at the windows of magazine stands and antique stores. Others, in ragged streams, still trickled up the sidestreets toward the parade.

The Perkins brothers came jogging uptown from Sheridan Square. They wove through the pedestrians, Oliver in the lead sometimes and sometimes Zach. Sometimes they split apart, running through the open ground at either edge of the sidewalk. Sometimes one of them fell to a fast walk to catch his breath, then started running again.

Zach clutched his red bag by the handles and it trailed behind him as he ran. His boyish face was flushed, his dark eyes were hectic. There was something disheveled and confused in his expression, as if he had just gotten off a plane and didn't quite know where he was.

Oliver didn't look at him much though. He just ran. He ran and there was the rhythm of his feet on the sidewalk. He listened to the rhythm and to the staccato of his breath. *Let us. Let us go,* he thought. *Let us go then. You and I.* Pat.

Pat. Pat. Pat . . . He ran and felt the rhythm of his heart inside his chest. He felt the emptiness in his chest. *Let us go then you and I* . . . The suffocating shroud of exhaust hung over the fender-to-fender traffic; he felt it poisoning the autumn air. The pinkish white of streetlight globes passed above him. *Let us go then.* He saw Avis sitting on his bed this morning, when she had gently stroked his brow. *Let us go.* Pat. Pat. The furniture in the passing display windows was like an empty room begging for company. He remembered how Avis's head had wobbled on its neck only minutes ago. *Let us. Let us.*

The two brothers turned up Christopher Street and jogged toward the library. They were shoulder to shoulder, both breathless. Perkins stared ahead and ran and saw the library's turrets above the trees. They were lit by spotlights now. The clocktower brushed at the bottom of the moon. It was almost eight o'clock. *Let us go then.* He ran and did not think, except in flashes of remembering. The thin, snowy cold against his cheeks as the sled rushed downhill. The weight of his little brother leaning against him on the sled. The library came closer. *Let us go.* He saw its thin-necked dragon gargoyles jutting into the empty air. He could feel Zachary running beside him.

A cluster of sycamores rose from the library's back lot. Now, in the shadow of their yellow leaves, he could see the parade on Sixth Avenue. A rolling stage, outlined in purple neon, was passing at the intersection. He saw a hairy giant gyrate on the stage, with attendant dancing girls on either side of him. The music, at this distance, melding with the traffic horns, sounded sour and discordant. They ran toward it, Oliver and Zach, side by side. Oliver carried the black weight in his stomach as he ran. His mind was black and heavy. He did not understand what had happened, how it had happened; how it had come to this. His mind was empty except for images. Avis holding her baby in her arms. The baby reaching out for him. "Pah!" The crowd grew thicker as they got near the parade.

Here, Oliver had to slow again. They both slowed, panting. They turned their shoulders to squeeze past the massing people, who were trying to squeeze their way, in turn, into the avenue crowd. Zach went first. Oliver followed him. Oliver's sweater was torn, his chest exposed. The sweater and his jeans were wet with Avis's blood. He could feel it, damp on his thighs, and his hands were sticky with it. He stared straight ahead, at the heads and faces of the crowd, as he pushed toward the library. *Let us go then, you and I,* he thought. *Let us go then, you and I.* He breathed through his open mouth. He did not care what happened. He wanted to get to the library fast. He wished he was there now. He would hold Tiffany until the police arrived. He did not care.

The crowd surrounded them, pressed in on them. They were near the corner. Near the library steps. The dancing beast was rolling past on his purple neon float, but the music was louder than ever. Oliver felt it drilling at his temple. He narrowed his eyes against it, twisting and turning in the crowd, forcing himself through, toward the steps. He saw Zachie's cap turning and pushing forward in the tide ahead of them. Then Zach was rising, up the steps, through the people there, toward the library doors. Oliver reached the steps too. He came up behind Zach. He had held the baby on his chest that morning, he thought. The pots had clanked as Avis made him breakfast in the kitchen. He reached into the pocket of his damp jeans. He brought out his library key.

Zach was already at the doors, the Invisible Zach in his coat and hat. He was waiting beside the black glass doors that were traced in stone. Oliver joined him, and Zach gazed hard at him with his frantic eyes. Zach licked his lips, waiting, while Oliver found the key he wanted. Oliver thought about sledding down the hill outside their house on Long Island.

Oliver pushed his key into the door. In the jangle of music, above the roar of the crowd, he heard the whirling strains of *Danse Macabre.* He looked up to his left as he turned his key. *Let us go,* he thought. He saw a giant paper skeleton, a puppet in the parade. It was grinning and bobbing and dancing in the sky above the avenue. The sight made his gorge rise. He shuddered and turned away. He pushed the door open and stepped into the library.

He turned. He saw Zach follow him over the threshold.

The door stood open for a moment behind him. He saw the people on the steps. He heard the music, still loud. He heard the voices of the people on the street. And he saw Zachary's shadowy figure on the spotlit night with the great puppet skeleton floating up the avenue behind him.

Zachary smiled a little, nervously, almost apologetically. "We better hurry," he said softly.

Oh, do not ask what is it, Oliver thought. *Let us go and make our visit.*

The library door hissed shut, unlocked now. The noise of the parade grew dim. The Perkins brothers stood in darkness together. They listened to one another's breathing.

THE WOMAN IN THE DOMINO

Death slithered through the crowd like a silverfish. The woman in the mask stumbled after.

Me. Supposed to be me, she thought dimly. Her vision had gone all misty red. It was hemmed in by the black of the mask. She panted and staggered, her arms wheeling. *Me. Supposed to be me.*

On the busy sidestreet, the costumed people milled and scuffled. There were shouts and barks of laughter on every side of her. Scarred faces swirled by, tortured with hilarity. Rouged lips grinned. Elbows levered up and down as masks sucked at bottles of beer.

She staggered through it all. Her breath came out of her lungs like dragon fire. Lances of pain went up her legs with every step. Her back twisted like a wrung rag. She ricocheted off the shoulder of a garrulous monster and nearly fell. A man, painted black and draped in red, snatched at her. A woman in spangles fell back a step and cried out "Hey!" She reeled drunkenly past.

Ahead, the swift, zigzagging figure of King Death drew farther and farther away. She saw the shiny white skull dodging this way and that, the colorful quilted shirt billowing. The running figure drew closer and closer to the intersection at Christopher Street, where Christopher slanted back up toward the parade. *Me!* the woman in the domino mask thought desperately. The spittle poured over her lips as she tumbled through the night, as she clawed at the night with her fingers. *Supposed to be me!* She peered at the dodging figure of Death through the thickening red haze. Nausea made her head spin, made her legs go wobbly. *Supposed to be . . . Oh shit!* she thought. She was going under. No doubt about it, fans. She was going down. Her staggering progress slowed. She was falling from each step to the next, bent forward. She was gasping hoarsely, hotly, for breath. The long corridor. Dimly, she remembered it. Crawling over the floor, the carpet against her belly . . .

He's getting away! King Death was at Christopher Street now, just at the corner, just about to rush into the intersection. The woman in the flashing domino was still half a block behind him. Still pushing against the wall of pain, another step and another. She was stumbling past the corner of Gay Street now, a small doglegged Village lane to her right. She was remembering the long corridor. The murmuring voice at the end of the hall. *Eight o'clock. You have to be there.* She had dragged herself down the hall, over the brown carpet that scraped softly at her belly . . . She remembered the voice murmuring: *King Death. The library. You won't forget now.*

"Oh God!" she rasped suddenly. The street and its revelers were swirling away from her in a sickening vortex. She fell. Dropped to her knees at the corner of Gay Street. She wavered there for a moment, her mouth open, the slobber dangling from her lip. Then she pitched forward to the pavement.

"Whoa there, lady!" said a long-haired boy above her. "I mean: party on!"

"Getting away," she tried to tell him, but the words

wouldn't come. She lifted herself on scraped palms. She could see him, the flash of his moving jeans. King Death had shot past the Christopher Street corner now. The strange, small, waiflike creature was braking at the curb, heels braced against the sidewalk. Around him, the clusters of masked people cheered and laughed and staggered aimlessly. Their elbows went up and down, their bag-covered beer bottles tilted up and down. King Death paused among them for only a moment. Then he dodged around the corner and he was gone, out of sight.

Prone on the pavement, her face barely raised, the woman in the domino mask stared at the spot where Death had been. To the right, she thought. He had gone to the right. He had gone up Christopher Street. He was slanting up toward the junction with Sixth, back toward the parade. Up toward that castle of a building she had seen in her dreams. And also, of course, back toward . . .

Gay Street.

He would have to go past the corner of Christopher and Gay.

"Oh," she said hoarsely. "Oh." She was trying to breathe. Trying to talk, to call for help. King Death had made a mistake. She still had a chance. She could still catch him. If she could just get up . . . She could run down Gay Street. She could cut him off. If she could just get to her feet . . .

"Help me. Help me," she whispered.

A hand slid under her arms. Hot beery breath washed over her cheeks. "Whoa! Whoa!" It was the long-haired teen. He yanked up on her. She struggled to get her knees on the pavement. She braced herself against him as he hauled her to her feet. "Party on, Dudette. I mean, party hearty! I mean . . . Jesus Christ holy shit!"

The woman in the domino mask had reached into the waist of her jeans and pulled out her .38. The long-haired teen fell back from her, his eyes wide, his chin glistening with drooled beer. He stared at the weapon.

"Whoa," he said solemnly.

The woman in the domino mask staggered backward a step. "Me . . ." she explained to him panting. "It was supposed to be me." Then she groaned. A gritty burst of vomit filled her mouth. The brick high rises around her tilted across the sky. The sky swung back up until it was overhead again. She swallowed what puke she could and spat out the rest. Now where the hell was Gay Street? She turned unsteadily, blinking hard behind the mask.

There. There it was.

"Oh, sweet Jesus!" she gasped as the agony went through her legs again. She pushed off and started running.

At the end of the hallway, she remembered, lay the body on the bed.

The little doglegged lane was lined with quaint brownstones. It was washed in the misty light of a single street lamp. There were fewer partyers here. The woman in the electric domino stumbled past them swiftly, giving little cries of pain and anguish. She tore around the bend with her gun raised up beside her ear. She could hardly see anything now. Just a blur of light and shadow. She felt the wet on her cheek, in her mask, but she hardly knew that she was crying. She only wished she could tear her head open; that she could reach into her mind and rip out the throbbing memory of that body. That headless body. She had seen it from the doorway. She had dragged herself into the doorway. She had dragged herself up along the jamb and then she had seen and she had reeled back, her arms before her eyes. The sight of the headless corpse had hit her in the head like a baseball bat. *Oh God, God, God,* she thought, *I was supposed to protect her. I was supposed to be her, to be Nancy Kincaid, so she'd be safe! If anything happened, it was supposed to happen to me! It was supposed to be me!*

Now, ahead, yawing under the tilted sky, the junction with Christopher Street came into view. She could see the thicker, swifter packs of revelers there. She could hear their shouts. She could hear the *Danse Macabre* again, the hammering music of the parade. One step more, she thought, hauling in the air as she stumbled to the corner. One step—and then another . . . She pushed herself on, the gun up by her ear, the muzzle up beside her flashing mask.

And then she was there, in the intersection. Plunging out

of the little alley onto the broader, slanting street. And there was King Death, right there, his skull gleaming white amidst the blackened and reddened faces all around him. He was running right toward her. He was looking back over his shoulder, as if he thought she must still be behind him. The woman in the domino mask halted. She swung around. She lowered the pistol, brought the muzzle to bear on the onrushing skull. A woman screamed somewhere, and then another. A man shouted, "Watch out."

Death collided with her head-on. He never even looked around; he just ran right into her. She was knocked off her feet, her gun hand flying wide. She went sprawling backward. Her back slammed into the pavement. Her breath went out of her with a loud "whoof." Still, she reached out, her hands like claws. She clutched desperately at the quilted shirt. She threw her arm around the frail figure of the King. The two of them went down together, clutched together, rolling on the pavement. King Death broke away. Struggled to his hands and knees. With a loud shout, the woman in the domino pushed up too. She was on her knees, both hands wrapped around the gun. She pointed the gun at the death's head.

"Aa-aa—ah," she said. It was all she could get out. Her whole body heaved and buckled with her breathing.

A crowd of people was gathering around them. No one said anything. The parade music filtered into the silence. The silence seemed bizarre. They could hear the wind blowing in the dying leaves.

Slowly, the death's head turned. The woman in the domino saw the pale blue eyes in the skull's sockets. She heard the heavy breathing beneath the mask.

"Dead," the King whispered—it was a strange, high whisper, almost melodious. "You're dead. You're supposed to be dead."

And then he began to cry. It sounded that way, at least. He stayed on his hands and his knees, his skull hanging down, his shoulders hunched. The sounds that came out from beneath the mask sounded very much like sobbing.

The woman in the domino let go of the gun with her left

hand. Just as she had in her dream, she reached out for the mask.

Me, she thought.

She felt the fleshy latex in her grip. She tugged it, almost pulling the figure forward. She tugged again. The mask started coming off. On the third pull, the skull was pulled away.

There was a cascade of black hair. The hair was streaked with silver. It spilled forward, hiding the face beneath. Then the figure sank to the pavement, rolled miserably onto its side. The woman in the domino looked on, appalled. It was *not* him. It was not the face she had thought to see. It was a woman. A woman with a lovely, porcelain face, her rose cheeks splotched with tears. A stranger.

The black-haired woman stared at the woman in the domino and shook her head, sniffling.

"You're supposed to be dead!" she complained, and she shook her head bitterly.

At first, the woman in the domino did not answer. She stared at the other. Slowly then, she brought her left hand back to the gun. She pulled back the gun's hammer. People in the crowd gasped and stepped back as the hammer clicked. The woman in the domino trained the revolver at the other's head. She was still gasping for breath, but she managed to speak clearly.

"Tell me where Oliver is or I'm going to kill you," she said.

The black-haired woman cried harder, staring into the gun's muzzle. Her whole body shook.

She said: "At the library."

On the word, a bell tolled sonorously in the library tower. It was finally eight o'clock.

ZACHARY PERKINS

The bell tolled again. Oliver and Zach moved deeper into the library. The music of *Danse Macabre* was dim now. The noise of the crowd seemed to have faded completely. The whole place was sunk in silence and shadow. Gothic arches hung blackly overhead. Blank-eyed busts stared out of sculpted medallions on the wall. The bell tolled in the tower again. They moved through the dark toward the stairs.

They began climbing. The stairs swept up in a graceful curve along the rounded wall. Oliver started up first and Zach trudged after. He climbed slowly behind his older brother. Slowly, he removed his cap and stuffed it into his coat pocket. He unbuttoned the coat for greater freedom. Now—now that the time had come—he found he felt almost calm. He felt almost nothing. Like the noise of the parade, the termite hum of mundane detail had sunk away from him. It was quiet inside him. He felt he was floating through a sort of liquid mist. A dreamy atmosphere. He watched his brother's back rising up the winding stairs ahead of him. He smiled sadly at the sight, and at everything he remembered. He did feel sad, in a wistful way. This was harder for him than for anyone after all. He suffered more than anyone, really. All the trouble and the pain and the killing: It had been forced on him. It had been all so unnecessary. And this, killing his brother. It was a shame. He really thought he would feel bad about this for a long, long time to come.

They climbed. They passed stained-glass windows set at intervals into the wall. The colored panes were dark and muddy, but sometimes they caught a streetlight's glow from outside. Images in the glass flickered out into the shadows on the curling stair. A queen with golden tresses and a pitying gaze. A knight with a noble brow and a razor-sharp goatee. They shimmered dimly for a moment like half-remembered faces, and then vanished as the brothers climbed on. For some reason, the sight of them made Zachary more nostalgic still. He felt himself pining gently for the past, and he remembered the smell of autumn around the house in Port Jeff. How sad it was! The smell of grass when there was still suburban sunlight through the changing leaves. The cool air and the distant jets in the blue sky. Damn all those people, he thought—the cops, the feds. It didn't have to be this way at all. It was almost a joke, a cavalcade of stupidity. The FBI. The FB-fucking-I, going into fits over a stupid twenty-five thousand dollars. That's all he had wanted. A little money. To get free. To get away from Nana and her psychiatrists. From Oliver and his . . . well, lust. From the whole world that held him down, that pinned him to the ground with its bullshit details. But the FB-fucking-I, in its wisdom, had thought it was all some kind of big-time mafia scam. They had thought they were finally going to bag Fernando Woodlawn . . .

So they had sent in their agent. They had sent in their goddamned bitch of an agent to impersonate Fernando's courier, Nancy Kincaid.

Oh, she had been good; he had to hand that to her. There was no doubt about it. She had the ID cards all made up; credit cards, a driver's license. And she had a kind of girlish patter that was all very convincing, very true to form. If he hadn't been so nervous about the whole thing, he probably never would have caught on to her in the first place. He would have taken the packet of money from her, handed over the photographs . . . And the next thing he knew he would have had a .38 down his throat and a hot-eyed federal bitch screaming in his face that he was under arrest.

But he had outsmarted them. He had outsmarted them all. He had talked the federal bitch into his car. Then he had jammed his automatic into her belly and searched her. The minute he found the listening device in her blouse, he had known she was a cop, no matter what she said. He had hit the gas hard, sped away from the scene. He had taken them all by surprise and lost whatever backup she had brought along.

Then he took her to the mews. All along, she kept at it; she kept at her patter. She kept claiming that she was really Nancy Kincaid. Oh, she was good all right. And God knows, he wanted to believe her. He was sweating bullets by then, figuring he was finished. Figuring he was going to prison. Prison!

It was his lowest moment, his greatest moment of trial. He seriously considered killing himself. Only his faith in God sustained him then.

Finally, he thought of Aquarius. He still had his stash of the drug under a floorboard in his bedroom at the mews. He just needed a little, just enough to calm him down. He knew he'd promised God, but he figured . . . just a little, just enough. He had tied the agent girl up in Nana's bedroom. He had resurrected his syringes and the stolen vaccutainers. He gave himself the injection on his knees beside his bed. He wept as he did it, praying for Christ's forgiveness.

And the drug worked wonderfully. In minutes, a great, warm calm descended over him. It was as if the hectic world had been cut away from him. As if everything but himself had been neatly excised and he was floating alone like a cloud in the luscious velvet blue. He could think clearly. Fernando wasn't going to say anything. The creep wouldn't ruin his career over twenty-five thousand bucks. Only the federal agent would testify. She and the Kincaid girl herself were the only ones who could make the case against him. As the drug took hold, he could see it all. He could see the connections clearly. All the connections everywhere. He was going into a sort of synaptic ecstasy. That was when he had developed his perfect plan.

He went to work at once. He killed the agent first. He overdosed her with the drug. He began by just doping her with it, hoping it would get her to talk, to give him more information about the case against him. But she was a tough girl, unfortunately. She would not surrender to him. Even as she was going under, she was still claiming to be Nancy Kincaid. Even as she began hallucinating, she kept up her patter. Finally, in disgust, he had simply pumped his whole stash into her. It was enough to turn her brain to Cream of Wheat. Hell, it was enough to cook it up hot and steamy for breakfast. But she had hung on. Christ. Tough. Tough as nails, he had to give her that. She had kept repeating her cover story until she was unconscious. She had babbled about being Nancy Kincaid even after she had gone under. Then she just lay there. Wheezing. The drug paralyzing her lungs. Pushing her heart to the point of explosion . . .

So Zach had left her there to die. And he had gone off to find the real Nancy Kincaid.

He smiled wider—he almost laughed—remembering that. That part had been just hilarious.

By then, the drug had spread all through him. He was in a kind of mystic wonderland. Everything had Meaning, nothing was simply what it seemed. And he had felt no fear.

He had taken the Kincaid girl's address from the agent's license. He had gone to her building and announced himself as Officer Toody Muldoon. She had almost been expecting him. He had walked right up to her and talked her right down into his car. And they were off. It was as easy as that. By the time he got the Kincaid girl back to the mews, his life, his mind, his soul, were a single symphony of comprehension. He had tied the real Nancy Kincaid to the bed in mental ecstasy. Now, as he climbed the library stairs, he could only recapture the faintest trace of it. He could only mourn the passing of its transcendent beauty. And of that electric moment when he had made his first entry into the flesh of the pleading girl . . .

The bell in the clocktower tolled again. And again as the two brothers climbed. It had tolled itself out by the time they reached the landing.

Zachary stopped there. He stood at the crest of the stairs. He sighed wistfully.

Oliver moved on into the library's long, thin upper room. Zach stood and watched him. The familiar shape of him, the old movements. Zach watched him fondly. When Oliver came to a stop near the center of the room, he stood slumped, his head hanging. Shelves and shelves of books lined the walls on either side of him. Above him, in the imposts of the low arches, bodiless heads, staring faces, gazed down at them both. Music reached them faintly from the parade. Faces in stained-glass windows shimmered.

Once again, Zachary felt his love for Oliver rise in a flood. Oliver was going to save him again, as he had since the beginning of this, out on Long Island. Oliver was going to kill himself up here. Remorse for the Kincaid killing and the killing of the agent was going to overcome him. It would be a point-blank wound delivered in his own workroom, a room to which only he had the key. A clear suicide. And in all the confusion outside, with his face hidden under his cap, and his colored shirt under his coat, no one would remember seeing Zachary come in here with him or leave.

They would only remember King Death. It was eight o'clock now. King Death was passing the library outside, right on time. Zach would put the bullet in his brother and rush downstairs to make the switch with Tiffany in the trees in the library lot. With the skull mask on, she had pretended to be him, even with his friends from the magazine. They—and tens of thousands of onlookers—would be able to say that they had seen Zachary as King Death in the street outside when the killing was going on in here.

He smiled in the library dark. He could almost feel a trace of that mystical comprehension. The incredible syncretic revelation that had hit him when he formed this plan. When he had called Tiffany on the phone to explain her part to her, he had been practically giggling with the excitement, with the truth of it all. She had been in her bookstore nearby. Sitting in the back of the closed store waiting for him to show up with the money. When he called her to tell her what had happened, to explain his plan, she became hysterical. *But it's not a good plan, Zach!* she kept saying. *It can't work, it's crazy, it's a crazy plan! Everything is crazy!* She just didn't see it, at first. The way it worked. King Death. Ollie. The library. The dead women in the mews. Symbolically, it was perfect. Symbolically, it just all made so much sense. *Just don't forget,* he said, sending his rhythmic, persuasive tones into the mews phone, *eight o'clock. That's the Animal Hour. You see? It all makes sense. You won't forget now, will you? You have to be there. Eight o'clock exactly. That's when he's going to die.*

Now then, the hour had come. Zach lifted the automatic out from under his quilted shirt. He felt so wistful, so sad. He loved his big brother so much just then. He extended his arm, leveled the gun at Oliver's back. He smiled fondly. His eyes were damp with sentimental tears.

Oliver turned around. He faced Zachary across the long room. He saw the gun and he stiffened a little, straightened a little. Even in the dark, Zach saw him open his mouth. He heard him catch his breath, as if he were surprised.

Zach's smile widened to a grin of affection. He shook his head. He laughed a little teasingly.

"Oh come on, Ollie," he said, his voice sudden and loud in the library quiet. "Don't look at me like that. You always knew."

THE WOMAN IN THE DOMINO

Above the trees, beneath the gibbous moon, the steepled clocktower of the library tolled the time. The woman in the domino mask ran toward it wildly.

She could barely think for the pain now. The fire in her lungs. The electric streaks up her legs. The numbing ache across her back. Still, she pumped her arms, clutching her gun.

Stay alive, Oliver.

She pistoned her knees, spitting grunts through gritted teeth. She wept with the effort, peering through the tears. Peering through the eyeholes of the blinking mask.

Stay. Please.

She saw revelers jumping aside as she charged toward them. She saw Death again, the great paper skeleton, dancing in the air above thousands of upraised faces. She saw the on-lookers clustered on the library steps. She saw it all through sheets of liquid red, and she heard the parade music broken into pieces: jangling, tuneless shards that seemed to be raining down around her. She ran, weeping. Black inside. She did not know who she was. She was black and twisted.

Stay alive!

"Oh!" she cried aloud in the agony of running.

Oliver.

Christ, she could not go on. She did not know who she was, and she wished she were dead rather than not knowing. It was so much blackness. So much blackness inside her, filling her. She ran faster, letting out another cry of pain. She ran as if the gargoyles were still after her; beating the air behind her with stone wings; bearing down on her with alabaster claws. The bell tolled yet again.

She had to elbow people out of her way now. The crowd was closing around her. Bright streaks of claustrophobic panic lanced her as she was surrounded by faces. So many faces, with melting cheeks and bloodshot eyes, sparse hair, vicious grins. They pressed in on her, thick as grass. Masks of torment. Men as women. Women as warty hags. She shoved her way toward the library steps, panting and sobbing at once. She twisted, waving the gun in the air. Just let him be alive, she thought, looking up at the library doors. And the thought, every thought, was washed away by the uncontrollable scream—*I don't know who I am!*—that sounded in the blackness of her.

Now she worked her way up the steps. Grabbing at people with her hand. Grabbing their arms, their shoulders. Pulling herself up by them, climbing over them. The bell tolled again. She heard them laughing at her. Shouting at her. Cursing. Her head rung with the shattered music of the parade. She felt the shadow of the great skeleton like a weight on top of her. She heard the wings of the gargoyles at her back, coming closer. She climbed toward the doors, thinking, *Still alive! Still alive! Oh please! Oh please!*

She was at the door. She was clutching the entrance bar in her hand. She was on one knee, trying to get up, trying to stand.

Locked. It'll be locked, she thought. The tears poured out around the sides of her electric mask. She moaned. Dragged herself to her feet, leaned against the door.

It swung open. She tumbled through it, fell inside. She heard people shouting at her. The cacophony of the parade. The wings of gargoyles. Again, she climbed to her feet. Slowly, behind her, the door swung shut with a pneumatic hiss. The noise of the crowd grew faint. The darkness grew thick in the recesses before her. She leaned against a gray wall, fighting painfully for breath. Her body convulsed with sobs. Her face was streaked with tears.

The bell in the tower tolled again, one final time. The sound seemed very far away. And then it was gone. It dissipated in the air. The quiet closed in around her, folded down over her. And she thought:

Eight o'clock. It's eight o'clock. It's the Animal Hour.

She gathered in a great breath. She stood off the wall.

Well, then, she thought. *Here I am.*

OLIVER PERKINS AND THE WOMAN IN THE DOMINO

Oliver saw the gun in his brother's hand. He shook his head. He turned his eyes away. The busts carved into the arches watched with blank eyes. The images in the stained-glass windows flickered all around him then disappeared. He said, "Zach. Man oh man . . ." But he couldn't go on. He pressed his lips together to keep from crying.

"Come on, Ollie. Oh, come on," said Zach again with a little laugh. He stepped toward him, the gun trembling in his hand. "You gonna tell me you didn't know? Come on!"

Oliver couldn't look at him. He couldn't say anything. He felt too heavy, too weary, to speak. It was an unexpected feeling. Not at all the way he had thought it was going to be; not as violent as he had thought it was going to be. The black batlike thing inside him had spread its wings finally. But it was only like the opening of a door—a door that led into more blackness. Oliver closed his eyes and looked into that dark. He saw Zach's face. The boyish, big-cheeked face with the huge black eyes. Peering up at him expectantly. *What do we do now, Ollie?* He shook his head.

"Come on!" Zach said. He laughed again, nervously. "You knew. You knew. You washed out the goddamned teacup, didn't you? You had to know."

Oliver breathed painfully in the dark.

Downstairs, for another moment, the woman in the domino stood still. The silence hovered over her. The blinking lights on her mask sent a little flash and glow into the dark around her. She sensed the library's glowering arches. She saw the faint glow of stained-glass windows; the gaze of their eyes. She was black inside; black and twisted. She staggered a step farther into the room.

Now, under the sharp, hoarse rasp of her breath, she heard something. She began to make out dim strains of music. The parade. The windy roar of the crowd in the distance. And something else . . .

Voices. The murmur of men's voices. It was coming from somewhere above her. She lifted her eyes. She swayed wearily on her feet. She saw the flight of steps curling gracefully away from her, up into the deeper shadows.

I don't know, she complained, shuddering. *I don't* know *who I am.*

Still, she came forward on stiff legs, dragging her body like a burden. Her gun hand was dangling at her side. Her other arm reached out. She felt her way. She touched cold stone.

She was standing under a lowering arch. She felt her way down along the wall until her fingers brushed a wooden banister. She clutched it. She began to pull herself forward. Her feet found the first stone step.

She began to climb.

Zachary took another step toward Oliver. Oliver heard it and flinched. He was all raw nerves now. Standing there, his eyes closed, peering into the dark. He could see his mother now. His mother's body. She was lying on the floor beside the coffee table. The teacup was on its side. The spurt-stain of tea stained the plush rug. The spurt-stain of poisoned tea. Unbearable. It was unbearable. He did not care what happened to him now.

Zachary peered at him, smiling. He crouched, hiding behind his gun. "What did you think?" he said. Oliver flinched again at the sound of that familiar voice. That familiar laugh: heh-heh, heh-heh. "I mean, why else would you wash the teacup at all? You knew it was me and my trusty chemistry set. I mean, right? Oh yeah. Come on, Ollie. You knew. I mean, I didn't ask you to wash the damn cup. Hell, I didn't even think, you know, the way her heart was; I didn't think anyone would even be suspicious enough to look for anything. You just covered up for me on your own, man." He grinned. "That's the symmetrical thing about it, see? You're covering up for me again. Now."

Oliver opened his eyes.

The woman in the domino climbed the stairs. She could not climb fast. Her legs were like slabs. She drew them up the high steps stiffly, slowly. She felt her way up along the banister.

Please, she thought. *Please.*

She climbed past stained-glass windows set in niches in the wall. Ghostly faces gleamed in them. The murmur of voices grew louder above her with every step she took. She became aware, too, of another sound. A distant sound that sent a chill into her. A dim howl, growing louder. Sirens. The police. They were coming to get her.

She dragged her legs up the stairs, clutching the banister, clutching her gun. *Please,* she thought, *Oliver. Please.*

The upper room came into sight above her. It was a corridor of a room. It was lined with books. She tried to breathe more softly as she crested the stairs. She bit her lips. She saw the two figures standing together in the center of the room.

"You see, you've got to look deeper into things sometimes," one of them said. "Then they begin to make sense."

That voice. She knew that voice. It was the voice she had heard as she dragged herself down the hallway. The urgent, murmuring voice: *Eight o'clock. You have to be there.*

The woman in the blinking domino mask reached out to one side. Her hand touched the wall. Her fingers crept along the stone. She felt a metal plate. The light switches. Three of them in a row.

She heard the sirens growing louder outside. She heard their scream pierce the rhythms of the distant music.

She pushed up the light switches, all three at once.

Oliver faced his brother. His breath came shallow, trembling. He saw Zach's black eyes suffering at him out of the shadows. He saw the outlines of the sweet, smooth face.

Don't go over the bumps, Ollie.

Oliver's lips parted and he wanted—something—to speak, to scream, to say . . . anything . . . He wanted to say: Remember? How Dad used to complain over dinner? Remember the time I pretended I'd caught that trapped ball? Remember how Mom burned the carrots and cried? He wanted to talk to Zach about the things they knew. The things only they knew . . .

But Zach's face jutted toward him out of the dark. His painful smile, his fever-bright eyes. The muzzle of his gun. And the words stuck in Oliver's throat. He was too weary to speak. He could not stand the effort. Every word he thought of was so freighted with meaning. Anything he said, anything he did, would give him away, would give it all away . . .

Because he *had* known. Somewhere inside him. He had always known. And every word that came to his mind was a confession of it.

Zach took one more step and they were face-to-face in the center of the room. The faint music filtered in to them. The sturdy books stood solemn in the shelves along the walls. The faces on the arches, at the windows, watched them. And Oliver looked down at his brother, and he did not care what happened anymore at all. He looked down at him and he looked so much like her. Zach looked so much like their mother that the yearning was unbearable and he just did not care. She had been, like Nana, a nervous, birdlike woman. Jittery gestures, darting eyes, fingers fiddling with one another. She had had gentle cool hands and they were only still when they were holding someone or stroking someone. When she could worry about you—when you were sick or you fell off your bike or something like that—then she could be calm for a few moments about herself.

Oliver knew that Zach had killed her. Somewhere inside him, he had always known. He had known without knowing. He had kept it hidden from himself forever. But he had known, too, every day. Every hour. In his sleep, minute by minute. He had always known.

Why? he wanted to ask. He shaped the words with his lips, but they didn't come. He was too tired. He just didn't care anymore. But he tried again. Looking down at Zach, at his face so much like hers. Hoarsely, quietly. He forced the words out: "Why'd you do that to her, man?" Then he made a noise and tears came down his cheeks. "She never hurt you," he said. "I mean, she *never* hurt you. You know? I mean, Dad—he—I know—he was angry, he . . . But she . . . I mean, gee, Zachie," he said, crying. "I mean, gee, I really *loved* her. What'd you go and do that for?"

Zach was inches from him. Oliver could see his face contorting. He could see the skin go red. The lips twisting together. The eyes glowing like coals. A mask of rage. Zach snorted once, and then again. And he said: "She *let* him hurt me, didn't she? Huh? Didn't she? Didn't she? And *you* . . ."

The two brothers stood facing each other, both in tears. Zach couldn't speak anymore. He let out a cry of frustration and anger. Grimacing, he stepped forward. He planted the muzzle of the gun against Oliver's head.

Oliver looked down at him. He didn't care what happened. He felt the cold steel of the gun. He saw Zachie's hand trembling.

Zach hesitated like that for one more second.

Then he smiled. His finger tightened on the trigger. "You broke the typewriter," he said.

There was a flash. A faint one. Like lightning at the vanishing point. The fluorescents in the ceiling crackled. They all started to flicker on at once. All along the length of the ceiling, they sent down a faltering purple glow.

The woman in the domino mask saw the two figures in that strange and strobic light. She saw Oliver

alive!

looking up in surprise. She saw the other man spinning toward her. His face whipping around toward her, his open raincoat fanning out.

That's him! That's him!

She recognized King Death, the real King Death. Zachary, that was his name. The man who was supposed to be beneath the skull mask. He was spinning toward her in the flickering light. His arm was whipping around with him. His hand was pointing out toward her. The purple light was flashing on the silver barrel of his automatic.

The lights snapped on. She saw it all frozen in glaring white. She started to bring her own pistol up from her side. She saw Oliver reaching out. She saw Zach aiming the gun at her: the twisted, scarlet, coal-eyed face of rage sighting her along the gun barrel.

Oliver cried out, "Zachie! No!"

She leveled her pistol.

And then Zach shot her.

OLIVER PERKINS
AND GUS STALLONE

Oliver had seen the woman first. He saw her mask wink red, green, and yellow out of the dark as she crested the stairs. Then the fluorescents above him were flickering on. He saw the woman's small pathetic figure. Her torn black jeans, the bloodied gray turtleneck. He saw the face in the cheap mask streaked with grime, sagging with exhaustion.

That was when Zach pulled the gun away from his head. He started spinning away from him. Spinning toward the girl in what seemed slow strobic motion so that Oliver had time to think, *Christ! Christ! He's going to shoot her!* And then he heard himself screaming, "Zachie! No!" His hand was flashing out toward Zach's gun arm. His fingers were scraping the slick raincoat sleeve, touching the sinewy arm beneath, pushing it to the side.

Zach fired. The automatic kicked and slammed. Oliver saw the masked woman thrown back a step as the bullet drove into her. He saw her stagger back to the edge of the stairs. She planted herself there, set her feet on the floor, bared her teeth in mindless determination. Zach was bringing his automatic to bear on her again, but the woman already had her revolver trained on him. Once more, Oliver shouted, "No!" but the word was blown away by the next explosion. The blast seemed to fill the room. To shake its heavy stone. To widen out to the walls in a deafening red roar. And then, slowly, the noise sank down, drifted down like ashes. The room became utterly silent, trembling. Then utterly still.

Zach stepped backward once and dropped his arms to his sides.

Oliver stared at him. "Zach?" he said.

He moved up behind the younger man and took him by the shoulders. Zach's shoulders felt flaccid and weak. His arms just hung down. Oliver heard a dull thud as Zachary's automatic dropped to the floor.

Zachary's knees buckled.

"Zach?" Oliver whispered. He held his brother on his feet for another moment, but Zach seemed drawn down by an irresistible force. Oliver wrapped an arm around him. He sank down with him. He sank down to his knees beside him. He held Zachary in his arms, pressed him against his chest. He stared at his brightly colored shirt for a long moment before he found the black hole in it. He saw the flesh of Zach's chest through the hole, and a red-black hole in the flesh. Frightened, he looked quickly at Zach's face. The large eyes gazed up at him, still alive. Zachary's lips moved. He licked them. They were white. He whispered something. Oliver leaned down close to listen.

". . . remember . . . ?" Zach said.

Oliver leaned closer, pressed his ear to Zach's lips. He thought Zach was going to ask him if he remembered sledding down the snowy hill behind their house. And he did remember. Yes.

But Zach did not go on.

Oliver looked at him again. Zach was still gazing up at him. The light of life was still in his eyes.

And then the light went out. Perkins lowered his head. He held his little brother close to him and patted his cheek, his hair. He rocked him back and forth, thinking: *Don't worry, Zach. Don't worry anymore.* His tears fell on Zach's face and rolled down his cheeks, as if it were the dead man who was crying.

Eesh, thought the woman in the domino mask. She dropped to one knee at the edge of the stairs. Her hand went lifeless. The revolver slipped from it, fell to the floor. *Eesh, eesh, eesh,* she thought. A wave of nausea rose up from her belly.

She blacked out for a second. And then she was tilting over the side of the top step. She was falling. A long, dizzying fall, it seemed. And then her head cracked against the stair. She felt a jolt, no pain. Her body tumbled to the side, and she went down another stair, and then another, her head thudding against the steps, thud, thud, thud.

She came to rest finally with her feet sprawled on the steps above her. Her arms flung out at either side. Her head thrown back. Her eyes staring up through the mask into a shifting blur.

Did I do it right? she wondered vaguely. *In the end, did I even do it right?*

The first agony burst all through her. She gasped. Her whole body went taut. She saw red. Then the pain subsided to a low throb. She lay on her back on the stairs, staring upward. She knew she had a bullet in her, somewhere high on her left side, somewhere around her collarbone. Her left arm was entirely numb. The rest of her was pulsing with that dull ache. She knew the real agony would flare again. Soon.

A lousy day, she thought, her eyes rolling. *A truly, truly bad day.*

She cried out in pain a second time before Perkins could let his brother go. He heard it and looked over his shoulder, and saw her foot sticking up above the top of the stairs.

Reluctantly, he lowered Zachary's head to the floor. Zach's eyes stared up like marbles. Perkins closed them with his hand.

The woman on the stairs was moaning steadily now. Perkins heard her babbling, a low rush of words. He stood away from Zach's body and took a deep breath to steady himself. He wiped the tears off his cheeks with his hand.

The sirens stopped. It was the first time he was aware of them. They had hit a squealing peak on the street outside and then gone off suddenly. That would be Mulligan, Perkins thought. Mrs. Wallabee had called him like he'd asked. That reminded him of Avis, lying in her apartment with her throat cut. He did not look down at Zach, but felt him there, lying at his feet. And Nana . . . He would have to break the news to Nana . . .

The woman on the stairs moaned again. Perkins turned to her.

Alone, he thought. Now he was going to be alone.

He moved heavily across the room to the top of the stairs. He saw the small figure sprawled there upside down. The lights that dotted her mask like jewels flashed ridiculously, dim now under the bright fluorescents.

The woman stirred. She moaned, mumbled. She was trying to get up.

Perkins moved around her, down the stairs. He crouched down next to her.

"Hold on there, kid. I got you," he said. "Just lie still."

The woman rolled her head back and forth. "Don't know. . . ," she mumbled. "Scared . . . scared . . . shoulda been me . . . so scared . . . please . . ."

"Ssh," said Perkins. He had to wipe his cheek again. He saw the woman try to open her eyes behind the mask. But the eyes fell shut heavily. Perkins reached down and pulled the mask up. Gently, he worked it up over her hair and tossed it aside where it blinked against the wall.

The woman's pile of reddish brown curls spilled out around her face. Perkins recognized her right away. The broad cheeks, the strong jaw. Mulligan had shown him a picture of her. She was the FBI agent they had sent after Zach. What was her name again? Stallone. Gus Stallone.

Her head thrashed back and forth on the stairs. She would not stop moving her legs. "Scared . . . Oliver . . . Oliver," she whispered. He stroked her forehead, brushing back the curls. She opened her eyes wide. She stared up at him. She lifted her hand weakly to his mouth. She pressed her fingertips against his lips. "You . . . Ol . . ." she muttered. "Know you. I know who you are."

She tried to turn to him.

"All right, all right," Perkins said. "You're gonna fall. You're gonna hurt yourself."

"Lousy . . . lousy day," she muttered.

He laughed mirthlessly. "Yeah. Me too. Come on, I better take you down."

He got her to hold her wounded arm close to her side. He

coaxed her right arm around his neck. He knelt and worked one of his arms around her back, the other beneath her knees. He stood up, hoisting her into the air, holding her against his torn sweater, her hair warm against his bare chest. He began to carry her down the stairs. Around the curve of the wall. Under the watchful windows shimmering in their fissures. Below him, beyond the darkness on the ground floor, there appeared a large rectangle of white-gray light. The library's front doors had been pushed open. A man was standing in the doorway, silhouetted against the streetlights' glow. Behind the man, there were crowds of people. Some were staring through the doors—eyes behind contorted masks, burning white in made-up faces, peering in at them. Most of the others were still gathered by the barricades. Perkins could see them pumping up and down, their hands upraised. He could hear the music still playing, the racy jangling brass from the parade. He saw some clowns still capering in the street, though they had to dance around the police cars. The police cars blocked the avenue, their white and red flashers whirling.

Perkins carried the woman down the stairs, holding her against him. Her head shifted and he glanced at her. He saw the purple bruises on her forehead. Streaks of dirt and scratches on her cheeks. He noticed that the bullet wound up by her neck was bleeding. The blood had soaked the upper left side of her shirt.

"Oliver," she muttered, turning in his arms. "Alive . . . Stay alive . . . Oliver . . ."

Perkins shook his head down at her. *Gus Stallone,* he thought. *Dumb name for a babe. Augusta. It must really be Augusta.*

"Do you . . . do you know . . . ?" she murmured. She turned her face to him, opened her eyes again. "Do you know the magic word?" Her eyes fell shut. Her head lolled to the side. He felt her cheek against his chest, her lips moving. He heard her babbling softly.

He turned away. He carried her down the stairs. Toward the masks. Toward the music. Toward the flashing lights.

Don't Say a Word

A Novel of Terror by Edgar Award-winning Author

ANDREW KLAVAN